WORKING MAN

"Aren't you forgetting who is supposed to be in charge here?" Julia asked with far more reserve than she actually felt.

"Could be that I am." Chad moved even closer, bending slightly at the waist, until his lips were but inches from hers. He noticed that her response to having him that close was to take a quick gulp of air. "I have been known to have an awfully short memory when I want."

"Then let me refresh it for you," she said. Her gaze dipped to his parted lips, all too aware that he was now close enough to kiss her if that proved to be his intention—although she doubted he would be so foolish. There was too much money at stake. "I happened to be the one in charge. You work for me. Remember?"

"Ah, yes, that's right. You hired me to be your lover," he said, his blue eyes twinkling.

"No, I hired you to be my sweetheart. And only a *pretend* sweetheart at that. I said nothing about us ever having been lovers. The closest I ever said was that I wanted you to convince my father that we are in love."

Chad smiled, then reached his arm around her slender waist and drew her close. "Which is why it is a good idea for me to touch you. It's possible he's watching us at this very moment," he said, finishing his remark by dipping forward and tasting her lips in a sweet, hungry kiss he could no longer deny himself . . .

ROSALYN ALSOBROOK

PASSION FOR HIRE

ZEBRA BOOKS
KENSINGTON PUBLISHING CORP.

ZEBRA BOOKS are published by

Kensington Publishing Corp.
475 Park Avenue South
New York, NY 10016

First Printing: December, 1993

Printed in the United States of America

Chapter One

Late April 1884

Julia Thornton drew in a slow, deep breath. She knew the time had come to take her fate into her own hands or risk forever being under someone else's control. Her heart pounded fiercely against her chest when she cut her gaze to the twin, off-centered doors that blocked much of the view into one of the bawdier saloons in Marshall, Texas.

She stood in the cool evening shadows only a few yards from where the saloon's bright glare spilled through the slatted doors across an uneven planked walk and out into the graveled street. She leaned forward and spoke in a voice so low only her maid could hear. Although there were very few people walking along the narrow boardwalks at that hour, she did not want to take the chance of being overheard by someone. "Remember, the man you bring out of there has to come across as being very bold and extremely disreputable. But don't choose anyone who acts *too* loud or unruly. The man still has to be manageable. I certainly don't want to end up with someone I can't control. The man I retain for this job must be willing to do or say anything I tell him, no matter how ludicrous it might seem. I

5

can't take the chance of anything going wrong. It's far too important."

"I understand," Pearline Williams said with a brief nod. Her dark eyes narrowed while she, too, studied the brilliant light that splayed through and around the batwing doors. Tilting her head, she listened to the raucous laughter and deep voices that overrode the other night sounds of the city.

In one of the other saloons farther down the block someone pounded on an out-of-tune piano and a woman squealed with delight. There also came the sound of a dog barking from inside one of the saloons, followed by a cat's screech and the sudden shatter of glass.

From where Pearline and her mistress stood across the darkened street, Pearline could not tell very much about what went on inside. But she knew from what she had been told about saloons in general, the Dry Creek was not a place she would want to stay for very long.

"Something else . . ." Julia cautioned, her attention drawn to a tall, slender man dressed in dirty work clothes and boots who had stepped outside to spit haphazardly into the street. She watched with disgust when he wiped the brown dribble from his mouth with his shirt sleeve, then paused to pet the nose of a nearby horse before turning and sauntering down the narrow walk toward another well-lit saloon, one of the many places around there where a working man could go for a quick meal and something numbing to drink.

"The man I hire can't be anyone Father might know or the plan will never work. He *must* be a stranger. And he must be a man who needs the money badly enough to do whatever I say, whenever I say, without question. He also has to be free to do whatever I want him to do for at least a month. Maybe longer."

6

She stared intently into Pearline's dark face. Even with the moon behind a small cloud and the nearest streetlamp almost a hundred yards away, she saw her maid's expression and knew Pearline had second thoughts about helping. "You do understand how important this is to me, don't you? I am almost twenty-three years old. Old enough that I should be allowed to do what I want with my life."

Pearline nodded that she understood, though her gaze remained on those slatted wooden doors while she listened to the rest of what Julia had to say.

"I can't spend the rest of my life doing only what Father wants me to do and seeing only the people he wants me to see. I care for Patrick and I do so want to marry him. And the only way for me to do that is to trick Father into accepting him."

Pearline frowned, then glanced back at Julia. "I know all that. I'm not stupid."

"Then go in there and find that perfect man for me."

"I'll do what I can." Pearline took several steps toward the noisy saloon Julia had chosen for no other reason than it was the largest and most popular in town, but stopped and turned back around when she realized her mistress had more to say.

"Remember," Julia continued, her pretty face twisted with concern, as if afraid Pearline had not paid close enough attention. "I only want the man to *look* like he's bold and unprincipled. But what I *really* want is someone who can be trusted to do whatever I say." Lifting her dark-plum silk skirts with a gloved hand, she stepped closer to be sure Pearline heard her every word.

"And even though I still think you should concentrate on finding a man who is several years older than I am so Patrick's age will look all the better in comparison, don't pick anyone who is either fat or ugly. He has to be

7

someone Father will believe I am attracted to despite his obvious character flaws. And please, make sure the man you choose has all his teeth," she added in afterthought. "I don't think I could tolerate pretending to be in love with someone who doesn't have all his teeth."

Pearline cocked her head to one side and planted her fists on amply rounded hips. "What am I supposed to do, Missy, stick my finger in his mouth and yank up on his lip? You're startin' to make it sound like I'm goin' in there to pick you out a good, sturdy work horse instead of some lowlife, two-bit scoundrel. Why don't I just stop and check some of these animals out here while I'm at it?" She gestured to the many horses lining the far side of the street. "I'd probably be less likely to get my finger bit off."

Julia sighed at Pearline's absurd response. "It's just that he has to be believable. I need someone who can be extremely annoying in his behavior yet at the same time not all that annoying to the eye."

"Wouldn't it be a lot simpler if you went in there and picked out the man yourself?" Pearline frowned when she turned to stare again at the noise-ridden saloon. "You know what you want a lot better than me." Her dark eyes widened when she heard the loud shriek of a woman followed by ribbons of male laughter. "You'd probably be able to pick out what you want right away. We could be on our way back to the house within the hour. Long before your father is due back home from his meetin' over in Jefferson. He'd never have to know we left the house."

"I told you . . ." Julia said, clearly irritated by Pearline's sudden qualms. "Saloonkeepers don't allow white women to go into such places unless they are the type who might work there. But they will let you in simply

8

because your skin is black and that you claim to be there looking for someone."

"Who do I say I'm lookin' for?"

"I don't know. If someone asks for a name, invent one. Tell them he's your boss and that you are trying to find him because you have an important message for him. Then while you walk around the room pretending to look for this man whom no once else knows and therefore can't help you find, search for someone who fits my needs. Quietly pull him to the side when you've found him and ask him if he needs a job. If he says yes, bring him out here to speak with me. I'll be waiting across the street, over in front of the bank."

Pearline hiked her dark-green skirt several inches to avoid the hem touching any of the horse dung that had accumulated along the street that day and marched determinedly toward the doors of the Dry Creek Saloon. Even though she did not particularly like the man from St. Louis, she was willing to do whatever it took to help Julia Thornton marry him, as long as it would mean that Julia could be able to live life the way she wanted. And it didn't hurt matters knowing that the three of them would return to the river city after the engagement was officially approved by her father—at least long enough for him to sell his house and his part of that big shipping company he owned.

It was still Pearline's hope that Julia would change her mind and decide to stay in St. Louis permanently and let Mr. Patrick continue to run his shipping company rather than return to Texas to have him take over Mr. Thornton's businesses. Oh, how desperately she yearned to be back where there were such wonderful things as electric lights and gas heaters, and where Negroes were allowed to attend the theater or opera as long as they sat in a special section on the top floor.

Pearline had the hope of falling in love with one of those tall, strapping men who worked along the St. Louis riverfront, eventually marrying one of them and having a family of her own.

But first they had to trick Julia's father into letting Julia marry Patrick Moore so they would have a reason to return. Julia had already told Pearline that she had no intention of returning to that school to be forced again into studying for nearly fourteen hours each day.

Poor Missy had never wanted to attend that business college in St. Louis in the first place. It had all been her father's idea, mainly because the college in Marshall did not allow women and the Masonic Female Institute did not offer such special courses. He wanted Julia to be prepared to take over his lumber companies, since he had no other children and it looked like Missy would never find a husband he considered capable of running them.

But Missy was far more interested in her drawing and painting, and wanted to spend the rest of her life perfecting her art. If only she could make her father understand that. But while Pearline stepped up onto the planked boardwalk and faced the swinging wooden doors, she doubted Charles Thornton would ever understand his daughter's desire to put what she saw down on paper and canvas. He had always considered it an idle waste of time.

While Pearline gathered the courage needed to enter the crowded saloon, Julia waited outside for her to return with at least one likely prospect. After watching Pearline lift up her head and disappear through the doors, she moved deeper into the shadows of the bank's elaborate overhang where it would be less likely that she would be noticed by those coming and going along the street.

She knew there was just as much danger in her being alone outside such a saloon as there was for her maid to be milling about inside. She bit deeply into the sensitive flesh of her lower lip as if that might help calm her rapidly hammering heart while she stood in the darkness listening to the boisterous laughter, the sudden shouts, and the loud, thrashing music that tumbled out of the various saloons.

It certainly sounded as if everyone was having a good time and, after several long minutes of waiting, she wondered if her sometimes adventurous maid might also be having a good time. She tapped her foot impatiently while she watched the street for anyone who might come close enough to catch a glimpse of her standing there. Not only was she in danger of being accosted by some stumbling drunk, she ran the very real risk of being seen in such an ungodly neighborhood by someone who knew her or her family. Her reputation could be forever ruined if she was caught lurking about in front of the Dry Creek Saloon at night.

But that was a risk she had to take if she wanted her father's permission to marry the man she loved. Her heart soared at the thought of one day becoming Mrs. Patrick W. Moore. How grand it would be. Not only would she finally be out from under her father's control, she would be free at last to do whatever she wanted with her life. Patrick had promised her that.

A sudden feeling of excitement rose inside her, but then spiraled quickly downward when she realized the difficult task that still lay ahead of her.

If only her father was not such a stubborn man. Then none of this foolishness would be necessary. She could simply choose the man she wanted to marry, marry him, and be done with it.

But he *was* a stubborn man. A very stubborn man.

11

He had thus far refused his permission for her to marry any of the young men she had fallen in love with in the past. None of them were ever good enough for her, nor wealthy enough, nor intelligent enough. Which was why she was twenty-two years old and still unwed. Practically a spinster.

She sighed unhappily and pressed her back against the cool glass of the bank window. If only her father had been more receptive earlier that afternoon when she had first tested the waters by bringing up Patrick's name during a casual conversation about some of the people she had met while attending college in St. Louis. But he had been unimpressed by what she had told him—even the part about Patrick owning one-third of a very large, very prosperous shipping company.

At the time, her father was still too concerned over the fact that no one had moved into the old place yet, even though someone had ordered several wagonloads of lumber dropped off, which now sat draped with canvas. "And it wasn't even *our* lumber," he had wailed, paying little heed to anything Julia had to say about the months she had spent in St. Louis. Which was the way it often was with her father.

Even after he had ranted and raved over the fact that Robert Freeport had recently sold almost everything he had ever stolen from them to some mysterious nephew from Charleston, South Carolina, he paid little attention to Julia's comments. Instead, he continued to rail about the young man who now owned the land that had once been theirs, claiming the place was headed for even further ruin for the nephew was probably an even bigger ass than his uncle.

"Which is why I think you would like Patrick Moore," she had responded in another attempt to bring her new beloved back into the conversation. "He happens to be a very shrewd businessman."

"If he's so shrewd why doesn't he own the entire shipping company? Why does he bother sharing his profits with two other men?" had been her father's response, sounding just as disgusted with this friend of hers whom he had never met as he was over the situation developing just three miles away. "Obviously this Patrick fellow does not have his goals set high enough."

After discovering how very unimpressed her father was with what little she had managed to tell him about Patrick, she had decided the time was not right to mention the very real fact that she hoped one day to marry him. Still, she knew she would have to tell him soon, because in just over a month, Patrick was due there for a two-week visit, at the end of which he intended to ask her father for her hand in marriage.

Sadly, Julia recalled that twice before likely suitors had gathered the courage to ask her father for her hand in marriage, and twice before her father had found reasons to disapprove of the marriages. One young man had come from a divorced family. The other did not have nearly enough education. And neither was earning enough money to keep Julia in the grand lifestyle to which she had so readily become accustomed.

Unless her father approved of their marriage, Patrick's plan to take over her father's timber businesses would fall through and she could end up completely abandoned by her own father. She would never be allowed back into his heart nor would she be given another cent of his money. Her father had made his position on that matter perfectly clear. If she ever married someone he had not first approved, he would disown her forever.

Which was why Julia had been forced to come up

with such a devious plan, one that had first occurred during that long, two-day train ride back to Texas. Since her father *never* approved of the men she chose and she no longer had a mother to intervene in her behalf, she would trick her father into finding Patrick acceptable by first pretending to be in love with someone she *knew* her father would not like. She would wait until he had become thoroughly appalled by this other man's intolerable behavior, then sadly agree that the first man was not for her before turning around and introducing him to her second and obviously better choice: Patrick W. Moore.

To her way of thinking, her father would be so relieved to learn that she had decided against marrying the first man, he would gladly agree to let her wed someone with Patrick's many fine qualities.

The strategy was simple. She would choose a man so bold and so obnoxious that Patrick would look like a godsend in comparison. It would no longer matter that Patrick was four years older than she nor that he was not making enough money. But then, with the approval of her father behind them and with Patrick's cunning for business, he should be able to take over her father's lumber businesses in her stead and within a very few years would be earning more than enough to take care of all of them in a fine manner.

There would be no reason for her to return to the college in St. Louis. It would no longer be important that she learn all there was to know about business management and accounting, not when she had a husband who could take care of such matters for her. She would be free at last to pursue her painting.

But first she had to convince her father that Patrick was indeed the perfect man for her. Which meant she had one month to prepare her father for Patrick's visit.

One month to find a man so crude and so objectionable that Patrick would look like a real treasure in comparison.

She pressed her gloved hands together and prayed that Pearline would make a good choice. Her happiness hinged on their finding just the right man.

Pearline stepped inside the noisy, smoke-filled, whiskey-drenched saloon and stood off to one side while she waited for someone to notice her. When all she received while canvassing the many faces in the boisterous horde was a passing glance from one or two of the men who sat closest to her, she realized no one really cared that she was there. Frowning while she continued her casual survey, she tried to decide the best way to go about approaching these rowdy men.

Should she simply walk around looking them over until she found someone she thought Julia would like, or should she try to maneuver her way across the room and make a few inquiries of the barkeeper first? She stood with a puzzled expression while she continued to search the crowd for likely prospects.

There were all manner of white men from which for her to choose. Short, tall, old, young, brawny, squat, fat, thin, dirty, clean, handsome, and dog-ugly. There were fancy men who smoked cigars, drank from small glasses, and played cards. Plain men who sat at the crowded tables, drank from large mugs, and laughed a bit too loudly. Some men stood at the bar with one boot on a rail while talking to the elaborately dressed women with unkempt hair, black-rimmed eyes, and dark-red lips. Other men stood at the food counter devouring large chunks of ham and cheese. Still others sat scattered across the two sets of stairs or along the gallery floor that ran between the two staircases, glasses in their hands, their legs dangling through the banister rails while they watched everything that went on below.

Pearline became so absorbed with everything going on around her that she did not notice the large, slovenly dressed man headed in her direction. Not until it was too late.

"You'll do," he said in a loud voice that she barely heard above the rest of the clamor just before he snatched her up off the floor and tossed her over his shoulder like a large sack of grain. "Let's get on upstairs and get to it."

"Put me down!" Pearline shouted an immediate protest, too stunned to consider a struggle. When the foul-smelling man failed to comply, she shouted again, louder this time so he could hear her above the noise. "I said put me down!"

When even that did not bring about the wanted response, she slapped him hard across his huge back. "Can't you hear me, white man? I said, put me down right now!" When he still did not obey, she started kicking her legs and screaming as loud and as hard as she could.

"Ahh, good, a fighter," the drunken man said, obviously pleased by her attempts to free herself. He laughed loud and heartily while he took the stairs two at a time. "I love a woman who likes to be tamed."

"I don't want to be tamed. I just want to be set free," she shouted. She looked down at the faces below, hoping to find one man willing to come to her rescue. But most of the Dry Creek patrons were looking elsewhere, as if they were completely unaware of her plight. "Someone *please* make him let go of me."

"What's the matter, whore?" the drunken man shouted angrily. "My money's not good enough for you?" He then slapped her bottom so hard it sent a sharp pain through her back and into her neck, causing her to fall limply over his shoulder for several seconds. "The way you're dressed, you're lucky anyone wants you at all."

"I am not a whore!" Pearline shouted back, frightened to realize just how badly the brute could hurt her if he chose. That one swat of his hand had caused both her legs to feel numb. "Please, mister. Put me down."

"Don't worry. I'll put you down. Just as soon as I get you upstairs. Which room is yours?"

"I don't have a room," she wailed, then reached around to pull his hair, wanting to bring him as much pain has he had brought her. "Don't you understand? I don't work here."

"Ouch! Let go of my hair, you black witch."

"Put me down or I'll pull every last one out of your head," she shouted. A hot rush of relief swept over her when the man came to a sudden stop just after he topped the stairs and had turned to head across the main gallery that looked out onto the floor below. She decided she had finally gotten through to him.

"Get out of my way," he blustered, clearly attempting to be heard over the clamor below.

Pearline twisted her body so she could see who stood in the man's way and was relieved to find a tall white man with dark-brown hair and angry blue eyes blocking their path. She could tell by the way he stood with his long legs spaced well apart and his arms crossed squarely in front of him that he had no intention of letting them pass.

"Not until you've put the woman down." He spoke calmly then shifted his weight to one well-muscled leg, giving the impression he had all the time in the world to wait this thing out.

"Look, stranger, this ain't none of your concern. I'd advise you to get on out of my way."

"Whenever I see a man mistreating a woman the way you are this one, I make it my concern." Again he spoke calmly while he flexed the muscles beneath the soft fabric of his pale-blue work shirt, as if to indicate he intended to use force if necessary.

"Who said I'm mistreatin' her?" The big man sounded truly baffled. "If you're worried that I ain't plannin' to pay her, don't be. I got plenty of money. I just won me four dollars and eighty cents playin' poker."

"I told you to put her down," the taller man repeated in a deep, determined voice.

"Why? *You* want her? Is that why you bolted up the stairs the way you did? You already picked her out for yourself?" Then, as if that had to be the reason and not prepared to fight this younger man for her, he quickly plucked Pearline from his shoulder and held her out away from his body, again as if he were handling nothing more cumbersome than a large sack of grain. "Here, have her. There's plenty more down there where she came from."

The other man continued to stare at him angrily, but made no move to unfold his arms and take possession of Pearline. His next words were edged with steel. "Set her down."

The large man grunted, then set Pearline abruptly on the floor. "She's too short for me anyway. I think I'll go see if Nicky is back yet. She's the one I really want."

Pearline stood before the stranger, too dumbfounded by what had happened to voice her gratitude. She watched in stunned silence while the large man who had held her captive quickly made his way back down the stairs before she finally turned to look again at the one who had saved her. It dawned on her that she should say something now.

"Thank you, mister." Even though the danger was clearly over, she felt suddenly weak and stepped over to the worn railing which she held on to for dear life.

The tall stranger looked at her curiously for several seconds before he finally spoke. "The name's not mister. It's Chad."

"And mine is Pearline. Pearline Williams," she said, still gripping the banister with both hands while she studied her savior further. Not only was he a tall man, broad through the shoulders, and extremely sure of himself, he was also extremely handsome—for a white man. She liked his pale-blue eyes, his longish thick brown hair, and the lean, muscular shape of his jaw. She also liked the way he had come to the ready defense of a helpless female. "I really am awful grateful to you. You just saved me from losin' somethin' very precious to me. Somethin' I hope to save for the man I eventually marry."

Chad continued to look at her with his dark eyebrows drawn into a puzzled expression. "Tell me, why are you here if not to earn a dollar of two behind those doors?" He gestured to the seven tall, narrow doors that lined the gallery wall behind him.

Pearline knew how the answer to that question might sound, but she was not about to lie to the person who had just saved her virtue. "I'm here lookin' for a man."

If Chad had taken her answer the wrong way, he did not show it. Instead, he tilted his head to one side while he continued to study her with eyes so blue and so pale they looked downright spooky.

"Any man in particular?"

Pearline's mouth twitched, amused by the answer she would have to give if she wanted to remain honest. "Yes and no. I am lookin' for a particular *type* man, yet I'm not lookin' for anyone in particular. I know that probably sounds a little peculiar, but that's only because it is."

Chad's eyes sparkled with answering amusement. "Would you care to elaborate?"

"My mistress sent me in here to find someone willin' and able to work for her."

"Oh?" Chad looked at her with a raised brow. Clearly he thought a saloon an odd place for a woman to look for employees. "And what sort of work would that be?"

Pearline grinned dimple-deep, then stepped away from the banister, her weakness having passed. "My mistress sent me in here to hire her a lover."

Chad blinked twice. "She *what?*"

"She needs me to hire her a lover," she repeated. "Or rather what she wants me to hire is a *pretend* lover," quickly she amended. "Someone who will call on her and act like he's her beau."

Trying not to look confused, Chad unfolded his arms and tapped his fingertips together lightly while he considered everything Pearline had told him. "Let me see if I have this right. The woman you work for sent you in her to find someone who will pretend to court her. For money."

Pearline shook her head, indicating that was not entirely correct. "Not just *court* her. She wants me to find someone who will pretend to be devoutly and passionately in love with her for about a month. He also has to be someone who can be very rude and crass. Enough so to cause her father to become so appalled by his behavior that he will later greet the man she really wants to marry with open arms." As if that should have explained everything, Pearline leaned forward to look at

20

Chad with an appraising eye, as if suddenly very interested in his mouth. "Do you got all your teeth in there?"

Finding her behavior a little odd to say the least, Chad took a tentative step backward. "Yes, I do. But why should that be important?"

Pearline shrugged, but continued to study Chad's face carefully. "I don't really know. Missy, she just happens to like teeth, I guess." She then tilted her head to one side and frowned, looking at him. "You aren't from around here, are you?"

"No. I'm from South Carolina. Why?"

"Not married, are you?"

"No. But what does that matter?"

"How long have you been here in Marshall?"

Chad could not help but grin again at this woman's bold nature. In the back of his mind, he could see Solomon hooked up with a woman just like this one and wondered if he should try to play matchmaker. His friend certainly could use the diversion, especially after having been recently jilted by that conniving little Rose Kane, who had found herself an older man with more money to offer and a better job. "I've been here for only a few days. Why?"

"Because I was told to find a stranger. Someone Missy's father ain't never met. It's the only way that scheme of hers can work."

"Are you implying that you want *me* to be the one to hire on as your mistress's pretend lover?"

"Why not?" Her dark eyes glimmered at the thought of pairing this man with her mistress, even if it was only for a month. "You interested? The pay is real good. Missy told me she'd got as high as five hundred dollars if her father ends up bein' completely fooled. That's almost all the money she got left from what her grandmother left her and more than most men make in two

21

whole years of workin' for the railroad. *Three* if you're just working in the railyards. And all you'd have to do to earn all that money is be loud and crude for about a month, sort of like that man you just sent away, all the while you pretend to be courtin' Missy."

Thinking Pearline's Missy had to be a very young and very naive girl desperate to convince her father to let her marry the boy of her dreams, Chad shook his head. "No. I don't think I'm the right type for what she needs."

"Oh, but you are. She told me to find someone older than she is and one who ain't ugly nor fat. You sure do fit all of that."

"How old do you think I am?"

"Oh, I'd say you're about twenty-seven or twenty-eight. And you seem like a very nice man to me. I think you'd be manageable enough." She pursed her lips into a persuasive pout. "At least come outside and meet her."

"She's outside?" His pale eyes widened at the thought of some young girl standing out in front of a place like the Dry Creek Saloon so late at night. "Doesn't she realize how dangerous this neighborhood is?"

"Of course she does. That's why she's waitin' over in the shadows where no one will see her. So, are you goin' out there to talk to her or not?"

Intrigued and unable to believe a girl would go to such lengths to trick her own father, he agreed to go; but with the intention of telling the foolish girl how very dangerous such a pursuit could be. Young women just did not go around hiring complete strangers out of local saloons.

"Okay, I'll go with you to meet her. But I'm not making any promises."

"Ain't askin' for none." Pearline smiled happily, then

22

turned to lead the way back down the stairs. "All I ask is that you keep yourself an open mind when you talk to her and if you do decide not to take the job that you don't tell no one that you ever talked to her. She needs to keep this a secret."

Chad shook his head while he followed Pearline across the crowded saloon. How could two young women be so foolish?

Chapter Two

"Where is she?" Chad asked Pearline as soon as they had stepped out onto the darkened boardwalk. He glanced around but did not see anyone lurking among the many horses, carriages, and buggies that lined the moonlit street.

"Over in front of the bank." Pearline motioned toward the largest building across the street from them.

Chad saw no one standing in the area she indicated. Worried the foolish girl had been abducted by some depraved drifter, he hurried ahead of Pearline.

Just before he reached the center of the street, he noticed a shadow move away from the windows near the entrance and he breathed a sigh of relief. But when she stepped farther toward the edge of the sidewalk where he could see her better, the sigh caught instantly in his throat.

Even before she had stepped out far enough for the silvery moonlight to catch the shimmering feathers of her hat or the elegant upsweep of her long dark hair, he knew this was no young innocent girl as he had first thought. Judging by the manner in which she filled out her stylish clothing and by her easy, graceful movements, this was a fully grown woman. And what a woman she was. Never had he expected Pearline's employer to be beautiful. Not when she thought it necessary to offer five hundred dollars to entice someone into merely pretending to be interested in her.

"Missy, I found you just the right man," Pearline called to her mistress in a low voice, then quickly stepped around Chad, who had come to a dead stop in the very center of the street. She gestured over her shoulder to the man she had brought with her, a wide, dimpled grin lighting her face. "Look at him. He's older than you by at least four years, maybe five, and as you can see even in this pale light there ain't one ugly bone in his whole body."

Julia stood at the edge of the boardwalk and stared at Chad, unblinking—and for a moment unable to swallow. She had not expected Pearline to find anyone quite so appealing, or anyone who walked with such pride and confidence. Considering the subservient nature of the job, it was hard to believe that she had found a man with any backbone at all.

"Have you explained to him that I will expect him to be at my complete beck and call for at least a month?" she asked in an attempt to dissuade him. Her silk skirts rustled softly when she stepped out into the graveled street to have a closer look at the strong lines of his clean-shaven face. If it were not for the fact that Patrick was every bit as attractive and already very much in love with her, she might be tempted to trifle with this handsome man. As it was, she felt a little afraid of him. Probably because of what Patrick might say if she hired anyone that striking in appearance. "It is important I find someone who is willing to do *whatever* I tell him to do, and that he do it the very moment I need it done. It has to look as if he is totally devoted to me."

"Yes'm, I already told him all that, and it turns out he

don't have nothin' better to do with his time anyway. He just got into Marshall a couple of days ago. He can't possibly have found himself work in so little time."

Chad opened his mouth to correct her, knowing he and Solomon had plenty of work ahead of them during the next few months, but before he could actually comment, Pearline interrupted.

"Ain't he just everything you wanted me to find?" She counted off his many attributes on her long fingers. "He's a newcomer to these parts, so your father can't possibly know him. He's older like you wanted. Not married. Real' nice-lookin'—that is, for a white man. His hair may be in need of a good barbering at the moment, but it is obvious he bathes regular and carries himself well. Why, he's even got all his teeth. And best of all, he don't have no job yet, so he'll be free to do whatever you need him to do." She turned to look at Chad questioningly. "You *don't* got no job, do you?"

"Not a job exactly," he started to explain, but was again interrupted before he could finish.

"Yes see? No job. That means he needs the money," Pearline responded then crossed her arms proudly when she turned to look at Julia again. "He's perfect. He's exactly what you wanted me to find."

Julia found it hard to argue with Pearline's glowing assessment of the man, still she was hesitant to hire him. Patrick would be angry enough with her for having instigated such a daring plan without first talking it over with him, but to allow this handsome man to play her sweetheart . . . Patrick would be furious.

"But is he willing to do whatever I tell him?" she continued while she purposely avoided his gaze. She found it easier to talk about him when she did not have to look into those probing blue eyes. Instead, she focused on Pearline. "He will be expected to devote his every wak-

26

ing minute to me for at least a month. I could need him day or night—but probably more at night, since that's when Father is usually home, and he's the one we have to convince."

She glanced at Chad's face again but still found his studious gaze disconcerting and quickly lowered her eyes so that instead of his handsome face, she gazed at his clothing.

Clearly he was a working man. Not only did he have the strong build of someone who worked outdoors instead of in the cramped confines of an office, but he wore dark-blue broadcloth britches like that type of man wore to work. He also had on a heavy twilled-cotton shirt that was unbuttoned at the throat, allowing a glimpse of the dark hair curling beneath. Although it was hard to judge colors in such darkness, the shirt appeared to be either white or pale blue and had been fitted against his tall, muscular body with a pair of black or dark-blue suspenders.

When Julia realized her attention kept returning to the narrow opening in his shirt, she swallowed hard, then forced her gaze back up to meet his. She refused to be intimidated by his deep, penetrating eyes. "What about it, mister? You willing to do whatever I tell you to do no matter how ridiculous or embarrassing?"

Although Chad had gone outside with every intention of lecturing this woman for her foolish attempt to hire some stranger from a saloon, and although he in no way needed the money being offered, still he nodded in response.

Julia's frown deepened. She had expected the man to swell up and become angry with her for even suggesting he bend to her will like that. She tapped a fingertip against the corner of her mouth while she considered the situation further. "I don't think you are exactly what

I wanted. I had hoped to find someone a little rougher around the edges than you. Someone a lot more offensive in nature."

Chad did not know whether to take that last comment as a compliment or a complaint. "Let me assure you, madam, I can be just as crude and insufferable as you want me to be."

To prove his point, he cocked his mouth into an off-centered smile that formed a dimple in his right cheek, then lowered his long silky black eyelashes and raked his pale-blue gaze over her in an extremely roguish manner. When he did, his attention fell immediately on the rapid rising of her breasts, the tops of which were visible above the lacy edge of her low-cut gown.

"Like your maid just told you. I am *exactly* what you want." *And you happen to be exactly what I want,* he thought with a devilish lift of his brow. He knew already that he would do whatever it took to win her heart away from whomever she thought she was in love with. "Pearline could not have found better had she searched for days."

Aware of what had caught his attention, a strange mixture of exhilaration and foreboding washed over Julia, causing her cheeks to flame bright red. Although she sensed a very real danger in letting this attractive and obviously arrogant man into her life, she finally nodded her agreement and motioned for him to follow her into the shadows where they could talk without being noticed. Pearline followed.

"Very well, sir. You have the job. You now work for me, Julia Thornton. Just remember that to earn the full five hundred dollars you will have to convince my father that you and I are very much in love. And he is not an easy man to fool. He must be made to believe that you are strongly attracted to me, enough so to want to marry me."

"That will not be a problem," Chad said with a slight shrug of his shoulders. The only reason he had agreed to participate in the scheme was because he already *was* attracted to her. Attracted enough to be willing to let Solomon handle all the work for a month.

"It also means that you'll need to make my father loathe you right from the start," she continued, wanting to make sure he fully understood the requirements.

"Again, not a problem. I can be extremely loathsome when I want."

He smiled again, this time so slow and easy, it caused Julia's pulses to race unexpectedly in response. She clasped her hands together to keep from pressing them against her pounding heart. She did not want this man to know how truly affected she was by his presence—not when she was soon to be engaged to marry another. "But don't be *too* hideous. I don't want Father to think I've lost my mind entirely."

"Don't worry," he answered, his voice deep and reassuring as he settled a more serious expression across his face. Even so, there was a look of pure amusement in his eyes. "Just let me know when and where I'm supposed to start courting you."

A strange shiver of apprehension washed over her, but she quickly pushed it aside. She had made her decision. She would stick to it. "You can start this Friday night by paying your first personal call at my house. That should give me enough time to prepare Father for you." She reached into the silk handbag dangling at her wrist and brought out a folded map she had drawn earlier. "Here are the directions to my house and my promise of payment. Although I am willing to pay you a ten-dollar advance to help you get by during these next few weeks, I do not plan to hand over the rest of the money until after the services have been rendered, and to my satisfaction."

"I don't need the ten dollars just yet," he admitted, not planning to take any of her money ever. "What time do you want me there Friday?"

"About seven o'clock. And should my father ask, you are from St. Louis, Missouri. That's where we met. If you've never been there, please go to the library near the college and read something about it."

"I've been there. But what I want to know is why St. Louis?" he asked while he accepted the folded piece of paper and slipped it into his shirt pocket. "What were we doing way up there?"

"I was attending a very prestigious woman's college. And you were working for . . ." She paused to think of something truly unimpressive. "You were working as a stable hand for a small livery near the riverfront."

Chad nodded while he committed those facts to memory. "And how did a college student of obvious grace and substance and this poor, destitute stable hand meet?"

Julia's forehead wrinkled with thought, then smoothed again when the perfect response occurred to her. She would make their meeting very similar to hers and Patrick's. "You approached me one afternoon in a small park overlooking the river to tell me I had dropped a letter I was carrying and we became deeply smitten with each other right away. In fact, you could hardly take your eyes off me."

Pearline shook her head and turned her back to them, as if not wanting to listen to such silliness. Instead, she focused her attention on the loud noises coming from the saloons.

Chad wanted to grin at such detail but kept a serious expression. Obviously, Julia Thornton was very serious about what she said. "Sounds very romantic," he admitted, then asked. "By any chance was I so smitten by your beauty that I tried to kiss you that first day in the park?"

Julia's hand flew to her throat, not having expected such a provocative question. "No. Of course not." Her neck grew warm at the mere thought of this man's lips stealing a kiss from hers. "You didn't kiss me until much later in our relationship. You're crude and annoying, but you're not *stupid*. You knew I would slap you silly for trying such a thing so soon."

She paused to give the sudden question of their kissing further consideration. Because her father was just the type to ask about something so personal, she knew it was a topic that could easily come up in conversation. "You did not try to kiss me until weeks later. Until late one night while you were walking me home from the theater. It was a cold, moonlit night and you had put your arm around me to help keep me warm when the temptation suddenly became too great."

"And did you enjoy the kiss?" His gaze darkened while he studied the fullness of her mouth, aroused by the mere thought of ever having kissed her. Suddenly he felt jealous of any man who had.

"Of course I enjoyed it," she answered. Unwittingly, she dampened her lower lip with the tip of her tongue, annoyed by the strange reaction that occurred inside her. She hardly knew the man and yet he had caused this complete turmoil just by asking questions. She glanced at Pearline and noticed her maid's green-clad shoulders shaking with mirth. That Pearline found the strange conversation so amusing annoyed her. "I had to have enjoyed it. We are in love with each other, aren't we?"

Chad was as intrigued by the situation as he was by

the anger reflected in her dark eyes and the high color that tinged her fair cheeks. He liked her passionate nature and wanted to see more of it. "And while kissing you, have I every once undressed you?"

Pearline stiffened. Without looking back, she headed toward the carriage they had left just down the street, as if suddenly aware of something else that needed her immediate attention.

"Of course not!" Julia crossed her arms, a gesture intended to warn Chad he had taken this conversation too far. Unable to meet his penetrating gaze, she glanced up and watched Pearline's rapid withdrawal. "Keep in mind that we are not married! We are only in love and *wanting* to be married."

"Oh," he answered, pleased. Her incensed response meant that if he ended up successful in attracting this beautiful woman as he hoped, he would undoubtedly be her first lover. "Just thought I'd better get the facts straight before I meet your father. I'd hate to say anything that might conflict with what you may have already told him."

Julia drew in several quick breaths to steady her rampant emotions, then answered calmly. "You don't have to worry about that," she said, bravely meeting his gaze again. She decided it was the thick, dark, incredibly long lashes that gave him such a roguish, sultry look. "The truth is, I haven't told my father anything about you yet. Until earlier this afternoon, I really hadn't given you any serious thought."

Chad did his best to look hurt while he continued to take in every detail of her stunning beauty. "How can you say something like that when we are so deeply in love? We should *always* be in each other's thoughts. By the way, how long have we been in love?"

"Four months," she answered, thinking it a most

plausible answer. It was how long she had known Patrick. "We have been in love for nearly four months now." She did what she could to calm the flutter of confusion his questions had caused. It was strange for them to be talking as if they really *were* in love when the truth was, they had just met. But she knew she needed to get used to such talk if they were to convince her father of the fact.

"Only four months?" His eyebrows knotted into a perplexed frown, as if she had not thought that answer through well enough. "Aren't we being a little hasty here, darling? Most couples know each other for at least a year before deciding on marriage."

"Four months is long enough. My father knew my mother only six weeks before they were married," she said in ready defense of herself, then narrowed her brown eyes as to warn him. "Besides, it isn't the length of time that really matters, it is the intensity of the emotions involved."

"Oh, I agree wholeheartedly," he said with another provocative smile as he reached out to trace the upward curve of her nose with the tip of his finger. The unexpected action caused her to take a nervous step backward.

He quickly countered her motion by taking a quick step forward, shortening what little distance lay between them even more. Standing closer now, he breathed the gentle scent of her floral perfume before proceeding with his questions. "And just when do we hope to be married?"

Julia's whole body tingled as a result of his touch. "As far as Father is concerned, our plans are to be married this summer." She took another tentative step backward, finding his nearness far too disconcerting. "We'll want to be married just as soon as the arrangements are made and the invitations sent out."

Aware of her continued discomfort, Chad followed with another step forward. His eyes sparkled with devilment. "Will it be a large wedding? Will my family be invited?" He notched his eyebrows when he gave that last question further consideration. "Do I *have* any family?"

"What does that matter?" she wanted to know, perplexed by the chaos his nearness caused inside her. Afraid he intended to touch her again, she continued backing away from him, moving steadily deeper into the darker shadows in front of the bank, wishing now they had stayed in the middle of the street where they could be more easily seen. "It's not as if we really intend to go through with the ceremony."

"But I have to know what to tell your father if he asks," he explained while he continued slowly advancing toward her, aware she was now only a few feet from the large bank windows. He could hardly wait to see what her reaction would be when she realized she had literally backed herself against a glass wall. "He will expect me to know our plans."

Julia frowned. "Very well. Yes, it will be a big wedding. My father would want only the best for me. And of course your family would be invited." She pressed her lips together while she considered the matter further, unaware that each tiny movement of her mouth drove Chad to total madness. "But I don't think I want you to have any family. Questions about them would just complicate things. The fewer details we have to remember about each other, the better."

Her eyes widened when she finally realized her whereabouts, and instead of taking that final step back, which would have planted her back solidly against a wall of cold, beveled glass, she put out her arm and held him back with an open palm. She tried not to concentrate on how solid his muscles felt beneath her hand nor how warm. "Now if you have no further questions, Pearline and I really should be on our way. Father is due back home in less than an hour and it will take nearly that long for us to make the drive back ourselves."

She glanced again to see that Pearline was still wending her way to the carriage—moving very slowly as if having second thoughts about having left so abruptly. "Oh, by the way," she said. "I need to know your name and where I can reach you in case there's some change in plans."

"The name is Chad," he responded, knowing he had already told Pearline that much. "And you can reach me at the Capitol Hotel over on Houston Avenue just down from the courthouse. Room 16."

He immediately turned and headed back toward the saloon without offering a last name. He knew that if she found out who he really was and that he was a man of wealth and was about to move into his own place out on Cypress Trail, she would question his reason for having taken the job so readily and might fire him on the spot. He certainly did not want that. He was already looking forward to the next few weeks.

"Chad what?" she called after him, thinking she had every right to know his last name.

"Just Chad," he answered with barely a backward glance. Taking several more long strides, he disappeared into the saloon, leaving Julia to wonder why he had all but refused to tell her his last name.

He must be wanted by the authorities somewhere for having committed some sort of terrible crime, she decided, and thought it would be best to remain extremely cautious of him while he was in her employ.

"We must never leave that man completely alone in the house at any time," she told Pearline shortly after having caught up with her, "and I think it would be a good idea to always check his pockets before he leaves."

Pearline looked truly puzzled. "Why?"

"I don't trust any man who won't give out his last name," she explained.

"Oh, but you can trust this one," Pearline assured her. "He all but saved my life while I was in that saloon."

Knowing how Pearline liked to exaggerate, Julia did not question such a ridiculous statement. "I don't care if he saved the life of President Cleveland. Until I know who he is and why he thinks it so necessary to withhold his last name from me, we are to be very cautious of him. When he's at the house, we do not let him out of our sight," she repeated.

"Even when he goes to the privy?"

"Pearline!"

"Just askin'," she responded with a wide grin, then climbed happily into the carriage. Pearline liked the fact that this Chad person had a bit of mystery about him. That made him all the more interesting.

Chad stayed inside the Dry Creek Saloon just long enough to collect his hat and pay for the drink he had ordered before he had bounded upstairs to save Pearline Williams. After he squared his account, he headed directly for the boardinghouse where Solomon had finally found a nice room that accepted both Negroes and dogs, for Solomon never stayed anywhere without Old Ruby at his side. The faithful red-and-white-spotted hound had been with Solomon for over nine years now, long before Chad had come into his life.

36

Despite the fact that it was after nine o'clock and there was a sign on the front door that declared room visitors not welcome after nine, he marched on inside the front door and walked directly to Solomon's room, which was on the ground floor at the back of the large Victorian house.

Not wanting to be caught in the hallway by the widow who ran the place, he rapped twice on Solomon's door, then tried the handle. Finding the door unlocked, he opened it and slipped inside the sparsely furnished bedroom.

"And what if I'd had a woman in here?" Solomon asked, looking up from the book on animal husbandry he had bought earlier that day at the mercantile.

He lay in bed on top of the covers, propped by three feather pillows. His boots were off and his ankles crossed but otherwise he was still fully clothed, right down to his one gray and one black socks. Ruby lay across a small rug on the floor at the foot of the bed near where Solomon had dropped his boots, and his favorite hat hung over the bedpost only a few feet above the old dog's head.

"You? With a woman?" Chad responded, amused by the thought. He dragged the only chair in the room closer to the bed so they could talk. "Little chance of that. You're still too busy pining away over Rose Kane."

"I'm long over *that*," Solomon said with far more emphasis than necessary. A scowl formed across his face as he watched Chad turn the wooden chair around and straddle it. "Is that what you came here to discuss? If so, I wish you'd go ahead and leave. I have some reading to do."

"You're the one who mentioned the possibility of you being in here with a woman," Chad pointed out. "All I did was explain why that was so unlikely. Besides, Mrs.

Haught wouldn't have let a woman past that front parlor. She's made it perfectly clear that this place is for men only." He glanced down at Old Ruby and chuckled. "I'm surprised she let that mangy old female mutt of yours in here."

Solomon closed his book and set it on the night table on top of a large dictionary he had bought to help him with some words he did not recognize, then looked at Chad through lowered eyelids. "Did you come here for a reason? Or did you just get so lost and confused on your way back from your night of drinking and debauchery that you ended up here instead of at that fancy hotel of yours? And why are you still in your work clothes? I'd think you'd want to dress yourself up a little more for the women in this town. A man of your means can't expect to stay a bachelor forever. Might as well try to find a woman worth having."

"Look who's talking. I don't see *you* asking anyone to marry you," Chad said, wagging a finger at him as if to issue a warning. "And don't you go trying to blame me because none of the hotels in this city allow Negroes. I tried my best to get you a room at the Capitol, too, but there was just no getting around their policies. And to answer your original question, yes, I do have a reason for being here. Although I doubt you'll like hearing it."

Solomon tilted his head back against the pillows and ran his hands over his eyes, seeming to be weary of Chad's visit already. Although Solomon was four years younger than Chad, there were times when he clearly felt he was the elder of the two. "What have you done this time?"

"Found a job."

Solomon dropped his hands and looked at his boss, not certain he had heard him right.

"A job?"

"Which means I won't be around to help you with the rebuilding as much as I'd originally hoped. At least not for the first few weeks or so anyway."

"A job?" Solomon repeated and uncrossed his ankles, his back remaining pressed against the pillows. "Why on God's green earth would you go out and look for a job? Especially *now* after we found out how much more work there is to do. You saw what that tornado did to the house and the cottages behind it. Even with us both working together along with a full crew of men, it will be a good two months before we turn that place into a working cattle farm. Are you *insane?*"

"That's a good question," Chad admitted. He pushed his hat to the back of his head while he studied Solomon's bewildered expression. His behavior that night *had* been a little bizarre. "A very good question indeed."

"And one that deserves an equally good answer, I'd think." Solomon waited several seconds, but when all Chad did was stare vacantly across the room, he tried again, "Why on earth would you go out looking for a job when we now have so blamed much work to do? It's not as if you need more money to help us get by. You deposited over fifty thousand dollars in the Garrett and Key Bank only this morning, and that's just from the sale of your house and land. You still have the money coming from the sale of the mercantile, which will probably be twice that."

"I didn't exactly go looking for this job. I guess you could say it sort of came looking for me," Chad explained, being purposely vague to annoy Solomon further. He loved to stir his friend's ire. "It's a very unusual job. One I just couldn't seem to say no to."

"Why not? What sort of job is it?"

Chad grinned and pushed his hat back even more. His dark hair fell forward across his forehead.

"It seems I'm now a paid lover." When that statement did not fully register with Solomon, Chad hurried to explain his strange situation further. "For the next month, I will be at the beck and call of a very beautiful, very high-spirited young woman named Julia Thornton. I have just hired on to be her sweetheart."

Solomon lifted his hand to massage his forehead with his fingertips while he considered everything Chad had just told him.

"Thornton," he repeated, as if testing the sound of the name. "That sure does sound familiar. Where have I heard it before?" A second later, he sat bolt right in bed and spun to face Chad squarely. "She isn't by any chance related to that same Thornton who wrote to you about a month ago offering to buy your new place. Who then penned that really nasty letter after you'd had me write to tell him that neither the house nor the land was for sale?"

Chad's eyes widened. "Was that man's name Thornton?"

Solomon nodded. "If I remember right, his name was Charles Cole Thornton, and gathering by what he wrote in his letters, he already owns the land bordering on three sides of yours and is very determined to have that, too."

Chad slipped Julia's map out of his pocket and looked at the penciled markings. The house she had indicated as hers appeared to be only a few miles from his. He exhaled sharply while he continued to stare at the hastily drawn map. "Looks like she must be some sort of relation to him. My guess is that she's his daughter."

"And you just hired on to be her *sweetheart?*"

"Sort of," Chad admitted, then explained the situation to Solomon as best he himself understood it.

"So what all this simmers down to is that you have

40

agreed to pretend to be the obnoxious sweetheart of the daughter of that same hostile man who has threatened to make your life here a living hell if you do not change your mind about selling out."

Chad grinned. "Yes, I guess that pretty well sums it up."

Solomon groaned as he ran his strong, mahogany hands over his face again. He had nothing more to say.

"Which is why I will be very careful not to let Julia or her father know my true identity," Chad promised, hoping to make Solomon feel better about what he had done.

Solomon dropped his hands to his lap and looked at Chad as if unable to believe what he had done. "What if he already does know your identity? What if he somehow found out that you and I arrived in Marshall a few days earlier than expected and he purposely sent his daughter out with this scheme to hire you as a way of luring you into some sort of trap?"

"I don't think that's the case." Chad was not willing to believe he could be so easily duped by a beautiful woman. "She seemed genuinely annoyed when I wouldn't tell her my last name. Besides, I met her maid, Pearline Williams, quite by chance. Remember that? She's the one I rescued inside the Dry Creek."

"That whole scene could have been staged," Solomon pointed out.

"No. I don't think so. I saw the terror in that poor woman's eyes when the man snatched her off the floor and started up the stairs with her. She wasn't acting. She was definitely confused and afraid."

"Well, if that's true, if Julia Thornton really does not know who you are, then you had sure better do what you can to keep it that way. Either that, or give up this foolish job before you find yourself in too deep."

41

"Too deep for what?"

"Too deep to get out with your life. What happens when the original sweetheart finds out you are serious about Julia Thornton? That you are out to steal her away from him no matter what you have to do because you've decided you want her for your own."

"When did I say that?"

"You didn't have to. I could tell by watching your eyes when you talked about her. I haven't seen you this attracted to a woman since Veronica Rourke came into your life, and that was ages ago. You do remember Veronica Rourke, don't you? The pretty little blonde who suddenly up and married that arrogant Frenchman about four years ago."

Chad scowled at the memory. Although his feelings for Veronica had died, her betrayal still angered him. "We both have made some pretty lousy choices in women through the years, haven't we?"

"Which is why I worry about this Julia Thornton," Solomon said with all sincerity. "She may be every bit as captivating and spirited as you say, but she means trouble for you, Chad. I can feel it in my bones. It may not be intentional, but it will be trouble all the same."

Chad smiled again while her beautiful image danced before him, stirring emotions he had thought long since dead. "You know me. I'm always willing to take a few risks if I believe the reward will be great enough."

"Unfortunate but true," Solomon muttered. "I still think pretending to be some woman's hired sweetheart to make her father despise you more than he already does is carrying the risk a bit too far."

"Oh, but he doesn't know he already despises me," Chad pointed out cheerfully, too enamored to care what dangers lay ahead. "He doesn't even know who I am."

"In time," Solomon added with clear forewarning,

"one of them is bound to discover who you are. Then what will happen?"

Chad shook his head, refusing to consider the possibility. "They won't find out unless *you* find some reason to tell them. Other than the clerk at the hotel and that one teller at the bank, you are the only man in this whole city who knows my real identity. And I imagine a well-placed coin or two will keep the clerk and that teller quiet long enough for me to win her over. Once I have her thoroughly infatuated with me, I'll tell her the truth. But until then, there's no reason for her to know my last name."

"And what if she *doesn't* become infatuated with you?"

"She will. Fact is, she is already intrigued by me. I could tell by the way she responded to my touch. It may take a little while, but eventually she'll come to recognize the attraction between us every bit as much as I do. All I have to do is find ways to be alone with her so it can have a good chance to grow."

"For your sake, I hope that's true. That is, if you are as determined as I think you are to see this thing through."

"And I am," Chad admitted. His grin widened. "And when you finally see what this Miss Julia Thornton looks like, you'll better understand why. There is just something about that woman . . ." His blue eyes glittered while he considered just how very attractive she was. "She's soft, beautiful, and poised. A true woman in every sense of the word. And yet she is more than that."

Solomon fell silent for several seconds, then asked, "Have you really thought this thing through? What happens when Charles Thornton eventually decides to pay a visit to his new neighbor in a last attempt to buy the place and finds out that his new neighbor is you?"

"If he did that, then he'd probably end up talking

with you," Chad answered, but knowing Solomon was right, his expression sobered. "To be safe, I think I'd better continue staying at the hotel for a while—even after we've made my uncle's house livable again."

"What do you mean *we?* Sounds to me like *I'll* be doing all the work while *you* are off chasing that pretty little lass all over these east Texas hills."

"I'll help out when I can. Surely she won't want me there every single day," he said, then grinned again. "But if it turns out she does, I'll have no choice but to do exactly what she tells me. I've given her my word."

"You and your word," Solomon muttered. "I wish you'd learn to do a little more thinking before you go giving your word on anything so important. I don't think you realize how much more trouble I'm about to face finding workers to help clear the fields and repair those buildings now that you won't be there with me. Very few people from around these parts are going to hire on once they find out they'll be working for a Negro—not if there's not a white man on the premises supervising."

Chad thought Solomon had exaggerated the problem. True, they had come across several men who had shown an instant dislike for Solomon simply because his skin was dark, but that did not mean everyone from that area was like that. "As long as the pay is good and the hours are decent, no one is going to care what color the foreman's skin is. Besides, you can always point out that their salaries will come from the pockets of a white man."

Solomon huffed, then reached for his book again. "We'll find out if my skin color is going to make a difference tomorrow. I went by the courthouse this afternoon and tacked up that notice advertising for workers."

"On that community bulletin board I told you about?"

"Yes. I wrote that we need several hardworking men who know how to work stock but who can also help with general farm repairs and signed the notice C. W. Andrews just like you told me. I also mentioned needing a woman to cook and clean. Whatever men we hire will have to eat. I figure that the first men to answer the advertisement should arrive bright and early tomorrow morning."

"Good. Hire anyone who shows any promise on the spot. That way we can get started with those repairs right away."

"There you go with that *we* business again. Don't you mean *I'll* be able to get started on the repairs right away. *You'll* be too busy doing whatever it is the beautiful Miss Julia Thornton orders you to do."

"I told you. I'll help when I can."

Solomon met his gaze directly, more out to prove a point than start an argument. "Can you help tomorrow?"

"Well, no. I've got to wait for that shipment of furniture to come in, remember?"

"And can you help the next day?"

"Well, no. I have to find someplace to store the furniture now that we know the house is not going to be livable for some time. If I can't find somewhere here in town to store everything, I'll probably have to bring some of it on out there and put it in the carriage house or the barn, since neither of those were damaged by the storm. But unless I end up having to do that, I probably won't even be out."

"And the next day you'll be getting ready for your first encounter with Charles Thornton," Solomon pointed out. "So tell me again why you keep saying *we*."

"Because it sounds so much better than *you*," Chad admitted sheepishly. He lifted his chin when he had thought more about it. "And because even though it has turned out that you will be the one having to supervise most of the beginning repairs, it is still my place. I'm the one who's forking out all the money. Doesn't that count for anything?"

"A little, I guess," Solomon admitted, then met Chad's grin with one of his own. "Just make sure you check in with me from time to time so I can ask your advice on some of the more important decisions."

"Yes, sir." Chad saluted his friend by tapping a fingertip to his forehead. "I'll do anything for the man who saved my life."

Solomon groaned, but with his wide grin still in place. "Why do you find it so necessary to keep reminding me of my past mistakes?" he said, then laughed as he opened his book and resumed reading.

Chapter Three

"I thought you'd want to know. The furniture we ordered from New York arrived a couple of hours ago and with only one mirror broken," Chad pulled his hat off his head, then sat down across the small table from Solomon.

"Which mirror? The small one attached to my bookcase or that big one that came with your dresser?" Solomon wanted to know.

"My dresser," Chad admitted while he twisted around to hook his hat over the back post of his chair. He combed his hands through his thick hair in an effort to remove the indentation the hatband had left. "A lot more furniture came in than I remembered us ordering at first. I told the freight company to hold it for me overnight until I could find someplace large enough to store it all."

Solomon signaled for the waitress. Although this was nowhere near the nicest restaurant in the city, it did have table service and it did serve all races.

"Did those crates and barrels we packed come in, too?"

Chad nodded. "Those arrived this morning along with most of my old furniture. The crates and barrels

I'm having sent directly out to the farm first thing in the morning since you'll probably be needing some of the tools and the clothing that are packed inside. You should have plenty of room in the carriage house to store them, at least until our two houses have been made weather-tight again. The old furniture I'll try to have stored with the rest. Any luck hiring the men we need?"

Solomon's expression darkened. "I managed to hire a few."

"Why only a few? Aren't any of the locals responding to that notice you put up?"

Solomon glanced toward the waitress who stood nearby gaping openly at Chad while awaiting their order. Used to having women gawk at his handsome friend, he cleared his throat to make sure he had her attention, then nodded toward the large chalkboard hat hammered to a nearby post where the day's selections had been neatly printed in bold white letters.

"We'll both have that second one listed. The steak and potatoes." He then gestured to his empty mug with a slight wave of his hand. "Also bring me another beer, and one for my friend, too."

He waited until the woman had finally torn her starry gaze off Chad and headed toward the kitchen near the back of the room before answering Chad's questions. "Oh, we've had plenty of men respond to the notice. I guess twenty or so made the hour-long ride to find out more about what jobs we were offering."

Chad shook his head, indicating he did not understand the problem.

"Most of the men who responded were white, and just as soon as they found out that they'd be having to take their orders from me, they were suddenly no longer interested in working so far out of town. Or they suddenly remembered they had another job pending. Or else they just came right out and admitted the truth." His nostrils flared and the muscles at the back of his jaw flexed. "To quote one of them, 'I don't work for no Negroes'."

Chad's eyebrows dipped. "How many men *were* you able to hire?"

"Six thus far, all Negro. I'll do what I can to take on a few more tomorrow."

"Six? Is that all?"

"It was enough so we were able to start work on both the side of your house and the front of mine this afternoon. Even with just the six of them, I should still be able to have the overseer quarters livable by the end of the week and a good portion of your house livable before the end of the month."

"Any women wanting to be our cook yet?"

"No such luck." Solomon sighed. "I guess that means I'll have to continue doing all the cooking and serving until some woman does finally appear."

Chad studied Solomon a moment, then cocked a good-natured grin. "I sure hope that happens soon, because if it doesn't, your cooking will likely end up running off what few men you have managed to hire. Until we find some woman willing to take over the job, we'll probably have to do our hiring on an almost daily basis."

Solomon lifted an eyebrow as if in silent warning. "My stew is tolerable."

"Barely," Chad continued to goad, then abruptly changed the subject. He was too eager to hear about any progress being made to spend more time baiting Solomon. Having grown tired of living in the cramped city of Charleston, he looked forward to making something worthwhile out of his uncle's land, even though he still felt a little guilty knowing he'd found such happiness as a result of his uncle's failing health.

If the man had not been told to move out west to a drier climate, he would never have sold everything to him at such a reasonable price. "Are any of the men you hired today stockmen who might be worth keeping on after the last of the repairs have been made and the fields cleared and seeded?"

Solomon's forehead puckered with concern. "You have to keep in mind that there are very few large cattle farms in this area. Though the land is right for it, most of the locals prefer to grow cotton or timber. But one man I hired does claim to have worked around cattle before, although he admits it has been a while. And some of the others might be trainable. All I can do is wait and see what kind of workers they turn out to be."

Chad pressed his mouth into a flat line. He had waited all his life for a chance like this. He did not like the thought of having to wait any longer.

Julia waited until her father was finished eating and had stepped out onto the veranda on his way to the stables to check on the new foal before broaching the subject she had waited all day to broach.

"Father, I have a little surprise for you," she said sweetly and fell into step beside him. It was something she had not wanted to bring to his attention until after he'd had a good, filling meal, especially considering the mood he had been in lately.

"What sort of surprise?" Charles asked. He studied his daughter carefully while he pulled his usual after-dinner cigar out of his breast pocket and ran it beneath his nose. He slowed his pace. "What are you up to now, young lady?"

"Nothing." Julia tried not to look annoyed by such an accusing response when he had every right to be suspicious of her. "It's just that I received a letter today from a dear friend I met while in St. Louis who now has plans to be in Marshall for a few weeks."

"A dear friend?" Charles came to an abrupt halt halfway between the house and the barn as he turned to meet Julia's innocent gaze. Although the sun had gone behind the distant hill half an hour earlier, there was still enough light to see her unusually round-eyed expression. He narrowed his gaze. "What sort of *dear* friend?"

"A very dear friend," she answered, all the while fighting the urge to look away. Lying to her father had never come easily. "His name is Chad and he should be arriving in Marshall sometime this week. He hopes to stop by for a nice visit with us Friday evening."

Charles continued to study his beautiful daughter with a skeptically raised brow. "And why haven't I heard of this Chad before?"

"Haven't I mentioned him?" she asked, then wrinkled her forehead as if trying to recall a possible conversation that might have included him.

"No. You have not." He continued to meet her questioning gaze with his own. A slight breeze tugged at his white hair, causing him to lift his hand to push the front locks back into place but the gesture did not lessen his attention. "Let's see. Since you've been home you have mentioned a Keith, a Paul, and a Patrick, but no Chad. Who is he?"

Julia was surprised he had remembered those three young men, as preoccupied as he had been these last few days. "He's very bright and handsome," she said with what she hoped was just the right amount of enthusiasm. "Someone I know you are going to like."

51

"And why is it he is coming here only several days after you yourself have returned?"

Julia jerked her chin up in response to the accusing tone in his voice. Why did he always suspect hidden motives? "Because I want you to meet him. He really is a very *special* person. Like no one you've every met before." Even though she had just spoken the truth, it still took all the control she had to continue meeting his gaze.

Charles studied her a long moment, then looked suddenly weary. "I take it you are in love again?"

"Yes. I am," she said with a shy smile, knowing that part of it was true. She *was* in love again. But with Patrick, not Chad. "I am very much in love."

Charles put the cigar back into his pocket and shook his head tiredly. That was not what he had wanted to hear. "And I suppose he's coming here to ask me for your hand in marriage."

"It might lead to that. But first he only wants to meet you."

Charles sighed with annoyance as he started toward the stable again. "Why now? Why when I have so many other problems?"

Julia did not bother to answer. Nor did she bother to follow him. It was obvious he was already lost again to his own thoughts and she had already said all she wanted to say for now.

"I'll tell Ruth to set an extra place at the table Friday night," she called after him, smiling at how easily she had introduced Chad into her father's life. If things continued to go this smoothly during the next few weeks, she'd have no problem convincing him to let her marry Patrick.

She clasped her hands together at the mere thought of finally being allowed to marry and get out from under her father's stern rule. Very soon she would be starting a new life, one in which she could finally make her own choices. And it would be Patrick letting her make those choices. She sighed at the fond memory of his smiling face, knowing there were not too many men who would have promised her such happiness.

"Father, you will adore Chad every bit as much as I do. I just know it." Her smile widened at the hidden meaning, for the truth was she could hardly tolerate the man. He was far too handsome and far too arrogant for his own good.

Which made him the perfect man for the job. Oh, how her father hated arrogance.

Solomon glanced up when he heard yet another horse headed toward the house but did not bother getting up off his hands and knees when he saw that the rider was another white man. Instead, he finished hammering in the nail he had started and reached for another of the four he still held in his mouth. He wanted to finish replacing the damaged boards along the veranda floor by nightfall so his new workers would not trip and injure themselves while going back and forth to repair the inside of the house.

"You Mister Andrews?" the tall young man asked when he brought his horse to a halt in the overgrown yard nearby. The years of neglect had caused the weeds to stand as tall as the horse's hind hocks.

When Solomon did not immediately answer or pause in his work, the rider climbed down from the horse. Because there was no hitching post directly in front of the house, he tethered the animal to the lower limb of a nearby spreading oak, then headed immediately toward the steps. He hesitated on the top stair when he noticed the hunting hound lying on the veranda floor only a few feet away.

"That dog bite?"

Solomon still did not look up. "Old Ruby? Only when she thinks I'm being threatened. You're not here to threaten me, are you?"

"Not me," he answered in earnest, then asked. "You that Mister Andrews who's looking for hard workers?" He divided his attention between Solomon's bent form and the dog who had done no more than shift the direction of her head so she could look at him.

Tired of dealing with the white men who refused to take orders from a black man, Solomon took the last nail out of his mouth and positioned it over the board before answering. "No. My name's Solomon. Solomon Ford. Mr. Andrews isn't here right now."

The young man glanced out at the four men working in the field, then at two others replacing shingles on a small building behind the house. "Are you the one in charge, or is one of them?"

"I am." Solomon gave the man a cursory glance.

"Well, my name is Raymond Porterfield." He snatched off his hat as if just realizing he had it on, revealing a head carpeted with unruly red hair. "While I was at the courthouse this afternoon, I saw where a Mr. C. W. Andrews is looking for men to work stock and help with repairs." He twisted his hat brim, looking truly earnest about wanting to work. "I can see you've already hired a good number of men, but I thought maybe you might need one more. I don't mean to brag now, but I know all there is to know about tending livestock and I can swing a hammer or a sickle as good as any man."

Not seeing any reason to waste time asking the man to be more specific when he would undoubtedly make a beeline for his horse the minute he found out a Negro would be giving most of the orders, Solomon got right to the point. "Before we discuss anything else, I think you should know that I'm more than just the man in charge while the boss is away today. I'm official foreman here. If you worked here, you'd be taking most of your orders directly from me."

"I got no quarrel with that, sir."

Solomon's dark eyes widened. He had not expected to be called sir by a white man. He laid his hammer aside and gave young Raymond his undivided attention. "It wouldn't bother you to have to take your orders from me?" His dark eyes narrowed again, causing his eyebrows to take a noticeable dip. "You did notice that I'm a Negro, didn't you?" He patted his sweating arm to offer proof.

"Yes, sir. I noticed," Raymond looked at him questioningly. "Kind of hard not to. But it don't matter to me none what color skin you was born with. Not as long as you're fair about giving whatever orders you give. You see, I really do need the work. Several of my friends and I just lost our jobs because of so many of the Mexican-Indians around here have proved willing to do our work for practically nothing." He met Solomon's gaze directly. Mister, I got me a wife and three offspring and we all five got to eat."

Solomon blinked at hearing that last statement. "This wife of yours," he asked. "Can she cook?"

"Sure she can." He gestured toward his lean frame. "Although you couldn't tell by looking at me, she cooks just fine. Why?"

"Would she be wanting to work here, too? We are in desperate need of a cook. The men I've hired don't particularly like having to eat my stew every day."

55

Raymond stroked his chin thoughtfully. "Is that all she'd do, cook?"

"For now. Later, if she wants, she could probably work for Mr. Andrews as a full-time housekeeper." To make the offer more appealing, he stepped off the veranda and pointed to several wind-damaged cottages set off in twin columns behind the house. "I'd even be willing to let you have your choice of any of those little houses over there. With a few repairs, a lot of cleaning, and a fresh coat of paint, those old slave cabins should make nice little homes for some of our permanent workers."

He then pointed to the overseer's quarters which were built off to the right side of the slave housing. On top of the building, two men worked steadily at replacing a small section of broken shingles. "In fact, I'll be living right out there not too far from you. I'm moving in to that larger house there just as soon as they finish mending the roof and replacing part of the floor. It'll be nice to have someone around to talk to at nights besides Old Ruby and the boss, once he finally gets here." He gestured toward the sleeping dog. "Old Ruby is a trusted friend, but she isn't much of a conversationalist."

Because it turned out that Raymond and his family were having to camp near the railroads just outside Marshall, he wasted no time in accepting Solomon's offer of both jobs and place to stay. When Chad appeared later that afternoon with part of the new furniture in tow, he was greeted by a very happy Solomon.

"You look like the cat who ate the canary," Chad observed as soon as he had hopped down from the new work wagon he had just bought. He turned to untie the tarpaulin he'd tossed over what furniture he had been unable to fit into the small storage room he had rented earlier that day. Since it was apparent Solomon would be ready to move in long before he himself was, most of the furniture in the wagon were pieces Solomon had ordered.

"That's because I have good news," Solomon said, flashing a bright smile. "I hired us a stockman this afternoon who's had a considerable amount of experience working with cattle." He continued telling Chad all about Raymond's background and qualifications.

"I think he's just the man to help pick out the stock when that time comes," he concluded. *"And* he says he has a few friends who might be willing to come work for us, too. He's going to see if he can get in touch with them. Everything seems to be finally falling into place. Looks like your dream of owning a prosperous cattle farm is about to come true."

"Where is this man?" Chad asked, eager to meet him. He looked out into the nearest field where three Negroes were clearing out the small trees and brush that had taken over during all the years his uncle had neglected the place, then at the roof of the main house where another two were removing a large uprooted pine, one limb at a time. He also noticed two more men atop Solomon's house tacking down fresh shingles. That made seven in all.

"Right now, he's gone to tell his wife they have a new place to live," Solomon answered, then explained, "I told him that if they wanted to help fix up one of those cabins out back, they could move out here permanently."

"Oh, you did," Chad pretended to be annoyed that Solomon had taken it upon himself to decide such a thing.

"There's no sense letting those cottages go to waste, and I had to do *something* to make sure they took the jobs."

"Jobs? They? I thought you said you only found one stockman."

Solomon beamed. "His wife is going to be our cook, at least until we can hire a permanent housekeeper later on. Who knows, she might want that job, too."

"What are their names?" He turned back toward the wagon to finish untying the tarpaulin. It had been three days since he was last there. He was in a hurry to have a look around the place. He was especially eager to see what repairs had been made on his house. He wanted the house to look especially nice, perhaps because the more he thought about it, the more he liked the idea of filling that house with a wife and family. Just that thought brought images of the beautiful Julia Thornton into his mind. *What an interesting wife she would make.*

"Raymond and Deborah Porterfield. They also have three sons, two of whom are old enough to take on odd jobs around the place."

"And what about school? Don't you realize that the nearest school for Negroes is over six miles away? How do they plan to get back and forth?"

"Oh, but they are white," Solomon announced happily. "And oddly enough, it doesn't matter to them one bit that I am not."

"Imagine that," Chad said with a grin, then tossed the tarpaulin back to reveal the several pieces of furniture underneath. "Well, get your carcass over here and help me put this furniture into the barn. I want to have a look at the work you and your men have done before it gets too dark to see."

Julia had put away her canvas and paints and was out on the veranda waiting for her father to climb down from his carriage when Pearline's brother Sirus hurried

58

across the yard, apparently anxious to speak to him. After several minutes, Sirus headed back toward the stables with the carriage in tow while Charles moved toward the house.

"What was that all about?" she asked, wondering what the man had to say that was important enough not to have waited until her father's nightly visit to the stables after supper. "Is the new foal sick?"

"No. The foal's fine," he assured her as he climbed the steps, then turned to watch Sirus approach several other men who worked there. "He was just giving me a report about a situation I've been having him keep a close eye on."

"What situation is that?" She watched her father curiously while he tugged out of his white summer coat, then folded it over his arm. He had already removed his string tie and had unbuttoned the collar of his shirt to allow him to breathe more easily.

He continued across the veranda, and Julia felt a surge of pride wash over her. Although he had recently turned fifty-one, he had yet to go soft like many men his age. Because her father liked to keep an active hand in the production of his mills and in the work at his two shipping yards, and because he rarely stopped anywhere for a midday meal, he was still as strong as he had been the day he'd married her mother twenty-four years ago.

Julia was also proud of the way he had taken over her grandfather's lumber mill so soon after her grandfather had fallen to his death in a freak accident involving a hay rake. He had managed to build the small family business into an impressive timber concern in the years since. Now, not only was the timber mill four times the size it had been when her grandfather died, her father had also opened an enormous lumber yard in Marshall, a smaller one in Jefferson, and had a large store that sold cut lumber locally and now shipped to areas all over Texas, Louisiana, and, most recently, into New Mexico.

He also had his own logging company that employed over thirty lumberjacks who harvested timber all over northeast Texas, then transported the huge, felled trees to his saw mill for processing, usually by floating the trees down the Little Cypress River which flowed by both their house and the lumber mill. Unfortunately, the river also flowed right beside the house her father had had built especially for her and her mother just over twenty years ago, a house that still stood between their present home and the lumber mill itself. The same house they had been forced to vacate back in the early part of 1875 when she was only thirteen.

Julia frowned at the upsetting memories. Shortly after her father had been so easily tricked into losing the homeplace and five hundred acres of prime timberland in a high-stakes poker game, Robert Freeport had quickly moved into the luxurious house they had called home since before her birth, then set up a series of dams and spillways across the portion of river that flowed past his house. Although the dams allowed most of the water to continue downstream so others could use it, they made it virtually impossible for her father to float logs beyond that point in the river.

It had taken six years for her father to get the legal papers he needed to force Robert to tear down the dams. In the meantime, her father was forced to remove the logs that came down from the timber-rich areas higher in the hills. He'd had to pull them out of the river, one by one, then drag them in groups of two or three several miles overland to the lumber mill, a distance which otherwise would have been less than two miles downstream. Hauling the huge logs overland had

60

been far more costly and far more time consuming, and had wedged further hostility between the two men. It was no wonder her father was so intent on getting that land back.

"I've had Sirus watching the old place for me so I would know the minute that new neighbor moved in," her father went on to explain.

Julia shook her head, wishing he could let the past go. But knew that would never happen. He had promised her mother he would one day get their house and land back, and even though she was dead six years now, he still yearned to keep that promise. "And?"

"And it appears he's either already there or about to be, because there has been a lot of work going on both on the house and in the fields these past few days. In addition, last night, Sirus rode over to have another look at what was going on and said there were lights burning in both the main house and in the old overseer's cottage. There were also hammering sounds coming from inside, as if whoever is working there intended to continue right through the night." Having paused just outside the door to answer her questions, he took his hat off and used it as a temporary fan. It was unusually warm for April.

"Now that I know the new owner is there, I plan to ride over tomorrow afternoon as soon as I'm finished in town and make another offer to buy the place. This one even better than the last. This one so generous he'd be a fool to turn it down."

"That won't make you late for supper, will it? Don't forget we have company coming. I would like you already here when he arrives."

Charles scowled as he headed through the door. "How could I forget? You reminded me twice last night

61

before I went on up to bed and once this morning before I left for Marshall."

She followed her father inside. "It's just that it is important to me that you two meet so you can see what a truly exceptional man Chad is." At having mentioned Chad's name aloud, she felt a strange quivering sensation somewhere inside her which she immediately attributed to the guilt she felt knowing she was about to do something so deceitful. Despite his strong, controlling nature and his sometimes short, uneven temper, she did love her father dearly.

"Exceptional?" Charles set his coat and hat on a nearby table, then turned to look at her. "What's so exceptional about him? You haven't ever said."

And she didn't intend to now. She wanted her father completely unprepared for what was to happen tomorrow night. "You'll see," she answered sweetly, then quickly changed the topic back to one she knew concerned her father more—the fact that the new owner of their original home had finally arrived. Her father had been waiting for the chance to talk with the man personally for several months now, since the day they had first heard that Robert Freeport had sold everything to his nephew.

"And what if the new owner still refuses to sell the house and land to you after you've gone over there tomorrow?"

"He won't. Not when he hears how much I'm willing to pay. I'm offering a full thousand dollars more than I offered before, and that's just for the house and the land that's on this side of it. I'm willing to leave him the other three hundred acres so he can turn around and build a nice little place of his own with the money he'll have made. After all, my grudge has always been with Robert Freeport, not his nephew."

"But what if he turns down the offer?" she asked, wanting him prepared for the worst. She would hate to see him disappointed yet again.

Charles looked at her angrily, incensed that she could even suggest such a thing. "He wouldn't dare."

Julia watched her father stalk off toward the wide stairs near the back of the foyer, his arms swinging stiffly at his sides. It occurred to her then that it might be to her advantage if the new owner did flatly refuse the new offer—at least for now. It would certainly put her father in all the worse mood for meeting Chad tomorrow night.

Chapter Four

When Charles turned his carriage down the narrow, grass-covered driveway that ten years ago would have carried him home, he felt a strange combination of hope and remorse knotted together inside him. Although he passed this way at least once each week to leave fresh flowers on his wife's grave, today felt different. Today, it felt oddly as if he were coming home again. Perhaps because he knew there was still a good chance he could persuade the new owner to sell the house and at least part of his land back to him. And in doing so, he would finally have fulfilled the promise he had made his beloved Virginia so many years ago.

Sadly, he thought back to the day he'd made that solemn promise. Virginia had tried to be so understanding about having to leave the only home they had ever known as husband and wife—the house he'd had built especially for her near a picturesque bend in the Little Cypress River just nine miles northwest of Marshall and eight miles southwest of Jefferson. It was her easy willingness to forgive him for the truly foolish thing he had done that hurt him even now. If only he had not made that bet and lost. If only he had seen Robert Freeport for the cold, conniving bastard he really was. Then all

64

that heartache could have been avoided. And Virginia might still be alive.

Charles's hands tightened on the reins until his knuckles were as white as the scant sprigs of hair that grew along their roughened backs, large hands that had suffered thirty-five years of hard, honest work in the timber business.

"By damn, I *will* get that house back for you, Ginny, and our grandchildren *will* play in the same yard our children played in just like you always wanted," he vowed.

His anger then fell into melancholy. If there ever *were* any grandchildren. He hated it that Julia was nearly twenty-three years old and had yet to find a man worthy of her so he could have that handful of grandchildren to spoil. Perhaps this new fellow, this Chad whoever, would be the right one. He certainly hoped so. But somehow he doubted it. Julia seemed to lean toward handsome, smooth-talking men who were far more interested in his money than her beauty. And that was a shame, for although his wealth was considerable, Julia's beauty was worth far more.

Again he was reminded of his dear Virginia. How very much alike those two were. Beautiful, strong willed, and more intelligent than most men—except when it came to affairs of the heart. That was the only area in which they both had proved lacking.

Grimly, he wondered if Virginia would still be alive if she had fallen in love with another man, one who had not been so easily manipulated. He forced aside the tears that threatened his hazel eyes. Tears would not help him in his quest to get back the house and land he had so foolishly lost.

If only he had known just how far Robert Freeport was willing to carry his hate. A hate born of jealousy, all because Virginia had chosen to marry him instead. A hate that had eventually taken Virginia's life.

Charles tried to push the bitter memories aside when, seconds later, he approached the divide in the road that in one direction led to the Thornton family cemetery. The other direction headed toward the house where he and his beloved wife had lived for fifteen of their seventeen years of marriage.

For the first time in almost ten years, Charles veered his carriage to the right instead of the left.

Again he became lost in thoughts of the past, wondering what it would be like to have Virginia waiting for him again. He was only vaguely aware of the tall, spreading broadleaf and pine trees that overlapped the road, forming the dark-green canopy that shaded large sections of the narrow drive. He barely noticed the brilliant blue-and-white wildflowers that grew in scattered abundance along the fence line.

Within minutes the house he had so lovingly designed and built for his wife came into his sight. When he first saw the damage and the general disrepair of what had at one time been a palatial two-story brick mansion, painted brilliant white with dark blue shutters and trim at either side of the oversize windows and doors, it felt as if someone had speared his heart with a fine-edged sword. He was glad Virginia was not alive, for it would have torn her apart to see the devastation that lay before him now.

Although he knew that last month's tornado had done a lot of damage throughout the area, until now he did not realize just how much. One side of the main house had been badly crushed by one of the huge, sweeping oaks that had at one time shaded much of the front yard but now lay torn out of the ground by the roots. At another section, the building had several boards and bricks missing, as if the high wind had simply peeled the walls away, laying it bare to the frame.

Many of the large, beveled windows he'd had brought in from Shreveport were completely gone, as were both front doors. Several of the old slave cabins that had been built toward the back of the house had also suffered severe damage, along with the old overseer's quarters. He could tell that a lot of repair work had already been done on that building because the walls and roof both looked as if they were constructed partially of fresh lumber. Lumber that had *not* been bought from his mill, which meant it had to have come from one of the mills over near Jefferson or else transported from Daingerfield.

When he continued his survey, he noticed that other hardwood trees not quite as large as the massive oak that had struck the main house had also fallen or snapped in two and had collapsed large sections of the slatted fenced that had surrounded the house. A tree had also destroyed a small windmill directly behind the cabins. Branches, dead leaves, and pine needles were strewn everywhere.

Yet oddly enough the carriage house, the smoke house, the chicken coop, the privy, the barn, the woodshed, and the river pier beyond had withstood the storm's wrath unscathed. Except for the fact that all the structures before him needed a fresh coat of paint, most of the buildings off to the far side, toward the river, looked to be in as good a shape as the day his workmen had built them back in 1860.

Snapping his reins after finishing his quick appraisal, Charles headed toward the house itself. When he got closer, he noticed several hired hands scattered about the area working in small groups of two or three busily repairing the storm's damage. For a moment Charles wished the storm had struck before Robert Freeport had left for Arizona. He would have loved to have seen the man's face. Unfortunately, Robert had already sold everything to his nephew by then and had already left town. As a result, Robert had never had to worry about the damage at all. The cost of all those repairs had fallen on his nephew.

Charles spotted a tall, slender young man with a brilliant shock of red hair standing beside a section of fence near the barn. He held a narrow board level to the ground while a tall, thickset Negro hammered it into place. Thinking the redhead must be the new owner, Charles turned his carriage in his direction. He avoided as much of the debris in the yard as possible.

"Hello, there," he called to the gangling young man, searching for any family resemblance in his features. He forced a smile, too apprehensive about all that could go wrong in the next few minutes for it to appear genuine. "Are you Robert Freeport's nephew?"

Raymond looked up but did not let go of the board when he shook his head. "No, sir. Mr. Andrews ain't here." He then glanced at the large black man.

Solomon finished hammering in the two nails he had placed, then stood to greet their visitor. "And he won't be here for at least a few more weeks."

Charles's smile fell to an immediate scowl while he watched the large man stretch and ripple his muscles. *A few more weeks?* He certainly did not want to have to wait that long. "But I need to talk with him long before then." Again he looked at Raymond. "When exactly will he arrive?"

Raymond, who had yet to meet Chad Andrews and knew only that he would be the one paying him at the end of each month, shrugged his shoulders before tugging at his sweat-soaked workshirt while he looked again at Solomon, waiting for him to answer instead.

Annoyed at the way Charles kept directing his questions to Raymond, Solomon took a determined step forward. His every muscle had tensed.

"Raymond's not the one in charge here. I am. And like I just told you, Mr. Andrews won't be moving out here for a few more weeks yet. There are some important matters he feels he must take care of first. He sent me ahead to see that all the repairs are started and he stays in regular contact with me."

Charles's eyebrows leveled into two flat lines above his piercing eyes. He did not like hearing that the new owner would not be there for weeks yet. "And what is your name?"

"Solomon. Solomon Ford." He stepped forward and extended his right hand even though he knew the fashionably dressed man in the high-springed carriage would not bend forward to accept a handshake from him. "I'm the foreman here."

"You're the foreman?" Charles's frown deepened with surprise. "And just what is it you are the foreman of?" He glanced around, trying to figure out what Robert's nephew planned to do with the place. Instead of planting new trees, they were busy tearing down many of those few that still stood.

"I'm the foreman of Mr. Andrews's new cattle farm," Solomon said, arching his glistening shoulders proudly.

"Cattle?" Charles looked at Solomon as if he were not all there. "When he could be growing trees instead? Doesn't he know how much money there is in timber? Especially these days, what with people moving out West in droves, out to those areas where there are hardly any trees to cut."

Solomon shrugged, then reached for the bright yellow

bandanna hanging out of his trouser pocket and wiped the sweat from his forehead and cheeks. "The boss has always wanted to live out in the country and manage his own cattle farm. And to tell you the God's truth, so have I. It's just something we both have wanted for a long, long time."

Solomon then looked at Raymond, temporarily forgetting their scowling visitor. "I've always preferred living in the country to living in a city. I came from a family that worked on a large tobacco plantation in Alabama when I was young. They were slaves who stayed on as free servants after the war. Because of that experience and because of all the schooling I've had since, I know a lot about agriculture and have also learned quite a bit about animal care, which is why Mr. Andrews asked me to be his foreman when the opportunity came to buy this land."

He looked back at the frowning white-haired man in the gleaming black carriage questioningly. "Who should I tell him stopped by?"

"His neighbor. Charles Thornton."

Solomon's face registered immediate recognition. "The man who has tried so hard to buy this place?"

"He told you about me?" Again, Charles looked surprised.

"I'm the one who sent the response to your lawyer explaining that he was in no way interested in selling his new land. Besides, by the time he'd received your letter, the boss had already sold his other home and already had a buyer interested in the mercantile."

"I thought that answer came from Mr. Andrews's attorney," Charles said, his voice gruff and accusing.

"No. It came from me. But I mailed the letter at Mr. Andrews's request after I'd sent him a telegraph message telling him about your offer. Is that why you're here? To make the boss another offer?"

"Yes. I'm here to make 'the boss' another offer," Charles admitted, reaching for the large envelope on the seat beside him. "This document will explain everything fully. I'm offering Mr. Andrews a thousand dollars more than I offered last time, even though the house has been seriously damaged since. Also, I now am including less than half his land in the purchase, which is the same as offering him over twice per acre what I'd offered the first time. And the new offer will leave him with nearly three hundred acres on which he can then build his own house."

Without climbing down from the carriage, Charles thrust the envelope in Solomon's direction. "See that he receives this as soon as possible."

"I'll give it to him," Solomon said. "But I don't think it will do much good. The boss has already told me he does not plan to sell any part of the land at *any* price. He's waited too long for this opportunity." Besides, Chad had made a promise to his uncle not to sell the land to anyone outside the family. That had been part of the agreement.

"Just see that he gets it," Charles repeated, then reached for his reins. "And the sooner the better, because my patience and my generosity will soon wear thin."

Thinking that sounded too much like a threat, Solomon opened his mouth to offer an appropriate retort, but Charles had already slapped his reins hard and was on his way.

"He's here!" Julia called up to her father, who had just appeared at the top of the stairs. Dropping the cur-

71

tain back into place, she hurried to meet him halfway. Her heart hammered hard and fast against the walls of her chest when she realized the time of reckoning had finally come. "Now remember, when you open the door, greet him with your warmest smile and don't you dare mention anything about his being fifteen minutes late. He probably didn't understand the directions I gave him, or else he read the time wrong."

"Why do I have to be the one to open the door?" Charles complained while he made his way across the foyer. "Why can't Abraham do that?"

"Because I want Chad to know how very unassuming and friendly you are," she said, fighting the urge to grin, aware he had been muttering angrily to himself ever since he had returned home from the old place. *Friendly* was the last thing her father wanted to be that night. "And because I want him to feel comfortable with you from the very start. I want you both to become very good friends."

Charles let out an annoyed sigh as he headed toward the door, hoping against hope that this one would be noticeably different from all the others. How he would love for Julia to find herself a good man who truly cared about her and finally settle down. How he would love a passel of dark-haired, dark-eyed grandchildren to spoil.

He paused in front of the mirror to check his appearance, knowing that Julia was drawn to men of impeccable dress. He certainly did not want this new suitor of hers outdoing him in evening attire. He had chosen to wear his newest dinner coat and had asked Abraham to polish his favorite boots until they gleamed like black onyx. He did not want the young man having even one advantage over him. "Are the loops of my tie even?"

"You look perfect," she assured him, then gripped her skirts with one hand then started up the stairs. She paused just long enough to turn around and caution him one last time. "Now, remember. *Smile.*"

Holding his head erect, Charles tried several different smiles while he stood in front of the small mirror but dropped them all like so much deadweight when he turned toward the door. He did not feel like smiling. Not tonight. Not after the disappointment he had had earlier that day.

Standing only a few feet away, he tapped his polished boot impatiently on the gleaming hardwood floor, waiting for this Chad fellow to twist the doorbell. It was while he waited for the summons that he realized he did not even know this young man's last name. He spun about to ask Julia for that information, but she had already disappeared back up the stairs so she could make her usual grand entrance.

After several more minutes of listening intently for evidence their visitor had approached the house, he finally heard the steady sound of footsteps on the veranda and was startled when there came a loud, clattering knock instead of the faint dingling of a bell.

Prepared to meet a dapper young man with stylishly cut hair, wearing the very latest in St. Louis fashion, he took just a second to give his lapels one last quick adjustment, then swung the door open wide. His white-fringed hazel eyes stretched to their limits when, instead of some fancy young dandy from the river city, he was faced with a tall, broad-shouldered man who looked to be in his mid to late twenties. He was dressed in form-fitting black broadcloth trousers and a freshly starched pale-blue workshirt with the top three buttons left purposely undone. He wore no dinner coat. Nor did he wear a necktie or a throat sash. *Nor* did he have on the latest in men's dress boots like Charles had expected, and instead of a narrow belt through the loops of his trousers, he sported black leather suspenders.

Suddenly, Charles felt grossly overdressed and wondered what his daughter had told this man about suppers there. Surely she had explained that unlike some families, they always dressed appropriately for the evening meal.

Well, at least he's clean, Charles thought when he stepped back to let the young man enter, desperately trying to find *some* reason for his daughter to be attracted to him. Something beyond the fact he was admittedly handsome—in a rugged, common sort of way.

"Hello, I'm Julia's father, Charles Thornton," he said, then extended his hand in proper greeting only to find himself holding the young man's hat instead of his hand.

"Pleased to finally meet you, too, Mr. Thornton. Sorry I'm so late," Chad responded quickly but offered no excuse that explained why he was so late.

Determined to play his role as the overbearing sweetheart as best he could so Julia would not realize he had far more personal motives for being there, Chad purposely paid more attention to his lavish surroundings than to the older man standing in front of him. He knew that pretending to be enthralled by the grandeur, even though his parents' house had been every bit as grand, would make Charles instantly wary of him.

Noticing how Julia's father stood staring at him with a baffled, almost startled, expression, he lifted his hand to the part of his chest exposed by the partially unbuttoned shirt and scratched at an imaginary itch in the dark, curling hair while he continued to study his surroundings.

Clearly the Thorntons had every bit as much money as the people in town had claimed. The house was extremely large and had been decorated in the grandest of elegance. Seeing it made him eager to do something equally as impressive with his own house.

The entrance of the Thornton home was so massive it could have served as a receiving parlor were there chairs and sofas scattered about instead of the six narrow tables stretched along the sides. Upon each of the large, decorative tables was at least one *object* carved from gleaming silver, and between the tables stood huge open doorways leading into rooms that were furnished in as grand a style.

Behind the tables stood the entrance walls, a full twenty-two feet in height and set spaciously apart. The walls were partially paneled with gleaming rosewood, from the decorative floor molding to the elaborately carved chair railing. A smooth, rich white stucco covered the remainder of the walls. Several large paintings hung in heavy ornate frames on opposing walls at or well above eye level. Most looked to be family portraits but some were of wooded landscapes and one was of the sea.

The floor was also made of gleaming rosewood with a thick, imported dark-blue carpet stretched across the middle. A carpet of the same color hugged the center of the wide, curving staircase that stood near the back of the entry while a huge crystal chandelier dripped exquisitely from the white, intricately sculptured ceiling high above the center of the room.

While Chad studied the glimmering effect of the white candles shining against the fat droplets of crystal, he noticed Julia's head appear briefly at the top of the stairs. Clearly she wanted to catch a quick glimpse at the proceedings below. He couldn't help but smile knowing she was upstairs spying on them.

"Sure is a right nice place you got here, Mr. T," he said in an overly loud voice so she could hear that he was sounding like a common livery hand. "I was especially impressed with how much land you got yourself. Why, your place goes on forever, don't it?" he asked, but without giving him time to respond. Instead, he glanced around as if hoping for his first glimpse of Julia. "Now just where are you hiding, my sweetcakes?"

"Sweetcakes?" her father repeated as he closed the door, more puzzled over this man's sudden request for sweetcakes than annoyed by the casual way he had just referred to him. "I'm sorry, son. We are not having sweetcakes tonight. We occasionally have those in the afternoon with our tea but never with our meals. What we are having tonight is roast beef with glazed vegetables, but I can assure you Ruth's roast beef is better than any you've ever had."

"Awh, no, you got it all wrong, Mr. T. I didn't mean the kind of sweetcakes you eat. Sweetcakes is what I call Julia. Didn't she tell you about all that? Didn't she tell you how I call her my little sweetcakes and she calls me her honey lips."

Charles ran a shaking hand over his pale face, then blinked twice and cleared his throat in a futile attempt to remain calm while he answered the original question. "My daughter is upstairs. I'll call her down for you."

"No need for you to do that. I can go on up and fetch her down myself. You just tell me which room is hers." He headed immediately toward the stairs as if he truly expected to be allowed to go up.

Charles stepped determinedly in his way, so agitated by now that he unwittingly crushed Chad's new work hat with his fingers. "I think it might be better for all concerned if you stayed right where you are and I called her to come down here instead."

Chad shrugged, then reached up to scratch the curling hair at the base of his throat again. "Whatever you think. You're the boss."

"*Julia!*" Charles shouted in a much louder voice than he normally used when announcing arrivals. "Julia, you need to come down here. Your . . ." He hesitated, unable to think of an appropriate word to describe this man. "Your guest is here."

Julia did not respond right away. She could not. She was too busy leaning against the wall, holding her sides with her arms and laughing silently at everything that had gone on thus far. Never in her wildest dreams had she expected the man to play his part quite so well. *Sweetcakes,* indeed!

She wished she could have seen her father's face when he first opened that door and found Chad standing there in those work clothes with that stupid look on his face. The man was behaving *exactly* as she had hoped. If he could just keep up his antics for the next few weeks, he would be worth every penny of that five hundred dollars.

Her happiness deepened. She and Patrick Moore were as good as married.

"Coming, Father," she finally managed from a short distance down the upstairs hall. She lifted her shimmering skirts just inches from the floor, then swept gracefully into sight.

Chad's eyes widened. Until now, all he had seen of Julia Thornton was that quick glimpse of her head at the top of the stairs and what little the street shadows had revealed to him earlier that week. He had known even then she was incredibly beautiful, but he had never dreamed she was quite *this* beautiful. Suddenly it was impossible for him to catch his breath.

Speechlessly, he watched while she floated down the

stairs in a smooth swirl of burgundy silk and ivory lace. His astonishment grew with each step she took.

Tonight Julia wore no hat to hide her luxurious mane of dark hair, which she had pulled up and away from her oval face, then shaped into an impressive array of long curls. Her dark-brown eyes were wide and round, and at the moment unblinking as they reflected the glimmering light of the crystal chandelier overhead. She closely studied her father's expression, carefully gauging his reaction thus far.

"Sweetcakes," Chad said, and rushed forward to take her hand as she stepped out onto the main floor. The closer he moved toward her, the more beautiful she looked—and the more determined he was to know her better. When he closed his hand around hers, he fought a very strong urge to pull her directly into his arms. "You sure look awful pretty tonight."

Julia blinked at the unexpected burst of sensations his touch had caused, and even though her gaze remained on her father's bewildered expression and had yet to be brought around to encounter Chad's, she responded ever so sweetly. "And you look very handsome tonight, too, *honey lips.*"

Her father paled, then scowled, boring his hazel gaze into hers as if unable to believe her comment.

Chad closed his hand around hers tighter, unaware of the turmoil he had stirred inside her but acutely aware of the startling emotions that had stirred to life inside himself. Just touching this dark-haired beauty had set his heart to thudding like some young schoolboy's, which was a ridiculous thing to happen. He had certainly touched his share of beautiful women before. Why should he react so strongly to this one?

"I bought me a new shirt just for tonight," he continued. Although he knew she had yet to look at him, he ran his free hand over the crisp blue cotton that covered his chest, as if to point out the cloth's durability. "I wanted to make just the *right* impression on your father. But I think I ruined all that by being so late. You should have told me it was such a far piece out here. By looking at that map you drew up back before you left St. Louis, I thought it was only going to be a few miles out. Why, it took me nearly an hour to find this place."

Finally Julia brought her gaze to meet his. The minute she did and noticed how very handsome he looked, she felt an immediate current pass through her. She swallowed hard while she tried to bring the subsequent burst of erratic breathing back under control. He had looked attractive enough in the darkness, but now that he stood only a few feet away beneath the bright, shimmering light of the chandelier, his appeal was devastating.

Another lavish shiver of awareness cascaded over her while she continued her study of him. It turned out he had a very beckoning smile, one that carved two deep sets of indentations in his lean, muscular cheeks while displaying a set of incredibly white teeth. Just as beckoning were his eyes. They had turned out to be a most startling blue with tiny flecks of white and silver, and were surrounded by the longest, blackest eyelashes she had ever seen on a man.

His hair was also extremely attractive. Although he had not yet had the dark-brown tresses cut back, he had gone to the trouble to comb the front part away from his face, where it blended neatly with the longer hair in the back. Even so, his hair gave him a roguish look that made her even more aware of his masculinity.

He also proved to be every bit as tall and intimidating as she had remembered, yet looked a little broader across the shoulder than she had thought. He certainly filled out his new cotton shirt to perfection, just like he did those black broadcloth trousers.

Julia swallowed again while her gaze continued to roam at will over his irresistible features, pausing momentarily at the slight opening of his shirt where the dark chest hair was in full view.

Never had she known a man who looked so dangerously virile. And never had she felt that instantly attracted to anyone.

Horrified that she could have such a powerful reaction to a man she hardly knew, she sucked in a startled breath and quickly looked away again. But did so too late to save herself completely. His handsome image had already burned itself into the back of her brain. Just as his touch was at that moment searing her delicate skin.

Feeling guilty to have had such a strong reaction to another man, she quickly summoned Patrick's image to replace Chad's, knowing that Patrick was the man she intended to marry. *He* was where her loyalties lay. She should be thinking of *him*. After all, Patrick was also very handsome and appealing, though in an entirely different sort of way.

Aware Chad and her father were awaiting a response to Chad's comments, she hurried to think of something fitting. "Sorry I made you late, but I'm sure my father is *very* impressed with you anyway." She then looked at her father and noticed he had taken his neatly folded handkerchief out of his pocket and dabbed lightly at his glistening forehead. "Aren't you, Father?"

"I can't tell you how much," Charles responded. Though his gaze remained firmly planted on the couple's joined hands, he forced a polite smile before tucking his handkerchief back into his vest pocket. "Julia, why don't you show Mr.—" He hesitated a moment, reminded that he had not yet been told this young man's last name. "I'm sorry, Chad. I don't believe I know your last name."

Chad looked to Julia with wide, questioning eyes. "You haven't told him my last name?" He did not bother telling it himself.

"Of course I have," Julia protested, all the while wondering what sort of last name to give him. "Don't you remember, Father? I told you his name is Sutton. Chad Sutton from St. Louis."

Chad repeated the name silently, committing it to memory while Charles shook his head adamantly.

"No, Julia, you have never mentioned your friend's last name to me. I'd remember if you had. Though that name does sound familiar for some reason, I feel certain it had nothing to do with this young man."

She pressed her free hand to her cheek in an attempt to look perplexed. "Are you sure? I could have sworn I'd told you all about him."

"No, dear, in truth, you have told me very little about him," he said, still remaining forcibly calm. "Each time I've asked you about him, you've always managed to change the subject to something else."

"Not *me!*" Julia looked truly affronted and pulled her delicate eyebrows into a pretty frown. "You're the one who keeps changing the subject around here. You're the one who is so obsessed with buying our land back. Why, the way you've been ranting and raving and carrying on lately, I have had little chance to talk with you about anything else. And believe me, I've tried."

The fact that his land had evidently belonged to Thornton at one time did not slip Chad's notice. He wondered why his uncle had never mentioned that fact to him and decided it could have something to do with the same reason his uncle had made him promise not to sell the land to anyone outside the family.

81

"You trying to buy up some land?" he prompted, hoping to find out the reason why Charles Thornton wanted the land so badly. Having stopped by on his way there, he had already heard all about Charles's angry visit and had also taken a few minutes to glance over the generous offer he had left.

"Just one particular parcel of land," Charles responded with a sudden glower.

"Oh, Father," Julia protested. "I really don't want to talk about any of that now." She did not want to bring Chad into such a personal discussion. The less this secretive man knew about them, the better. "I'd much rather we talk about Chad. It's time you two got to know each other."

"Fine with me," Charles said with a quickly raised brow, as if there might be *plenty* he wanted to know. "You two go on into the dining room while I head to the back and tell Ruth that our guest is here and we are ready to be served."

Chad waited until Charles had headed down the corridor that led on past the stairs, which put him well out of earshot, then dropped all pretenses when he turned to Julia with a curious look, all the while continuing to absorb her overwhelming beauty. "Why Sutton?"

"It's the first name that came to mind," she answered in a deep, throaty whisper as she quickly snatched her hand out of his. It was befuddling enough to have him touch her whenever her father was there. She certainly did not need him touching her during the time he was gone.

"But why Sutton of all names?" he said, aware of how abruptly she had broken contact. It delighted him that she appeared just as affected by his presence as he was by hers. "We used to have a preacher name Sutton where I came from and was he ever hellbent on saving me and my whole family from the eternal possession of the devil."

"Well, I had a teacher with the last name Sutton," she explained in a continued low voice, "And I guess you could say she was more bent on saving herself—*from me.*" She smiled impishly.

Chad's dark eyebrows perked with interest while his pale gaze studied every tiny detail of her beautiful face. "That's interesting to know. And just how threatening a person are you?"

"To a teacher who has been ordered to keep all the young women in her charge under close scrutiny, I guess you could say I was *very* threatening. During my last few months at the school, I developed a nasty little habit of slipping off at night, leaving her with an empty bed to worry about."

Knowing Julia was probably slipping off to be with the sweetheart she so desperately wanted to wed, Chad felt something very much akin to jealousy and his eyes darkened accordingly. "Why would you do something like that? So you could be alone with that man you're hoping to trick your father into letting you marry? Is he from St. Louis?"

"Don't say that quite so loud." Julia gasped. She turned her hand outward and pressed it over his mouth before she realized what a mistake that would be. Her whole body warmed, then tingled in response to having touched him there, but she fought the sudden urge to jerk her hand away and pressed her fingers harder against his soft, pliant mouth while she warned him stridently. "Father could hear you."

"Hss thll ad de bk oh th howth," Chad tried to explain, though his words came out too muffled to be understood.

Aware of the problem she had created, Julia quickly

removed her hand and waited for him to repeat whatever it was he had said.

"He's still at the back of the house," Chad restated. He smiled inwardly when he noticed her peculiar expression while she stared at the hand she had just used to silence him. It was obvious she continued to feel the same strong reactions he felt. "How can your father possibly hear me?"

"You'd be surprised at how reliable my father's hearing is," she cautioned him, all the while rubbing the warm yet tingling sensation from her hand. "That's why I don't want you ever to as much as mention Patrick again—not while my father is home."

Patrick? So now his adversary had a name. "All right. From now on, when your father is home, I'll only say things you would want him to overhear," he promised in a quiet voice, then lifted the volume and took on the country accent he had used earlier. "Like how very tempting you look in that pretty dress of yours." He nodded appreciatively while he let his gaze fall on the tiny gold-and-diamond pendant that dangled suggestively between her breasts. He was pleased she had chosen a gown with such a low, revealing neckline. "I don't know if I can wait until after the wedding to bed a firebrand like you."

Julia's eyes widened at such an unexpected statement, then narrowed again when she cut her gaze toward the back of the house where she had last seen her father. She would not put it past the man to be standing in an empty doorway listening to every word. "Well, darling, you have no choice but to wait," she answered with forced calmness, turning back to glare meaningfully at Chad. "Remember? We agreed that I should come to you on our wedding night a pure and chaste woman."

"Oh . . ." Chad played the role of the obnoxious

sweetheart to the hilt. "I guess I was only half listening at the time. I thought you said something about wanting to be *chased* on our wedding night. *That's* what I thought I was agreeing to. To chase you around the bed a few times before stripping you naked and ravishing you thoroughly." Again, he trailed his gaze slowly downward until it rested suggestively upon the rapid rise and fall of her rounded breasts. Such flawless white skin she had. How he yearned to trail his fingers over it. "I had no idea that what you really wanted was to protect your virtue until then. But if that's true, why do you respond to my kisses the way you do? Don't you know that a shared passion like that can only lead to one thing?"

Julia felt the color rise in her cheeks just before she abruptly changed the subject, aware that the mere thought of what he had suggested had set her heart to racing at a brisk pace. "I think we should do as Father suggested and go on into the dining room now." While fighting an overwhelming desire to reach into her pocket for the tiny white folding fan she kept there so she could cool her burning cheeks, she presented Chad with her arm. "Father will be back at any moment and will expect to find us already seated."

"Anything you say, sweetcakes," he responded happily, but instead of taking the proffered arm, he pressed the flat of his hand against the small of her back with shocking intimacy. "I am here to please you in *whatever* way I can."

Chapter Five

Julia wondered if her father's scowl would become permanently embedded into his features. He had been in a foul mood since before her return early last week—mainly because he had again devoted himself to reclaiming the house and land Robert Freeport had stolen all those years ago—but until now his expression had never been quite this grim.

Ever since the three of them had sat down at one end of the family dining table and Chad had started to eat, her father's thick white eyebrows had locked together to form a solid line across his face.

And no wonder.

Thus far Chad had managed to shatter nearly every known rule of accepted table etiquette.

Rather than cut his roast into manageable pieces that could be easily pierced with a fork then placed neatly in the mouth, he had speared the liberal slice of beef Ruth had served him with his cutting knife, then proceeded to tear off large, ravenous bites with his teeth.

When he wasn't ripping into his meat like an animal, he was using pieces of his dinner roll to push his broccoli and his carrots into the large spoon he had taken out of one of the serving bowls Ruth had left on the table. He'd then toss the sodden bread on top of the vegetables and eat the entire concoction in one gluttonous bite.

Interrupting at will, he talked often and loud, usually while he still had a noticeable amount of food in his mouth. Rarely did he have anything interesting to say and usually it had nothing to do with anything either of them had said previously, thus sending the conversation in odd tangents that rarely made sense. Never did he discuss himself.

Julia supposed that was because he knew so very little about himself to tell—or rather he knew so very little about this person he was *supposed* to be. Still, he was doing an incredible job of being just the type of man she had wanted.

Instead of sitting properly erect and placing his napkin across one knee like a gentleman, he sat hunched forward with both elbows pressed firmly into the tablecloth. He also had wadded his napkin into a rumpled heap and tossed it onto the table where it went largely ignored, only occasionally to be snatched to wipe some of the meat juices off his face.

Additionally, every time he reached for his water glass, he managed to slosh a part of the contents onto her father's favorite lace cloth and usually in the direction of her father, who sat at his customary place at the head of the dining table. Whenever Chad bent to take a drink from his water glass, he made loud slurping and gulping noises much like a small child might.

Too interested in Chad's behavior to do much more than pick at her own plate, Julia watched from across the table with mortified fascination while Chad shoveled food into his mouth at a remarkable speed.

When he had finally finished everything on his plate and even part of the roll that had sat perched on the edge of her father's plate, rather than sit and wait politely for the others to indicate they had also finished and were ready to leave the table, he reached into his shirt pocket and pulled out a small wooden smoking pipe and a couple of sulphur matches.

Not waiting until they had all retired into another, more suitable room like a gentleman would, he struck one of the matches across a metal clasp on the front of his suspenders, then touched the sputtering flame to the already filled bowl. He blew his first big draw of smoke directly into her father's face, who unfortunately had just opened his mouth for a last bite of carrots but ended up choking on the heavy smoke instead.

Amused by it all and feeling safe again now that she had the entire width of a dining table between them, Julia had a difficult time keeping a guileless expression when her father cut his hazel gaze toward her, as if to ask if she had witnessed this latest infraction.

"Doesn't that pipe smell wonderful?" she asked, and breathed deeply, ignoring the fact that her father was still coughing and sputtering from the unexpected lungful of smoke. She glanced at Chad adoringly, albeit without really looking at him. Even though she felt his table manners were wonderfully atrocious, she still found him too dangerously handsome to give him any real notice. Especially in the soft light of the candelabra hanging just overhead. The warm glow seemed to bring out the glimmering paleness of his blue eyes. "Isn't he everything I told you he was, and more?"

Charles turned his head away from Chad and waited until his coughing had subsided enough to allow him to draw in several quick, quelling breaths. He had been reared to be the perfect host, and he refused to let his annoyance get the better of him. "Actually, Julia, you haven't told me all that much about him. Nor has he. Just where did you two meet?"

"We met in one of those lovely city parks along the river," she answered with a soft sigh and, while purposely avoiding Chad's watchful gaze, she related the same love-at-first-sight story she had told Chad nights earlier.

Charles's scowl deepened upon hearing how quickly taken they had been with each other. He glanced at Chad, who was busily puffing his pipe and looking only halfway interested in the conversation.

"And just what is it about my daughter that attracted you so readily? Perhaps you were lured by the fact that she dressed so well and was accompanied by her own lady's maid. That meant her family obviously had a lot of money."

"Lured by her money? Are you blind?" he asked, and looked at Julia, thinking that last remark had to have insulted her, for she was a truly beautiful woman. But instead of appearing offended, he saw a hidden laughter in her dark-brown eyes and realized the little scamp was enjoying every minute of her father's discomfort. Enjoying it too much to care that her father had in any way indicated that men were attracted to her solely because of his money. "Who *wouldn't* be attracted to such a beauty?" he answered honestly, then decided to help the cause more. He quickly dipped his gaze to where the single diamond she wore twinkled from between the rounded swells of her breasts. "Haven't you noticed the way your daughter fills out a dress these days, Mr. T?"

Julia's eyes widened at the shattering burst of warmth his wandering gaze had caused. Even though she knew his being so bold and so interested in her was all a part of his act, she could not help but respond.

Charles shifted uncomfortably in his seat. He was so

upset now that the muscles along both sides of his jaw quivered with outrage. "I'd rather that sort of thing not be noticed. And I'd rather not be called Mr. T, especially by someone I hardly know," he commented through tightly pursed lips.

"Then what *should* I call you?" Chad looked truly perplexed. When he saw that Charles had glanced away, he winked at Julia. "Pa, maybe?"

Charles cringed, unaware Julia had to turn her head to keep from laughing. "No! Mr. Thornton will do nicely." A vein at the base of his neck bulged in a resolute attempt to remain calm and cordial. "What sort of work do you do, Mr. Sutton?"

Chad hesitated. Having always believed a man should be honest above all else, he was not at all comfortable with the sort of lies he had agreed to tell this man. He felt awkward pretending to be someone he was not. "I can do all sorts of work," he answered carefully. "What did you have in mind?"

The muscles in Charles's jaws remained rigid while he rolled his gaze ceilingward. When he looked back at Chad, it was with renewed determination. He carefully clarified the question. "Where do you work and what do you do?"

Believing Chad had given such an evasive answer because he had forgotten that part of what she had told him, Julia hurried to intervene. "Right now he's working as a stable hand at a small livery near that college you have me attending."

Charles's face fell slack, stupefied by that latest bit of information. He found it hard to accept that his daughter has fallen for such a common man. "He's a *what?*"

"He's a stable hand at one of the nicer liveries near the college," she restated, then quickly added, "But as you can clearly tell just by looking at him and by having talked with him, he has the potential to become something much, much better than that."

"He does?" Charles looked at Chad, baffled by his daughter's evaluation.

"Yes, sir," Chad responded with a brisk nod, ready to defend himself, or rather the person he was supposed to be.

Aware he had Julia's father's full attention, he lifted his pipe and poked the mouthpiece deep into the thick waves of his dark hair, then used it to scratch his scalp. "Someday I want to own a nice place of my own and raise lots of animals."

"Animals?" Charles turned up his palms, as if to ask if Chad could possibly be more specific.

"Yes, Father," Julia intervened again, eager to pursue that statement. She knew her father's feelings on the subject of growing anything other than timber. "That's why he went to work in a livery in the first place. Chad just loves animals."

Charles blew out an annoyed huff, then wrinkled his mouth with disgust while he met Chad's gaze. "Well, maybe you should ask our new neighbor for a job. He's planning to raise *cattle* on that land he just bought from his uncle."

"What's wrong with raising cattle?" Chad asked. "People have to eat."

"Father thinks the land should be used to reproduce more trees," Julia explained. "Especially here in east Texas where trees grow so straight and tall. He thinks cattle should be grown in those areas of the country where trees don't thrive so well."

Charles nodded his agreement. "What with more and more of the people around here clearing out fields to grow more and more corn or cotton instead of replenishing their trees, we are starting to have fewer and

91

fewer forested areas," he grumbled, reaching for his water glass while he glowered angrily at Julia for having made the matter sound so unimportant. "Soon there won't be any trees left to cut, and where will that leave us? How will we get the wood to build our houses and sidewalks? How will we get the wood we need to make paper or fuel our homes?"

"Oh, Father, there will always be trees. Especially in northeast Texas." Julia leaned forward, seeming to tell Chad some deep, dark secret. When she did, she again became aware of the blueness in his beckoning eyes and felt another strange rush of awareness flow through her body. "The truth is, my father would find fault with whatever the new owner planned to do with that land. You see, he wants it for himself."

"Oh, is it that same land you mentioned him wanting to buy earlier?" Chad asked, as if that fact has just registered.

"The same." Aware she was practically gaping at a man she hardly knew, she pooled her feminine pride and looked away. Even so, she could feel his gaze burning into her while she watched her father take a long, slow sip of water—aware he was very near exploding with rage.

Although Julia hated that previous circumstances had dictated her problem be handled this way, she felt an extreme sense of accomplishment in knowing, for the first time in her life, that *she* was the one in control of a situation that also involved her father. Thus far, he had responded to Chad exactly as she had predicted, and by the time she and Chad had finished, her father would literally beg her to marry Patrick instead. "Father has wanted that land for years."

"And I will have that land again before long," Charles put in, his face filled with determination. "Just you watch. Robert Freeport's greedy nephew is no match for me. With my wit and my cunning, that land and that house is as good as mine. The new owner doesn't stand a chance against me."

Chad tried not to appear in any way angered by those last comments, although in truth they had made him all the more determined to keep the land to himself. Even if his uncle had never made him promise to sell only to family members or some close friend, he would not let Charles Thornton have that land.

"And you really think I should ask this new neighbor of yours for a job?" Chad asked. He looked from Julia to Charles, then back to Julia. He did not want that suggestion to get away just yet. It would give him the perfect excuse to be over there helping Solomon during the day. He could simply pretend to be another hired hand.

"But you already *have* a job," Julia pointed out, then narrowed her brown eyes, a silent reminder that he worked for her. His time was taken.

"Oh, but that job is in St. Louis and I don't really want to have to go back there until you do," Chad responded happily. "I'd sure rather find me a second job right here in Texas. That way I could earn a little extra spending money, yet still be able to come by and see you every day. Or at least I could come by every *night.*" He lifted one dark eyebrow. "I know how you love the dark."

Charles's water glass fell to the floor with a crash, startling them all. He made no move to clean up the mess.

Nor did anyone else.

Instead, Chad offered Julia another of his most winning smiles. He smiled so deeply, in fact, that the fascinating lines formed not only around his liberal mouth, but at the corners of his eyes, too. "Just think, sweetcakes. If I got me a job with this new neighbor of yours, we wouldn't have to be apart again. I could stay in Texas for as long a time as you do."

"But I was hoping to see more of you than just an occasional evening," she pouted, all the while sending a silent message beneath lowered lashes. If he needed money why hadn't he taken the ten dollars she had offered him Tuesday night? "You promised we would go on several picnics and that you would take me on long rides through the country. You also said something about wanting to visit my father's timber mill on the Little Cypress and his shipping yards and his lumber store in Marshall while you were here."

"Then I'll just work part of the time," Chad said, thinking it better to bend a little than risk having her fire him for insubordination before he had even had an opportunity to be alone with Julia. Besides, those picnics and long rides through the country sounded far too tempting to decline.

"Picnics?" Charles interrupted. His dark scowl was back. "Rides through the country? Certainly you don't mean alone. Just the two of you?"

"Of course not," Julia responded, though without much sincerity, fully aware of the nerve she had just struck. "Until we announce our engagement, Pearline will continue to act as our chaperone." She tried not to look too amused, aware that Pearline would suffer a very convenient illness the day she had Chad drive her to her father's mills. Just knowing the two of them were off somewhere alone together would cause her father to lose control completely. "Besides, it shouldn't be all that long before you give us your blessing and we can be married."

"How many grandchildren do you want?" Chad startled them both by asking. He looked at Julia again and

94

offered a slow, sensual smile that formed such long, deep crescents in his cheeks, that Julia wondered what it would be like to touch the indentations.

When Julia glanced at him then, she noticed that his blue eyes glittered with something she could not quite identify. A floodtide of warm, pleasant sensations swept through her body, causing tiny goosebumps to prickle beneath her skin.

Chad continued to look at her with an odd sparkle while he directed his next comments to Charles. "Personally, I'd like to have at least two little girls who look just like Julia, then maybe a couple of boys who look more like me. I've always liked the idea of having at least four children."

Julia felt a funny little leap deep inside at the mention of children. Her gaze locked with Chad's for a moment. Oh, how she wished she could read whatever thoughts were going through his mind!

Resting her hands on the table in front of her in a demure fashion, she forced aside any speculation of what those children might look like. It occurred to her then that she and Patrick had never discussed children. She wondered how many he'd want to have and hoped he, too, would want at least four. Having grown up an only child, she did so like the idea of having a large family. "Father has always claimed to want as many grandchildren as I could possibly provide."

"Good. Then maybe we'd better get started on that just as soon as possible," he said with a playful wink. He turned to Charles with a wide grin. "Of course we'll probably wait until after we're officially hitched before we do too much about having any children."

Consumed with anger, Charles leaned forward in his chair and met Chad's gaze head-on. "You'd damn well better wait until *afterward.*"

"Oh, then we already have your permission?" Chad asked. "Wonderful."

"No, you do *not* already have my permission. Not in the least."

Julia hurried to intervene again. "At least not yet," she explained patiently to Chad. "It will take Father a little while to get to know you, darling. But after he does, I just know he will grow to love you as much as I do."

Seeing that comment as the perfect opportunity to touch her again, Chad set his pipe aside and reached across the table to cover her hands with his. He was struck by how warm and delicate they felt beneath his fingers. "I sure hope so, sweetcakes. I wouldn't want us to have to go against your father's wishes."

Julia's pulses sprang into rapid motion. She fought a renewed urge to pull away, knowing her father might think it odd if she reacted adversely to his touch.

"He'll come around in the end. You'll see," she responded in a voice that was amazingly controlled, considering how her whole body trembled as a result of his sudden touch.

As if unaware of her discomfort, Chad continued to gaze intently into her dark-brown eyes. "Good, because I don't want anyone ever coming between us. Not *anyone.*"

Julia felt another strange stirring of her senses and she wondered if he had actually meant that. Surely not. Surely he understood that her only interest in him was that of an employer. Surely he had not taken any of what she had said about him that night seriously.

Chad's gaze again met the glimmering darkness of her startled round eyes. "I don't think you really understand just how very much I do want you, and have since the first moment we met. I realize that we have not known each other all that long, but it feels as if you have already become a very real part of me, a part I never want to be without. I am willing to do anything or take on anybody if it will mean making you a permanent part of my life."

Julia felt a tightening knot form inside her stomach, causing her already rapid pulse to hammer at an alarming rate. Unnerved by the serious tone of his voice, she tried to look away but could not force her stunned eyes from his. Nor could she think of a proper retort, one that would make him understand he had no real chance with her without alerting her father to the same fact.

The frightening truth was, with Chad looking at her like that, she could hardly think at all. The man was amazing in his ability to muddle her senses. A floodtide of conflicting emotions washed over her while she tried again to read his thoughts through those impossibly blue eyes.

Charles did not like the dazed look on his daughter's beautiful face and wondered yet again what she saw in this crude man. He cleared his throat in an obvious effort to regain everyone's attention by reminding them he was still there. When that did not bring about the intended result, he tried again, louder. When still the two did not break apart, he leaned forward and physically removed Chad's hands from Julia's.

"That's quite enough of that, young man," he scolded, glowering at them both. "You two are not officially engaged, therefore it is improper for you to be holding hands like that."

Julia was actually relieved that her father had intervened when he did, not knowing how long she might have stared mindlessly at Chad's handsome face before she finally regained her senses. Gently, she rubbed the backs of her hands to make them stop tingling and wondered how long until her heartbeat finally settled back into a more normal rhythm.

"There's nothing wrong with a little *hand*-holding," Chad argued in an affable tone. He took up the neglected pipe again, then glanced over at Charles with a playful wink. "Not when you consider the other areas of her sweet body that I'd rather be holding."

Julia's mouth flew open in disbelief as did Charles's, and if Ruth had not chosen that very moment to enter the dining room and ask if anyone was interested in a slice of freshly baked apple pie, her father probably would have hauled Chad out of his chair and thrown him directly out of his house. As it was, every muscle in her father's body had turned rigid in the effort to contain the anger churning inside him.

"Apple pie?" Chad responded to the suggestion with a raised brow then glanced down at his flat stomach as if trying to decide if he had enough room.

When he looked back at the small, fair woman who awaited his answer, he shook his head. "A piece of pie certainly does sound inviting, ma'am, but I guess I'd better say no to any sweets. I ate far too much of that splendid roast of yours. My, but you sure do know how to cook a fine meal."

Ruth smiled timidly, then lifted a wrinkled hand to touch the tidy bun of graying brown hair at the back of her neck, as if pleased but somewhat embarrassed by the unexpected compliments. "Why, thank you, Mr. Sutton. I do what I can using what skills my own dear mother taught me."

"Well, she sure must have taught you right," Chad said with an affirming nod. "I enjoyed every last bite of that meal. What are we having tomorrow night?"

Ruth glanced at Charles questioningly, clearly unaware Chad was to return so soon, then looked again at

98

Chad. "Tomorrow is Saturday. We almost always have either goose or turkey on Saturday. That's because I have fewer other chores, which gives me more time to prepare the meal."

"Sounds good to me." Chad patted his stomach, then looked at Julia who was still absently massaging the backs of her hands. She divided her attention between him and her extremely angry father. "When should I be here tomorrow, sweetcakes? Same time as tonight?"

"No," Julia quickly answered, not giving her father time to respond. "Not tomorrow."

Charles let out a captured breath, deeply relieved to hear that answer, but then sucked it back in a strangled rush when she continued with the rest of what she had to say.

"You'll have to come much earlier tomorrow. Father doesn't normally go to the mill or the lumber yard on Saturdays. He stays home and takes care of matters around here. And because of that, we normally eat a lot earlier on Saturdays and Sundays. Usually about six o'clock."

Turning so only she could see his face, Chad winked playfully, causing her heart to take another unexplainable leap forward.

"I'll try to see if I can't get here on time tomorrow night," he said, then waited until Ruth had left the dining room carrying several empty food bowls and pieces of the glass Charles had broken before he turned his pipe over and knocked the bowl against the side of the table several times.

In keeping with the character he'd portrayed thus far, he let the cold ashes fall directly onto the dining-room rug, though he felt a little guilty knowing that some blameless housekeeper would be the one to have to clean up the mess. "And since we'll be eating so much earlier tomorrow evening, that should leave us plenty of time afterward for a little moonlit ride along the river. The moon should be just full enough to let us see the water." He kept his gaze trained on Julia while he awaited her response.

Even though Julia knew Pearline would be ordered to tag along as chaperone, she felt an alarming jolt at the mere thought of being out on a moonlit ride with this daring man and knew that Patrick would be furious with her if she went.

"Oh, yes, that sounds wonderful." She turned to her father, eager for someone else to go along. Someone Patrick would approve more readily than he would Pearline—who had let them get away with some very ardent kissing during those last two months. "Would you like to come with us, Father? It would certainly give you two the chance to get to know each other a little better."

"Yes," Charles responded even before she had finished her sentence, then glowered at Chad. "I wouldn't miss it. I haven't been on a moonlit ride along the river in quite some time. I think it would be just the thing to help take my mind off the problems I'm having with that new neighbor. I think we should go right after it turns dark."

Aware Charles was deadly serious about joining them, Chad's expression fell into a dark, gloomy frown when he reached into his shirt pocket for the tiny pouch that held an extra ounce of pipe tobacco.

It looked as if he would have to wait at least until Sunday for his first chance to be alone with Julia.

Pearline waited outside in the shadows, snuggled in a light woolen shawl. Although the temperatures had climbed well into the eighties during the day, the night

100

remained uncomfortably cool, making her long wait outside seem all the longer.

Following Julia's orders, she had sat on a small wooden stool for nearly an hour, wondering when that man Julia had hired to help her hoodwink her father into letting her marry Patrick Moore intended to leave. She knew for a fact that supper had been over since just after eight o'clock and yet it was nearly ten now. By adding the hour it normally took a horseman to make the ride into town after dark, it was evident the new hired man would not make it back to Marshall before eleven.

Finally, after several more minutes of waiting and watching and rubbing her sleeves to keep her arms warm, the left half of the front door opened. Because the lanterns that hung from chains along the high-ceilinged veranda still burned brightly, she could tell that the three people who stepped out included Mr. Thornton, Missy, and Chad.

Aware that her time for action was finally at hand, she quietly stood and moved closer to Chad's horse. She was careful to stay in the shadows of the huge pine and oak trees that dotted the front yard, keeping well out of everyone's sight. Although still irritated that he had stayed so long, she watched with amused interest when Chad slapped Charles soundly on the back as if they were long-set friends just before he turned and sauntered down the veranda steps and out across the main yard.

Having peeked in the windows several times that night, Pearline was already aware of what a fine job the man she'd found for Missy had done thus far. He had been perfectly dreadful at the table and had behaved even worse after they had all retired to the front parlor. She had heard his deep, thunderous laughter all the way outside and noticed that only occasionally were the loud guffaws accompanied by Missy's girlish giggles and *never* by Mr. Thornton's more discreet laughter. Clearly the older man was not enjoying himself.

As promised, Missy made certain her father did not follow Chad to his horse, which was still tied to an elaborate hitching rail at the edge of the front lawn. Instead, the two Thorntons turned and strolled casually back into the house while Pearline waited for Chad to come around the low-limbed trees that stood between her and the house to untie his horse.

"Mr. Chad!" she called to him in a harsh whisper the second his hands had touched the reins.

Chad spun about, startled to discover that someone else was there. His tense expression gave way to instant relief when he noticed Pearline standing nearby.

But the look of relief was short-lived because, although she stood in the shadows wearing clothing every bit as dark as her skin, he could see her well enough to know she was not smiling.

"Why are you out here this time of night?" he asked, also whispering. Aware she obviously did not want anyone else to know she had waited for him, he quickly moved away from the hitching rail and into the shadows surrounding her. Since Pearline knew the truth about him, or at least a large part of the truth, he did not continue to talk in boorish fashion. "Shouldn't you be in bed by now?"

"Yes, but I got orders from Missy to have a good look at what's in your pockets before you ride out," she stated matter-of-factly, then glanced down at his clothing. She stared pointedly at the noticeable bump in his shirt pocket. "She said I was to make sure you didn't take nothin' while you was here."

Chad's eyebrows arched. "What would I take?"

102

"I don't rightly know. But Missy told me to have a look anyway. Seems she don't trust people who don't give out their last names." Pearline held out her hand, then wiggled her fingers as if to hurry him. "Come on. Empty them so I see what you got and then get on to bed. I got me a pile of laundry to do in the morning."

Cocking his mouth to one side, debating whether or not to obey, Chad reached slowly into his shirt pocket and came out with his pipe, a small pouch of tobacco, and his last match. After handing them to Pearline, he slipped his hands into one of his pants pockets and next handed her the key to his hotel room. After a moment's hesitation he pulled out a small money clip that held several large bills.

Pearline's eyes widened when he placed the money in her palm.

"Missy already pay you some of your money?" she asked, wondering when that could have happened. As far as she knew, Julia had not been back to town since Tuesday night.

"No," he answered quickly, aware that claim could be too easily refuted. "That's money I brought with me from Charleston."

Pearline poked at the money with her finger and noticed that several were five and ten-dollar bills. "You got enough here to buy a horse and fine rig if you had a mind to. Haven't you never heard of banks?"

Rather than admit that he had over a thousand times that much money in the bank, that this was just the amount he carried with him for essentials, Chad leaned forward as if about to reveal some long-kept secret to her. "I don't trust banks. They tend to get robbed."

"So do foolish men who carry all their money around in their pockets," Pearline warned with a sharp wag of her finger. "You'd do better to hide them bills somewhere than carry it around with you like that. You're just askin' to be hit over the head with a rock and knocked out cold."

"You're probably right," Chad agreed, patting his other trouser pocket to indicate that one was empty and thus not in need of a search. "I'll see if I can't find someplace safe to hide it. Where do you think I should put it?"

"You ain't goin' to get me to tell you where to hide your money," Pearline said, then thrust her empty palm toward him, as if to push the idea away. "If I was to tell you to hide it up under your mattress or inside your pillow and it then suddenly turned up missin', you'd sure as the world think I took it. I don't need nobody goin' around thinkin' I'm some sort of thief."

"In that case I'll think of someplace to hide it on my own."

"Good," Pearline said with a nod, pleased that at least she had convinced him to be more cautious. "By the way, I think you did a real fine job tonight. After the way you acted up in there, Mr. Patrick Moore is goin' to seem like a true saint."

Chad's body tensed at the mere mention of his rival, but he managed to keep his tone noncommittal when he spoke again. "This Patrick Moore you just mentioned, is he really that special?"

Pearline shrugged, then handed his property back to him so he could slip it back into his pockets. "I guess so. Leastwise, he sure seems to think he is."

Chad's dark eyebrows rose slightly. Obviously Pearline was not all that impressed with the man Julia had chosen. "And is he in love with her?"

"Says he is. Says he can't wait to marry her," she responded in a factual manner, unaware of just how interested Chad was in her answers. She watched while he quickly returned everything to his pockets. "But I'm not really too sure what it is he feels towards her."

Chad paused in his efforts to shove his money back into the unusually snug trousers he had picked to wear that night. "Why do you say that?"

"I don't know. I guess it's the way he looks at her." She crossed her arms and tapped her fingers while she thought more about that answer. "Or maybe it's the way he *doesn't* look at her. He always seems to be lookin' around at other things most times they're together. But then I guess that could be because he doesn't have the courage to look her in the eye. That's the way some men are when their hearts get involved."

"What do you mean?"

"You know. They have a hard time lookin' the woman they favor in the eye. Even so, I think he'll probably be good for her. And it's high time Missy got herself married and settled down. She's almost about to pass that age where she should be raisin' a family. Why she's even older than I am, and I should have been married years ago."

"So you believe Julia *should* marry him?"

"Might as well. She sure not gettin' any younger, and at least this one has some of his own money."

"This one?" he asked, encouraging her to continue. He wanted to find out as much as he could about Julia's past so he could figure out the best way to work himself into her future.

"You mean there have been others to ask for her hand in marriage?" he asked, though not at all surprised. As beautiful as Julia was, there had to have been plenty of young men haunting her door.

"A few. But none Mr. Thornton ever approved of, mainly because they didn't have much money of their own and he suspected they were just after *his*. Or else they didn't have the good sense God gave a deaf mule and would never be able to provide for her properly on their own. At least this Mr. Moore has his own shipping business. Or *part* of one. And he's been to college and made himself pretty smart."

"So you think he'll make her happy."

"As happy as any man, I guess. He's promised not to try to control her after they get married like some husbands do. She'll be allowed to make all her own decisions and do whatever she wants with her life. It's a sad fact that most men don't make promises like that."

"And is that sort of freedom important to her?" he asked, though he already knew the answer to that question. It was obvious that Julia Thornton thrived on having things her own way.

"Very important. She's awfully tired of being told what to do all the time. And I don't blame her. She's lived all her life doin' exactly what her father tells her to do for fear he'll become angry enough with her to disown her like he sometimes threatens to do. She doesn't want to end up bein' a family outcast. Why, the only reason she went off to that fancy women's college in Missouri was because *he* wanted her to. He wanted her to take some business classes so she'll be able to take over the family business one day when what she'd rather do is enroll in an art school."

"She's an artist?" For some reason that did not surprise him.

Pearline nodded vigorously. "And a very good one. But Mr. Thornton doesn't see that as bein' a very worthy pursuit for a woman these days, and is determined she take over the timber mill and lumber yards when he's ready to retire." She sighed tiredly. "I guess since he doesn't have a son to follow in his footsteps, he thinks Missy should. He sure doesn't want it all to go to ruin.

Not after the hard work he and his father put into it. That's another reason for her to marry Patrick Moore. Seems he's got a real good head for business and has promised Missy he'll take over the running of both the lumber mill and shipping yards for her. That'll leave her free to paint whenever she wants and free also to raise herself some children."

Chad's stomach knotted at the thought of Julia bearing another man's child. He could not allow that to happen. "What if some other man came along who also had a lot of money and a fairly good head for business?"

"What do you mean?"

"What if there were *two* men for Julia to choose from instead of just one? What would you have to say about her marrying Patrick Moore then?"

Pearline looked at Chad a long moment, then slowly grinned. "You got yourself a good head for business, do you?" Her smile widened further even though he did not answer her question. She tapped a finger against the corner of her mouth while she considered his question. She stared at him with a knowing twinkle in her dark eyes. "Would this other man also be a little on the mysterious side yet pretty darned handsome, leastwise for a white man?"

"It's possible."

"And would this other man also be willing to let Missy paint or draw whenever she wanted to?"

"If it made her happy, he would *demand* it of her."

"Then I'd simply shrug my shoulders and say, may the better man win." Pearline studied Chad for several more seconds, then winked as if she had just promised to keep whatever suspicions she had to herself. "This is sure goin' to be an interestin' next few weeks." She chuckled softly before turning and heading back toward the house with a lively bounce in her step.

Chapter Six

Julia tried to keep her mind on her artwork, but found it an impossible task. The more she tried to concentrate on the scattered splashes of blue, yellow, coral, and white wildflowers strewn across the grassy tree-spotted field before her, the more her thoughts drifted back over the more disturbing events from the night before. Even the brilliant sun-sparkles on the slow-moving Little Cypress River that wound through the center of the picturesque scene before her was not enough to hold her attention. Nor was the hushed swaying of the tall pines or the gentle nodding of the massive oaks or the trailing cypress trees.

Although Julia was pleased with Chad's performance that previous night, some of what he had said while supposedly pretending to be her sweetheart still bothered her. Or perhaps it was more the peculiar, almost penetrating, look she had seen in those incredibly blue eyes when he had spoken the words that she found so unsettling. Or maybe what disturbed her more was the way she had caught his gaze focused on her mouth several times, as if contemplating what it would be like to kiss her.

Her heart vaulted at the thought of what might happen if he actually tried such a thing, though she was certain he wouldn't dare. He would not want to risk losing such a well-paid job.

Almost as quickly as the unbidden image had formed, she pushed it aside. She knew that if he ever did try to kiss her and Patrick somehow found out, her soon-to-be-fiancé would be furious with them both. So furious, he might decide to abandon her forever as punishment not only for the kiss, but for having even lured a man like Chad into her life to begin with. Patrick might even try to *kill* Chad for having tried to defile what he rightfully believed was his.

Although Julia had never witnessed Patrick's rage, she had heard through mutual acquaintances how extremely volatile his anger could become when confronted with matters of the heart. He had shown that temper just two years earlier when a young woman he had been casually courting suddenly announced that he was not to pay call on her anymore. In a fit of rage, Patrick had later destroyed the inside of a small tavern and beaten an innocent patron senseless.

Julia knew Patrick would become even more angered should some tall, handsome stranger try in any way to seduce the woman who had already vowed her love and her life to him. But was that really Chad's intention? Did he truly desire her or was his saying that he did just another part of his act?

While she continued to dab lightly at the canvas with the coral-pink paint she had just blended, she heard Chad's deep-timbred voice speak those puzzling words again and again: "I don't think you really understand just how very much I do want you and have since the first moment we met. I realize that we have not known each other all that long, but it feels as if you have already become a very real part of me, a part I never want to be without."

Julia's face drew into a pensive frown while she tried to decide his motivation. Had he said those words because her father was sitting there listening so intently to every word that ventured from his mouth—or had he said them because he actually meant them? Knowing so very little about the man, it was impossible for her to decide which of the two possibilities was true.

It was possible that the words had been nothing more than part of a well-planned and extremely elaborate performance. She had to admit that Chad had done an amazingly good job of acting the previous night and those devout words of longing might have been merely a declaration designed to capture her father's full attention.

Still, something inside told her that Chad had indeed meant what he said. Meant every word of it. And if that was true, then he had probably also meant it when he said he would do anything and take on *anybody* as long as it resulted in her becoming a permanent part of his life.

Her heart twisted with uncertainty. Had she made a grave mistake by hiring someone she had not investigated first? But then, there had not been time to investigate anyone. Patrick would be arriving within a very few weeks and her father had to be primed for the response she wanted long before then.

She paused with her paintbrush just inches from the canvas. Did Chad plan to provoke some form of trouble between her and Patrick? But why would he? What could he possibly hope to gain by starting trouble between them. Surely he had enough sense to know that he was not the sort of man she could ever become interested in.

Not only was Chad the sort to find his entertainment in the town's rowdiest saloon, he had secrets in his past so horrible he was afraid to speak his last name aloud for fear of what might catch up with him. And, too, he had absolutely *no* chance of ever winning her father's approval, so it would be futile to become interested in him. Especially after his horrendous behavior last night.

Chad might be undeniably handsome and have the bluest and most captivating eyes she had ever seen, but he had no chance of ever becoming a permanent part of her life. Surely, he *had* to know that no matter how attracted she was to him—and she had to admit she *did* find him attractive—she could never let herself fall in love with him. They were just too different. Besides, she already had plans to marry Patrick and Chad knew that.

So why was she plagued with a nagging feeling that he planned to do more than collect the five hundred dollars she had offered him? Why did it feel as if he planned to start some very serious trouble for her?

She bit the sensitive flesh inside her bottom lip while she tried to decide if there was anything she could do to head off any such trouble. She considered sending a letter to Patrick, warning him about what she had done. But, no, that might encourage him to come to Texas too soon, and it was still possible she had misjudged Chad's intentions completely. If that was true, if she *had* misjudged him, then her plan to trick her father into accepting Patrick could still work.

Her frown lifted into the slightest of smiles, knowing how well her plan to manipulate her father had worked thus far. Already he did not approve of Chad. He had made that perfectly clear last night. He should be willing in only a matter of weeks to agree to just about anything to keep her from marrying someone so barbaric.

To make sure her hastily planned scheme worked

adeptly, Chad had to continue visiting her with annoying frequency. And he had to continue acting like that same outrageous clod while pretending to be devotedly in love with her. She had to be absolutely certain that her father's initial impression of Chad and his fear that she might actually marry him lasted until Patrick finally arrived.

If only she could get over the uneasy feeling that Chad intended to cause trouble for her. The sort of trouble she would have a hard time rectifying. Then she could better enjoy the wonderful job he had done thus far.

But there was just something about the way Chad looked at her that bred this growing sense of foreboding.

Suddenly it occurred to her that Chad could very well be the type of man to try blackmailing her later on. Chad knew how important it was that her father never find out what a manipulative thing she had done, that he must never know Chad was not her sweetheart.

A cold, apprehensive chill rippled across her spine when she thought of what could happen if Chad threatened to expose her secret if she did not come up with more money.

Why hadn't she thought of that possibility earlier? After all, until she had hired him to help her trick her father, he had been a man with no visible means of support, yet he was staying in the nicest hotel Marshall had to offer. *That* should have told her something. He lived too well to be just another out-of-work drifter.

How would she ever manage to pay him if he did suddenly demand more money from her? She'd already promised him nearly all the money she had left from what her grandmother had left her. How would she ever come up with more money? Would Patrick be willing to help pay him for his silence, or would he rather risk having Chad tell her father the truth?

Her heart sank at the thought of what would happen if her father ever discovered what she had done. He hated conniving people of any sort. He would become so angry with her for having tried to manipulate him, he would immediately disown her as his daughter—which was exactly what she was trying to avoid.

Julia blinked back the sudden rush of tears. She knew her father. He was the type to hold grudges forever. Just like with Robert Freeport, who had tricked him into that card game. Her father would never forgive her for what she'd done. Nor would he allow her inside his home again.

Dropping her paintbrush into the small jar of turpentine she had brought with her, Julia realized she needed to find out more about the man she had hired. She had to know if he was really the type to do such a thing or whether she was simply borrowing trouble because she was starting to feel guilty about what she had done.

Hurriedly, she gathered her canvas and paints. She had to get back to the house and find Pearline right away. If anyone could uncover the truth about that man, it was her daring and resourceful maid.

Pearline could follow Chad at a distance and ask questions of anyone seen talking to him until they finally found out exactly who he was and whether or not she should continue worrying about what he might eventually do.

Because it was Saturday and there was little work to do, Charles had eaten a late breakfast and was on his way to the stable when he heard a lone horse approach from the main road. He was surprised to see that same tall, gangly young man he had earlier taken to be Robert Freeport's nephew headed toward the house.

Aware the younger man had to be coming there to see him, Charles waited in the yard until the rider had come to a stop several yards away and then took several steps toward him.

"Can I help you . . . ?" He frowned while he tried to remember the young man's name. But the only name that came to his mind at the moment was Solomon Ford and he knew that name belonged to that pompous Negro foreman.

"Yes, sir. I got a message for you here," Raymond answered readily. Without bothering to climb down from the horse, he pushed his wide-brimmed, high-crowned hat to the back of his unruly dark red hair, then reached for a small postal-size envelope he had tucked into his belt. "It's a letter from Mr. Andrews."

Charles's hazel eyes widened. He had not expected a response quite this quickly and decided that either the letter was from Solomon writing in Andrews's behalf again, or the new owner had to be staying in some city far closer than Charleston.

"Is it an answer to my last offer?"

"I don't know." Raymond pulled the envelope out, flattened out the wrinkles as best he could with his roughened hands, then held it out to him. "I was just told to bring it over here and give it to you personally."

Charles took the rumpled envelope and held it reverently. His heart drummed hard and quick against the lining of his chest while he tried to decide whether to open it now or wait until after the young man had left. If by chance Freeport's nephew had finally agreed to sell him the house and the section of land he'd asked to buy, he would want to send a word of thanks and arrange a personal meeting. But if the message inside was another blatant refusal to sell even part of his new holdings, Charles would not want this young man to witness his disappointment. He was too proud for that.

Raymond, on the other hand, saw no reason he should stay. "Now that you got your letter, I'll be on my way," he stated matter-of-factly, already taking hold of the reins again. "Mr. Ford told me not to be dawdling none. We got way too much work to do if we want that place ready for that first herd of cattle next month."

Charles glanced up from the bold lettering across the envelope and frowned. That statement had sounded like Andrews still intended to go through with his plans to put together a cattle ranch. "But what if after I read this I have a return message for him?"

"Then I guess you'll have to send it over by your own man. I was told not to stay around after I gave you the letter, and I need this job far too much to be going against a direct order like that." He then prodded his horse into a high-stepping trot and left the same way he had entered.

Charles's frown deepened just before he turned and headed back toward the veranda. He had a strong feeling he would not like whatever was inside that envelope and decided it might be better to be sitting down when he read it.

He slid into the first chair he came upon after climbing the stairs and, as predicted, when he tore open the back flap and pulled out the folded piece of paper inside, he was gravely disappointed. The neatly written message was short and direct:

April 26, 1884

To Mr. Charles R. Thornton:
    I have received and read your latest offer to buy all the buildings and part of the land I recently ac-

quired from my uncle. I admit it almost tripled the low price I paid for it myself, but again I must decline your offer. I have important plans for both the house and the land and will not be selling even a part of it to you or anyone else for any price.

Your new neighbor,
C. W. Andrews

Charles's eyebrows arched with immediate interest when he noticed the signature. This time the letter had been written *and* signed by the nephew himself and not by Solomon Ford in his stead. That meant "the boss," as that arrogant Negro had so often referred to him, had finally arrived. Unfortunately he had arrived still determined not to sell any part of his new holdings.

Angered to have been turned down yet again and in such a cold and discourteous fashion, he decided it was time to make a far more convincing offer for the house and land. And this time he would not go to the trouble to deliver the papers himself. This time he would have them delivered by men who were far more persuasive than he could ever be.

Remembering there had been approximately eight or nine workmen scattered across Andrews's place repairing buildings, clearing fields, and mending fences, he decided to bring together twelve or fourteen of his largest and roughest lumberjacks to carry the papers over there for him.

He stood and headed back into the house with long, determined strides. If he hurried, he could have a group of his men ready to head over to the house by late afternoon.

* * *

Solomon bent down for the large wooden bucket Raymond held up to him, paused to splash a little of the water it held in his face and across his brown, sweating shoulders, then set it down beside the other two. "Well, if we put those new shingles on here as good as I think we did, then that roof of yours shouldn't leak another drop."

"I hope not," Raymond answered. After handing Solomon the fourth and final bucket, he stepped back to rub his neck muscles wearily while he gazed out at the dark clouds that had gathered in the northwest. Because he did not feel as comfortable about taking his shirt off as Solomon did, fearing what the sun's rays might do to his pale skin, Raymond still wore his workshirt. But he had unfastened the top three buttons and had tugged the hem out of his waistband to allow more air to circulate. It clung to him like a wet rag. "It looks like we might be in for another shower this afternoon and I'm just plain tired of hearing my wife complain about all that water dripping down on her newly polished floors. You'd think that after having had to live the last three months in a tent, she would appreciate whatever shelter was given us. But no, she's bound and determined that this place be absolutely perfect. Why, she spent all last night making curtains for the front room out of some fresh-washed flour sacks she'd saved. Sat up until after two o'clock finishing them."

"No wonder she looked so tired this morning when she and Noah headed off into town to get those supplies we need. But then, she's no worse than most other women. They are always looking for a way to improve things. It's just part of their nature. Which is probably to their credit."

"Yeah, I guess so," Raymond admitted, although reluctantly. He looked back up as Solomon poured the first bucket of water across the roof, then stepped back to avoid the overflow. He waited until all four buckets had been emptied before heading inside to see if there was still a leak.

While he was inside, his three sons came running out of the barn with Old Ruby at their heels.

"Where's Pa?" Eric, the oldest of the boys, asked. His green eyes sparkled with excitement as he hurried toward the house. At ten years of age, Eric was the tallest of Raymond's three sons and the only one to inherit that thick shock of unruly red hair. Although the boy kept his locks cut much shorter than his father's, it still managed to stick out in all directions. He was not quite as fortunate as his brothers, who had both inherited their mother's straight brown hair.

"I think our cow is about to have that calf," Eric said, wrinkling his freckled nose. "She just put out one awful smell."

"Yeah." Eight-year-old Craig nodded vigorously. "And she's startin' to bleed right where Pa said she would."

"He just went inside," Solomon told them, already climbing down to have a look at the animal for himself. They had been expecting that milk cow to either calf or burst wide open for days now.

Just when the boys entered the side door of the small, renovated slave cabin that had recently become their new home, Raymond came out the front wanting to know what all the shouting was about. By the time the trio had clamored through the small house and come back outside, Solomon was on the ground standing beside their father.

"Looks like the first calf is about to be born on the Big A," he said with a wide smile, using the same name the boys had come up with for the place early the day before. It was a name Chad had admitted he liked, too, when he had stopped by the previous night on his way back from Thornton's house.

"I just hope Shirley don't end up having a lot of problems with this one," Raymond said, headed toward the barn. "That last one of hers tried to come breech and we nearly lost them both."

Solomon followed behind Raymond while the three sons bounced eagerly in front. He paused and glanced out across the north pasture when he heard a group of riders headed toward them at a fast trot. Because there were no other houses along that particular road, he knew the men had to be headed there.

A cold, sick feeling washed over him and caused his stomach to curl into a tight, hard knot when the group turned down the narrow drive toward them. He saw how many of them there were and saw also the determined expressions on their faces. Memories of nearly twelve years earlier flashed before him, causing his stomach to coil tighter.

Although Solomon had been only twelve at the time, the images of that day were still as vivid as if the incident had happened yesterday. Images of a similar group of men who came riding up to the tiny house where his family lived and snatched his father up right out of the fields. Three of the men had carried his father off screaming and kicking while the rest set fire to the two fields next to their house. The men were angry because his father had put what he knew about growing tobacco to good use and had also managed to grow a big crop of yellow corn on the land he had been given by the government. They'd wanted him to know his efforts were not appreciated.

Their mother was not home, and by the time his father had returned, swollen and bloodied from the beating the men had given him, their entire corn crop had burned to the ground. Solomon remembered how hard he and his sister had fought to put out the blaze, but it had been too much for the boy and his eight-year-old sister to manage. They were just lucky the flames had never reached the cabin because everything they owned had been stored inside.

But they had lost their first crop, which was intended to make them self-sufficient. And Solomon had been so deeply affected by the terrible events of that day, he could never stand to watch a group of white men riding together—not even in a parade.

And he sure didn't like the sight of this group.

"Raymond, we've got company coming. Send the boys on into the barn to help take care of Shirley, but you stay with me." He spoke without taking his eyes from the men riding four and five abreast, their horses kicking up dust as they approached. They completely filled the narrow lane formed by the two fences that had recently been put up to eventually protect the gravel drive from the trampling of cattle.

Knowing the men who were out clearing the fields were too far away to hear him, he shouted to the three me working just inside the main house and ordered them to come outside. By the time the band of riders arrived in the yard there were five men waiting to greet them.

Aware he could have misjudged the riders' expressions, Solomon put on as friendly a smile as he could manage, then slowly stepped forward, away from the others.

"Hello there," he said, wiping his sweat-dampened palms on the sides of his trousers in case one of them would shake his hand. "You gentlemen out here looking for a job?"

"No," the largest of the fourteen men called out just before he signaled for the rest of the men to bring their horses around to form an uneven line behind his. He was obviously the spokesman for the group. "We're looking for the man who owns this place." He barely glanced at Solomon. Instead, he looked from building to building as if expecting to find that owner present. "I've got a letter here for him."

He snatched his short-billed, cloth cap off his head, revealing a shock of dark-brown hair every bit as dirty and matted as the wiry beard covering his face, then hooked the stained woolen cap over the saddle horn. He continued to scan the area while he patted one of the four pockets on his sun-faded green workshirt, where the edges of a large white envelope that had been folded in half protruded.

"He's not here right now," Solomon answered, and wondered why it took fourteen fully grown men to deliver one small letter. Pushing aside the uneasiness he still felt, he took another step forward and extended his hand for the envelope. "But I'll make sure he gets the letter."

The large man scowled. Clumsily, he swung one meaty leg over the saddle, then dropped to the ground with a heavy thud. He signaled for several of the others to do the same, then curled his upper lip against his teeth and looked at Solomon with obvious disdain. "And what makes you think I'd leave an important letter like this with you?"

Solomon tried to show neither anger nor fear, although he felt both. "Because I'm the foreman here. And I am the only one who happens to know where Mr. Andrews is."

"You're the foreman?" The burly man cut his glance to those standing closest to him and laughed. "Can you be-

lieve that? This man says *he's* the foreman of this here place."

The other men laughed, too, and exchanged amused glances.

"That's because he *is* the foreman," Raymond said as he stepped forward to take a stand directly behind Solomon. "And if you plan to leave that letter for Mr. Andrews, then Solomon is the one you'll want to leave it with."

The large man's eyebrows vaulted while he studied Raymond more closely, as if unable to believe a white man had just come to the defense of a Negro.

"Is that so?" He stepped around Solomon so he could position himself directly in front of Raymond, who stood nearly as tall but weighed only half as much. Judging from the man's solid build, he was accustomed to working hard and eating plenty, and judging from the scowl on his face, he was not used to anyone speaking out against him. "You work here, Red?"

Raymond cut his gaze to the two men who had also come forward and flanked the angry one standing in front of him. He swallowed hard. "The name's not Red. It's Raymond. And yes, sir. I work here."

"Does that mean you take your orders from this nigger?" the leader asked with a frightening sneer, then indicated who he meant with a short, backward jerk of his thumb. Narrowing his eyes, he leaned forward until his woolly face was only inches from Raymond's.

Raymond stiffened but did not back away. Instead, he answered the question as best he could without antagonizing the abrasive man further. "I take my orders from Solomon. Yes, sir."

"*All* these men take their orders from me," Solomon put in, not wanting Raymond to be singled out to fight his battles. He waited until the three men had turned around and faced him again. They looked surprised by his comment. "And they all do a good job."

Solomon again held out his open hand to the tall, burly man. "So if you would just leave that letter with me, I'd be happy to see that Mr. Andrews gets it as soon as possible."

The large man scowled, then cut his gaze to the others as if suddenly undecided. "No. Mr. Thornton told us to give this letter to Mr. Andrews ourselves. He told us not to leave here until we'd done just that. He didn't say nothing about leaving it with no foreman."

"Then I guess you'd better do what you can to make yourselves comfortable," Solomon said, crossing his arms over his chest. He wanted to show how little impressed he was by these threats, believing that if the men had truly meant to harm anyone, they would have done so by now. Obviously their mission was to be aggravating and intimidating without actually bringing physical harm to anyone. "And I suggest finding someplace where you will be less likely to get rained on."

He gestured toward the approaching storm with a slight nod. In the last few minutes the sky to the northwest had darkened and wind had picked up considerably. Off in the distance thunder rumbled its first warning. "Because if you men are planning to wait around until my boss arrives, it does look like you'll have an extremely long wait ahead of you."

"Don't get smart with me, boy," came the man's angry retort. He leaned his bearded face forward, much like he had just done to Raymond only moments earlier, then jabbed Solomon in the shoulder with his finger.

Solomon flinched from the rancid smell of the onions and peppers the man had undoubtedly eaten for lunch, but said nothing in response to the man's sudden outburst. He merely stood there with his arms still crossed, waiting for them to tire of their harassment and leave.

The angry man tried again to provoke him. "I ain't the type to put up with no smart-mouthed niggers." He placed his face only an inch from Solomon's and jabbed him in the shoulder again.

Barely able to tolerate the large man's foul breath, Solomon felt a definite urge to put more distance between them. But he knew how a step back might be misinterpreted and decided to stand his ground—even if it meant having to fight this man physically.

"Mister, my name is Solomon. Solomon Ford. Not *Boy,*" he said calmly, aware his continued composure only frustrated the man more. He unfolded his arms, then lowered them to his sides so he would be ready to block any sudden punches that might come his way as a result of having refused to cower. "And I was not trying to be smart-mouthed. All I was trying to do was make you understand that Mr. Andrews is not living here yet and he won't be living here for several weeks, long after most of this repair work has been done. If you really want him to see that letter before that, then your best choice would be to leave it here with me. It is possible I could have it in his hands within two days." *Probably within two hours,* he thought, but did not want to tell them that. He would rather they not know Chad was that close at hand for fear they would return.

The giant man looked at one of the others standing nearby, then at those still on their horses. "What do you think? Should we leave it?"

Most of the men either shrugged or gave no response at all. One finally threw up his hands and said, "Hell, Clay, we can't hang around here forever. That nigger's right." He glanced off at the darkening sky. "It's fixin' to rain somethin' fierce."

The man known to Solomon now as Clay turned back to face him with another angry glower. "All right. I'll leave the letter." He snatched it out of his pocket and thrust it toward Solomon. "But you sure better see to it that Mr. Andrews gets his hands on it right away, because we are supposed to ride back out here some- time late Wednesday afternoon to get his answer." He lowered his lashes while he continued to meet Solo- mon's dark, stolid gaze. "Do you understand that, *boy?*"

Certain that inside the envelope was yet another offer to purchase Chad's new house and a good part of the land, Solomon let out an annoyed breath. Why was Thornton having such a hard time accepting the fact that Chad wanted to keep both the house and all the land? Couldn't that man understand the meaning of the simple word no?

"He will have the envelope within two days— probably sooner," he finally answered, then tilted his head to one side as if more bored than angry with the way the man kept calling him "boy." "Which means you men won't have to bother resaddling those horses Wednesday. I happen to know for a fact that my boss will not be any more interested in this offer than he was in that last one and will have sent a response stating so long before then."

"You know, if I was your boss, I'd sure think twice be- fore refusing Mr. Thornton again. The way I under- stand it, Mr. Thornton is about fed up over this Mr. Andrews's stubborn refusals to sell," Clay responded in a deep, threatening voice, then turned his back and strode toward his horse.

Solomon felt an odd combination of dread and relief while standing stiffly there watching the men slowly re- mount their horses.

Distant flashes of lightning darted ominously across

the windswept sky while the men turned their horses around and rode back the same direction they had come.

Chapter Seven

Chad arrived at the Thornton home still angry over what that young messenger Solomon had sent into town, and later Solomon himself, had told him about the incident earlier that afternoon. He wondered if he could make it through the evening without totally destroying his chances with Julia by telling Charles Thornton exactly what he thought of his abusive actions.

His stomach knotted at the thought of what might happen if he did. Julia would be furious with him for having intentionally neglected to tell her that he was the new neighbor she and her father seemed so determined to loathe. She also would never forgive him for having ruined her plans by letting her father find out that he was not the St. Louis sweetheart he pretended to be. He certainly did not want her upset with him.

That was why he had been so careful not to come right out and lie to her while pretending to be in her employ. He knew she would be angry enough with him when she found out that he had kept such a vital secret from her. To add his own deliberate lies on top of those she herself had suggested he tell would forever ruin his chance of ever winning her heart. He did not want to add to her reasons not to trust him when the time finally came to reveal who he really was.

Even so, Chad seethed with anger because of what Charles's men had done that afternoon and knew that during the course of the coming evening it would be very hard if not impossible not to say *something* to him about the way Solomon and his men had been terrorized.

Didn't the man know that by having harassed his men like that, he had only made matters worse? After he had stopped by the ranch and found out from Solomon himself what had happened, Chad was more determined than ever to keep his land out of Thornton's hands. Even if he had not already promised his uncle not to sell the land to anyone outside the family, he would never agree to give up even one of his five hundred acres to a man like Charles Thornton.

Besides, the land and what it represented was too important to Chad to want to sell it to *anyone* at any price. It was his one true chance to do with his life what he had always wanted.

Scowling while he tied his horse to one of the ornate wrought-iron posts at the edge of the immaculately manicured lawn, he wondered if Julia had any idea what her father's hired men had done. And if she knew about her father's attempt to intimidate and harass him into selling him the land he wanted, did she condone such vicious tactics?

For some reason, Chad doubted it. Although Julia was clearly a clever and manipulative young woman who was obviously used to having things her way, he did not believe her to be either cruel or malicious.

Chad's scowl lifted when he thought of Julia's charming smile and her dark, expressive brown eyes that missed nothing of what went on around her. No, there was not a cruel bone in that entire beautiful body. There couldn't be.

Stepping lightly over a small water puddle left from the brief storm that had passed through earlier, Chad removed his high-crowned, wide-brimmed hat. He raked his fingers through his thick dark-brown hair to remove any dents while he strode hurriedly toward the house. Although he did not care for the idea of having to put up with Charles Thornton for the rest of the evening, he could hardly wait to see Julia. Just thinking about her set his heart to pumping like a young schoolboy's.

Julia frowned while she watched Chad tie his horse to the post then head across the rain-soaked yard. She did not like the way his dark scowl suddenly lifted into a pleased smile when he neared the house, as if some sinister thought had just entered his mind.

Although she tried her best to heed Pearline's advice and give the man the benefit of a doubt, she had a hard time actually doing so. There was just something about Chad that caused her to keep her guard up.

Pushing away from the window, she hurried across the bedroom toward the large wall mirror to check her hair and her clothing one last time and wondered yet again if the man crossing her yard with such long, determined strides might be out to cause her more trouble than she could ever handle.

Glimpsing the long brown curls she had spent nearly an hour shaping to perfection and the smooth lines of the dark-plum silk evening gown she had so carefully chosen, she adjusted the high collar one last time, then headed toward the door to await her father's call.

Disturbed over the way Chad's blue eyes had repeatedly dipped to peruse that which her plummeting neckline had revealed to him the evening before, she had decided not to tempt him with a similar view again. Even though the low, plunging necklines were the latest in women's fashions, for the next few weeks she would put aside her newer gowns and make a point of dressing much more demurely than usual. If nothing else, Patrick would appreciate her efforts not to interest this man in any way.

With her heart hammering hard and fast, still worried about what Chad's true intentions might be, Julia opened the gleaming white bedroom door several inches. After hearing her father's call, she counted to ten, then moved gracefully down the hall.

She paused a moment at the top of the stairs to catch a needed breath before affixing what she hoped was an adoring smile on her face and descending. She smiled briefly at Abraham, who stood off to one side waiting to be properly dismissed, then headed immediately toward where her father and Chad stood quietly talking.

"I want to thank you for that suggestion you made yesterday," she heard Chad say to her father, though his gaze was now on her.

Julia knew by the way his eyes had rounded and his harsh expression had softened that he liked what he saw, and that made her even more uncomfortable. It took all the resolve she had not to look away. Instead, she met his gaze straight on, and as before, she was struck with how handsome he looked under the glittering light of the chandelier.

"I stopped by the Andrews place on the way here and got that job you told me about," Chad continued while watching Julia come to an agile stop only a few feet away. "Although they don't have any cattle to tend to just yet, they're going to go ahead and put me to work mending fences and clearing fields. Said I could start first thing Monday morning."

Julia's eyes narrowed. She was paying this man enough so that he should not have to work elsewhere, and she wished now she had made that point perfectly clear from the beginning.

"But you promised to take me on a picnic Monday." She slid her hands into the folds of her skirts and crossed her fingers to ease the guilt she still felt at lying to her father. She narrowed her dark eyes further, warning Chad not to dispute her, then pursed her lips into a childlike pout. "I had my heart set on being with you all afternoon."

Chad blinked twice before a dimpled grin creased his face. "Don't worry, sweetcakes. I explained to the man who hired me that I could work mornings only. That way I will have all my afternoons free to spend with you. We can still go on that picnic. In fact, I'm looking forward to it—far more than you could ever know."

Julia's forehead notched briefly when she realized the full impact of what she had just done. In her attempt to let him know she was upset with him for having taken that job, she had just obligated herself to spend part of Monday afternoon with him. She wondered how she could ever get out of that, for spending time with Chad when her father was not around to watch would accomplish nothing. It would also be extremely hard to explain such a thing to Patrick.

"Picnic?" Charles interrupted. His neck stretched to its limit, reminding Julia of an old bandy rooster preparing for a cockfight. "Just the two of you?"

"Of course not. Pearline will be with us," she replied, then quickly added, thinking she now had the perfect solution to this sudden dilemma she had so unwittingly created. "And you, too, if you'd like. We'd love to have you along." That way, she and Pearline would not be at this man's mercy. She really knew so very little about him. He could be a violent murderer for all she knew. "You haven't been on a picnic in years."

Chad's expression flattened, but he made no comment while he awaited Charles's response, certain he would join them.

Charles's neck slowly shrank back into place but his mouth remained compressed into a harsh line while he cut his gaze from Julia to Chad, then back to Julia. "You know that's impossible," he said in a tone clearly accusing. "You know I have too much work to do at the mill. Especially on Mondays."

"Then it looks like it'll have to be just you, me, and Pearline," Chad put in quickly, not about to give Julia the chance to back out. He stepped away from Charles and quickly drew one of her delicate hands into both of his, amused when he found her fingers still crossed. "What is Ruth preparing for us?"

"Chicken," Julia answered quickly, thinking that would be easy enough to cook on such short notice. Her whole body trembled in response to his unexpected and somewhat possessive touch—a response she attributed to all the unknowns about him. Now that she and Pearline might end up having to be off somewhere alone with him, she was obviously frightened.

She tried to look away long enough to calm her pounding heart but could not find the willpower needed to liberate her stunned gaze from his. Like the night before, it was as if he held some strange, hypnotic power in the crystalline depths of those incredibly blue eyes.

"Chicken with fresh rolls, pickles, and fruit salad," she elaborated, wondering why her father could not have found the time to join them.

"Sounds tempting." Chad brushed the tip of his

tongue across his lower lip while he continued to hold both her hand and her gaze captive. "Almost as tempting as the thought of spending the entire afternoon with the woman I love and hope to marry. I can hardly wait."

A foreboding chill washed over Julia, making her wonder if there had been a veiled message in the words he had just spoken. But she was too frightened over the prospect of being alone with him to try to figure out what that message might be.

Knowing her father had already warned Chad against holding her hand and not wanting him evicted from the house before her scheme had more of an opportunity to succeed, Julia quickly pulled away. By doing so, she finally broke the strange spell Chad had cast over her.

"Nor can I, dearest. I just hope it doesn't rain," she said ever so sweetly, though in truth a dark, rainy day was more what she wanted. A good, heavy rain would keep them from having to leave the house.

Rather than continue standing before this man like some mindless dolt, she immediately turned and headed toward the dining room. "Come, let's eat. I'm famished."

Chad quickly moved to follow and again placed his hand intimately at her waist. Julia closed her eyes against her body's quivering response, so overwhelmed by the disturbing reaction that she barely heard his next words, though they were spoken very close to her ear.

"Well, if it does rain, we'll just have to find something *else* to bide our time." He pressed his hand harder against her lightly sashed waist while he continued walking at her side.

Charles waited until they were all three seated at the dining table and Ruth had set several of the food platters in place before trying to lure Chad's attention away from his daughter. "You said something about having stopped by the Andrews place on your way here. What were the people like?" He narrowed his eyes while he studied Chad's face carefully. "Did they perhaps seem a little *edgy* to you?"

Chad fought hard to ignore his wrench of anger. He knew what information Charles was after. He wanted to find out what effect his hostilities had had on Solomon and the rest of the men he had working for him.

"Not that I noticed." He met Charles's gaze directly but did what he could to conceal his anger by twisting his face into a questioning frown. "Why would they be edgy? Something going on over there I should know about?"

Charles looked disappointed by that answer. "No. It's just that some folks tend to get a little edgy when they have so much hard work ahead of them. I was over there just this last Thursday and was surprised by all the damage. That tornado that came through last month really took its toll on the place."

"Which is probably why they are so eager to hire men like me," Chad said, then grinned when he realized how his next comment would strike Charles. "But it looks to me like they must be taking it all pretty much in stride because when I rode up they seemed to be in a pretty good mood. They were all joking about some letter they'd gotten."

Charles bristled. "What sort of letter?"

"Don't rightly know," Chad said, then reached for his neatly folded napkin, which he popped open with a loud snap, eager to annoy Charles further. "All I know is that someone came by there a couple of hours before I did and left them a letter that must have been downright humorous because they sure were laughing a lot while they discussed it." Which was true. By the time he had

134

written a response to the letter and left, he had calmed most of their fears and had left them in a very jovial mood.

Chad felt pleased when Charles sank back in his chair with an annoyed frown. "They seemed to think that the owner of the place would find the letter every bit as amusing as they did and could hardly wait to show it to him. The way I understood it, the letter was addressed to him."

Julia studied her father's peculiar reaction a moment, then returned her attention to Chad, who was now busily dabbing tiny patches of mud and wet grass off his boots with the corner of his table napkin. Having come to expect that sort of behavior from him, she didn't as much as flinch. "Did you get to meet the new owner while you were there?"

"No. It seems he's not living there just yet. I guess that's because the house still needs so many repairs. But I did get to meet the foreman," Chad answered readily as he placed the soiled napkin back on the table and looked pleased as punch that his new boots were again clean. "He's a real nice man named Solomon Ford. You'd like him. He seems like he'll be a fair man to work for."

Although a gentleman would wait until whoever was seated at the head of the table had started to serve himself, Chad lifted his plate and immediately started filling it with the food nearest him. "I think I'll really like working over there."

Julia looked at her father, puzzled, then glanced back at Chad. Her father had given a far less flattering description of the new foreman. "Is he really a Negro like Father said?"

"As far as I can tell," he answered, then paused in filling his plate, annoyed by the amazed tone in her voice.

He still did not see why the color of Solomon's skin matter as much as it seemed to around there. After all, slavery was no longer an issue in this country and hadn't been for nearly twenty years. "He's sure got the dark skin."

Julia's eyebrows drew together as if trying to make sense of that fact. "And this Negro foreman, he has white men working under him?"

"Obviously," Chad responded, holding up his own hands to indicate that he was white. He then met her gaze directly, wanting to know if she was really that bigoted. Perhaps he had misjudged her. "Why do you ask?"

Julia looked away, feeling a little foolish. "I don't know. I guess I'm just not used to hearing that a white man has hired a black man to be his foreman. It is very unusual in these parts."

"That might be true, but is there anything wrong with a white man hiring a black man to take care of his place?"

"No. Not really," she said, then shrugged when she realized there really wasn't anything wrong with it at all. "I guess all that really matters is that the man is capable of doing the job. Besides, who Mr. Andrews hires to do what is really none of my concern. I don't even know the man, nor do I want to."

Chad blinked when he heard the sudden animosity in her voice. It was the second time she had spoken of him in such an ill tone. "Why not? Do you have something personal against the man? Something I should know about before starting to work over there?" He studied her reaction closely, curious to know why she felt so strongly about a man she had never met—or did not *realize* she had met.

"No. Like I said, I don't even know him." Her eyes

darkened with remembered pain. "But I *do* know his uncle, and I know that I *don't* like him."

"Why?" Chad set his plate aside, curious to know the reason she had spoken of his uncle with such obvious bitterness. He had always thought of the man as very likable.

Charles decided to be the one to answer that. "Because of something he did to us a long time ago. Something that really does not concern you."

Aware he had just been put in his place and that no further information about his uncle would be forthcoming, at least not yet, Chad slumped back in his chair and resumed his earlier manner. He thrust his chin forward, then crossed his arms as if deeply offended by that last comment. "Anything that concerns Julia concerns me."

"No it doesn't," Charles said with certainty, leaning forward to emphasize his next words. "You two are not engaged yet, and as long as I have something to say about it, you will *never* be engaged. Therefore nothing about our family truly concerns you. And nothing ever will."

"Oh, Father, you don't mean that," Julia protested with an immediate pout, eager to steer the conversation to a different, less hostile course. "You are just angry because he plans to work for Robert Freeport's nephew. Why, you don't even know Chad yet. Once you do, you are sure to love him as much as I do. Which is why I'm so looking forward to our carriage ride tonight. I've told Sirus to have the Stenhope ready for us by seven."

Charles rolled his eyes with disgust as he reached for the large carving knife Ruth had placed beside the goose. He studied the sharp blade, as if contemplating a different use for the gleaming utensil, then quietly carved several thick slices of white meat and laid them to one side.

He hesitated before finally placing the knife back down, then fell into a deep, reflective mood and remained quiet for the rest of the meal, speaking only when directly spoken to and sometimes not even then. It was not until they prepared to climb into the carriage that he finally appeared aware of his surroundings again. Immediately he returned to his old domineering self.

"You get in first, Julia. Then I will sit in the middle," he stated firmly, though he gave no reason for wanting such a seating arrangement. He crossed his arms to indicate his determination.

Knowing that would put her father right beside Chad, who was giving another remarkably irritating performance that night, Julia quickly agreed to let her father sit between them. She went as far as to suggest her father take the reins, wanting him to have the feeling of being in full command of the situation when for the first time in her memory, *she* was the controlling one. She marveled at how good that felt.

Charles immediately turned the shiny black, high-springed carriage onto a narrow dirt road that ran along one side of the winding river.

The three then spent the remainder of the evening riding slowly along the riverside, listening to the pleasant sounds of the horse's hooves clopping on the hard earth and the dark water lapping gently against the steep bank right along with the not-so-pleasant yet consistent sound of Chad sucking small food particles out of his teeth.

When Julia noticed how rigidly her father sat at her side, wincing with each little sucking sound Chad made, it was all she could do to keep from laughing. Although she was still a little leery of Chad and his intentions, she could not help but enjoy tonight's antics.

While glancing out across the glimmering black water

to the moon-glistened trees beyond, she marveled yet again at what a fine actor he had turned out to be. If only she could be certain he meant her no harm, she could relax and truly admire this splendid performance. But as it was, she still had the nagging worry that he fostered plans to blackmail her. She had already promised him nearly every cent she had, something she had done willingly, knowing that after she married Patrick money would never be a concern—especially after her new husband had taken over her father's businesses and made them even more prosperous than they were already with his constant ideas for improvement.

She also worried what Patrick would do if Chad did decide to try to extort more money from her. Would he be understanding and help her pay him what he wanted, or would he become so annoyed with her, he would decide to forget about all their plans and return to St. Louis without having married her.

She shuddered at the thought of losing him. She so wanted a husband who would help take care of her father's business so she would be free to live her life the way she wanted. A husband who understood her passion for art and would not resent the endless hours she devoted to her paintings. A husband who, unlike her father, understood that she was an adult, fully capable of making her own decisions.

Pearline waited in the shadows, annoyed that Julia had demanded that she not only check Chad's pockets again, but now wanted her to follow him into Marshall that night and make a note of every place he went and everyone he talked to. Believing Chad to be a good man with the right to keep his last name a secret if he wanted, she was put out with Julia's foolishness.

When Chad finally emerged from the house shortly before ten o'clock, she moved to stand just to the other side of his horse so he would more readily see her. She saw no need to frighten him again, like she had that previous night.

"You again?" Chad asked when he bent to unloop his reins from the iron post and noticed Pearline's dark figure standing just a few yards away.

Pearline grinned at the teasing quality in his voice, having expected him to be annoyed that she had turned out to be such a nuisance. "I suppose we really should stop meetin' like this, Mr. Chad."

Chad nodded and returned her grin while he stepped closer so he could see her better in the dim moonlight. He held his hat in his hands. "Yes, I suppose we should put a stop to it. Before people start talking." He reached immediately for his shirt pocket. "I suppose you have been sent out here to make sure I didn't steal anything while visiting again tonight."

"Those are the orders," she said, then held out her hand.

Moving his hat to his left hand, Chad used his right hand to empty his pockets, but this time he had only a small folding knife and a few coins to show her. He had accidentally left the pipe and his tobacco inside Solomon's cottage and had purposely left most of his money behind in his hotel room. He did not want to chance another lecture on the careless handling of his cash.

"There now, are you satisfied that I have taken nothing from the house?" he asked after he had handed her everything, including his hat. He then patted the remaining pockets to show they were empty. "Or do I need to pull them all inside out to prove my innocence?"

Pearline handed his knife, hat, and coins back to him.

"I never thought for a moment that you'd taken anything. Missy's the one who still doesn't trust you—all because you keep refusin' to tell her your last name. She can't stand not knowin' everything there is to know about someone who's in her employ. That's why she's now determined to find out what your last name is and why it is you act so secretive about who you really are."

She paused a moment, then tilted her head to one side, as if that might give her a better perspective in the dark. "I don't suppose you'd be willin' to tell *me* what your last name is."

When he did not immediately answer, she shrugged, knowing it really did not matter to her what name he went by. "I thought not." She then leaned her head to the other side while she continued studying him. "Tell me, if someone like me were to climb onto a horse and follow you into town tonight, just where all would that person end up?"

Chad felt an immediate rush of apprehension but tried not to show any alarm. "She has you following me?"

Pearline nodded. "Like I said, she's determined to find out more about you. She worries that you might end up bein' the type to cause a lot of trouble for her."

Chad dampened his lips with a quick flick of his tongue. It had never occurred to him that Julia might have him followed. He wondered how much both of them already knew. "How long has she had you following me?"

"She didn't tell me to start until this afternoon. But the truth is, I'm just too tuckered to go trailin' along behind you all night. You'd sure be doing me a big favor if you'd just tell me everywhere you plan to go after you leave here and why."

Chad lifted an eyebrow while he studied Pearline's

dark face. Was she really that trusting? Or did she plan to follow behind anyway to see if he actually went everywhere he claimed he would go.

"Well, although some nights I do stop by the Dry Creek for a cold beer, tonight I'm headed straight for the hotel. Like you, I've had a long day and am just too tired to do anything but go straight on to bed."

"You still stayin' at the Capitol Hotel?" she wanted to know.

Chad nodded. "I'm headed straight for room 16. Most I might do is stop to say hello to the desk clerk when I pass. That is, if he's still awake."

Pearline's eyes rounded with a sudden thought. "And that desk clerk. Would he know your real last name?"

Chad felt another sharp stab of apprehension, for the desk clerk was one of the few people in that town who *did* know his full name although he had already been well paid to keep that information to himself.

Hoping to put an end to such a notion without having to lie to her, he shook his head and asked a question of her in return. "Now why would I go giving a complete stranger my real name and then refuse to give it to Julia?"

Pearline's hopeful expression fell. "You're right. I guess I wasn't really thinkin' too clear. I should have known you would have give a false name when signin' the register. What name did you use?"

Chad looked thoughtful for a moment, then shrugged as if to indicate he had forgotten. "Whatever came to mind at the moment. I don't think it really matters to the hotel what name a person uses as long as that person pays for the room in advance, which is what I did."

Pearline sighed, disappointed. "So no matter what I do, I'm not goin' to be able to find out your last name, either."

"I do seem to be very good at keeping such matters a secret."

Pearline's playful grin returned. "You seem to be very good at a lot of things," she agreed. "You sure do have Mr. Thornton believin' the worst. And Missy, too." Her grin widened. "I can hardly wait for Mr. Patrick Moore to get here. He sure isn't goin' to like findin' out that Missy went and hired herself someone like you—even if it was to help him. The feathers are sure goin' to fly."

"Oh? And when will that be?" he asked, curious to know how much time he had to conquer Julia's heart before the "other man" became more of a problem.

"Should be in about three weeks," Pearline supplied readily. "That's when he is supposed to come here for an unannounced two-week visit at the end of which he is to ask Mr. Thornton for his permission to marry Missy."

"In three weeks?" Chad stroked the strong lines of his chin while he thought of everything he had to accomplish in so little time.

"Doesn't give you long," she agreed, her dark eyes twinkling over some private thought. "But then I don't really think a man like you needs three whole weeks to win a woman over. Your problem isn't goin' to be the lack of time you have to win her, because in some small way you've already started. I can see that in the spirited way she talks about you. No. Your problem will be gettin' Mr. Thornton to accept you afterward. Especially after the way you've been behavin' around him these past two days." She chuckled softly. "You sure do seem to have a real knack at knowin' just what annoys that man."

"To tell you the truth, I don't really care if he ever accepts me or not," Chad answered abruptly, then realized that was not entirely true. Even though he did not care for Charles Thornton or his way of doing business, the man was Julia's father and she obviously loved him. "But that's something I'll worry about later. I have enough to worry about for now."

Pearline nodded her agreement as she lifted her heavy skirts in preparation to leave. "That you do, Mr. Chad. More than I think you really know."

Chapter Eight

Patrick Moore's heart slammed hard against his chest. He had not expected to find anyone inside his office that late at night or he never would have chanced returning for those last two thousand dollars he had taken.

Curious to know who was inside, yet not wanting his presence discovered, he edged his way along one wall of the darkened corridor that divided the company's many offices, closer to the partially opened door where he had heard the voices of at least two men.

Stopping just short of the area where a pale yellow light spilled out across the hall floor, Patrick felt icy prickles spread across his skin, as if he had brought the cold night air into the building with him. Closer, he recognized the voices. They belonged to the two men who owned the shipping company where he had worked as an accountant for almost a year now.

"Looks like you were right," James Oakley, the older of the two men said. His deep voice quaked with anger. Patrick swallowed hard. He could almost see that tiny vein in Oakley's forehead standing prominent against his leathery skin. "Patrick Moore *has* been stealing us blind."

"And by the looks of this, I'd say he's made off with

well over forty thousand dollars," Donald Bunn added, obviously just as angry as his partner.

Of the two, Patrick feared Donald Bunn more since he was younger, and stronger. He also was known to carry a small, ivory-handled derringer beneath his finely tailored coats, which eliminated all hope of rushing in and killing them both. Even if he had not left his own pistol lying in the bottom drawer of his desk, he wouldn't dare go up against a man like Donald Bunn. Not face-to-face anyway.

"I think you're probably right, but we can't know the exact amount until we have these books completely audited," Donald continued angrily, unaware Patrick was right outside the door listening to every word.

"So what do we do? Call the police and have him arrested?"

"Damn right. That bastard belongs in jail."

A hard, throbbing ache filled Patrick's chest, making it hard for him to catch his breath. *How could they already be on to him?* He had started pilfering only a few months ago.

"Do you know where he lives?" James wanted to know.

"Over on Bellomy Avenue somewhere. The exact address should be in his file."

"Then let's go find it."

Knowing the files were kept in Mrs. Burt's office directly across the hall, Patrick quickly stepped back. He could not let them find him there.

Panicked, he headed for the only door he knew would be unlocked at this time of night, the one to the back stairs.

Knowing time was short, that as soon as they had the address they would head directly to the police station to report his crime, he hurried silently down the stairs, then across the building and down another set of stairs that led directly outside.

He had been found out. He had to get back to his rooms. Once there, he needed to get out that small trunk where he kept what little money he had not yet spent in the bottom and toss in as many clothes as would fit. Now that Oakley and Bunn knew he had been secretly "borrowing funds" from the company at a rate of about two to four thousand dollars a month to help pay his gambling debts, he needed to get as far away from St. Louis as quickly as he possibly could.

Narrowing his dark green eyes to enable him to see better in the dark, damp alley, he ran as fast as his new Italian boots would let him on the worn red brick. The way it looked now, he would be headed for Texas much earlier than originally planned.

Until he could come up with enough money to pay back all those funds he had secretly "borrowed" from the North Bend River Company, he did not dare show his face again in St. Louis.

Chad, Julia, and Charles had just finished their noonday meal and stepped out onto the veranda to enjoy the clear, balmy air when Julia noticed a lone rider approaching from the east at an unhurried trot.

"Are you expecting company, Father?" She shaded her eyes against the bright sun to try to make out whom the rider might be. It being Sunday, their visitor could be just about anyone.

"Maybe it's the parson come by to scold us for not being in church today," Charles retorted, then scowled at Chad, who had already sunk into one of the large padded chairs that was positioned near the banister facing the yard.

Until Chad had arrived shortly after nine o'clock, Charles had had every intention of attending services that morning. But after having discovered that Julia had no plans of going to church that day—and knowing that she would be there alone with Chad if someone did not stay to chaperone, because Pearline and Ruth had both finished their work and already left to attend their own churches—Charles had felt it best that he forget church and stay home.

"No, it's not the reverend," she responded. The rider was close enough now she could see his dark-brown skin and bright red shirt. Not only was the Reverend Cross a white man, he never wore anything but black or dull gray. And the good reverend was nowhere near as large as the big man now rapidly approaching their house.

Chad, who was already comfortable in the nearby lounge chair, watched Charles's face carefully, curious to see his reaction. He already knew who the visitor was and why he was there. But rather than take the chance that Noah might recognize him from having met briefly the day before and thus say something that could indicate who he really was, he turned his head just enough to keep the new hired man from getting a good look at him, yet not enough to make it appear he was hiding.

"I don't know who that is," Charles said, and frowned while he watched the large man ride through the gate then turn directly toward the house. "But I'll find out what he wants."

He paused to adjust his tasteful white summer coat before stepping quickly out into the yard and heading toward the edge of the drive. Julia stepped closer to the banister.

Aware neither Charles nor Julia was looking in his direction, Chad held his hand up to hide a portion of his face from Noah, then proceeded to watch Charles cross the neatly trimmed yard with long, steady strides.

"Are you looking for someone?" Charles called out when he neared the rider.

"Yes, sir. I'm lookin' for a Mister Charles Thornton." Noah pulled the large black horse Solomon had loaned him to a nervous stop at the edge of the drive. "I got a message to give him."

He did not give Charles time to respond before he reached into his shirt and pulled out a folded piece of paper and bent forward to thrust it at him. "If you ain't him, would you see to it that he gets this? It is supposed to be important."

"I *am* him," Charles acknowledged, then accepted the rumpled paper. He shielded his eyes again while he stared up at the rider, who had not bothered to introduce himself or even dismount. "And you are . . . ?"

"In a hurry to get on my way," Noah responded, already nudging the horse with his heels. "I came here directly from church and ain't had nothin' to eat since six o'clock this mornin'. My insides are rumblin' like some oversize freight wagon for a big plate of that beef pie I know I got waitin' on me."

With Noah already headed out, Chad dropped his hand and watched while Charles read the note he had quickly penned the day before. After finishing it, he wadded the paper into a tight ball. Chad tried not to appear too pleased when the stocky, white-haired man turned and stalked angrily toward the house, the wadded note still in his hand.

"The nerve of that man!" Charles shouted when he was near enough to the house to be heard. The angry words had been directed to no one in particular. His thick eyebrows formed a deep scowl. "It's obvious he does not know who it is he's dealing with here, nor what I'm capable of."

"What foolish man is that?" Julia asked, hurrying toward her father. "Who was that man?"

"I don't know other than he obviously works for our new and as-of-yet-absent neighbor, Mr. C. W. Andrews," he answered with a bitter expression, displaying the wadded paper while he continued toward the veranda steps with long, angry strides.

"What is that?" Julia was puzzled.

"The answer to my latest offer." His expression hardened more.

"But I thought he answered you yesterday." She reached up to play with a strand of her dark hair. "Or at least that's what I thought you said."

"He *did* answer me, but then I turned right around and made yet another offer. This one a little more persuasive than the last—or so I thought." Again, he sounded bitter.

"And the man has turned you down yet again," she surmised, looking truly sorry for him.

The muscles in Charles's cheeks flexed. "And he was in such a hurry to do so, he didn't even bother to put his response in an envelope." Again, he held the wadded paper out for evidence while he took the front steps two at a time. "He didn't even bother to use a letterhead, just wrote his words on plain tablet paper."

"What exactly did he say?"

"I'll read it to you." He paused only a few feet away, quickly unrumpled the page, and held it in his trembling hands while he read the brief message through tightly clenched teeth. "Thornton. Like Solomon Ford has tried to tell you twice now, I am not interested in selling my land or my house at any price. Don't bother making another offer like that one yesterday."

"Is that all?" She stretched forward on tiptoes so she could see the actual words over her father's shoulder. "He doesn't say *why* he won't sell?"

"That's all he wrote," he said while he stared at the offending words. *"Not interested.* I'm getting awfully tired of hearing those words." He thumped the rumpled page with his finger. "Those were the exact words that blasted foreman of his used the first two times I offered to buy the place. 'Not interested in selling at any price.' " He paused a moment, and his angry expression deepened while he thought more about the situation. "That black foreman of his has far more influence than I first realized."

"What do you mean?" Julia stepped back and studied her father's angry glower worriedly.

"Isn't it obvious? Freeport's nephew is letting that Negro tell him what to say. The nephew obviously does not have a mind of his own. He'd rather let someone else make all his decisions for him."

"What do you plan to do now?" Julia asked, still studying her father with a worried expression.

Chad watched and listened with amazed interest. Giving up had obviously not occurred to either of them.

"Look's like I'll have to try a whole new approach," Charles responded with a determined gleam in his hazel eyes. He curled his fist around the already rumpled paper, then headed into the house.

Chad blinked with disbelief. For the first time since early Friday evening, Julia and he were alone.

"Father, I know how much you want that house and land, but don't you dare do anything that will get you into any trouble," she called after him, her forehead notched with daughterly concern. "I mean it, Father. Don't you do anything foolish."

"You sound worried," Chad observed when there

came no response from inside the house. He uncrossed his legs and stood, eager to take advantage of their time alone.

"I am," she admitted, then turned to look at Chad. "I know my father, and I know how very much he wants that house and the land surrounding it."

"But why is this particular house and land so important to him?" he asked, curious to know why the man was so determined to buy his property. The man already owned enough to form a small county all his own.

"It's a very long story that has nothing to do with you," she answered, then sank wearily into a nearby wicker chair. Her pale-blue skirts puddled softly around her. Sighing deeply, she tilted her head back to rest it on the scrolled back.

"But maybe I could help," he prodded.

Julia shook her head, as if she thought the situation hopeless. "Not unless you know a way to make a man we've never met do something he obviously does not want to do." She turned her large brown eyes to his. "You just concentrate on continuing to be as brash and as annoying and as offensive as you possibly can. Which you do very well, by the way."

"Thank you," he said, and offered a most disarming grin. "I'll take that as a compliment."

Julia gazed at him for several seconds, her attention again drawn to every magnificent detail of his smiling face. From the crinkled corners of his blue eyes, to the strong, curved lines of his jaw, to the bronzed skin that seemed a shade darker with each passing day. She also noticed the smooth shape of his dark eyebrows, as well as the perfectly proportioned nose that flared ever so slightly at the end. Her gaze moved to the splendid dimples that formed in his lean cheeks whenever he smiled—which she noticed was often.

A delicious shiver of awareness cascaded over her. She knew by the appraising way he looked at her that he was also studying her intently. Her heart slammed hard against her chest when she noticed how his eyes sparkled when he again met her gaze.

Aware he must think her very brazen, she pulled her gaze away, but there was just something in his expression that kept her from looking elsewhere. Something about him commanded her attention. Slowly she returned her eyes to his.

"And since we are handing out compliments, I'd like to mention that you are a very beautiful woman," Chad told her. His eyes darkened with an emotion Julia could not quite identify when he then dropped his gaze to take in more than just the intricate details of her face. "Very beautiful. In every way."

"Don't say that!" Julia gasped, then threw her hand to cover her heart, as if that might help to calm its violent response. Never had she felt it beat with such rapid force.

"Why not? It's the truth." He knelt on one knee beside her chair so he could have a better view into her dark-brown eyes, which had grown very large and very round in the last few seconds.

"Because I am practically engaged to marry someone else. It is not right for you to compliment me like that."

"Why? What harm can an honest compliment cause?" He continued to stare deeply into her eyes in an attempt to read her thoughts.

"It can cause *plenty* of harm," she responded, although she was too affected by his nearness at that moment to think of a sound reason why.

"I don't see what kind of harm." He leaned forward so he could touch her cheek lightly with his hand. "I only spoke the truth."

The unexpected touch caused a startling array of conflicting sensations to scatter through her body. Eager to put some distance between them, she slid out of the chair and hurried several steps away before turning to face him again. "Don't do that, either!"

"Don't do what?" Chad asked, also rising. Eager to touch her again, he immediately closed the distance she had placed between them. "Don't touch your cheek? Why? What's wrong with me touching you?"

Julia's pulses continued to race at a frantic rate, aware he looked very much as if he planned to touch her again. She could not allow that to happen. It would not be fair to Patrick.

"Because it's not right." She took another small step back but stumbled against a small wooden table that lay in her way. Glancing behind her, she saw that the table was flanked by two heavy wrought-iron chairs, which would be impossible to move. She had nowhere to go.

Keeping his gaze on her startled expression, Chad wasted no time countering that backward step with a forward movement of his own. He was reminded of that first night when he had tried to back her against the bank window. That time she had realized his ploy and stood her ground. He wondered if she would stand her ground today. "I don't know—it certainly felt right to me."

Julia swallowed hard while she tried to focus her thoughts on a way out of her current predicament. Even though Chad was not actually touching her at that moment, for he was still several feet away, she knew that was his intention. Already she felt a very strong, very vibrant warmth radiating out of his body and into hers, a warmth so strong and so beckoning, she almost wished he *would* touch her again. And that frightened her more.

"Aren't you forgetting who is supposed to be in

charge here?" she asked with far more reserve than she actually felt.

"Could be that I am." He moved closer, bending slightly at the waist, until his lips were but inches from hers. "I have been known to have an awfully short memory when I want."

"Then let me refresh it for you," she said. Her gaze dipped to his parted lips, all too aware that he was now close enough to kiss her if that proved to be his intention—although she doubted he would be so foolish. There was too much money at stake for him to risk losing it over something so trivial. "*I* happen to be the one in charge. You work for me. Remember?"

"Ah, yes, that's right. You hired me to be your lover."

He was clearly amused by her predicament. He smiled so deeply, it formed the most fascinating lines at the corners of his heavily lashed eyes and along the outer edges of his mouth.

"No," she immediately corrected, her eyes stretched wide. "I hired you to be my sweetheart. And only a *pretend* sweetheart at that. I said nothing about us ever having been lovers. The closest I ever said to that was that I wanted you to convince my father that we were in love."

"Which is why it is a good idea for me to try to touch you when we are alone. It's possible he's watching us at this very moment," he said, then reached his arm around her slender waist and drew her close, praying she would not pull away before he'd had a chance to really hold her. His pulses raged with desire when he felt her soft curves meld lightly against his.

Aware he had left her momentarily speechless, he let his gaze wander again while he drank in the smoothness of her flawless white skin then noted the slight upward curve of her pert little nose, and the regal shape of her high cheeks that tinged while he continued his bold perusal.

"But it is more probable that he is not," she finally responded in a rasped voice. She tried very hard to concentrate on his words instead of the disturbing fact their bodies now touched. "In the state my father was in, he's probably gone directly to his study to take whatever steps he plans to take next."

"But just in case he hasn't . . ." Chad said, then finished his sentence by dipping forward for the kiss he could no longer deny himself. His desire for her was too strong and raged uncontrolled inside him.

Not having believed he would actually kiss her, Julia's initial response was surprise, followed almost immediately by outrage. She tried to push him away, but his determination to hold her proved too strong.

Her next thought was to kick him, but because she had worn silk slippers that day instead of a pair of sturdy leather boots, her efforts only served to send a sharp, curling pain through her foot. Quickly she discarded that plan and moved on to something else; she clenched her hands into tight fists and pummeled his back and shoulders as hard as she could. Finally, he broke the kiss, but not the embrace.

"What's your father going to think if he sees you fighting me like that?" His blue eyes sparkled with amusement while he looked down into her shocked expression. "Do you want him to believe that we are truly in love with each other or not?"

"You already know the answer to that," she muttered, then slid her hands to his chest with every intention of pushing him away. Despite her outrage, it amazed her to discover how firm his body was. Obviously, Chad did not sit behind a desk like Patrick did. His sleek muscles were much harder and far more developed than Patrick's. "What on earth do you do for a living?" she asked, too curious to care that she had yet to break Chad's embrace.

"You mean besides hire on to be the insufferable lover of attractive women I've never met?" He dipped his head slightly so he could better gaze into her compelling brown eyes. How truly beautiful this woman was.

Julia's eyebrows flattened with warning even though somewhere deep at the very core of her, she had an unexpected urge to laugh. "Yes, besides that. What do you do that makes you so strong?"

As pleased that she considered him strong as he was that she had given up her struggle for freedom and was now allowing him to hold her gently in his arms, Chad thought for a minute. He had to answer that question very carefully. "I used to work in a large mercantile where I often had to load and unload large boxes of freight; but here lately, since having come to Texas, about all I've done in the way of hard work is help to move some furniture and haul a little freight."

Thinking he had been unable to find better work, Julia frowned. "Did you try to hire on with one of the railroads? They are almost always employing strong, healthy men like you."

"No, I hadn't gotten around to talking with anyone associated with the railroads. I guess I was hoping to find something a little more to my liking first."

Julia tilted her head back and studied the way his dark hair fell softly away from his handsome face while she considered his answer. She felt a sudden unbidden urge to touch the locks but managed to keep her hands where they were—on his virile chest. "And what would that be?"

"And what would *what* be?" he asked, as pleased by

157

the way she was looking at him as he was to be holding her close.

"What would be more to your liking?"

Chad's answering grin was immediate.

"Actually, this would be more to my liking," he said, and quickly dipped to take a second kiss, this one even more surprising and more persuasive than the last.

Julia let out a startled moan but did not try to push him away like she had done earlier. She had decided he was right, her father very well could be watching them through a window or an open door and would wonder why she had refused a kiss from a man she was supposed to be deeply in love with. She decided what she should do instead was focus her thoughts on something else and allow Chad to have his kiss. Surely he would tire of his actions soon enough—after he realized he would earn no true response from her.

But to Julia's dismay, by the time she had decided to stand there and let him have his kiss, a response had already started to form. A strange and unaccountable sensation of bubbling warmth had entered her bloodstream unexpectedly. It now spread slowly through her body and made a very real attempt to take possession of her senses while she waited for him to give up his tender quest and finally break the kiss.

She fought the disturbing sensations by trying to bring forth Patrick's handsome image. But to her growing horror, she was unable to focus her thoughts on anything outside what was happening to her at that very moment. Her eyes drifted softly shut and to her further dismay, she felt herself actually starting to enjoy what Chad was doing to her. The slow, simmering warmth that had so easily taken over her body was really quite nice.

A deep, soothing ache filled her body and she felt

herself wanting to yield to the wondrous sensations he had created. But to respond in such a way would be the wrong thing to do. She was already in love with someone else. Where was her reasoning? Where was her normally strong resolve?

More than ever she wished Chad would tire of his kiss and pull away, before she gave in to these strange new feelings—and ruined her chance to marry the sort of man she had always dreamed of marrying. The sort of man who would love her enough not to want to control her. The sort of man who would allow her to do what she wanted with her life.

She pressed her eyes harder shut and continued to fight the strong, fluid emotions that raged inside her. She felt guilty knowing she actually enjoyed this man's kiss. Enjoyed it every bit as much as Patrick's—if not more.

But Chad showed no signs of lessening his ardor. If anything, the kiss intensified. Soon the strange warmth that had entered her with such languid ease filled her entire body. It caused her to feel lightheaded and breathless.

She had to wonder about the strange, dizzying effect. Patrick's attentions had never caused such an utter daze. It was as if she had suddenly been blanketed in a thick, rolling fog—a fog that made it hard for her to concentrate on anything but the feel of his seductive mouth against hers and the wild rhythm of her heartbeat.

Wishing she better understood what was happening to her, Julia did her best not to surrender to the peculiar sensations. She remained determined to ignore any and all of the feelings this man had awakened inside her while she prayed fervently that Patrick never found out that she had allowed such a kiss.

Panicked by that last thought, Julia gave another valiant effort to push away. Patrick would be furious with her for having been so weak. But the effort to free herself only caused Chad to tighten his hold more. Her breasts were suddenly flattened firmly against the hard planes of his chest, causing her to suck in a startled gasp. No man had ever been that bold with her. Not even Patrick, whom she would one day wed.

Her blood raged frantically through her body while she wondered what could be done to stop him. She had already tried pushing him away yet that had only brought them closer still, and if she tried hitting him again, her father might be watching and realize something was amiss.

While she tried to keep her thoughts collected, Chad slowly lifted one hand to gently massage her upper back. He continued to hold her body pressed against his with the other. The wondrous feel of his strong fingers softly kneading the tense muscles across her back and shoulders made it instantly harder for her to breathe—much less be able to think clearly. It also further weakened her resolve to push him away, causing her to instead lean against him for the needed support to remain standing.

Such a powerful response both amazed and alarmed her. He was not the man she loved. Yet there she stood, melting in his arms like some mindless schoolgirl—and enjoying, at least to some degree, the strange new feeling of helplessness he had created inside her.

Overwhelmed by her own response, she moaned softly, then unexpectedly pressed herself harder against Chad's body while the whirling sensations inside her quickly deepened. There was such warmth and such pleasure to be found in his embrace.

Becoming more breathless by the minute, Julia parted her lips in an effort to draw needed air into her lungs. No sooner had she parted them than she felt the tip of

Chad's tongue dip inside and lightly tease the sensitive flesh just inside her mouth. What a strange sensation that caused!

At that same moment the hand that had been so skillfully massaging the rigid muscles along her shoulders and upper back edged slowly downward until he finally reached the rounded curve of her buttocks. There he immediately curled his fingers to fit the shape and pressed the lower part of her body more firmly against his.

Startled that he would attempt such a thing, Julia's brown eyes flew open, and to further the sudden mortification, she spotted Pearline standing only a few feet away with her green-clad arms crossed casually in front of her, watching the two of them curiously.

That's when Julia found the strength she needed to push Chad away.

"What are you doing here?" she asked Pearline, her voice ragged and her face pale while she quickly backed away from Chad.

"My sister was feelin' a might poorly today, so I decided to let her rest and come back early. Since no one was expectin' me, I came in the back way, and when I stopped by your father's study to let him know I was back, he sent me out here to keep an eye on you two." Her brown eyes sparked with amusement, although her expression revealed nothing of her thoughts. "And that's exactly what I was doin'. Keeping a close eye on you both."

The continued racing of Julia's pulses coupled with the inability to breathe enough air to fill her lungs made it hard for Julia to think of a logical explanation for the kiss, though her mind desperately sought one.

Chad, too, was having a hard time regaining his composure and leaned heavily against a wooden post, as if suddenly needing its support.

Finally Julia caught her breath enough to speak. "That was *not* what you think it was."

"Oh?" Pearline questioned. The corners of her mouth quivered with an overwhelming desire to grin when she stepped closer. "And just what *was* that?"

Julia frowned, still too addled to explain what had happened. Finally she lifted her chin and took a defiant tone. "What that was is none of your business. And if you dare tell anyone that you saw what you think you just saw, I'll see to it that you never go with me to St. Louis again. Not even when I travel there to shop."

Pearline's forehead notched, obviously not taking Julia's threats seriously. "But if what I just saw is not what I think I just saw, then why would you care if I tell anyone that I saw what I just saw? And even if I really *did* see what I thought I saw, why would I tell anyone about what I saw? After all, I have seen that sort of thing before."

Julia closed her eyes for a moment while she tried to sort through what Pearline just said, not sure she had gotten the crux of it.

"Don't worry. Your secrets are safe with me," Pearline continued, then seeing that Julia's eyes were still closed, winked at Chad before stepping back to sink happily into her favorite chair.

Chapter Nine

Unable to push aside the intense emotions Chad's kisses had stirred to life inside her only moments earlier, and feeling both guilty and embarrassed to know that she had actually enjoyed what the man had done while kissing her, Julia decided it was time to take to her bed with a headache.

Rather than continue having to face Chad after having reacted so profoundly to his kisses, knowing he had probably credited her reaction with all the wrong reasons, she ordered Pearline to turn back her bedcovers. After a feeble apology to Chad, she quickly followed Pearline upstairs, leaving him alone on the veranda.

Chad saw no reason to stay longer. Since it was barely midafternoon and there were still several hours of daylight left, he decided to take advantage of the unexpected free time and headed directly toward his own place, eager to have a good look in the sunlight at the repairs done thus far.

He purposely left without bothering to say goodbye to anyone so Pearline would not realize he was leaving. Although he did not think she had followed him into town last night after all, he was not all certain she would continue being so lax. At some point, she might start feeling guilty about her neglect and actually follow him. Which was why he cut through a wooded field rather than stay on the main road.

Taking the longer route also gave him more time to think about the amazing response he'd had to Julia's kiss. Just knowing she had the power to affect him like that made him all the more determined to have her as a permanent part of his life.

Because it was Sunday afternoon and the men who worked for him had the day off, only Solomon, Raymond, and Raymond's wife, Deborah, were outside when he rode into the yard. Since what little outdoor furniture his uncle had left behind after he moved had been destroyed by the recent storm, the trio sat in three dining-room chairs that had been brought outside and placed in the cool shade of one of the few spreading oaks left.

Although it was still April, though barely, the temperatures that day had been unseasonably warm and the shaded area off to one side of the house looked terribly inviting, even to Chad.

"Hello!" he called to them when they did not look up from their conversation. Then he chuckled when Raymond quickly jerked off his hat and stood to greet him properly only to be signaled to sit back down by Solomon, who saw absolutely no reason for either of them to get up out of their chairs.

Instead of rising and extending a hand in greeting, Solomon shifted his weight to one side so he could better watch Chad's approach. He looked too tired to do much more than that.

It was then Chad noticed that Solomon's purple workshirt was unbuttoned and hanging loosely behind him, and that Raymond's clothing was soaked with sweat. It was obvious the two had worked that afternoon, even though it was supposed to be their day of rest. But for the moment, the two men had set their work tools aside and sat slumped in Solomon's new chairs while sipping fresh lemonade.

"Pull up a piece of sod and join us." Solomon gestured to the neatly cropped grass beside them. It was then Chad noticed that the whole yard had been cut to an even height, as had the bushes that grew in front and to the side of the house. He also noticed that some bright red flowers had been planted near the front steps and in the planter's boxes at both corners of the veranda.

"Don't mind if I do," Chad responded agreeably, already swinging his leg over the saddle in preparation to dismount. He waited until his footing was again on solid ground and he had looped the horse's reins around the saddle horn before pulling his hat off and nodding politely to Mrs. Porterfield. "You three sure look comfortable."

"We are," Solomon agreed, then took a long sip of his drink. "We've just been sitting here enjoying this fine day without a care in the world."

"But there must have been a rain shower because you and Raymond look soaked to the bone," Chad commented. "Odd, though, it didn't rain over at the Thorntons."

"You know how these spring showers are," Solomon said, then looked at Chad with a puzzled expression. "Speaking of the Thorntons, why aren't you still over there? I thought you planned to stay the whole day."

Chad's senses gave a perplexing little leap. He could still feel Julia in his arms. "I did, but Julia suddenly came down with a headache."

Solomon was too interested in other matters to pursue that particular topic. "So tell me, did Noah remember to deliver the note?"

"He did," Chad said, then moved closer to the group. "About two hours ago while the three of us were all sitting out on the veranda."

"And how did Thornton respond?"

Chad tossed his hat onto the grass, sinking down beside it. He frowned when he felt how sharp the grass felt, then realized the ground had more weeds than anything else. "About like we expected."

"Pretty upset, was he?" Solomon asked, looking very pleased to hear it. He took another drink of his lemonade then held it out to Chad, offering him a drink. "And has he finally given up trying to buy this place?"

Chad shook his head to both the lemonade and the question, then sighed heavily. "Not at all. Truth is, he said something to Julia about trying a whole new approach."

Solomon sat forward. His strength had instantly returned. "What sort of new approach?"

"I don't know. I wish I did so I could tell you what to expect next, but he didn't take the time to elaborate."

"You don't think he's going to send his pack of ruffians back over here, do you?" Raymond asked, clearly as worried as Solomon by the news.

Chad looked at Raymond, then Solomon, then back to Raymond. He wished he had more to tell them. "I really don't know *what* he plans to do. After he read my note, he wadded it up for the second time, then carried it with him into the house. I never saw him again after that."

Images of what had happened not long afterward set his heart to thudding again like a schoolboy's, making it hard for him to concentrate. He wished more than ever that Pearline had not shown up when she did. No telling how far he could have taken that last kiss if he had just had a little more time. It was then Chad decided he needed to find something *or someone* to occupy more of Pearline's time. His gaze fell again on Solomon.

Unaware of the directions Chad's thoughts had taken, Solomon's expression hardened as he nodded toward something behind Chad. "Really doesn't matter much if Thornton sends those men back over here or not. Because no matter what that man plans to do next, I for one will be prepared."

Chad turned to see what he'd indicated and was not too surprised to find Solomon's hunting rifle propped against the trunk of the tree. A strong feeling of apprehension washed over him when he turned to look back into Solomon's determined face. Surely it would not come to that.

Charles pushed the swinging door open and peered apprehensively into the kitchen. When he did not see Julia or Pearline anywhere in sight, he cautiously stepped inside and headed toward Ruth, who stood at the counter with her back to him.

"Have you seen Pearline this morning?"

Ruth spun around, startled, at Charles's voice. "Mr. Thornton, what are you doing here?" She glanced at the clock, then at him, clearly mystified. "It's after nine o'clock. Why aren't you gone off to the lumber mill?" Her weathered face drew into a puzzled frown. "It *is* Monday, isn't it?"

"Yes, it's Monday. And I'll be leaving for the mill in just a few minutes. But first I need to ask Pearline something. Have you seen her?"

Ruth nodded, then pointed the small meat cleaver she held toward the back door. Because of Julia's last-minute announcement that she planned to have a picnic with her new fellow, Ruth had been busily cutting apart a small chicken when Charles first entered. "Pearline said something a few minutes ago about getting started on Missy's laundry."

Charles cut his gaze in the direction of the door. "Is Julia with her?"

"No." Ruth tilted her head and looked up at him questioningly. "Missy gathered up her paint case and that canvas she's been working on for the past week and headed off toward the river about an hour ago. Not too long after she finished eating. She said she wanted to get in at least a few hours of painting before her young man came by to take her on that picnic."

Charles bristled at the reminder of his daughter's plans. "Then Pearline is out there alone?" He let out a short, relieved breath that caused Ruth's questioning expression to deepen.

"As far as I know, she's out there alone. Abraham has already brought in the eggs and gone upstairs to put your room in order, and Sirus decided to wait until this evening to do any work in the garden. Lisa, she's out in the summer kitchen getting it ready for use."

"Good," he answered, then headed immediately for the door. What he had to say to Pearline, he wanted said in private.

Relieved that Julia was nowhere near the house, he hurried across the back porch, then down the nearest stairs to the area of the yard where Pearline busily poured hot water into one of the two wooden tubs she had brought out of the laundry room just minutes earlier. She paused with the steaming kettle still in her hands when she heard Charles call out her name.

"Yes, sir?" she answered, looking just as surprised to

discover him still home as Ruth had. "Did you want me?"

Charles looked around to make sure no one else was nearby, then motioned for her to put the kettle down beside the others she had brought from the kitchen.

"Come here. I have something I want you to do for me." He gestured toward a small group of white wrought-iron chairs that were positioned in the shade of a large maple tree. The grouping was on a small bricked area at the edge of the main garden. It was the closest comfortable place to sit.

"But I have to get this washin' done," she protested, then indicated the three large baskets of clothes she had brought outside with her. She pursed her mouth to one side, clearly not wanting to add another chore to her list. "I promised Missy I'd have it all done in time to go with her on that picnic." Her worried expression relaxed again when she realized what she had just said. "Or is that what you want to talk to me about? The picnic."

"Yes, I want to talk about that, too," Charles admitted, gesturing toward the chairs again. "But first I want to ask you to do me a small favor."

"Favor?" Pearline looked at him with a cautiously raised brow while she finally set the kettle aside, then stuffed the pot holders into her apron pocket. "What sort of favor?"

"A very *special* favor," Charles answered. He waited for her to join him before he, too, sat down, eager to explain.

Pearline eyed him warily, not used to such courtly behavior from her employer. Although Charles Thornton had never treated her badly, he had also never bothered to wait until she was seated before sitting down himself.

Charles wasted no time. "As you probably know, I

169

have been trying to buy back that land I lost to Robert Freeport in that crooked poker game years ago."

Pearline nodded that she did indeed know, but clearly did not see what that had to do with her. Her eyebrows formed tiny points in her forehead while she waited to hear more.

"And I'm sure you also know that the nephew who just bought that land refuses to sell to me."

Pearline nodded again. "Missy mentioned it to me. But what's any of that got to do with me?"

"I need your help with a certain matter. But before I tell you what sort of help, I want your promise that you won't mention a word of what I'm about to say to anyone."

"Not even to Missy?" Pearline's right eyebrow shot up higher than the left one, as if leery of having to make such a promise. "I don't usually keep no secrets from Missy." Although she did know of *one* secret she was keeping. One that she felt certain would eventually affect them all. That secret had to do with Chad.

"You'll have to keep this one. Because the fewer people who know about this plan the better."

Pearline's left eyebrow shot up until it was level with the right when she leaned slightly forward, curious to know more. *"Plan?* What sort of plan?"

Charles shook his head, then ran his hands through his thick white hair. "No. First you have to promise not to tell anyone what I'm about to ask you to do."

Pearline tapped one foot on the painted brick while she studied Charles's determined expression. "But what if I don't want to do whatever it is you ask me to do?"

"Then you won't have to do it, but you will still have to keep it a secret." He paused a moment while he met her gaze directly, then added, "I assure you if you do me this one little favor, you will be well rewarded. Espe-

170

cially if you are as successful in doing it as I think you'll be."

Pearline tapped both feet in rapid unison, causing the hem of her dark-green skirt to bounce spiritedly, then suddenly stopped when she made her decision. "All right," she finally conceded. "I promise I won't tell no one. What is it you want me to do that is so important? And what's it got to do with that land you want?"

Charles smiled, leaned forward, and spoke in hushed tones so his words would go no further than Pearline's ear.

"Tomorrow morning, when Julia goes off to do her painting like she does most mornings, I want you to put on your very best dress . . ." He studied her for a moment, then corrected himself. "No, put on one of *Julia's* nicest dresses—one of the low-necked ones she brought back from St. Louis. You two look to be about the same size, so you should have no problem fitting into any of her gowns that you choose. Then I want you to ride over to the new neighbor's house and leave off a message for me. I've decided to make one last appeal to purchase that house, and I want you to be the one to deliver it."

"Is that all?" Pearline asked, as if wondering why all the secrecy.

"Well, no. There's more." He directed his gaze to his hands, tightly laced in his lap. He was not too sure how she would respond to the rest of what he had to say. "You see, the main reason I can't get Freeport's nephew to sell me that land is because that foreman of his has some sort of hold over him and refuses to let him get rid of any of it."

"How do you know that?"

"For one thing, the nephew keeps using the exact same words and phrases in the letters he's written that the foreman himself used when talking directly to me or my men. Obviously he has a lot of influence over his boss."

"But I still don't understand what that has to do with me. Why can't someone else deliver this final appeal of yours?"

Charles hesitated before answering. "Because you are better suited for the job. I don't know whether Julia mentioned it to you or not, but that foreman over there is a Negro."

Pearline's eyes widened with surprise. "No, she didn't tell me nothin' about no foreman. All she told me was that the nephew wasn't moved in yet but that the work had already begun and you was none too pleased. You say he's a black man?"

"Yes." Charles lifted his expression into a wry smile. "Which is why I want *you* to be the one to carry my next offer over there. And it's why I want you to go over there wearing one of Julia's frilliest dresses. And perhaps a bit of that new lavender perfume she just bought." His smile deepened. "I do want you to look and smell your very best when you first turn on your feminine charms."

"My *what?*" Pearline blinked several times, looking at him as if unable to believe she had heard him correctly.

"Your feminine charms," he repeated, then leaned forward to convince her. "You are a very beautiful young woman, Pearline, though you do tend to be a bit too choosy when it comes to the men you see."

"Just because I happen to want one who bathes regular and can talk sense?" Pearline asked, looking perplexed, clearly not certain whether to be flattered or offended. "What's wrong with that?"

"Nothing," Charles answered, and held his hands out in a calming gesture. "It's just that this man is probably

172

not going to interest you, either. But even so, I want you to pretend that he does. At least long enough to sweet-talk him over to our side."

"Our side?" Pearline tilted her head forward while she looked at him with a sharply raised eyebrow. "Don't you mean *your* side? What do I get out of this? What's the reward you mentioned earlier?"

Charles shifted. "His name is Solomon Ford, and if you can persuade him over to my way of thinking, and he in turn helps convince his boss to accept the new offer you'll be leaving with him, then you will be rewarded royally."

"How royally?"

"If this thing goes through and I finally get that house and land back, then I'll deed you an acre of land by the river to build your own little cabin on one day. I know how you love the river."

Pearline's eyes stretched to their limits. *"Where* by the river?"

"Anywhere you choose except directly in front of either of the two houses," he answered, then explained. "Even though I plan to move out of this house and into the other one just as soon as I've bought it back, I'd like to keep this one nice for Julia just in case she ever does find someone worthy of marrying her," he said, then grumbled, "although I'm beginning to think that will never happen."

"But I thought Negro women couldn't own land."

Charles frowned, not having thought of that. "That could be. But even so, I could still put the land aside in your name to be deeded over to whomever you marry for when you finally do find the right man. Or I could deed it to your brother."

Pearline gazed off toward the river. "Can my acre be

a part of that small clearin' over near the persimmon trees?"

Knowing the spot was about a half mile upriver, Charles nodded. "But first you have to help me win that Negro foreman over to my way of thinking. You'll have to explain to him that I'm not after everything the man owns. All I want is the house, the outbuildings, and part of the surrounding land. The new owner would be left with nearly three hundred acres of prime land on which to build his own house and outbuildings. He could do that by using the money he will have made by selling the property I want at over twice what it is really worth. And he'd probably have enough left over to buy all the cattle he wanted."

Pearline pressed her hands over her face while she considered everything she had just been told. "But what if I can't persuade him to help convince Mr. Andrews to sell? Do I still get that land for havin' tried?"

"No," he answered firmly. "You only get the acre if the deal goes through."

"But what if somethin' goes wrong that's not my fault? What if he takes one look at me and decides he doesn't even like me?"

"Then I'll have to think of something entirely different, because you will have failed." He paused for a moment while he rubbed the curve of his jaw with his hand. She needed some sort of incentive to try. "Although you still wouldn't get any land for your efforts, if you can somehow convince me you tried your best, I'd be willing to double your wages for that month. How's that sound?"

"Tempting. Very tempting," she answered, then sat forward, clearly excited about the offer, yet still a little apprehensive. "But how do I explain away havin' taken one of Missy's new dresses out of her wardrobe?"

"You don't. Wear one of those . . ." He nodded toward the three large baskets filled with the clothes she had brought outside to wash. "All you have to do is pretend you didn't get around to washing them all because you were too pressed for time getting ready for today's picnic. Then after you've worn the dress you picked, you simply return it to the dirty clothes and wash it again with the next bundle. If you wait and put the dress on tomorrow morning right after she has left to go do her painting and then get back here and change back into your own clothes before she returns for lunch, she'll never know you wore it."

"But what about my ironin'? I usually do Missy's ironin' on Tuesday mornings. She'll wonder why I didn't get it done in the hours she was gone. She'll be angry and want to know what I did with that time instead."

"No she won't. I'll have Lisa do Julia's ironing tomorrow when she does mine. That way Julia's clothes will be pressed and hanging in her wardrobe like they are supposed to be and she will have no reason to question what you did with your time."

"But what if Missy finds out that Lisa was the one who did all the ironin'? Wouldn't Missy want to know why *your* personal maid was suddenly havin' to do both our jobs?"

"I'll just tell her that I asked you to run an errand for me, which is true enough. It's none of her business what sort of errand." He paused again while he studied Pearline's wide-eyed expression. He could tell she was sorely tempted. "So will you do it?"

"If it means me gettin' that land I like, you know I'll do it. You just have that letter or whatever it is I'm suppose to carry over there ready when it comes time for me to leave out," Pearline said. "Too bad I can't go on

175

over there today." Her dark-brown eyes lit with hope. "Maybe I could. Maybe I can find some excuse not to go on that picnic after all."

"No," Charles responded with a sudden scowl, then held up a finger in warning. "I want you on that picnic. I don't want those two leaving this house alone."

"Why?" Pearline asked with feigned innocence. "Don't you like Missy's new beau?"

"No, I *don't* like him," Charles answered honestly. "And I don't trust him. There is just something about the young man that does not ring true with me."

Pearline grinned, as if she fully understood what he meant. "Don't worry. I'll be right there with them when they leave."

"Good," Charles said, then thinking he had accomplished all he had come to accomplish, he stood to brush the creases from his ivory-colored summer suit with the backs of his hands. "I'll leave the papers you'll need to take with you tomorrow in your bedroom. Look for them under your pillow."

Pearline watched, still a little stunned by what she had just been asked to do, while Charles Thornton headed off toward the front of the house where his carriage awaited. Her heart hammered excitedly while she hurried to the clothing baskets, eager to decide just which dress she should wear.

Chapter Ten

"Aren't you plannin' to change your clothes?" Pearline asked when she entered Julia's bedroom and saw that she still had on the same pink-and-white cotton dress she had worn to do her painting.

"No," Julia answered, looking very disgruntled as she leaned forward on the vanity stool to comb several unruly locks of hair back into place. She could not stand to have her hair in her face. "Why should I? Father isn't here to see what I look like, nor will he be."

She picked up a hairpin and stabbed it into the loose strand she had tucked at the base of the coiled twist she had shaped high at the back of her head earlier that day. "And I certainly have no reason to want to impress Chad. If anything, I should be trying to do all I can to *un*impress that man."

"Oh?" Pearline asked, her tone clearly doubtful.

Julia could tell by the glint in Pearline's eyes what she was thinking.

"Now don't you start with me again," she warned, then turned away from the mirror to wag her finger. "I have gone over this with you once already." She narrowed her brown eyes. "That was not a real kiss. It was just something Chad and I did because he thought Father might be watching."

"I don't know if I quite believe that. It sure did look like a real kiss to me," Pearline said. "Real enough to set my heart to racin' about fast as it can go—and I was just standin' there *watchin'*. I can just imagine what it must have been like to actually take part in a kiss like that."

"It *wasn't* a real kiss," Julia repeated then set her comb aside and rose from the stool to face Pearline. "When are you ever going to get that one simple little fact through that thick, stubborn head of yours. You know very well I don't care for that man. All I want from him is help in convincing Father to let me marry Patrick. After all, I'm twenty-two years old now. I should be allowed to marry the man I choose and start a life of my own. I can't let Father control me forever. I have to break free *sometime*. And if it takes having to pretend to kiss a man I don't love to accomplish that, then so be it. But that is all that was, a *pretend* kiss." Not wanting to be reminded of her own responses, she pushed image of the rakishly handsome man to the back of her mind, still outraged by the fact he had suddenly kissed her like that. "Quit reading more into it than was there. Those were *not* normal kisses."

Although Pearline decided not to come any closer to Julia, staying just out of strangling range, her grin deepened until two fat dimples marked her brown cheeks.

"I think maybe you are right. I can't recall Mr. Patrick ever kissin' you like that," she taunted, knowing full well how annoyed Julia would become over that remark. "Not even when he thought you two were alone."

"That's because Patrick respects me far too much to try something like that," she replied with a stubborn lift of her chin.

Pearline nodded, but then took a precautionary step back. "Either that or he just doesn't know how to go about it. Maybe you should have him watch how Mr. Chad does it so he can learn."

Julia pursed her mouth into a short, flat line that showed her annoyance.

"Speakin' of love . . ." Pearline decided she had been given the perfect opportunity to find out just how Julia felt. "Do you really love Mr. Patrick?"

Had that question come from any other servant, Julia would have been outraged, but because it had been posed by one who was also her lifelong friend, she felt she should answer.

"I want to marry him, don't I?"

"But do you love him?" Pearline pressed.

Julia looked away. "Patrick and I have similar backgrounds and we have a lot of the same interests, including art."

"But do you *love* him? Is he in your every wakin' thought? Does he make your legs feel like melted jelly while settin' your very soul on fire?"

Julia arched her eyebrows at the melodramatic way Pearline had posed that last question. "You have been reading too many of those paper books your cousin Nora keeps sending you."

"You still have not answered my question. Do you *love* Mr. Patrick?"

Julia tapped her foot a moment. "Of course I love him," she finally answered, wondering why it had been so hard for her to say that. She'd had no problem declaring her love for him before. "That is to be one of the reasons I want to marry him."

"Then he *is* in your every wakin' thought?" Pearline asked, wanting to be sure.

"Of course he is," Julia lied, knowing it was no longer

true, because for the past few days her thoughts had more often strayed to Chad. But *that* undoubtedly was because he remained such a mystery to her. As soon as she managed to solve some of the questions surrounding him, she should be able to keep him from invading her thoughts quite so often.

"And you don't care even one little bit for this Mr. Chad?" Pearline continued, all the while studying her face carefully.

"I've only known the man a week." Julia gave an annoyed sigh, then crossed her arms, not caring in the least that she could be wrinkling her dress. "Did you come up here for a reason?"

"Just to see if you needed any help. And to remind you of the time. Mr. Chad should be arrivin' any minute." She walked to the open window and peered out across the yard toward the front drive. Her dark eyes widened with recognition. "Fact is, I think I see him comin' already. I wonder where he got hold of such a fine-lookin' carriage."

"He brought a carriage?" Julia hurried to the window to see. "Why would he bring a carriage? I thought we'd just walk down the path to the river and have the picnic there." That way they would still be in full sight of the house, which would sound much better to Patrick should he ever find out how she had spent that day.

"Guess he's got other plans," Pearline said, her eyes sparkling with amusement at the *be*musement she saw in Julia's round eyes. With Chad only a short distance away, she turned and headed back toward the hallway. "I'll go on down to get the food basket and meet you both outside. That is, of course, unless you've changed your mind about wantin' me with you. I know how you always like to be alone with Mr. Patrick. Mayhap you'd like to be just as alone with Mr. Chad."

Julia felt the heat staining her cheeks. "I enjoy being alone with Patrick because I am in love with Patrick, and because I will one day marry him." Odd, she had found that word *love* a little easier to say when using it as a form of rebuttal. "But as you well know, I am *not* in love with Chad, nor could I ever be. We are far too different for such as that. The truth is, I can barely tolerate the man."

"Are you sure?" Pearline asked casually, then glanced back at her with a questioning expression.

Julia planted her fists on her hips. She wanted to show just how sure she was. *"Yes,* I'm sure."

"Then why do you seem so flustered about goin' on this picnic with him? If you don't even care for the man, what harm could possibly come of it?"

"I'm not flustered. I'm just worried that Patrick might find out."

"And what if he does? The only reason you hired this other man was so that your Mr. Patrick would be more readily accepted, isn't it?"

"Yes."

Pearline looked truly perplexed. "Then why are you so worried that he might find out? It's all bein' done for his benefit. Seems to me like you'd want him to know what sort of trouble you're willin' to go to just so your father will be more likely to take to him right off."

"The problem is that Patrick might not understand why I allowed myself to go off on a picnic with a complete stranger. Especially if he ever has the occasion to meet this particular stranger and sees for himself how very—very . . ." She paused, looking for just the right words to explain the fears that nagged her.

"Handsome he is?" Pearline supplied promptly. "You think it might bother Mr. Patrick to find out that Mr. Chad is so very handsome?"

Julia nodded. "Yes I do. Patrick is not going to like the fact that I hired someone as attractive as Chad."

"Then you do admit Mr. Chad is attractive?" There was a definite sparkle in Pearline's dark eyes.

"Yes, of course I do," she conceded, wishing her heart would not jump every time Pearline so much as mentioned the man's name. "I'm not blind. And neither is Patrick."

"Oh, so, *Mr. Patrick* is who you meant when you told me not to be tellin' nobody about that kiss yesterday," Pearline said, as if just having figured that out.

"Of course he's the one I meant. If Patrick ever found out about that kiss, even though it meant *nothing* to me, he would be furious." He would be even more furious if he found out that for a moment she had actually enjoyed the strange but wondrous effects of Chad's mouth on hers. And he would be just as furious to know that she had been unable to sleep the night following all because she could not stop thinking about the wild stirring those two unsolicited kisses had caused inside her.

"Maybe not after you explained everything to him," Pearline supplied, though with little conviction. "Why, you don't even know the man's full name. How could he possibly think you are attracted to some man you don't even know?" She paused a moment to give Julia time to consider that last point, then asked, "You don't suppose that's goin' to make Mr. Patrick even more angry, do you? Finding out that you went and hired a complete stranger like you did. A man you'd never even met."

"But I did so on your recommendation," Julia reminded her. "Besides, I should know more about him by the time Patrick arrives. It shouldn't be too much longer before you and I finally find out who he is and why he is so determined to keep his last name such a secret."

Pearline shook her head. "Won't know nothin' if he keeps slippin' off unannounced like he did yesterday. You can't expect me to follow the man if I don't even know when he's leavin'. Yesterday he got away without me even bein' able to check his pockets. Good thing he wasn't inside the house much."

"We'll just have to keep a closer watch over him. Today when he leaves here, I want you following right behind him, making careful note of every place he goes and of every person he talks to. I want to know all there is to know about him long before Patrick arrives in three weeks."

"I'll do my best," Pearline agreed, although as far as she was concerned, they already knew enough about him. He had stepped in and saved her virtue that first night when he certainly did not have to. That alone said a lot about him. "But for now, I'd better get on downstairs after that picnic basket. We don't want to keep Mr. Chad waitin' any longer than we have to."

Julia watched with growing apprehension while Pearline disappeared into the hall. She was not ready to spend the afternoon in the company of a man she hardly knew and whose kiss held such an unexplainable power over her. Especially when he had already proved he could not be trusted to keep his hands nor his eyes off her.

Still, she knew she could not back out of the picnic now, not after having made such a fuss earlier. How would she explain such a sudden change in plans to her father? Even feigning another headache was out of the question. Her father would wonder why she continued to allow such a thing to get in the way of true romance when she never had before.

With little choice but to see the afternoon through, Julia paced the floor of her bedroom waiting for Abraham to announce that her guest had arrived.

Patrick pressed his cheeks between his hands, unable to believe his bad luck. How could he possibly have lost while holding three kings and a pair of eights? It just did not seem possible.

"Read 'em and weep," the brawny man with the bulging arm muscles and long, drooping handlebar mustache said as he reached for the large pile of money and bits of jewelry scattered across the center of the table. "Never have four little threes looked so good."

The elderly gentleman to Patrick's right took one last gulp of his whiskey then reached immediately for his hat. "That pretty well takes everything I had on me today."

"Me, too," the portly man to Patrick's left said, also reaching for his hat. Both men were dressed like store owners. Easy pickings, or so Patrick had thought.

"Guess I'd better get on back to work and try to sell something to help make up the loss."

"Ah, gents, don't go away just because you're out of money again," the brawny man said, laughing deep from inside his barrel chest. "I take IOUs, you know." He looked at Patrick. "What about you, stranger? You still game for another hand?"

Patrick stared at the winning cards a moment longer, then at the ones he had thought would win for him. He shook his head. Why was he having such a terrible run of bad luck? First, his thefts were discovered far sooner than they should have been, then he had been unable to buy a train ticket that would carry him all the way through to Texas, which meant changing lines in this godforsaken town, and now this.

"I don't have any more money, either. You just won my last two hundred dollars."

"What a pity," the burly man said, and laughed again as he continued to pull his winnings toward him. "But then, it was your idea to raise the stakes. I was content to keep things like they were."

Patrick grimaced, running his hand through his cropped blond hair. "Don't remind me. I really thought I had a winning hand."

"I can see why," he responded good-naturedly, then frowned at the way Patrick continued to stare at the cards intently—never blinking. "Say, that really was all the money you had, wasn't it?"

"Every last cent. I don't even have enough to get a room now. And all I was doing was killing time while I waited for the Southwest Railroad ticket office to open at noon." He reached into his pocket and felt for his watch, temporarily forgetting that he had included that as a way to raise the bet. Julia had given him the expensive gold watch with the sparrow engraved on the case for his birthday. He would have to tell her it was stolen. "Now I don't even have enough to buy the ticket I need."

"Tell you what," the man said, reaching into the pile of money he had just pulled toward him for a small gold coin. "Take this and go get yourself a room, then come around to my place as soon as you have settled in and I'll have Reggie find you some temporary work so you can at least earn yourself enough money to go back west."

"What place is that?" Patrick asked, annoyed that he could not be on his way now. He had so hoped to be in Texas by mid-week.

"My name is Hiram Buchanan. I own that little carriage repair shop right next door," he said, tossing the coin in Patrick's direction. "I can always use more help when it comes to mending carriages, especially this time of year when the roads are in such bad shape."

"But I don't know anything about mending carriages," Patrick admitted, scowling at the thought of having to do such menial work. Especially when he was now only a couple of hundred miles away from having all the money one man could ever need. All he had to do was marry that fiery wench, Julia Thornton, then get rid of her father. He wished he had never stopped into the small tavern while waiting for that blasted ticket office to open. He should have known he would end up in some poker game.

"You'll learn all you need to know," Hiram assured him. "Nothing hard about it." He was still smiling when he raked his winnings into his dark-gray bowler hat and stood. "I pay by the job. If you work hard enough and fast enough, you just might earn what you'll need to be on your way again sometime next week."

Patrick sighed while he quickly pocketed the coin, aware he had little choice but to accept the offer. He certainly couldn't hope to rob this giant of a man in a dark alley somewhere. Not without a weapon of some sort, and unfortunately he had none. He had been forced to leave his pistol behind in his office inside the shipping company.

Blast his continued rotten luck. The way it looked now, it would be at least a week before he could surprise Julia by arriving at her door early.

"I'll be ready to work just as soon as I can find a room," he promised reluctantly, then pushed himself out of the chair and headed towards the door.

* * *

Pearline watched Julia's disgruntled expression while she climbed unassisted out of the handsome new carriage Chad had obviously rented in a futile attempt to please her. She wondered when Julia would finally realize that the man was interested in far more than the five hundred dollars she had offered him.

"I still don't understand why we couldn't have had our picnic along the section of river that passes in front of the house," Julia muttered, purposely avoiding Chad's attempt to help her down. She refused to let him touch her, knowing only too well the strange effect his touch had on her. She would not allow today to end up being a repeat of the previous day. "It would have been much more convenient than riding all the way out to this place."

"But it would not be nearly as beautiful as it is here," Chad responded, gesturing toward the grassy knoll near a sharp bend in the lazy river. He planned to spread their quilts there in the shade of a pair of large sweet gum trees that grew within yards of each other near the water's edge. "Nor would it be quite as private."

Julia cut her gaze at him. "And why on earth would we need privacy?" She quickly stepped away, afraid he might try to capture her elbow and escort her to the area where he planned for them to eat.

But instead of attempting to touch her, he turned his back to her.

"Well, for one thing, to worry your father." Chad's gaze met with Pearline's, but he tried not to look too amused while he helped the maid down from the carriage. He waited until Pearline stood firmly on the ground before explaining anything more to Julia. "I'm sure your father will demand to know exactly where we picnicked and exactly how long we were there, so the lovelier the spot the better. And what could be lovelier than this?" He gestured toward the scattering of colorful wildflowers that peeked out from beneath the thick green grass that grew along the shaded riverbank.

Julia crossed her arms. She certainly could not argue with that reasoning. Her father would indeed demand to know all the particulars, if not from her, then certainly from Pearline. "Just as long as you understand that the only reason we are out here is to aggravate my father."

"Why else?" He looked back at her with a most innocent expression while he reached inside the carriage for the basket and quilts he had placed in the back.

"I just want to make sure you understand that you are not to try to kiss me."

"Why would I? That was done for your father's benefit, remember? He's not even here today," Chad explained with a curious expression, as if the thought had never occurred to him. "Isn't the only reason we are out here is so that you and Pearline can go back and report what a wonderful time we had? We don't even have to talk to each other if it bothers you that much. You said you wanted me to go on a picnic with you. I figure this is all just a part of my job."

With the two quilts he had brought tossed over his left shoulder and the food basket gripped in his right hand, he headed immediately for the spot he had chosen. There they would have the benefits of both a beautiful view and the slight breeze curling in from the northwest.

Julia stopped to consider what he had just said for a moment, then hurried to follow him. There was too much she wanted to know about him to agree to an afternoon of total silence. The sooner she uncovered his many secrets, the sooner she could push him out of her thoughts completely. Then she could start to think about Patrick again. "I don't mind talking to you. It's just that I wanted to make sure you understood there was to be no more touching."

"Unless of course your father is present to see it," he corrected, then set the basket down so he could spread the quilts across the grass, one atop the other. When he finished, he reached for the basket and placed it in the center of the pallet he had formed. "There, now, if you ladies will do the honors of getting the food ready, I'll go make sure the horse is tethered in an area where there is plenty of both shade and grass."

Julia watched while he walked away, noticing how very tall and lean his body looked in the dark colors he wore—and how he always walked with such obvious male confidence. She also noticed the way his black broadcloth britches hugged his long legs with each step he took, and how the loose-fitted dark-blue cotton shirt clung to his broad, muscular shoulders. Shoulders that she remembered he kept strong by taking on such strenuous jobs as moving furniture and carrying freight.

An intense fluttering of warmth and giddiness poured over her when she recalled just *how* strong those muscles had felt when he'd held her in his arms, but she quickly pushed the unwanted memories aside. It was not fair to Patrick for her to be thinking about another man in such an intimate manner.

"You want me to wait and serve myself later?" Pearline asked, bringing Julia's attention back to her surroundings and to the main reason they were there. "Or should I go ahead and fill my plate, too."

Julia glanced down and saw that Pearline already had most of the food Ruth had prepared unpacked and now held three empty plates in her hands. "I see no reason we shouldn't all three eat together."

"Good," Pearline answered, and started to do just that. "I'm about as hungry as a she-wolf with pups in winter."

Julia sank down onto the quilts beside Pearline, leaving plenty of room on the opposite side for Chad. She liked the idea of having the bulky picnic basket and most of the food Pearline had unpacked between them, and tucked her feet beneath her skirts to make herself more comfortable.

By the time Chad had returned, Pearline had his plate ready. She handed it to him as soon as he had sat down and crossed his legs Indian-style.

"You've got a choice between milk or water to drink with that," she said, gesturing toward the two stoneware bottles that she had taken out of the basket. "I guess Ruth didn't have enough time to make any lemonade like she usually does."

"Water will be fine," Chad told her, then tossed his hat into the grass to get it out of his way before carefully balancing his plate on one knee. He glanced across at Julia and noticed she had only a fraction as much food on her plate. Hardly enough to feed a small child. "Aren't you hungry?"

"Not especially," Julia admitted, then laid her plate on the quilt beside her where it would not be in her way and she could pick at it at leisure.

Pearline, on the other hand, had no problem with her appetite and already held a large piece of crusty fried chicken in her hands, ready to devour. "She's worried that her real sweetheart will somehow find out that you two went on this picnic together," she supplied, obviously finding no reason to keep the matter a secret. "She's afraid he'll be jealous."

"Pearline!" Julia admonished, thinking it was none of Chad's business why her appetite was so wan.

"Well, it's true," Pearline replied, in ready defense of her actions. She jutted her chin forward. "You said so yourself."

"But you don't have to announce that particular truth to the world," Julia complained and narrowed her gaze with warning.

"I didn't announce it to the world," she returned and looked unduly chastised. "I only told Mr. Chad."

Chad waited until he had finished chewing the bite of chicken he had just taken and had dabbed his mouth with the folded corner of his napkin before commenting. "I don't see why you're worried about something like that. How's he ever going to find out? I certainly don't intend to tell him." Although he might be sorely tempted. Anything to bring a rift between the two.

"That's because you'll never meet him," Julia responded quickly. "He won't be arriving for a few more weeks. You should be finished and gone long before then."

"You sound like you don't *want* me to meet him," Chad observed, then looked to Pearline for a reason, knowing of the two women, she was the more likely one to offer an explanation.

Pearline did not disappoint him.

"That's because she *doesn't*," she explained while she tore a large piece of crust off her chicken and held it between the tips of her fingers. "She doesn't want Mr. Patrick ever findin' out what you look like. She thinks it might upset him if he ever got a good look at how handsome you are."

Chad's eyebrows arched immediately. He looked to Julia to see if that was true.

"Pearline!" Julia admonished again. "You said something about being hungry. Why don't you *eat* instead of talk?"

"I was just explainin' to him why he won't never be meetin' up with the man you hired him to help you marry." Pearline said with a childlike scowl, then plopped the piece of crust she had torn into her mouth. "Just thought he'd like knowin' why."

"I really don't want to talk about Patrick," Julia said with certainty. "I'd rather talk about Chad. There's so very much we don't know about him."

Pearline cut her gaze to Chad, clearly not opposed to knowing more about him herself.

"And what is it you want to know about me? I'll answer just about any question you might have."

"Except for any that pertain to who you really are," Julia reminded him flatly. For lack of anything else to do with her hands, she picked up an olive from her plate and rolled it between her fingers. "Or have you finally changed your mind about that?"

"No, I haven't," he admitted. "For reasons you will one day understand, I have no intention of telling you what my last name is. At least not yet."

"But you will someday?" she asked. Her face wrinkled into a questioning frown while she studied him, noticing the way the tiny splashes of sunlight that had found their way through the two trees played with the golden highlights in his dark-brown hair. She also noticed the intent way he looked at her with those crystal blue eyes of his. Eyes that were surrounded by the longest, thickest, darkest eyelashes she had ever seen on a man. Eyes that made her feel guilty just to be looking at them.

"Yes," Chad promised, aware he finally had her full attention and pleased by that fact. "Someday, I will tell you everything there is to know about me. Just not right now."

"Why not?" Rather than continue rolling the olive awkwardly between her fingertips, she slipped it into her mouth and chewed it, glad Ruth had remembered to re-move the pit. "Just what is it that you have to hide?"

Chad dropped his gaze to watch the slow, sensual movement of her mouth while she slowly chewed. When she finished, he swallowed, then lifted his gaze back to hers. "Why don't we talk about something else?"

Julia arched her eyebrows then relaxed them again. "All right, so you won't tell me your last name. Will you at least tell me why you are here? By that I mean why you decided to come to Marshall, Texas, of all places?"

"I came here looking for a new way of life," he said, wanting to keep his answers as honest yet as uninformative as possible. Having finished his chicken, he wiped his hands with his napkin, then picked up his fork to take a bite of the mixed fruit salad Pearline had piled on his plate. "I was not happy where I was."

Julia continued to study his expression while she reached for another olive. "Do I assume then that you have already grown tired of whatever type of life you led before?"

"Definitely."

She knotted her forehead. He seemed sincere enough. "So, whatever it was you did that makes you want to hide your identity now *bothers* you to some degree?"

"Yes," he said with a confirming nod, though the question had been a little confusing. He watched again while she ate the second olive, still finding the slow motion of her mouth oddly provocative. "I don't like having to keep secrets. I'm normally a very open per-son."

Julia leaned forward slightly, glad to finally be learn-ing something about the man she had so hastily hired. "Was what you did that now bothers you against the law? Is *that* why you are so afraid for anyone to find out your full name? Are you afraid they might make the connection?"

Chad met her curious gaze with one of pure amusement. She certainly had a lively imagination. "No. I've committed no crimes; at least none that I know anything about."

"Then why don't you want anyone to know your last name?"

Chad paused to consider his next answer and chose his words very carefully. "Because there are certain people who would use the information against me, and it might cause me to lose something that has become very dear to me."

"See?" Pearline interrupted, looking very pleased with that answer. "He ain't no blackmailer after all."

"Blackmailer?" Chad repeated. He looked at Julia, clearly surprised. "You thought I was a blackmailer?"

Julia lifted her pretty chin defiantly. "To tell you the truth, I didn't know what to think. I still don't."

"Well, I can assure you that I'm no blackmailer. I'm not even all that certain just what it is you think I could blackmail you with."

"Oh, she was afraid you planned—" Pearline started to answer, but was quickly interrupted.

"Keep quiet," Julia snapped. "I think you've said quite enough about me already."

"So what you're sayin' is that you have certain secrets you want kept from *him*, too," Pearline said with an impish grin while she reached for the last bit of roll on her plate.

When Chad saw how quickly Julia stiffened, he felt the urge to grin right along with Pearline. "Is there anything else you want to know about me?" he asked. "Something other than my last name and the fact that I'm not a blackmailer?"

"Yes, there is." Julia's expression went from angry to just plain annoyed. "I'd like to know why you accepted that part-time job working for our neighbor when you know I didn't want you to."

"Because I need to work," Chad answered simply, then set his empty plate aside so he could take a quick drink from his water glass.

"But why? I told you I'd advance you ten dollars to help you get by until the job is complete. I'm not insensitive to what you need. I realize you are a drifter who looks for odd jobs where you can find them, and that the hotel where you're staying is one of the most expensive in town—which brings me to another thing I don't understand. If you are all that broke, why are you staying there of all places? Why not somewhere less expensive like a boardinghouse?"

"I didn't say I need the *money*," he corrected her, then wiped his mouth and hands one final time with his napkin before tossing it on top of his empty plate. "What I said was that I need to *work*. I *like* working. I like staying fit."

Julia's gaze dropped to the powerful lines of his body, aware he was certainly that. The muscles at the base of her throat contracted when once again the unbidden memory of the kiss they had shared the day before invaded her thoughts, causing her to become momentarily silent.

It was not until Pearline had finished the last morsel of food on her plate several minutes later that anything else was said.

"I think I done ate too much." She patted her middle soundly to emphasize her point. "I need to get up and walk around a little."

She glanced off toward a thick stand of trees just to the north of them while she quickly gathered the dishes and set them back into the basket. She left out only Julia's plate and the bowl that had held the six rolls Ruth had packed. "If you don't mind, I'd like to walk out to that little field over near the persimmon trees and see if there are any blackberries yet." She also wanted to sit there after she was through picking any berries and imagine what a small house would look like nestled on that acre of land she might soon own. She also needed to consider the best way to go about convincing that foreman to see matters their way.

Before Julia could think of a logical protest that would keep her there, Pearline picked up the empty bowl and quickly stood. Since Mr. Charles had said he did not want Missy and Chad *leaving* the house alone, but had said nothing about their *being* alone at any time after they had left, she felt no guilt in absenting herself for an hour or so.

Chad stood, too, though he had no intention of following. "Where are you headed?"

"Through those woods there," she said, and pointed. "There's a small little meadow near the river that I like to go to on those days I don't work. The water is a little deeper there, perfect for swimmin' and splashin', and there are no roads nearby to bring unwanted visitors."

"You know how to swim?" Chad asked, not having thought of Pearline as a swimmer.

"Sure do. My grandmother taught me," Pearline responded proudly. "She was a good swimmer."

"Her grandmother was a Caddo squaw," Julia explained, having heard the story many times. "Her name was Weeping Branch."

Chad looked at Pearline with surprise. "Your grandmother was an Indian?"

"Yes, but my grandfather was a runaway slave from Louisiana. His name was Toby Potter. He was hidin' out with the peaceful Caddo when he met and fell in love with my grandmother. While he was there, they were married, and before bein' recaptured and sent back to Louisiana, my mother was born. Eventually, she was taken from the tribe by white hunters to Shreveport and sold into slavery, which is how she ended up workin' for the Thorntons. She was only nine years old when Julia's grandfather bought her to have someone to help out in the kitchen. She liked workin' for the Thorntons so well that even after she got her freedom papers, she stayed on as their head housekeeper right up until she died eight years ago. That's how Sirus and I came to be workin' there. We were born there, were given work there, and never found no reason to leave."

"Sounds like you have a very colorful past," Chad commented.

"Oh, I do. I'll tell you all about it sometime. Just not today. Today all I want to do is go put my feet in that water and see how cold the mud feels between my toes." She glanced up at the brilliant blue sky and smiled contendedly. "It shouldn't be too much longer until the days get warm enough for me to start up swimmin' again. Why, it will be May in just a few more days." She looked at him again, her eyes twinkling with untold thoughts. "I'll be back in about an hour. You two just sit here and let your food settle."

Chad stepped back and watched while Pearline hurried off in the direction she had indicated, her dark-brown skirts held high enough to reveal the bright red stockings she wore beneath.

When he turned back to face Julia again, he found that instead of watching Pearline, she was looking at him.

Julia felt a strange fluttering in her stomach when she

197

noticed that Chad now bore a deep, almost sinister-looking smile on his handsome face.

"Looks like it's just the two of us," he told her in a deep, mellow voice that sent fresh shivers of awareness cascading over her.

She swallowed hard, thinking he sounded just a little *too* pleased by that fact.

Chapter Eleven

Julia's dark eyes widened when Chad settled himself only two feet from where she sat.

"Don't you think you'd be more comfortable over there?" she asked, and pointed to the area of the quilt where he had sat earlier.

"No. I'm just fine right here," he responded in a voice so deep and so sultry that it sent another wave of tiny shivers trickling over Julia's body.

She watched with bemused fascination while he slowly stretched his hand forward and pushed a loose strand of her dark hair back into place with the tips of his fingers. Her pulses jumped when she realized just how close he had to be to do that. Close enough she could now see a sprinkling of silver in his deep-blue eyes. Eyes that looked very much like they were devouring her.

"Would you care for some dessert?" She hoped to distract him in some way, afraid of what his intentions might be. She gestured toward the huge wicker basket still resting in the center of the quilt, then dampened her lips with a quick flick of her tongue. Suddenly her mouth had gone dry. "There's a large apple pie in there just waiting for one of us to cut it."

"Yes, I think I am ready for a little dessert—but apple pie isn't what I had in mind," he answered.

His gaze never left hers, even when he bent to one side and moved first the food basket then her plate out of the way, setting them both in the grass nearby. He then scooted several inches closer. "What I have in mind is much sweeter than that."

He changed to a kneeling position. His face hovered just inches above hers.

Julia stared at him, unblinking, her mind unable to form a rational protest when he slowly dipped forward and nudged her cheek lightly with the tip of his nose. Another wild array of unfamiliar sensations scattered through her.

Reacting to his playful touch, her pulses raced. Only inches separated their bodies.

Although no part of him other than the tip of his nose and the ends of his fingers had yet to touch her, she felt a very strong, very vibrant, warmth rushing through her, as if it had radiated right out of his body and into hers. It reminded her of the wondrous tangle of emotions she had felt back when he'd kissed her. Emotions so strong and so overpowering, they left her temporarily weak. Her heart drummed a frantic rhythm at the mere memory of what had happened between them.

"Chad, I don't think you should touch me like that," she said, knowing it was not fair to Patrick for her to allow such behavior to continue. "Especially when Father is not around to see it."

She held her breath while she waited for his response, hoping he would agree. But it was as if she had never spoken.

His next words sounded seductively soft yet terribly masculine when they fell with a gentle vibration against the sensitive lobe of her left ear. "Prepare to be kissed."

"*Kissed?* But *why*, when no one is here to witness it?" She swallowed hard. Just knowing that his mouth hovered only inches from hers made it very difficult to concentrate. It also made it just as difficult for her to breathe.

"I don't think I really need a witness," he countered, his lips almost touching hers while he gazed deeply into the large round eyes that peered at him so apprehensively.

"Yes you do." Although she had tried to speak with anger and resolve, her voice had come out sounding raspy and uncertain. Her whole body quivered in response to his nearness.

"Then *you* can be my witness." He let his gaze wander, eager to drink in the smoothness of her ivory skin. He memorized every detail of her face, right down to the compelling way her cheeks blushed while he continued his bold perusal. Unable to resist, he lifted his hand to caress one soft cheek with his warm fingers.

Her dark eyes stretched to their limits while she tried to bring her racing heart back under control. She had to do something to stop him before something happened she would later regret. "I don't think you understand. There is no reason for you to kiss me now. Besides, you promised me you wouldn't even try. Remember? Back when we first arrived?"

"No I didn't," he told her, all the while continuing to drink in her beauty with glittering blue eyes. "All I did was ask why I would want to. I never promised anything."

"But there's no reason for you to kiss me now," she tried again, frightened. She already felt her resolve growing steadily weaker. Something about having him that close made her long to be touched. "No reason at all."

"Ahh, but there is. Plenty of reason."

He slipped his hands to her shoulders before he finally dipped forward to claim her lips in what turned out for Julia to be another very powerful and very persuasive kiss.

Although she silently vowed to remain indifferent toward the unwanted kiss, she found it impossible not to respond to the peculiar effect his touch always had on her.

Again, a staggering wave of desire washed over her, leaving her feeling instantly weak yet at the same time vigorously alive. Despite her resolve not to respond to him in *any* way, her eyes closed while the tantalizing sensations he had created continued to wash gently over her.

The powerful feelings he had so easily aroused grew even stronger when his hands left her shoulders and trailed slowly downward to the small of her back. Tenderly, he pulled her into a kneeling position, then pressed their bodies together. She was overwhelmed by the wondrous feel of his firm upper body pressed intimately against her soft curves, as well as by the fresh, clean scent of his hair and skin. Almost as overwhelmed as she was by the kiss itself.

Again, a strange, shimmering warmth had already developed in the vicinity of her rapidly pounding heart and spread quickly through the rest of her body, flooding her senses with euphoria. The alluring sensation swelled inside her until it filled her completely, making her instantly light-headed and breathless.

Such a powerful response frightened her. Especially when she knew she should not respond at all. She was in love with another man for heaven's sake! If anything, she should push this man away and chastise him for his continued bold behavior.

But she couldn't. All she could do was lean against him and wonder where such mindless pleasure could lead.

Again, it felt as if Chad had splashed her very soul with some evil magic. Instead of shoving him away like she should, her hands slowly lifted from where she had held them stiffly at her sides so she could curl her arms around his strong shoulders. Gently, she caressed the sleek muscles along the back of his neck with her fingers.

To her surprise, that tiny action caused the already amazing kiss to deepen more, and for the moment all was forgotten but the wild yearning that had flared to life the moment his mouth had claimed hers.

It was not until a few seconds later that she felt one of his hands working to remove the many pins from her hair. A tiny voice echoed a warning from somewhere in the back regions of her mind, reminding her that this was not Patrick. This was not the man she planned to marry. She had no right to be kissing him like that. Finally she found the strength needed to push him away.

"Don't do that!" she said, and sat back so he could not continue to hold her. Her next few breaths came in short, rapid bursts while she tried to calm the wild tempest still raging inside her.

"Why not?" he asked, his eyes nearly black while he, too, drew in several long breaths of air. Desire for her still pulled at every part of his body and surprised him with its sheer intensity. It felt like his whole body was on fire.

Quickly, Julia gathered the pins he had pulled loose and started jabbing them back into her hair. She was glad she had come to her senses before he had completely undone the small twist, for she had brought no comb for repairs. "Because it isn't right. I belong to another man."

"Not yet you don't," he reminded her. "And until your engagement is finally made official, you remain free to kiss whomever you want."

"But that's just it. I don't *want* to kiss you," she said, her senses still reeling from the effect of a kiss that she never should have allowed. As soon as she had her hair secured again, she turned to face him directly. "I don't want to do anything that might jeopardize my relationship with Patrick."

"And how does my kissing you when we are completely alone jeopardize your relationship with Patrick?" he asked. Unable to resist, he again reached out to touch her soft cheek with the tips of his fingers. He still longed to seduce her. Now more than ever. He had to find some way to make her his. And not just for right then. He wanted her to become a permanent part of his life. He wanted to marry her. Have children with her. But first he had to win her heart. And obviously he still had a long way to go before accomplishing that goal. "How will he ever know?"

"He just will," she answered, and felt more guilty by the moment. "He'll see it in my eyes."

"What will he see when he looks into your eyes?" He touched her cheek again, pleased by the shuttering effect that obviously had on her. "Will he discover that you have started to develop feelings for another man? Is that what you're so afraid he will see?"

"No, of course not," she answered a little too quickly, then scooted farther away from him so he could not keep touching her. It made it too hard for her to think. "What he'll see is the guilt I feel. He'll know just by looking at me that I've been unfaithful."

"Unfaithful? Just because you kissed me?"

"I didn't kiss you," she corrected. Her face filled with indignation. "You kissed *me!*"

"Ahh, but you kissed me back," he countered.

"I did not!" she quarreled, although in her heart she knew that was not true. She had indeed kissed him back, and with far more passion than she had ever kissed anyone else in her life. "I just didn't push you away as soon as I should have."

"And I wonder why that was?" he asked. His eyes sparkled with pure devilment while he slowly moved closer again a tiny inch at a time. "Could it be because you actually enjoyed it? Could it be that you are in some way attracted to me?"

"Of course not. It's just that you caught me off guard. I was too surprised to think clearly." That much was true. "That's why I don't want you trying anything like that again."

Aware the distance between them had again diminished considerably, she scooted farther away. An odd sprinkling of apprehension washed over her when she met his gaze then, causing tiny bumps to scatter across her delicate skin.

"But I thought I was *supposed* to be openly courting you. I thought we were *supposed* to act like that."

"Only when Father is around."

He looked at her questioningly. "But don't you think it would be a good idea to rehearse our parts while we are alone?"

"No, I don't," she answered, wondering if that really was what he had been doing. Rehearsing his part. Somehow she didn't think so. It had all felt too real. "There is no reason for such bold behavior when Father is not around to witness it."

He finally stopped his slow pursuit of her. "Don't you think it's a good idea for me to play my role whenever we are together? That way we don't take any chances of ever being caught off guard."

"Not when Father's nowhere around," she said again. "There's no need for it."

Deciding that now was not the time to force the issue, he nodded that he understood and immediately sat back down beside her. "Have it your way, ma'am. You are the boss." Then, as if it had been his intention all along, he leaned over, plucked a nearby wildflower, and twirled it between his strong fingers.

Julia let out a relieved sigh, still trembling from the effect of what had just happened. She studied him a moment longer. The breeze played lightly with his long hair while he divided his attention between the tiny yellow flower and her. Suddenly, he looked about as threatening as a small child.

"I wonder how much longer Pearline is going to be gone," she asked, wanting to break the awkward silence.

Chad glanced in the direction the lively maid had gone and shrugged. "Probably depends on how enthralled she becomes by her surroundings." He looked back at Julia. "Maybe you should have brought your paints and a canvas with you. I'd think this would be the perfect place to paint. I know I'd love to have a scene like this on my wall."

"How did you know I paint?" She met his gaze questioningly. She tried to remember it having come up in a previous conversation.

"Pearline told me."

"When?"

"One night while you had her out there fleecing my pockets."

Julia dropped her gaze a moment before looking at him again. "Did she also explain why I asked her to do that?"

"Said something about you not trusting me," he said

206

with a disarming grin. "Said you didn't trust anyone who purposely kept secrets from you."

"What else did she tell you?"

"Just that you are an artist who would rather spend the rest of her life painting than working in a lumber mill."

Julia lifted her chin as if to defend herself. "And I suppose you also think that it is foolish of me to want to spend so much time painting."

"Not if you truly enjoy it and are good at it. And according to what Pearline told me, you are very talented."

"She said that to you?"

"Yes, she did. But if that's true, if you really are talented, then why aren't any of the paintings in your father's house painted by you?"

"Father does not appreciate my talent nearly as much as Pearline does," she admitted sadly. "But then, I'm not too certain I do have talent. All I know is that I truly enjoy painting. There is just something about re-creating the images I see on canvas that I find personally rewarding."

"Pearline seemed pretty sure that you have talent," he reminded her, then looked at her with a curious expression. "What do you paint?"

"Landscapes mostly."

"Then I don't understand why some of them aren't hanging in your father's house. It's obvious he likes landscapes. There are so many hanging on his walls."

"My mother bought those. She loved art. Besides, I wouldn't want to see any of the paintings she chose replaced by anything else. They remind me of her." Her brown eyes glimmered with sad memories. "She was such a very special person."

"When did she die?"

"When I was sixteen. She accidentally stumbled onto a hornet's nest and was stung several times. She had some sort of terrible reaction to all those stings and died within a few hours."

Her gaze became distant while she thought back to that day. "If only she hadn't been out there overseeing the clearing of that field. She'd still be alive today."

She pressed her lips together for a moment to quell the pain, then added, "If she was still alive, I wouldn't be having to go through all this. She would make Father understand how important it is for me to live my life the way I want. She would understand my need to paint."

When she looked at Chad, she was surprised to see how intently he sat listening to her. "I don't mean to complain, but Father was so much less controlling back when my mother was still alive."

Chad continued looking at her for a long moment, then asked, "What do you do with your paintings if not hang them in your own home? Do you sell them?"

"No. What I don't give to friends, I put away in the attic. I probably have enough up there to cover the walls of a small palace." She grinned at the thought.

"But why not sell them?"

"Who'd buy them?"

Chad frowned, unable to believe the insecurity he'd just heard in her voice. He had always thought of Julia as such a strong, self-assured person. "People who appreciate art, people like your mother would buy them."

She shook her head, looking almost embarrassed. "I'm not that good."

"How do you know? Have you ever had an art expert look at your work?"

"I don't know any art experts. Besides, I don't paint because I see money to be made. I paint because I enjoy it. Simple as that."

"But what a waste to have your work hiding in an attic somewhere. True art is meant to be seen," he argued, then hesitated before asking, "could *I* see some of your work?"

Julia felt both pleased and a little surprised that he would ask. "Why would you want to?"

"I'm a curious sort," he said with a slight shrug. He didn't want her to feel intimidated by the idea of sharing something so personal with him. "Besides, I might want to buy one myself." He offered yet another disarming smile. "After all, I'll soon have five hundred dollars burning a hole in my pocket. And I can't think of a better way to spend it than by buying something that came directly from your soul."

Julia stared at him a long moment, not knowing how to respond to such a comment, but then noticed a movement off in the distance.

"Here comes Pearline," she said, relieved not to have to respond after all. "I guess it's time we started back for the house. We've been out here long enough to worry Father with what might have happened."

Chad watched while she hurriedly tossed what food remained on her plate into the grass for the wild animals, then put the empty plate into the basket. He decided then and there that even if it turned out that Julia was not to be a lasting part of his life, he would see to it that her artwork had a chance to be seen and appreciated. If he was allowed to give her nothing else, he would give her that.

Chapter Twelve

"Where were you a few hours ago when I first came home?" Charles asked Pearline after looking both ways to make certain they were alone in the hall outside the kitchen.

"I had somethin' I had to do for Missy," Pearline answered vaguely, knowing he might find it a bit odd that Julia had asked her to follow Chad into town.

"And are you finished with that?"

"Yes, sir. What is it you want? To know all about what happened at the picnic?"

"No. I've already heard more than I care to know from Julia," he answered gruffly. "Seems Mr. Sutton ate so much while you three were out gallivanting about the countryside that he didn't care to stay for supper. For the first time since that man arrived, Julia and I were able to eat our evening meal alone."

Pearline fought the urge to grin, knowing that the real reason Chad had not stayed was because Julia had not wanted him to and had told him to go on back to town. Evidently what had happened between her and Mr. Chad during that hour she was gone had made Julia feel extremely uncomfortable.

She smiled when she thought about that, knowing she

should never have left them alone. But she'd been too eager to start daydreaming about owning her own land and had gone to the small field where one day she hoped to build her own little cottage. Just the thought of someday finding a good man to settle down with and the two of them owning their own home right there by the river sent her pulses racing.

"If you already know all about what happened at the picnic, then why you've been lookin' for me?"

"I wanted to be sure you found those papers I left on your bed. The ones you need to take with you tomorrow. You *do* remember about tomorrow, don't you?"

"Of course I do. And yes, I found them right where you said they'd be. Or at least I figure that's what's inside that big white envelope you stuck up under my pillow."

"Yes, that's what's inside," he confirmed with a brisk nod, then glanced around again to make sure no one had come up on them. He ran his hand nervously through his thick, white hair. "Does that mean you are all prepared for tomorrow?"

"As prepared as I'll ever be." Her wide grin was flanked by two round dimples. Now that she had had the time to get over the shock of what Mr. Thornton had asked her to do, she was starting to look forward to such an unusual challenge. She especially looked forward to the reward she had been offered should she succeed. "I got the dress I plan to wear hangin' in my room behind the door all pressed and ready where nobody will see it."

"Which dress did you choose?"

"The real pretty one made up of burgundy red satin with tiny rows of ivory lace." Her dark eyes sparkled at the thought of wearing such an expensive garment. "The one with the low, rounded neckline and those short, puffed-up sleeves, and with a waistline that can be made bigger or smaller by a sash so I can be sure to have plenty of breathin' room. You remember the dress. It's the one Julia wore her first night home. The one you said she was practically spilling out of, the one you told her she was not to wear outside the house."

Charles smiled appreciatively. "Good choice. And with the way you're proportioned, that young buck will have little choice but to sit up and take notice. What time does Julia usually leave to do her painting?"

Pearline glanced down to see what he had meant by the way she was proportioned and was reminded that she had been blessed with what her mother had referred to as a "brimming figure." She smiled, knowing how men like to gaze at such things. "Missy usually leaves right after breakfast. And she don't usually come back until at least one o'clock or a little after. That should give me plenty of time to get on over there and have a friendly little chat with the new foreman."

Her dimples sank deeper into her dark cheeks at the thought of releasing the full force of her womanly charms on some hapless stranger. She knew from experience the sort of effect she could have on a man when she wanted to. "I should have that old man eagerly agreein' to help you buy back whatever land you want long before I leave there."

"Even if you don't have him eagerly agreeing, you should at least do what you can to have him thinking favorably about you before you go. The man isn't really all that old, as you apparently think, but he might be a little more mulish than most, so it might end up taking more than one visit to finally convince him that I really do have everyone's best interest at heart. If that's so, I'll find other reasons for you to go over there."

Pearline's playful smile dropped into an immediate frown. "I hope it doesn't take *too* long to convince that man. I don't think I can stand not knowin' for too long whether or not I'm goin' to be able to get that land." She closed her eyes at the torture it would be not to have a promising result right away. When she finally opened them again, she looked at Charles questioningly. "Did you remember to fix it with Lisa to do my ironin' tomorrow?"

"Yes, and I told her not to mention the extra duties to Julia, or anyone else for that matter."

"And she agreed?" Pearline knew what a snit Lisa could be when she wanted.

"Willingly—after I agreed to pay her an extra half dollar for the day. Seems that girl is always in need of an extra day's wages."

"I can understand *that.*" Pearline smiled again, reminded that even if she failed to persuade that foreman to help Mr. Thornton, she would still end up doubling her earnings for a month. Either way, the venture would be profitable.

The thought of what she could do with that extra fourteen dollars sent her pulses racing again. "Well, then, I guess I'd best be off to bed now. I'll need to be gettin' me plenty of sleep if I want my womanly wiles in prime workin' order tomorrow."

She turned and headed off in the direction of her room with such an exaggerated sway of her well-rounded hips that her long black skirts danced a lively jig behind her.

Charles smiled contentedly, then headed off in the opposite direction.

Julia lay on her back staring into the darkness that filled her bedroom, too restless to sleep. For the fourth straight night, she could not stop thinking about Chad. It was as if his image was permanently burned into her feeble brain. She could not stop the memory of how handsome he looked when he smiled at her, nor how *dangerous* he looked when he stopped. For the life of her, she could not push aside the vivid memory of his kiss, or how dramatically that kiss had affected her. She was outraged, yet at the same time intrigued to recall how splendidly his mouth had felt against hers—and how splendidly it had felt to be held in such strong arms. It was like nothing she had before experienced. And it was something she did not ever want to experience again.

Her cheeks stung with mortification when she remembered the passion with which she had responded to his unbidden kisses. What inside her caused her to behave like that?

She had always believed herself to be a woman who possessed both a good mind and sound principles—a woman who was always in control of her every emotion. But the moment Chad's strong arms closed around her, pulling her body firmly against his, and his warm, hungry mouth descended upon hers, devouring her hungrily, she lost her ability to think rationally. She responded to his every touch like some wanton fool.

Moaning at the shameful memories that continued to plague her, knowing how disgracefully she had behaved and what problems it would cause if Patrick ever found out, she rolled over onto her side and stared idly at the dark, lacy curtains that billowed away from her window. She had not taken the time to bind her hair into a fat braid like she normally did and played nervously with a strand that had fallen across the pillow in front of her.

If only she could rid herself of the unwanted feelings she had for Chad. Then perhaps she could finally push his image out of her mind for good and again concentrate on what really mattered instead of worrying about what might happen the next time she found herself alone with him. If only she could come to terms with what she felt toward him, then she would be free to dwell on the future again—and she would no longer have to suffer such an enormous feeling of guilt.

Julia closed her eyes despite the total darkness. She wished she had never met Chad. If he had never been lured into her life, then her relationship with Patrick would not be in such jeopardy.

Her stomach twisted in a hard, painful knot when she considered what Patrick might do if he ever found out that she had let Chad kiss her like that. Not only would he refuse to marry her and eventually take over the responsibility of running her father's businesses for her, he would probably commit the same sort of bodily harm to Chad that he had to the stranger in that tavern several years ago.

The thought of harm coming to Chad as a result of some petty scheme to outsmart her father made her feel guiltier still. Especially now that she believed Chad had no plans to blackmail her for more money later—or cause her any other trouble, for that matter.

Pearline had followed Chad twice now and both times reported that he had gone straight back to his hotel. He had not even stopped in at one of the local saloons for a drink beforehand, although most of the rowdier establishments were still open at that hour.

Whenever he did come out of his room, it was usually for a late-night dessert at the hotel's own restaurant. Afterward he usually took a simple stroll around town, then went directly back to his room. There was certainly nothing sinister in any of that.

Sighing, Julia turned onto her back again and stared at the empty shadows overhead. None of what she had done thus far would have been necessary if only her father did not still view her as his little girl. She never would have met Chad, and Chad would not now be plaguing her every waking thought. Why couldn't her father just accept the fact she was a grown woman capable of making her own decisions? Why did he still find it so necessary to tell her how to live her life? Moaning softly to herself, she wondered if he would ever change.

Pearline giggled when she looked into the small mirror just above the dresser in her bedroom and saw her reflection garbed in Julia's new gown. Expensive clothing certainly became her.

"Mr. Solomon Ford, you poor, poor man, you don't stand a chance," she said as she bent forward and dabbed the perfume she'd taken from Julia's room between the rounded tops of her mahogany breasts, which the low-cut of the gown displayed in a most flattering manner. Setting the bottle aside again, she lowered her dark eyelashes seductively and pursed her mouth into a playful pout. "Oh, that land is as good as mine."

Stepping back, she turned her head to make sure her braid was anchored in place, then picked up the envelope and headed immediately for the front door. Because she did not want to chance either Ruth or Lisa seeing her while she was dressed in Julia's gown for fear they would ask questions that would be difficult to answer, she had requested that Mr. Thornton have her brother bring the buggy around to the front and leave it there for her.

Minutes later she was on her way, glad it had turned out to be such a wonderful day. The morning sun gleamed from an almost cloudless blue sky while a slight breeze tugged at the dark-green treetops overhead. Much of the land in that area was wooded, largely because it's owner, Charles Thornton believed in keeping the timber supply plentiful. Nevertheless, there were still several open fields along the way, covered now with tender green field grass and dotted with an abundance of the same blue, pink, yellow, and white wildflowers that had formed a colorful pattern along the fenceline.

What a perfect day for a friendly seduction, she thought when she glanced up into the trees and caught sight of the dark-feathered birds that chirped merrily from the higher limbs. Her heart throbbed with growing anticipation while she considered what she should say to this Solomon Ford when she first arrived.

She decided that first she should compliment him about something. Even if the man turned out to be hound-dog ugly and jackass stupid, she would find something about him worth praising. That sort of thing was always important to a man.

Batting her eyes flirtatiously while she leaned slightly forward, Pearline glanced toward an upcoming oak tree, then smiled prettily while she practiced her wiles. "My, my, Mr. Oak Tree. You certainly do have a handsome head of leaves there. How did you ever manage to grow branches so thick and so strong?" She then ducked her head coquettishly and sank her dimples deep into her cheeks. "Who, *me?* Beautiful? Oh, how you do carry on. You are a rascal, aren't you, Mr. Ford?"

Thinking she had her technique down to a fine art, she leaned back against the thick-upholstered seat and wagged her head happily. The deed was as good as done. Now all she had to do was find herself some man worth marrying so the land could legally be hers forever. Maybe she should reconsider Otis Marshall's latest proposal of marriage. He might be ten years older than her, but he did have a good job working over at the Hardin's place and might even have some money already put aside so they could start building themselves a house right away. It was certainly worth thinking about. Especially if she ended up owning her own land.

It could be that Julia had been right all along. Maybe it *was* time she quit trying to find herself a man who caused her heart to race and her pulses to pound. Maybe that sort of thing *did* exist only in those paper books she loved to read. Maybe it was enough that she and Otis got along together, and that Otis seemed to respect her a little more than most men might. At least he had admitted being in love with her and it was possible that in time she could learn to love him, too.

If nothing else, Otis would be a good provider, which meant she would no longer have to work for the Thorntons. Although she enjoyed working for Missy and they got along almost like sisters at times, she did not want to spend the rest of her life having to clean up after someone else or wash someone else's clothes.

Unless, of course, she was married to that someone. She supposed it wouldn't be too bad washing and cleaning up after Otis. He seemed like a fairly tidy man. At least he'd be good company in her old age.

The thought of ending up like Ruth, mostly alone and destined to work as a housekeeper for the rest of her life, made Pearline all the more determined to have that land and a husband to help take care of it. The land represented freedom to Pearline. Freedom not to have to work for anyone else. Freedom to be able to do whatever she wanted with her life. In that respect she was just like Julia. She hated being told what to do all the time. Hated having so little say over what went on around her.

And now, suddenly she and Julia both had a way out.

Humming happily, Pearline waited until she reached the final turn before she quickly sat forward again and arranged her burgundy skirts just so. Her stomach fluttered with growing anticipation when she drove the small buggy over the next rise and the house finally came into sight.

Pearline had forgotten just how large the house really was. Probably a third again as large as the house where they lived now. In addition to a wide, column-supported front, there was a porch-lined back with a small wing of bedrooms along the far side, giving the house a sort of L shape. There were also more buildings behind it than she remembered from the years they had lived there, even though one of them had been her own home.

Slowing the buggy, she breathed deeply of the scent of freshly cut grass while she studied the area. She wanted to refamiliarize herself with the buildings. The summer kitchen and smoke house both still stood a few dozen yards off to one side of the house directly across from the bedroom wing, although the elaborate flower garden that had filled the area between was gone now.

Behind the kitchen was a small wood shed and several cottages lined in two even rows, each with its own tiny yard. All were the same size but one, which she remembered had been the overseer's house. It was positioned so it had a view of the old slave quarters and the barn, which had been built off to the other side of the house along with the stable, the carriage house, the hen house, and the tool shed.

The stable and more than half of the main house had been freshly painted bright summer white with a dark-green trim. The rest of the buildings were still faded and had the same pale-blue trim the house had sported when she had lived there.

While she continued to study the area, she noticed that the main house, along with several of the cottages directly behind it, had been patched recently with unpainted brown brick or freshly cut lumber. Even the roofs had yellow spots where new shingles had been set in place and not yet painted.

While surveying the storm damage that had yet to be repaired, she spotted a small group of men standing on ladders busily painting the rest of the main house while another small group stood just outside the barn, bent over a large double plow, as if working on it or trying to adjust it. It was not until she rolled into the yard itself that she realized one of the men working with the plow was Chad.

Her heart slammed hard against her ribs when she realized who he was. Even though Julia had told her he had taken a job there part-time, it had not occurred to her that she might run into him while she was there. How would she ever explain her being there dressed the way she was? And how could she keep him from turning around and telling Julia about it? Mr. Thornton was adamant that no one know about this plan.

Knowing Chad was destined to see her anyway, for he was only a few dozen yards away, she took a deep breath and headed toward the area where the men worked on the plow. She had no idea which of the many negroes working there might be Solomon Ford and realized it would be easiest to ask Chad.

One by one the three black men working with Chad either turned or lifted his head to see who had ridden up, and one by one they stopped what they were doing to stand and stare at her with open mouths and unblinking brown eyes. Eventually Chad realized that he was no longer getting any help from the others and he, too, stopped working to watch her approach.

"Pearline?" he asked, as if not quite sure it was her. He dropped the tool he'd been using and wiped his hands on his trousers before reaching for his shirt, which hung on a nearby post. "What are you doing here?"

He cut his gaze to the men around him, hoping none of them would say anything that might indicate he was the boss. They had been cautioned not to, but still, he did not know how well they could keep their wits about them.

"I am here to see the foreman. I believe his name is Solomon Ford," she answered, smiling prettily at the men standing around him. Seeing their foolish expressions gave her the encouragement she needed to go through with her scheme despite the fact that Chad was there to witness it. Chad had always seemed like a reasonable man. Surely he would not tell Julia if she asked him not to. After all, she had kept his secret. It seemed only fair he should keep hers. "Would you be so kind as to point him out?"

She waited to see if one of the three men with him would step forward. When none did, she looped her reins through the tether ring and scooted toward the side of the buggy.

Seeing that Pearline was about to alight, Chad hurriedly shoved his arms into his shirt, then, without bothering to button the front, stepped forward to help her down.

Pearline looked at him with surprise.

"You came here to see Solomon?" he asked, waiting for her to take his hand. "He's inside the house. Working on the wiring."

"Wiring?" she asked, and continued to look at him oddly while she allowed him to assist her. It was the second time Chad had helped her out of a carriage and that seemed a little odd to her, being that he was a white man.

"Yes. The, ah, *owner* of this place is planning to buy a generator and run it off a windmill so he can have electricity in the house. I guess he's too used to having electric lights and electric fans, coming from a big city like he does." He glanced back at the other men with a meaningful expression, letting them know they were to keep any comments to themselves.

"Electricity? Way out here?" she asked, clearly impressed. "This Mr. Andrews must be very wealthy."

"I don't think he's really what you would really call wealthy, but then again he's not hurting all that much for money, either," Chad responded, choosing his words carefully. He then glanced down at the beautiful burgundy gown Pearline wore and arched his eyebrows questioningly. "Just what business do you have with Solomon Ford?"

"I have been asked to deliver something to him," she answered, then reached back into the buggy for the thick envelope. She took a deep breath and swallowed hard when she realized her hour of reckoning was upon her. Bravely, she glanced at the house again. "Did you say he was inside?"

"Yes. He was in the kitchen last I saw of him. You want me to show you where?" He turned his head slightly in an attempt to glimpse the handwriting on the envelope and showed no surprise when he recognized Charles's bold script.

"No," she answered a little too quickly, not wanting him anywhere near when she spoke with Mr. Ford. Then, aware how abruptly she'd spoken, she softened her tone. "You look busy. I'm certain I can find him without any help." Especially when the kitchen was where she'd spent so many hours watching her mother work back when she was a child. "You just get on back to what you were doin'. Oh, and there's no real need in you telling Julia about any of this. I don't think she knows I'm here."

"As long as she doesn't ask, I won't tell her," he said,

then quirked a grin while he watched her lift her shimmering skirts barely an inch off the ground and walk smoothly across the yard, remembering that yesterday she had hiked a set of less elaborate skirts high enough to reveal several inches of the red stockings she wore underneath and had stomped across the open field like a small child marching in a parade. Obviously Pearline hoped to impress somebody with this sudden show of grace and charm—and he could well imagine who. He could also well imagine *why*. So that was Thornton's latest plan. To try to get to him through Solomon.

Chad just wished he could be in the kitchen to see Solomon's face when he first saw Pearline standing there in that beautiful burgundy red gown with her head held at such a haughty angle and her dark hair shaped into such a handsome, braided coil. Even Solomon would have a hard time resisting such a woman, even *after* he realized she had come there as a part of Thornton's latest scheme.

Having wanted the two to meet but not knowing how to go about introducing them, Chad did nothing to try to stop Pearline from entering the house. Instead, he turned back to the men still standing in the yard, mouths agape, and ordered them back to work.

Relieved that Chad did not intend to follow her inside and feeling somewhat exhilarated just knowing she was about to step inside the house that had been home to her for so many years, Pearline walked as gracefully up the familiar steps as she knew how. She paused to smooth her skirts with her free hand and check her hair one last time before entering the house through the closest door.

She was shaken by the disarray and destruction that

surrounded her. The floor of the hallway where she stood had been stripped bare of its carpets as had a set of stairs just off to her right. Both had been patched in several places with fresh lumber, along with a small section of the wall. Although some work had been done in that area, the floor was strewn with tiny bits of wood, brick, and broken glass, undoubtedly the result of damage done by the tornado.

Remembering that the kitchen was in the back part of the house, not too far from where the summer kitchen stood outside, Pearline turned left and walked as far as the dining-room door, which was off to her right. She stood just outside the doorway and was about to call out and let her presence be known when a tall, lanky white man with flaming red hair suddenly burst through the open door, nearly knocking her down in his bumbling haste.

"I'm sorry, ma'am. I didn't see you standing there," he said, and stopped just in time to catch her arm and prevent her from falling. His eyes grew wide as saucers when he glanced down to see if he had hurt her and noticed the interesting view given from that angle of height.

Quickly he blinked and returned his gaze to her face. "Who are you?" he asked bluntly.

"My name is Pearline Williams," she answered in as polite a voice as she could muster considering she had nearly been knocked to the floor. She hurried to readjust her clothing while making a supreme effort to speak clearly and properly, eager to make a good impression. "I am here to see a Mr. Solomon Ford. Could you tell me where to find him?"

"Sure," Raymond pointed in the direction he had just come. "He's in through that door there waiting for me

MORE PASSION AND ADVENTURE AWAIT... YOUR TRIP TO A BIG ADVENTUROUS WORLD BEGINS WHEN YOU ACCEPT YOUR FIRST 4 NOVELS ABSOLUTELY *FREE* (AN $18.00 VALUE)

Accept your Free gift and start to experience more of the passion and adventure you like in a historical romance novel. Each Zebra novel is filled with proud men, spirited women and tempestuous love that you'll remember long after you turn the last page.

Zebra Historical Romances are the finest novels of their kind. They are written by authors who really know how to weave tales of romance and adventure in the historical settings you love. You'll feel like you've actually gone back in time with the thrilling stories that each Zebra novel offers.

GET YOUR FREE GIFT WITH THE START OF YOUR HOME SUBSCRIPTION

Our readers tell us that these books sell out very fast in book stores and often they miss the newest titles. So Zebra has made arrangements for you to receive the four newest novels published each month.

You'll be guaranteed that you'll never miss a title, and home delivery is so convenient. And to show you just how easy it is to get Zebra Historical Romances, we'll send you your first 4 books absolutely FREE! Our gift to you just for trying our home subscription service.

BIG SAVINGS AND FREE HOME DELIVERY

Each month, you'll receive the four newest titles as soon as they are published. You'll probably receive them even before the bookstores do. What's more, you may preview these exciting novels free for 10 days. If you like them as much as we think you will, just pay the low preferred subscriber's price of just $3.75 each. *You'll save $3.00 each month off the publisher's price.* AND, your savings are even greater because there are never any shipping, handling or other hidden charges—FREE Home Delivery. Of course you can return any shipment within 10 days for full credit, no questions asked. There is no minimum number of books you must buy.

4 FREE BOOKS

TO GET YOUR 4 FREE BOOKS WORTH $18.00 — MAIL IN THE FREE BOOK CERTIFICATE T O D A Y

Fill in the Free Book Certificate below, and we'll send your FREE BOOKS to you as soon as we receive it.

If the certificate is missing below, write to: Zebra Home Subscription Service, Inc., P.O. Box 5214, 120 Brighton Road, Clifton, New Jersey 07015-5214.

FREE BOOK CERTIFICATE

4 FREE BOOKS

ZEBRA HOME SUBSCRIPTION SERVICE, INC.

YES! Please start my subscription to Zebra Historical Romances and send me my first 4 books absolutely FREE. I understand that each month I may preview four new Zebra Historical Romances free for 10 days. If I'm not satisfied with them, I may return the four books within 10 days and owe nothing. Otherwise, I will pay the low preferred subscriber's price of just $3.75 each; a total of $15.00, *a savings off the publisher's price of $3.00.* I may return any shipment and I may cancel this subscription at any time. There is no obligation to buy any shipment and there are no shipping, handling or other hidden charges. Regardless of what I decide, the four free books are mine to keep.

NAME

ADDRESS _____ APT _____

CITY _____ STATE _____ ZIP _____

(   )
TELEPHONE

SIGNATURE _____ (if under 18, parent or guardian must sign)

Terms, offer and prices subject to change without notice. Subscription subject to acceptance by Zebra Books. Zebra Books reserves the right to reject any order or cancel any subscription.

ZB1293

GET
FOUR
FREE
BOOKS
(AN $18.00 VALUE)

ZEBRA HOME SUBSCRIPTION
SERVICE, INC.
120 BRIGHTON ROAD
P.O. Box 5214
CLIFTON, NEW JERSEY 07015-5214

to fetch him another saw blade. He just stripped the teeth off the one he's got."

He indicated the largest of three doors that stood on the opposite side of what Pearline knew had at one time been the main dining room. Now, though, it was hard to tell *what* the room had been. There were no table or chairs to mark its use, only a small china cabinet, which stood in one corner, and a large, broken mirror that dangled crookedly on the far wall. Again, there were tiny bits and pieces of wood and glass everywhere.

Pearline was glad her mother was not alive to see such a mess. She had always loved this house so.

"Excuse the litter," Raymond said, aware by her unblinking expression she was taken aback by what she saw. "But these folks had a real bad tornado tumble through here a couple months ago and are just now gettin' around to repairin' some of the damage."

He then glanced around with a wrinkled expression, as if trying to view the surroundings through her eyes. "It'll probably continue to look like this for a while longer, but when these folks get through, this place will look better than any home you've ever laid your eyes on. I've heard some of what they plan to do here and this place is going to be downright elegant eventually."

Pearline swallowed hard. For the first time, she doubted her ability to convince these people to sell even a small part of what they now owned. Obviously they had plans of their own for the property. Plans that included making this a very special place to live.

When Pearline spoke again, she continued trying to make her words sound refined. "I gather then that they are pretty set on restoring this place back to the way it was and then living here for quite some time."

"I don't know if they want so much to fix it back the

way it was, but they do have plans of making it a home to be proud of."

"You keep saying *they* when you talk about who owns this place. Does the new owner have a family?"

"No. Not yet. But I do think he's got somebody already in mind for sharin' this house with him. He keeps talking like there's someone mighty special he plans to show it to someday."

"Oh? Then you've met him?" Pearline asked, then frowned. She had been led to believe that the owner had not yet arrived.

Raymond's green eyes widened, wondering if he had just said something he should not have. "Solomon is always telling me some of what he says. He hears from him regular."

Reminded of her reason for being there, Pearline lifted her skirts just enough to avoid the debris, then nodded toward the kitchen. "Would it be permissible for me to go on in there?"

Looking relieved that Pearline did not plan to pursue that particular subject, Raymond nodded eagerly. "Sure. Go on in. You'll find him standing up in a chair over by the sink. He's decided that's where to put one of those new electric lights that came yesterday."

Raymond nodded politely then to excuse himself, then headed immediately toward the back door. Meanwhile, Pearline took another deep, sustaining breath and slowly picked her way across the debris-strewn room. She did not want to cut her boots on the tiny pieces of glass.

When she neared the kitchen door, she heard a loud, clattering crash, followed almost immediately by a dull thud.

She hurried to find out what had fallen.

Chapter Thirteen

When Pearline entered the kitchen, she was only vaguely aware that unlike the rest of the house, this room was tidy and swept—except for a small area near the sink where a large man lay in a toppled heap beside an overturned chair on a sawdust-scattered floor. A large but rail-thin red-and-white dog stood over him, poking at his back with its nose as if testing to see what damage had been done.

Aware the injured man had to be Solomon Ford, the very man she had come to influence, Pearline hurried forward to help.

"Are you hurt?" She quickly knelt beside him, her borrowed skirts puddling to form a small pool of burgundy. The dog looked at her oddly, then sat back on its haunches as if waiting to see her intentions.

Although the man lay with his back to her so she could not see the expression on his face, she could tell by the way his broad shoulders hunched forward straining his black shirt that her question had been a ridiculous one. He was indeed very hurt.

Solomon quickly jerked his head around to look at the owner of the female voice. Although his teeth were clinched from the pain in his shoulder, his eyes rounded with surprise. "Who are you?"

"My name is Pearline Williams," she answered quickly. Still concerned for the man's welfare, she tossed the envelope she carried aside so she could grasp the tops of his shoulders with both hands and turn him to face her squarely. The second her hands touched the work-hardened muscles, she felt such an immediate jolt to her senses, she stopped searching for possible injuries and looked him directly in the face. When she did, she felt yet another alarming jolt to her senses. This one caused her heart to slam hard against her ribs and her eyes to stretch as wide as saucers. Was *this* Solomon Ford? Was this the man she had been sent over to entice? Her body tremored at the mere prospect, for he was absolutely the handsomest man she had ever laid eyes on. "A-are you hurt?"

"I don't know," he said, still too stunned by both the fall and her presence to be sure of anything just yet. "But I must have hurt something. I think I'm having delusions."

Pearline watched while he closed his eyes and then slowly opened them again as if that might clear whatever was wrong with his vision.

"Should I go for help?" she asked, then gestured toward the door. "There are several men outside."

"No. Don't go," he said, reaching out to touch her. His eyebrows arched when he realized she was not just an image that had formed in his clouded mind. "You are real," he said, more a question than a statement.

"Of course I am," she said, then, realizing just how disoriented he was, she pressed her mouth into a tight frown. "Maybe I'd better go get Mr. Chad. You must have hit your head on something during that fall."

Solomon grasped her by the arm to prevent her from leaving. "No. Don't go. I'm fine."

"You don't look fine. You look half dazed with pain."

"It's not pain that dazes me." He continued to look at her oddly. "All I hit was my shoulder, which has already stopped hurting."

"Then can you get up?" she asked. Still kneeling, she reached over to right the toppled chair that lay behind him.

Aware of the magnificent view he was granted each time she leaned forward, Solomon's eyes widened further still. "I can, if you help me." He extended his arm for her to take hold.

Thinking he must have been weakened by the pain he had felt when he first fell, Pearline did just that. She bent forward and grasped his arm with one hand and reached around to help support his back with the other, completely unaware that her ministrations caused her breasts to press upward. "Here, sit in this chair until you're sure you can stand."

After she helped him to the chair, she bent to brush much of the sawdust from his clothing. It was then she noticed a tiny blood-soaked tear near his right shoulder. "Oh, my, you're bleeding."

Solomon looked down, too distracted by the beauty before him to have realized his own injury. He glanced curiously at the floor where he'd landed, then pulled his shirt up and peered beneath at a small puncture wound. "I guess I landed on the drill I was using when I fell."

"On the drill?" Pearline also glanced at the floor and noticed a wood drill nearby. Beside it she noticed a small stain of blood. Her forehead notched. "How bad you hurt?"

"Not ba—" Solomon started to say but then quickly recanted. "Hurt badly enough to be bleeding." He fumbled with the buttons of his shirt to show her the wound.

Seeing that the movements were difficult for him, Pearline quickly leaned forward to help. After she helped him tug out of the bloodied garment, suddenly he sat shirtless in front of her. Her heart skipped two beats when she realized just how solid and smooth his muscles were, how his skin gleamed like dark chocolate.

Aware now of how truly virile this handsome man was, Pearline took a tentative step backward and blinked while trying to decide what to do next. Clearly she should try to tend to him in some way. "That wound needs washing. Are there any laundered cloths anywhere?"

"I think in that drawer there," he said. Though he dipped his head toward the top of the three drawers nearest the sink, his gaze never left her face.

Feeling a little awkward to have this handsome stranger staring at her so openly, Pearline went to the drawer, took out a small dish towel, and dampened part of it with water. She then returned to dab away the blood with quick, gentle strokes. When she did, she realized his gaze had dipped to the low cut of her dress, which caused her to feel even more awkward. Self-consciously she cleaned the wound, then pressed the dry portion of the cloth over the cut to stop any further bleeding.

Rather than continue to stare at his muscular build, she glanced down at the dog, who now rested only a few feet away watching her every move.

While they waited for the bleeding to stop, Solomon continued his bold study of her. "Are you one of those guardian angels that appears whenever someone has hurt themselves?"

Pearline smiled at his comment. "No. I'm no angel."

Dimples sank into her round cheeks at the mere thought.

"Then who are you?" He glanced down at his shoulder when he felt the pressure slacken and watched while she lifted the cloth away to see if the wound had stopped bleeding. It had. "And why are you here?"

"I told you. My name is Pearline Williams. And I think I'm here to see you." Aware there was no more blood, thus no more reason for such close attention, she set the cloth aside and stood erect again. "That is, if your name is Solomon Ford."

Solomon flashed a big smile. "Even if it wasn't, it would be now." He glanced again at the wound, saw that it had not resumed bleeding, then stood to greet her properly. "How can I be of service to you?"

Pearline registered immediate alarm when she saw how quickly he had gotten to his feet.

"You sit yourself back down before you start that shoulder to bleeding again," she admonished. When he did not immediately obey, she reached forward to forcibly set him back down. She did what she could to ignore the odd stirring that occurred whenever she touched him.

But Solomon did not want to sit. He wanted to stand so he could gaze at her better. "I'm fine, now," he insisted, then grasped her hands with his so he could stop her attempts to push him back down. "I don't need to sit."

Even after she stopped trying to push him back into that chair, he continued to hold her hands. "Now just what was it you wanted to see me about?"

Pearline's brown eyes stretched as wide as walnuts when she realized he had no intention of letting go of her. Her heart rate increased. "I was sent here to deliver something."

Solomon cut his gaze to where a large envelope lay on the floor not too far from the bloodstains, then quickly returned his attention to Pearline's beautiful, flushed face. He fought a very strong desire to pull her closer to him. To feel those soft, supple curves pressed hard against his body. "That envelope?"

"Yes." She nodded, aware his gaze had darkened considerably in the last few seconds, making him look every bit as dangerous as he was handsome. "It's from my boss. He asked me to bring it here and give it to you personally."

Although Solomon continued to study her every movement, he found it difficult to grasp completely what she had just said and decided the fall had affected him far more than he first realized. It took a few seconds for the words to finally sink in.

"And just who is your boss and why would he be sending *me* something?" Solomon's gaze lingered on her mouth while he awaited an answer. There was something about the way it moved that stirred him.

"Before I tell you his name, I want you to promise to listen to everything I have to say," she said. She knew he might become angry enough to demand she leave the minute he learned the answer—especially when she had not yet had the opportunity to flatter him like she had wanted. She had so wanted to win his notice first. But she then realized that certain parts of her had already done that.

Solomon's expression had revealed instant distrust but he still did not let go of her. "Why? Who *is* your boss? Someone from town?"

She paused to gather the courage needed to answer. She had already been warned what this man thought of her boss. "No, he's Charles Thornton."

Solomon released her hands as if they had suddenly

burned him and quickly stepped back. "Charles Thornton? What on earth could he be sending me?"

Pearline felt an immediate ache from having been so abruptly shunned. "It's another offer to buy this house," she answered honestly. "Only this time he has sent me to explain to you how important it is that he be allowed to buy it."

Solomon's broad nose flared with anger. He took yet another step back. "So what he really did was send you over here to lure me into helping him convince *my* boss to sell. Does he really think I can be so easily swayed?"

Pearline looked at where the dog still lay on the floor watching them while she tried to decide just how to answer that question and was startled when almost as suddenly as she heard footsteps she was drawn into a powerful embrace. She glanced into Solomon's eyes again, and was alarmed to find they had grown darker still.

"Did Thornton really think that you could come here all sassy and prissy flaunting that beautiful body in front of me and persuade me to do his bidding?" Solomon's eyebrows lowered with angry intent. "Or were you supposed to do more than just flaunt? Perhaps you were supposed to lure me into a ravenous kiss that would lead me to want more."

Having said that, he dipped forward and took that kiss, pulling her soft body firmly against his.

At first his lips felt hard and punishing, and Pearline did all she could to squirm out of his ironlike embrace, but after only a few seconds the painful pressure of his hands and mouth lessened and the kiss became maddeningly seductive. So much so, Pearline found herself not wanting to fight him at all. Instead, she allowed the sensations he'd aroused to completely overwhelm her.

When, a few seconds later, Solomon suddenly let go, they both took a step back.

"Did Thornton really think something like that would affect me enough to change my stand?" he asked between deeply drawn breaths. "Does he really believe I am that simple?"

"He just wants this house," she answered, her thoughts a jumbled mess. "He'll do anything to get it. Anything at all."

"And what about you? Will you do anything for him to have it?" His gaze dipped once again to the rounded tops of her breasts so prominently displayed by the deep cut of her gown. When it did, he noticed how rapidly they now rose and fell. Obviously the kiss had affected her, too. "Is that why you wore that dress?"

"Of course not," she said, and quickly covered what she could of her exposed flesh with her hands. "I was just sent here to talk to you is all. To try to get you to listen to reason. I just wore this dress to get your attention."

Solomon huffed, his face still hard with anger while he stood facing her with crossed arms and braced legs. "Too bad. I think I might have been more easily swayed had I been allowed to sample more of your pleasures."

Pearline took a precautionary step back. She did not like the way his gaze raked her body, as if trying to decide what she looked like beneath Missy's clothing. "Well, I'm sorry, but no land is worth that."

"Not even *this* land?" he asked, and gestured to his surroundings, unaware she meant the land Thornton had offered her.

"Not even this land," she answered defiantly.

"Why? Would making love to me be *that* repulsive?" he asked with an upward thrust of his chin, suddenly insulted.

"Yes, because love would have nothing to do with it," she snapped as she took another step back. She continued to hold one hand flat against her cleavage to prevent him from having another glimpse when she bent to pick up the envelope and quickly thrust it at him. "Here! Have your boss read this. It's a very generous offer to buy the house and part of the land. He'd be a fool to pass it up."

"He's no fool, believe me. And he doesn't want to sell," Solomon told her, but accepted the envelope anyway.

"He might change his mind after he opens that and reads just how much Mr. Thornton is offering," she replied with a narrowed gaze. She was so filled with anger and the disappointment that nothing had gone according to plan, she trembled in response.

Solomon tucked the envelope under his arm and continued to study her stormy expression with cool certainty. "He won't."

"He might when he sees the amount involved."

"He won't."

"How do you know?" she asked, infuriated by his unshakable confidence. "It could be your boss is not quite as mule-headed when it comes to the matter as you are. It could be that he is actually smart enough to recognize a real bargain when he hears one. Smart enough to realize he can sell part of what he owns for over twice what it's worth and use that money to build himself his own house." She then planted her fists on her amply rounded hips and hardened her gaze. "It could be your boss has a lot better sense than you could ever hope to have."

Solomon's eyebrows arched with surprise. He had not expected such a fine display of feminine temper, especially when she had obviously been sent there to placate him. He uncrossed his arms and tossed the envelope onto a nearby counter before taking a challenging step forward. "Did you just call me a mule?"

Too angry to be intimidated by such action, Pearline lifted her chin and continued to glower at him. Then, remembering that he had some sort of hold over his boss and was therefore the most important person standing in the way of her getting that land she so wanted, she calmed her tone but did not change her expression. "I said you were mule-*headed*. Too mule-headed to listen to reason, no matter who gives it."

"And do you think you might have better luck talking with my boss?" He stopped advancing long enough to peer deeply into her glittering brown eyes, eyes so full of determination, he hated to see the fire doused.

"Probably." Her expression went from angry to cautious. "Why?"

"Because I've decided you should have the chance to talk to him yourself," he said. Just as suddenly as he had tensed, he relaxed, aware he had no real reason to be angry with her. She was just doing what she had been told to do. The one to be angry with was Charles Thornton.

"You have?" Pearline blinked several times while she considered this new development. Perhaps she could convince the man herself—and get that land yet. "Why?"

"Because contrary to what your boss may have told you, I'm a fair man. And being a fair man, I think you should have a chance to present your side of things to him."

"When?" she asked, suddenly filled with renewed hope. "When will he finally get here so I can talk to him?"

Solomon stroked his chin while he studied her further, determined to get to know her better. "That's hard to say. I guess if you really want a chance to talk with him, your best prospect would be to drop by here every day. That way you will be able to talk with him as soon as he arrives. Before I could have a chance to do the harm you obviously think I can do."

"*Every day?*" she repeated, instantly disappointed. "But I have to work. I can't be coming over here every day just to see if he's arrived yet. I'll fall behind in my chores. Missy won't like that."

"Then stop by every night," he suggested, thinking that idea even better. His eyes glimmered at the thought of what he might accomplish if he saw her every night. "Surely you don't work at night, too."

Pearline's mouth flattened. She remembered it had recently become her duty to follow Chad into town every night—although she had yet to actually do so. "Lately I have been working nights, too."

"All night, *every* night?" he asked, hoping to tempt her yet. Now that he had sampled her fiery kiss and had felt her firm, young body pressed against his, he was determined to have more of her pleasures.

"No, of course I don't work all night. I do have to sleep sometime," she answered, and continued frowning while she thought more about it.

"Then come by every night just before bedtime. Thornton's place isn't all that far. And if Mr. Andrews is here when you come, I'll let you talk to him no matter how late it is."

Deciding she could always stop back by after having followed Chad into town, or better yet, *instead* of following Chad into town, Pearline quickly agreed. "Okay. If it means getting a chance to talk with Mr. Andrews, I'll do it. When do you think I should start coming by?"

Solomon shrugged, then winced at the dull pain the

sudden movement had caused his shoulder. He glanced down to be sure he had not started his injury bleeding again. "The man is unpredictable. He could arrive any day. Could even be this afternoon for all I know." Spotting no fresh blood, he looked back at her again. "I guess the smart thing would be to start dropping by as soon as possible."

"All right, then I'll stop by here tonight if I can," she said with a determined nod, then frowned again. "But how will I know whether he's here or not? Or if he's still awake? I'll have to come by late. He may have already gone to bed by the time I arrive."

"Come around to my cottage first and knock. Mine is that largest one out back. I should be able to tell you if he's here or not and if he's still awake."

Aware Solomon meant the old overseer's cabin that stood well away from the other cottages, she asked, "Why don't I just knock at his door instead?" She looked at him suspiciously.

Solomon sighed. "Because you are right. He may have already gone to bed and he might not appreciate being bothered so late at night by someone he's never met. It would be better if I was the one who disturbed him. It would also be a good idea for me to be the one to introduce you and explain why you are so eager to talk with him and why you had to come so late. Besides, even if he's not here yet, it is still possible I will have heard from him and might know when to expect him."

Pearline realized that made sense. Reluctantly, she agreed. "All right. I'll stop by your door first. But if he's here, I'll want to talk with him alone. I don't want you reminding him that he already has plans for that land."

"Fine with me," Solomon said, then offered a wide smile that revealed gleaming white teeth and made Pearline suddenly wary of him again. He was certainly a handsome man, maybe too handsome for his own good. Not only was his skin a deep, rich mahogany brown only a shade darker than her own, he was taller than most men she knew and his body more powerfully built. His eyes were wide and his nose prominent but not what she would call large, and his lips ample but not thick. His black hair was clean and cropped close to a perfectly shaped head.

"Good," he responded, his smile still in place. "I'll be watching for you."

For a long moment, the two stood stone-still staring at each other, then Solomon blinked twice and turned away. "I hear Raymond coming. I hope he was able to find that saw blade I sent him after." After he bent to pick up the drill he had dropped as a result of the fall, he moved the chair back to its original position and climbed onto it.

Thinking the manner in which he had just dismissed her very abrupt, Pearline snatched up her skirts and started out of the room, then decided she should comment on his rude behavior first. She spun about to face him but before she could actually say anything, he turned to look at her with an unreadable expression. "You are a beautiful woman, Pearline Williams. I just thought you should know that."

Too stunned by the unexpected compliment to say what she had started to say, Pearline stood staring at him while he turned his attention back to his work. She wondered if she should return the compliment in some way, but before she could gather the courage to admit that she found him equally attractive, Raymond came bursting into the room. He waved a saw blade high into the air as if it were some sort of trophy.

"I have it!" he shouted, then stepped over the dog and headed toward Solomon.

"I'll talk with you later, Mr. Ford," Pearline said, her voice deep and sultry as she turned away. "Be sure to put some salve on that cut so it doesn't go swelling up on you. I'd hate for you to end up in bed over something like that."

"Solomon," he corrected, pausing to look at her again. "The name is Solomon."

"I'll try to remember," she said, but did not actually make use of the name before heading on out the door. She was not quite halfway across the littered dining room when she heard the other man ask in a curious voice, "Who was *that?*"

"One of the most beautiful women I have ever met," Solomon answered quickly. "And one of the most exasperating."

Pearline smiled at the thought of being both beautiful *and* exasperating while she continued across the room, down the hall, and out into the yard.

Obviously, there was still hope. She might have that land she wanted yet.

For the next several days, Chad continued to spend his mornings at the ranch helping Solomon and the nine men he now had working under him. From tacking on new shingles to erecting new fences strong enough to hold cattle, to cutting down the tall grass and weeds, to pulling up small trees and bushes by the roots, he was impressed by the progress they had made in such a short time.

He knew at the present rate, it would not be long before the house would be repaired enough for him to move in. It also would not be long before the pasture nearest the house would be ready for the first small herd of cattle. Although he still did not intend to move into the house until he revealed his true identity to Julia, he liked seeing such progress in so little time. He also liked the idea of the house being ready to show Julia when the time finally came.

He liked the idea of sharing both his home and his life with her. Liked the thought of coming in after a long, hard day and having her there waiting for him. He could visualize her sitting in the parlor sharing a few moments with the children or standing on the front veranda gazing occasionally at the river while creating another of her paintings.

Even though he had yet to break whatever barriers still lay between them and she had yet to take his interest in her seriously, he had already chosen a large room upstairs to be her studio. There she could set up her easels and paint to her heart's content, while covering the walls with whatever paintings she did not want scattered throughout the house.

The hope that one day Julia would indeed join him in his new home made Chad work all the harder. Eagerly, he rose before dawn and worked hard until midafternoon each day. He then cleaned up, changed into the clothes Raymond's wife always had ready for him, and headed over to Julia's, arriving in plenty of time to be there when Charles Thornton returned home, which was all Julia had required of him since the day of their picnic.

During those hours he pretended to be formally courting Julia—and while being served some delicious meals—Chad managed to pick up bits and pieces of what went on in the Thornton household. He also learned a little about Charles's different attempts to buy his land from him. He felt increasingly uncomfortable knowing *he* was the contrary new owner Charles and Julia discussed in such angry tones.

It was clear that both Julia and Charles disliked him immensely, although he had yet to figure out exactly why. At times, their anger toward him became so intense, he knew it had to stem from more than the simple fact he had refused several times now to sell them his land.

He was just glad they kept referring to their hated new neighbor as "C. W. Andrews," which was the name Solomon had suggested he use right from the start because he thought it sounded more official. Chad knew that if and when either Charles or Julia finally did find out what the C in C. W. stood for, Julia would immediately make the connection and would know who he was and why he had been so determined to keep his last name a secret. She would be furious with him for having kept that information from her.

He shuddered at the thought, not at all ready for that to happen. At least not yet. Not until after he had found a way to become a far more important part of her life. He knew that if she found out the truth too soon, she would immediately turn against him, and he would no longer have the chance of winning her heart. She would be too angry to care that the whole reason for what he had done was that he had hoped to use his employment as a way of getting closer to her.

And get closer to her he would. Even if it meant having to play the charade for several more weeks.

Julia stood staring idly at the tip of her paintbrush, not actually seeing the pale-blue paint that clung precariously to its bristles. As was rapidly becoming a habit with her, her thoughts were no longer on the magnificent view stretched before her, but were instead on the most recent events involving Chad.

242

Two weeks had passed since that day she had introduced Chad to her father and she was both pleased and alarmed by the way things had progressed. Her father was becoming increasingly more annoyed with Chad's absurd behavior while she was becoming increasingly more intrigued over his ability to be two such entirely different men.

He was such an annoying pest when her father was present, but whenever the two of them were alone and he no longer had reason to be a bumbling oaf, he proved to be quite interesting and at times even charming. He was also courteous, intelligent, and enthusiastic about whatever topic they discussed. She hated to admit it but she thoroughly enjoyed being with him—except for those occasions when he was in one of his playful moods and attempted to touch her or tease her for whatever reason.

She had tried several times to convince him that unless her father was around to witness it, such forward behavior was not to be tolerated. But even after he had agreed, there would be moments when he would taunt her by touching her cheek or tapping the tip of her nose with the end of his finger. There were also times when he lowered his eyelashes in a sultry fashion and leaned forward with his mouth slightly parted, as if planning to kiss her again, but then would turn away at the last minute without actually having done so.

His impulsive, unpredictable behavior was as disturbing as it was baffling. Part of her wanted him to stop teasing her before his playful nature again got out of hand like it had during the first week, while another part of her enjoyed the splendid feelings such teasing aroused. Eventually, she decided that as long as he did not actually kiss her again, she had no real reason to protest.

Her only real objection concerning Chad was that she could not seem to stop thinking about him. Not even when she knew she should be concentrating on Patrick and figuring out the best way to go about introducing him to her father. After all, the man who was soon to be her fiancé was due to arrive in just a few more weeks. Shortly afterward, they would announce their engagement. By then Chad should have finished what he had been hired to do and she would no longer need his services. He would then be out of her life.

Tilting her head while she continued to gaze down at the paintbrush, she wondered why that made her feel so sad. She had known all along that their association was a temporary one.

So why couldn't she stop the ache that spilled from her heart whenever she thought of never seeing him again?

Patrick glanced around him. He wanted to make sure no one had entered the back of the small shop before he jammed the flat end of the small chisel he had borrowed from Reginald's tool box into the narrow space between the office door and the doorframe.

Earlier he had watched Hiram Buchanan place over six hundred dollars in a small wooden box then lock it inside his desk. If that money was still there, and if neither Hiram nor Reginald came back from eating lunch during the next ten minutes, Patrick's problems would be over. He would finally have the money he needed to get on to Marshall, Texas, and would have more than enough left over to buy a new summer suit and hire a nice horse and buggy so he could arrive at the Thornton home in grand style.

But first he had to break both the lock on the door

and the lock on the desk. Then he had to grab the money, go by the hotel to get his belongings, and still make it to the train station in time to buy a ticket and be on the next train headed anywhere before either Hiram or Reginald returned to discover the damage.

Patrick frowned while he positioned the chisel just below the latch. If only Reginald had not taken so long repairing that last wheel, he would have left earlier and Patrick would not be so pressed for time. As it was, Hiram had already been gone for nearly half an hour. He was not a man to linger over the noonday meal.

When he found the huge door as willing to give as that half-breed he had bedded the night before, Patrick grinned and headed immediately for the desk. Pulling open the drawers one at a time, it took only seconds to discover which was the locked one.

Kneeling so he could fit the small chisel into the tiny gap between the drawer and the desk itself, he chuckled at how easily the wood gave way, leaving the lock intact but not the drawer. He tossed the broken pieces aside, then slid what was left of the drawer out. There was the box that held Hiram's latest winnings, and beside it was not one but *two* small caliber handguns!

Deciding it was his lucky day, Patrick quickly pocketed both pistols, then slid the box up under his coat. He decided to wait until he was safely inside his hotel room before smashing it open since Hiram could return at any minute.

It was not until Patrick had stood again and was about to head toward the broken door that he realized he was no longer alone. Without actually looking up to see who was in the room with him, he slid his hand into his pocket to feel for the pistols and hoped they were loaded. It had not occurred to him earlier to check.

"What are you doing in here?" Hiram asked, his large frame filling the door, his face an angry glower.

"I need money to get out of here," Patrick responded, then quickly pulled one of the pistols out of his pocket and pointed it at Hiram. "And I got a little tired of having to work for it." When he saw the color drain from Hiram's face, he felt a great sense of relief. The pistol was indeed loaded. He was as good as out of there.

It was not until after Patrick had fired the fatal shot that he decided he should be the one to find Hiram's body. That way he could direct the guilt away from himself, toward some nameless thief.

Even though having to stick around long enough to satisfy the curiosity of both the sheriff and his men would delay his departure another day or two, it also meant he would not have to be looking over his shoulder for the next several years, wondering if they had figured out yet that he was the culprit.

Patrick hurried out into the side alley to hide the money box and the two pistols in a place where he easily could come back for them later, then hurried across the street to eat lunch at his favorite saloon.

With any luck, he could again be on his way to Texas as early as the first of next week.

Chapter Fourteen

"Did you follow Chad again last night?" Julia asked Pearline when the sleepy-eyed maid stumbled into her bedroom to inform her that breakfast was ready.

She had already pulled her long brown hair into a loose twist at the back of her neck and had put on her laced boots and the pale-yellow-and-white dress she planned to wear that day. She was almost ready to go on downstairs; all she needed to do was make a few adjustments to her skirt.

"You bet I did. I was right in behind him when he rode out of here," Pearline answered, not about to admit that she had stayed behind him only a little while. Missy would never understand why she had gone to visit Solomon last night instead of following Chad into Marshall as she had been told to do.

"And did he go straight back to his hotel as usual?" Julia wanted to know while arranging the white sash of her skirt just so.

"No. Not last night," Pearline answered, thinking it was time to change her story a little, before Missy decided it was no longer worth it to continue her vigil. Pearline was getting far too much enjoyment out of visiting with Solomon each night to do anything that might put an end to it. At least not yet. Besides, she had promised Mr. Thornton she would continue with her nightly visits for a while yet.

He liked knowing she was over there each night learning all she could about their new neighbors. He also liked the idea of Pearline talking with the new owner himself when the man finally decided to make an appearance. That was why it would not fit into either his or her plans for Missy suddenly to change her mind and decide she would rather her maid be there at the house helping prepare for the coming day as she normally did.

"Oh? And just where did he go last night?" Julia looked at her questioningly but continued to work with her sash, trying to make the bow lay flat and even.

"To see a young woman." Pearline had no idea why she chose that to be her response. She could have come up with any number of places for him to have gone. "Seems Mr. Chad has found himself a new friend in town—although *when* he found the time, I'll never know."

Julia's hands froze with the sash still between her fingers. "He *what?*"

"He, ah, stopped by to see a young woman."

Pearline could see she was angry.

"That late at night?"

Pearline dampened her lower lip. She had not expected Julia's reaction. "But he left here early last night, remember?" Early enough that she had been able to spend a whole extra half hour sitting out beside the neighbor's newly planted flower garden with Solomon. Her heart fluttered at the memory of his deep voice and his dark, smiling face while they sat on a small bench he'd built, with him gently holding her hand between his. It was all she could do not to close her eyes and relive every delicious moment.

"But the only reason he left early was because Father had told him to. Father was angry with him for having dumped his tobacco ashes into the umbrella stand instead of waiting until we were outside. Chad couldn't have known that Father had had a difficult day and would end up throwing him out of the house as a result. Not when he had done so much worse in the past and not been ordered to go. He could not know that Father had finally reached his breaking point."

"That may be, but the fact is, he was still on his way out of here long before eight o'clock and was standin' at someone else's door with his hat in hand by eight-thirty. Also, you have to remember, eighty-thirty isn't all that late for town folk. Especially on a Friday night."

Julia's forehead pulled into a deep frown. "Who was she? I demand to know her name. Who was the woman he so brazenly went to see?"

Pearline studied her mistress a moment, thinking her reaction excessive. Suddenly she wished she had thought of somewhere else for Chad to have gone.

"Don't rightly know who she was. I figured he might be a while, so I didn't stay too long. But I don't think there's any reason for you to be so concerned. No one but me saw him there. He didn't jeopardize anything by payin' her a visit. Your secret is still as safe as it ever was."

"How do you know?" Julia demanded, tapping her boot at a rapid rate. "If you didn't stay, how can you be so sure that no one saw him leave?"

"What if they did?" Pearline wanted to know, still not seeing a problem. "Hardly anyone around here knows he's supposed to be your new beau. Your father has seen to that."

"But *she* might know. She might know all about me. It is possible he told her everything so she would not be jealous of the time he spent here."

"He wouldn't do that."

"How do you know what he'd do? Besides, it is just as possible that she is also having him followed. If so, she would know that he had gone there to see her *after* having been here to see me. What if she gets angry about that and tells someone? What if she decides to come here and confront me with the fact he is her beau, too?"

"I doubt she knows anything about you. Most folks are a lot more trustin' than you. Most folks don't go around havin' other folks followed."

"Still, he shouldn't have gone," Julia responded with a stubborn lift of her chin, looking more hurt than anything else. "He should have had better sense than that." She curled her hands into small fists and held her arms stiffly at her sides. "Just wait until I see him!"

"You plan on mentionin' it to him?" Pearline was worried that she might have stirred up far more trouble than she had realized. Mr. Chad would not like such a lie told about him. "How you goin' to explain knowin' where he went?"

"I will tell him the truth. I will tell him I've been having him followed. There's no law against an employer having an employee followed. No law at all."

"But what if hearin' about it makes him angry?"

"So what if it does? What do I care? I'm *already* angry. Seems fair he should be angry, too."

Pearline shook her head in an attempt to better understand Julia's explosive reaction. "But why are *you* angry? Because he's courtin' another woman?" Her questioning expression relaxed, aware she had just uncovered the root of the problem. "Are you jealous of this other woman?"

"No of course not," she answered a little too quickly. "Why would I be jealous? I just don't like the thought of him doing something so foolish. What if someone besides you saw him? What if Father somehow finds out?"

Pearline lifted her hands, indicating she did not understand. "What if he does? It would just make him like Mr. Chad all the less."

"But it might also make him realize that there is something wrong with the situation, and I certainly don't want him questioning what we've told him so far."

"But you don't really expect Mr. Chad to stay away from other women the whole time he's workin' for you—or for other women to stay away from him for that long do you? Not as attractive and manly and as unmarried as he is. Women are going to flock to such a man. There's not much that can be done about that."

"Considering how much money I'm paying him, you'd think he'd at least make an effort to keep them away," she responded flatly. "Doesn't he know the trouble it could cause if someone found out that he was attracted to someone besides me? Especially if the someone to find out was my father. It could ruin everything."

Pearline fell silent while she continued studying Julia's troubled expression then narrowed her gaze and slowly shook her head. "That's not what's worryin' you. You're not worried about your father findin' out like you said. You *are* jealous of that woman. You jealous because Mr. Chad went to see her the minute he had some free time."

"*Jealous?* Why would I be jealous?" Julia demanded. "Why should I care if he's interested in some other woman? Why, when I am already in love with another man and have plans to marry him?"

"Because I think you are also in love with Mr. Chad," Pearline pointed out, then fought the sudden urge to grin, fully believing Missy had finally met the perfect man but was too blinded by what she still felt for Mr. Patrick to see it. "You may not like it, but it's as true as a fact can be. I can tell by lookin' at your face. You love Mr. Chad every bit as much as you love Mr. Patrick. If not *more*."

Julia opened her mouth, prepared to argue Pearline's claim, but realized her words would fall on deaf ears. Pearline knew what was in her heart better than anyone. Sometimes even better than herself. Finally, she admitted the truth. "You're partially right. I have developed certain feelings for Chad, feelings I have no right to feel. But I *don't* love him. I haven't known the man long enough to be in love with him."

"Oh, yes you have—and you do," Pearline said softly, then reached out to rest a comforting hand on Julia's shoulder. "You just don't know it yet. Or maybe you do know it but feel so guilty because of Mr. Patrick that you won't admit it—even to yourself."

"What am I going to do?" Julia asked, looking sadly bewildered. "I can't let this go on. I can't continue feeling this way about Chad, my heart fluttering like it had grown wings every time I see him. Not when I know that one day I will marry Patrick. It's not right."

"Don't ask me what to do," Pearline said with a helpless lift of her hands. "I am the last person you should be askin' when it comes to matters of the heart."

"But I thought you were the authority," Julia reminded her. "You are the one who reads all those romantic paper books your cousin sends over here."

"Doesn't help none when it comes to real life,"

252

Pearline admitted solemnly. "To tell you the truth, I think I just might be fallin' in love myself, but can't be sure because I really don't know that much about what love really is. Only about what it can do."

"Falling in love? With Chad?" Julia asked, thinking that preposterous, but aware he was the only man they had discussed lately—and she *had* called him handsome and manly.

Pearline shook her head, then laughed. "Oh, no. No, the man I think I might be fallin' in love with is named Solomon Ford."

Julia recognized the name. "The foreman next door?"

Pearline nodded, then reluctantly told Julia about her visits there and how she had been reporting regularly to her father everything she found out about the new owner.

"You mean you've been going over there every night after you've followed Chad into town?" Julia's brown eyes were wide with surprise.

Pearline hesitated, not knowing if she should admit the whole truth or not, then nodded again. "Haven't missed a night yet."

Trying to set it all straight in her mind, Julia stared at Pearline blankly for several seconds. "All because Father asked you to go over there and try to charm the man into helping him get that house back? Is having your own land really that important?"

Pearline grinned and dipped her head sheepishly. "The chance of gettin' my own land might be what sent me over there the first time, but I don't think that's the only reason I keep goin' back."

Julia's puzzled expression slowly relaxed into a pleased smile while she considered what Pearline had told her. "And you say this new foreman is very handsome?"

Pearline's dimples sank even deeper into her cheeks. "As handsome as any man I've ever laid eyes on. And strong. Why, he's even stronger than those big, strappin' men in St. Louis who work down on the docks. You should see the muscles in his arms and across his back. He also smart. Not only did he graduate high school, he even been to college some. That's why Mr. Andrews chose him to be his foreman. Solomon knows an awful lot about raisin' cattle. Plans to have some of his own someday."

"And you've been going over there to see him every night for almost a week?"

"More than a week," Pearline corrected. "A week and four days. But then who's really countin' the actual days we been seein' each other?"

"Sounds to me like *you* are." Julia could not remember seeing Pearline quite so happy. "And in all this time has he kissed you?"

"A couple of times." Pearline shivered visibly at the arousing memories that wrought. "And he holds my hand every night while we talk."

"And what sort of first kiss did he give you?" Julia's eyes glimmered at the mere thought of someone having finally captured Pearline's heart. In all the years she'd known her, Pearline had only been in love once and then only for a few months. "Was it on the forehead or on the cheek?"

"You remember that kiss Mr. Chad gave you out on the front veranda that Sunday about two weeks ago?"

Julia's eyes rounded and she nodded that she did remember, remembered quite vividly. "He kissed you like *that?*"

"Ummmm-hmmmm." Pearline closed her eyes so she could remember the kiss better. "Exactly like that—if not better."

"And you didn't slap him?"

"Never occurred to me." She opened her eyes and laughed. "I guess I was too busy enjoyin' the kiss to think about nothin' like that. That Solomon is a mighty fine kisser. I can just imagine what real full lovemaking would be like with him."

"Pearline!" Julia admonished, but was laughing too hard to sound too very shocked. "How can you think about such things?"

"Don't you?" Pearline asked, then quickly sobered, although a glimmer remained in her eyes. "Don't you ever look at a man and wonder what kind of husband he'd be?"

"You've actually thought about marrying him?" Julia was truly stunned. "What does your brother think about all this? Does he know that you've been going over there late every night?"

"Sirus? Heavens no. Why would I tell him where I go? Besides, your father has asked that I keep my goin's on over there a secret from everyone. That's why you can't go tellin' him how I already up and told you about it. I don't think he wants *anyone* knowin' about any of it in case I end up failin'. Especially not you."

"But he's told me about everything else he's done thus far. Why wouldn't he tell me about that?"

Pearline shrugged. "Maybe he's afraid you wouldn't approve, sort of like *I* didn't approve at first. Or that you might try to talk me out of helpin' him like I am. You know how your father can be."

Julia nodded that she did. "He doesn't like interference of any kind. Especially from me." She flattened her mouth into an annoyed frown, then wrinkled her brow with a new thought. "Why didn't you tell me about all this before? Why did you wait until now to mention Solomon to me?"

255

"Because, like you, I'm not all that sure of what it is I am feelin' towards him just yet. It could be love. Or it could just be that I am flattered by all the attention he pays me and all those pretty words he says. All I know for sure is how he makes me feel when I'm around him, sort of like I been runnin' a race even though I'm sittin' still. I also can't stop thinking about him, no matter how hard I try. It makes sleepin' next to impossible. And no sooner have I left there than I want to go back. I can barely wait until the next time I see him."

She paused a moment, then tilted her head to one side while she thought more about her complex feelings. "At least I only have *one* man to try to decide about. You got two." She shook her head at the complications that had to cause for Julia. "I'd sure hate to have to try to decide between *two* men. I'm confused enough just trying to decide how I feel about my one."

"There's nothing to decide," Julia put in quickly. "I told you. I love Patrick. We are very compatible. Enough so I plan to marry him. It's just that I also have these confused feelings for Chad, too. But whatever these feelings are, they're certainly not strong enough to be considered *love.*"

Pearline hiked her eyebrows, as if planning to challenge that last remark but shook her head questioningly instead. "If that's so, then why are you so jealous about that other woman?"

"But I am *not* jealous."

"You sure do seem to be jealous. And since you do seem that way, if I was you, I wouldn't mention even knowin' that he went over to see that other woman at all. You sure don't want him to start thinkin' like me, that the real reason you so upset about his sudden interest in this other woman is because you wish it could be you."

Pearline watched Julia's contemplative expression closely, hoping she had convinced her not to approach Chad with the outright lie she had told. "You wouldn't want him to start thinkin' that he had a real chance with you. Not when you're still so dead set on marryin' someone else. It wouldn't be fair to him or to Mr. Patrick."

Without giving Missy a chance to respond, wanting her to have time to think more about what might happen should she mention that other woman to Chad, Pearline shook her head and headed toward the door. "Better hurry up and get on downstairs if you want your breakfast still hot. Ruth made your favorite this morning. Egg toast, and plenty of it."

Julia watched while Pearline hurried out of the room, more uncertain of her feelings than ever. What if Pearline was right? What if her anger was really just some form of jealousy? What if what she felt toward Chad really *was* love? And if it was love, or something very close to it, would he be able to tell just by talking to her?

The muscles at the base of her throat constricted at the mere thought of Chad discovering how she felt about him. What would she do if he found out that she had developed such a deep yearning for him? Or that whenever she looked into those pale-blue eyes of his she longed for him to hold her. Longed for him to take her into his arms again and kiss her like he had that first weekend.

But more important than what *she* would do was what would *he* do were he to find out her true feelings. Would he try to use such a discovery to his advantage by attempting to come between her and Patrick in some way?

Finally Julia decided Pearline was right. She should

not mention knowing about Chad's visit to that other woman. At least not until she better understood and could better control her feelings toward him.

She sighed softly, wishing that life did not have to be so complicated. All she had ever wanted was to marry a man who would be kind to her and not try to mold her into something she was not. Someone who would love her for who she was. All she had ever wanted was a man who would not try to control her. A man willing to let her do what she wanted with her life.

Remembering that Patrick had promised to be just such a man, she finished adjusting her sash. When she headed downstairs to eat, it was with a renewed resolve to put Chad out of her heart. She could not continue longing for a man who could never be all the things Patrick had promised to be.

"Are you still planning to bring Chad to the mill Monday afternoon?" Charles asked Julia while he sprinkled a thin coating of powdered sugar across the three slices of fried toast laid across his plate.

"Yes, I am," she answered, then glanced up from her own plate with the sweetest of smiles, aware the idea did not set well with him at all. Apparently he did not want his employees meeting Chad. Nor did he want anyone *else* meeting him. In the two weeks and one day he had known Chad, her father had not invited one single visitor to the house. "Chad has heard you talk so much about your work, he is curious to see what the mill is like. He also wants to visit the lumber store and the Marshall shipping yards later in the week. Probably Wednesday. That way we can visit while you are there."

"Why?" He lifted the powdered toast to his mouth

but did not take a bite. "Why is he suddenly so set on seeing my businesses?"

"I told you. He's curious to find out what they are like. After all, once we are married, it is likely that he will decide to go to work at one of them. That way he can be near me when the time comes that I finally take over everything for you." She tried not to show the annoyance she felt even discussing the likelihood of having to work at either place. She knew that if she ever allowed herself to take over her father's duties, she would end up being kept busy with them at least five, and possibly six, days a week. Her father would see to that. He would see to it that she was thoroughly involved with every aspect of his different timber concerns. And *that* was not what she wanted to do with her life. "It's the only way Chad and I will ever see much of each other."

Charles huffed so hard at the thought of Chad ever having anything to do with his businesses, the powdered sugar billowed into his face. He scowled and reached for his napkin to wipe away the white dust. "I don't really think you'll want him working for you. He's not very adept."

"Father!" She tried to sound deeply insulted when what she really was was pleased. Very pleased. It meant that thus far Chad had accomplished exactly what he was supposed to accomplish. "Surely you don't mean that."

Charles set the napkin back down and drew his thick white eyebrows into a perplexed frown. "Just what is it you see in that man?" Again he held his toast near his mouth, still not taking a bite.

"You mean Chad?" She arched her eyebrows, as if not quite understanding why her father would ask such a thing.

"Of course I mean Chad. Just what is it you see in him?"

"Do you mean besides the fact that he is so incredibly handsome and so terribly strong?" she asked, then gave a whimsical sigh. "Aren't his eyes the bluest blue you've ever seen in your life?" Her heart trembled when she thought of those eyes, for they were indeed the deepest, most penetrating blue she had ever seen.

"There are lots of strong, handsome, blue-eyed men in this world. Why did you have to pick *him?* Why not someone who has a few manners and shows at least a trace of common sense? That man can't tell an ashcan from an umbrella stand. He is a complete misfit."

"Chad has plenty of common sense," she responded in ready defense. "And he isn't a misfit at all. He's just not the type of man you are used to being around."

"That's an understatement," Charles muttered. "And he's not the type of man I ever *want* to get used to being around. I really don't like the thought of you marrying him. There are so many other men who are better suited for you."

One in particular, Julia thought smugly but did not dare say so aloud. It was important her father continue to believe that Chad was the man she loved.

"You just don't understand him. Chad is really a very good person," she argued with a sharp wag of her head. She did not dare surrender too easily. She wanted her father to believe that he had gradually worn down her resistance. She wanted him to come away feeling like the victor instead of the victim. "Why can't you see how good he is?"

"And why can't you see that he is not the man for you?" he countered, and waved his toast for emphasis. "You could never be happy married to a maladroit like that."

"But he's not a maladroit," she argued with a determined lift of her chin, although Chad had been nothing *but* awkward and inept while around her father because that was exactly what he was being paid to be.

"He's *not?*" Charles asked, his tone challenging.

"No. You just make him nervous is all. And he *is* the perfect man for me. We were made for each other," she said, and found it odd that she was now able to look directly at her father while stating such a thing. She hoped her lack of remorse had nothing to do with those strange new feelings she and Pearline had discussed earlier. "I couldn't ask for anyone more kind or more considerate. I just hope you are not planning to deny us your blessing."

"What if I did? Would you marry him anyway?"

Julia pouted, her forehead wrinkled with false concern. "You can't have made up your mind about Chad already. You've known him for only a couple of weeks. That's not long enough for you to have discovered the true person inside him and you know it. You should give him at least another week before passing any final judgments." She felt certain that one more week was about all her father could take, which would work out perfectly, since Patrick was due to arrive in just a little over two weeks.

Charles studied her determined expression a moment longer then sighed with reluctance. "All right. I will give him another week."

Julia's expression brightened. "Do you mean it? You won't make any decisions or say anything else ugly about or to Chad for at least another week?" She wanted his words verified, all the while knowing she had just asked the impossible. He might try, but he would never succeed. She and Chad would see to that.

"He has until next Saturday. But if that man doesn't

show at least some indication of intelligent life before then, you may as well know that you will not have my blessing. I will not sanction such a marriage."

"Oh, Father, you will find reason to like Chad yet. I know you will." She renewed her smile. "Wait until you see how truly interested he is in the lumber business. You'll be very pleased."

Charles looked at her with clear skepticism.

"His interest is probably more in the money that business brings in than in the business itself," he muttered, then dropped his toast back on his plate and excused himself from the table.

"Now remember, you are to act especially obnoxious while we are here," Julia cautioned Chad after he pulled the carriage to a halt just outside the main offices of her father's mill. "I want this to be one of the events that pushes Father over the edge."

She laughed despite the apprehension she felt knowing that what happened during those next few minutes was to be very important. She then explained the promise she had extracted from her father. "I want this coming week to become the longest and most trying week of his life," she concluded.

Chad chuckled when he noticed the devilish glimmer in her dark-brown eyes and the high color in her otherwise fair cheeks. She was truly the most beautiful woman he had ever seen. And the most conniving. And why *that* should draw him to her was beyond reasoning.

"I promise, I'll be on my very best worst behavior," he vowed, then climbed down from the carriage and turned to face her. Gallantly, he held out his hand to help her alight. "I'll have your father pulling out large handfuls of hair before we leave here."

"His or yours?" she wanted to know, then laughed again while she accepted his proffered hand. As usual, just touching him made her feel all giddy and warm inside, but she did what she could to ignore her body's mutinous reaction and quickly took her position beside him. "Yes, do be as bad as you know how. I want him cringing inside."

Deepening his smile, Chad reached back inside the carriage to retrieve his wide-brimmed, high-crowned hat, then followed Julia across the sawdust-covered drive toward a small side door. He waited until they were about to enter before plopping the hat haphazardly on the back of his head instead of pushing it forward to its usual angle. He then tugged at the front and sides of his pale-blue shirt to make him look even more unkempt.

"Good touch," she said with an appreciative grin, then quickly sobered as they were about to enter the house. "Now remember. You are supposed to be madly, deeply, *insanely* in love with me. So much so, you are willing to make me your bride despite what my father has to say about you."

"*That'*ll be easy enough to do," he muttered softly so that she barely heard, then quickly opened the door, not giving her a chance to respond. He already *was* madly, deeply, insanely in love with her. So much so she haunted his every waking thought.

He waved his hand forward. "After you, my future bride."

Even though she knew he had not been serious in calling her that, Julia felt a strange, hollow ache inside her, but quickly attributed it to the guilt she continued to feel whenever she was around him. But rather than dwell on the strange sensation his words had caused, she instead set her mind on the matter at hand. She nodded toward a narrow door at the far end of the hall that looked to be made of heavy oak and opaque glass.

"That last door leads into Father's office. Wait until he hears we have come without Pearline." Her brown eyes sparkled at the thought. "He will be furious to learn we are unescorted."

"Yes, it is amazing how quickly the poor dear woman fell ill this morning," Chad responded with a knowing smile, pleased finally to have some time alone with Julia. He quickly closed the door behind them, then offered his arm.

Julia accepted the arm, aware they really should enter the office together. Again the simple act of touching him stirred her senses.

"Now remember, your primary interest in coming here is to find out how much money the business makes," she whispered, leaning close enough to his ear that she caught the now familiar scent of his perfumed soap. "I want you to come across as being very mercenary. He's to think that the real reason you want to marry me is so you can get your hands on my family's money."

"I know my part," he responded, already using the voice he used when pretending to be her sweetheart, then winked. "Before I'm through, he'll think the absolute worst of me. In fact, he will probably end up despising me every bit as much as he does that new neighbor of yours."

Aware of how determined Julia's father was to hate the neighbor, for whatever reason, Chad had accepted the fact that as Robert Freeport's nephew, there was little hope he would ever earn Charles's friendship. No matter what he did. Therefore, it did not bother him to be purposely doing what he could to turn the man against him. Not when he would eventually rise in Julia's estimation for having done so.

"And keep in mind that Jean Boswell is Father's most treasured employee. She's been with him for nearly fifteen years. It would be a good idea to have her dislike you, too. Father values her opinion immensely." She paused. "Maybe too much so. Sometimes I think there is more between those two than a working relationship."

"Oh?" Chad arched his eyebrows, clearly interested.

"Yes. I think that if Father would only ask her, Miss Boswell would gladly marry him. You'll know what I mean when you see the two of them together. She's the one we will have to talk to first. No one gets in to see Father without first obtaining her approval."

Chad glanced at the door curiously, wishing he could see through the smoky-gray glass that filled the upper half. He was curious to see the woman who had such an important place in Charles's business life.

Julia paused just outside the door to take a deep, steadying breath, then nodded for Chad to open the door, which he did. Seconds after they stepped inside, a tiny, dark-haired woman who appeared to be somewhere in her middle to late forties glanced up from her typewriter. Although her initial expression had been that of annoyance, the tight scowl melted into a genuine smile when she saw Julia. She came immediately out of her seat.

"Julia, I was wondering when you were going to pay us a little visit," she said as she walked quickly but gracefully around the large desk with her arms extended. "It has been months since we last saw you."

Julia hurried forward to accept the woman's embrace. "You mean Father didn't tell you we were coming?" she asked.

"We?" Miss Boswell glanced then at Chad as if just

265

now aware of him. "Who do we have here?" Her dark eyebrows arched questioningly while her gaze slowly swept his lean, muscular form, but then flattened again when her gaze came to rest on the large, wide-brimmed hat he still wore atop his head.

"He's a dear friend of mine from St. Louis." Julia stepped away so that the woman could have a better look at him. She noticed that Miss Boswell had seemed to be impressed with him until she'd noticed the hat. "His name is Chad Sutton. Chad, this is Miss Boswell, Father's secretary, and if the truth be known, the person who really runs this place." She winked at Chad but then frowned when she looked again at the slender secretary. "I can't believe Father hasn't mentioned him to you. He's been here for over two weeks now."

Miss Boswell cut her gaze from Chad to Julia, then back to Chad. Again she stared pointedly at his head covering. "Sir, would you like for me to take care of your hat for you until you are ready to leave?"

"No. I like wearing it," he answered, as if unaware it was rude of him to wear it inside the building. He then glanced at the inner door that carried Charles's name engraved with bold white letters. "Is her father in? We came here to see him. Julia wants him to show us around."

Miss Boswell frowned while she continued to stare at the hat. "Yes, he is in. But he is with Tommy Sanford at the moment so it will be a while."

"Who's Tommy Sanford?" he asked, looking first to Julia then, Miss Boswell for the answer. "And why is it more important for him to be in there than it is for us to be in there?"

Noticing the annoyance in Miss Boswell's expression, Julia did what she could to keep a straight face.

"Tommy is the mill supervisor. It's his job to take care of operations on the days when her father is not here."

"And that makes him more important than *us?*" Chad asked with an indignant wag of his head. He crossed his arms to show how insulted he was.

"Sir," Miss Boswell replied, trying to remain calm and composed. "He *was* here first."

"What does that matter? Sweetcakes here is his daughter. His flesh and blood. She shouldn't have to wait around to see her own father. Especially when we got so many better things we can do with our time."

Julia turned away while she made a valiant effort to keep from laughing. Chad played his part beautifully. Miss Boswell's eyes were bulging with outrage.

Taking advantage of the moment, Chad stepped over and laid his arm around Julia's shoulders. "Why, this is the first time in weeks that we finally got a whole day to ourselves. Just the two of us." He drew her body firmly against his. How good it felt to hold her like that, as if she belonged at his side. "We don't want to spend too much of what little time we got left cooped up here in this old office building. Do we, sweetcakes?"

"No, of course not," Julia responded, her brown eyes rounded. She had not expected him to pull her against him like that and was ill prepared for the resulting jar of her senses. Wetting her suddenly dry lips, she glanced at Chad and felt a twinge of annoyance to see such a wide, devastating smile. He looked as if he was enjoying all this a little too much.

When she returned her gaze to her father's secretary, who still stared at the couple, Julia decided not to pull away. Instead, she leaned against him and pretended that she was not quite so affected by his nearness.

"We do have a lot of things we need to discuss," she admitted, then tilted her face up and smiled adoringly at

Chad. "That is, if we want our wedding to be absolutely perfect." Her voice had wavered just a bit when she made that last remark, but she decided that was because she had never seen Miss Boswell look so shocked. She could well imagine what all the prim little secretary would say to her father after they left! "But I think it would be a good idea to wait until Father is through talking to Tommy. We don't want to do anything to anger him just now. Not until we finally have his blessing."

"Whatever you say," he responded, then bent to press a gentle kiss against her temple. He marveled at how good it had felt to do that just before he flattened that same mouth into an exaggerated frown. "But I still don't think *you* should have to wait for anyone. Not when one day you will be the person running this place." He bent to give her a second kiss, but Julia pulled away before he could succeed.

"We shouldn't have to wait too long," she said, then looked nervously to the clock on top of one of the filing cabinets. "We'll still have plenty of time to ourselves."

"I hope so," Chad muttered. He watched her closely for several seconds, wondering if that kiss he'd given her had anything to do with the reason she suddenly seemed so fidgety, then glanced down at some of the papers scattered across Jean Boswell's desk. Tilting his head, he bent forward, picked up a small writing tablet, and skimmed over it as if he had every right to know what was written there.

"Sir, those are my notes," Miss Boswell's tone was sharp and her body rigid while she made a futile grab for the tablet. Chad held the pad high enough so that it was just out of her reach, which frustrated her more. "I'd thank you to leave my things alone."

"Why? You got something to hide?" Chad looked at Julia with a puzzled expression. "Looks like this was written in some sort of secret code." He held the pad out for her to see. "Can you read this? If you're going to be running this place one day, I think you should be let in on any secret codes. That way you can know about everything that goes on in every department." He arched an eyebrow. "Maybe we should look over some of the financial statements while we're here. Put some of what you learned in that fancy woman's college to use."

"It's not a secret code. It's called shorthand," Julia explained as she carefully took the tablet from his hand and returned it to the desk. She knew only too well that her father's secretary did not like anyone tampering with the items on her desk. She only wanted to offend the woman enough to make her voice her disapproval, not alienate her forever. "And for today all I want to do is have Father show you around. I'm not interested in seeing the books yet."

"Are you sure? Could be interesting to see how much money a place like this brings in," he said, then tilted his head again so that he could look at other items scattered neatly across Miss Boswell's desk. He poked at several other papers and a small stack of files with his fingertip, then picked up one of the fatter files and opened it. "How long you figure that supervisor fellow will be in there?"

"I'll go check," Miss Boswell responded, suddenly reversing her decision not to disturb Charles. She hurried immediately toward the closed office. Keeping an eye on Chad, who was busily pulling papers out of the file and setting them off to the side, she tapped on the door lightly, then opened it just a few inches and peered inside. "Mr. Thornton. Your daughter and her—*friend* are here to see you."

There was a low, deep, grumbling sound from inside the office that continued for several seconds before the prim woman finally turned back to face Chad and Julia with an obvious look of relief. "He said he will see you now. You may go on in."

She pushed the door fully open, then stepped aside to let them pass. It was not until Chad was nearly to the door that she bent forward and grabbed the yellow folder he still held. At the same time she reached up and snatched the hat off his head. When he turned and looked at her with a startled expression, she narrowed her gaze. "The hat will be waiting for you on my desk when you are ready to leave."

When he looked as if he was about to make an issue of what she had done, she added in a low, controlled voice, "It is for your own benefit. Believe me."

Deciding it not worth his effort to do battle with her over something so unimportant, not when it was now time to focus his attention on aggravating Charles instead, Chad let her keep the hat.

He followed Julia inside and was not surprised to find the large office so ornately decorated. In addition to the expected desk and storage cabinets, there was a small scroll-backed sofa with matching armchairs off to one side and another set of less comfortable-looking armchairs directly in front of the large, oak desk. The wall nearest the desk was composed of all windows with stacks of freshly cut lumber stacked beyond. The wall next to that was lined floor to ceiling with dark-stained shelves that held books and notebooks of all manner. On the wall opposite the windows hung a massive painting of how the mill must have looked years earlier. And on the final wall, behind them, was a lighted portrait of a much younger Charles seated beside a beautiful woman who looked very much like Julia.

After quickly committing his surroundings to memory, Chad turned his attention to the two men who

270

stood only a few feet away from the desk. The taller one was Charles. The other he assumed to be Tommy Sanford, the mill supervisor.

Smiling broadly, and knowing Charles had warned him not to as much as hold Julia's hand while he was there, he plopped his arm around her shoulders again, then practically dragged her across the thick gray carpet in his eagerness to get on with this latest confrontation. The sooner they finished there, the better. He was eager to be alone with Julia again. "We're here to see the mill. Just like Julia promised."

Chapter Fifteen

"Sorry we couldn't get here a little sooner," Chad continued, all the while holding Julia close to his side, "but we decided to take the river road since there's no problem for me to be crossing Mr. Andrews's land."

"The river road? Why?"

"More romantic," Chad answered, then winked. "I couldn't believe my luck when I got over to your house and found out that Pearline had come down with a sick stomach and was asking to stay in bed for the day."

"Pearline is not with you?" Charles cocked an eyebrow with disbelief. He glanced at the doorway behind them as if he expected to see the young maid waiting patiently in the other room. When all he saw was Miss Boswell, who stood watching the proceedings from a few yards away, the cocked eyebrow quickly joined the other in a full, angry scowl.

"Not today," Chad answered happily. He gave Julia's shoulders a demonstrative little squeeze, then bent to press his cheek against the top of her head. "Must have been something she ate."

Charles continued to glare at Julia while Tommy Sanford edged toward the door.

"If Pearline is really so sick, why didn't you ask Lisa

to come with you instead? You really should have an escort."

"I probably should have asked Lisa, but she looked too busy and I didn't want to bother her." Julia turned her adoring gaze to Chad and smiled. Her heart fluttered when she found him looking back at her with an equally adoring expression. "With Pearline sick, poor Lisa was left with both her own chores and Pearline's. I didn't dare ask her to drop everything just to come with us."

She glanced over her shoulder to see if Tommy had left the room yet and was pleased to discover he had not. The short, stocky man was still close enough to hear everything she said. "Besides, I see nothing wrong with being alone with my future husband. It gives us a chance to talk about our plans without a lot of interruptions from other people. Have we told you yet that we have already decided to have children right away? With any luck you could be a grandfather within a year or two."

She watched with growing satisfaction while her father bristled over those last comments.

To provoke him even more, she leaned against Chad's chest, amazed at how firm his muscles felt beneath her soft cheek. She fought a strong desire to press her fingers into other areas of his body to see if he could possibly be that solid all over.

While continuing to enjoy the comfort of Chad's arm around her, she provoked her father further. "You've always claimed to want grandchildren."

Tommy Sanford's eyes had rounded immediately, but he made no comment before slipping out of Charles's office and quietly closing the door. Julia could well imagine the shocked whispers that would pass between him and Miss Boswell during those next few minutes.

Charles's scowl deepened. "Do you have to behave like that in front of my employees?" He was so angry now that his whole body shook with a poor attempt to control his rage. "What will they think? You two are not even engaged yet."

"No, not *yet*," Julia agreed, then again gazed adoringly up at Chad. This time she noticed a strange look of contentment in his eyes and wondered what had caused it. "But we will be married soon enough."

"I don't—" Charles was interrupted before he could finish that statement.

"Are you ready to show Chad around?" Julia asked, as if unaware her father had planned to say something else. "He's very eager to see the place. Aren't you, darling?"

"Anything you say, sweetcakes." Chad gave her shoulders yet another loving squeeze. His blue eyes glittered with something more than amusement when he looked at her then. "My only goal in life is to make you happy."

Charles's eyes narrowed and a tiny muscle pumped rhythmically near the back of his jaw while he stared at them. When he finally spoke again, it was in low, even tones. "Would you please take your arm from around my little girl. You don't know how much seeing you hold her like that bothers me."

"Little girl?" Chad's face stretched with surprise. "Sir, I don't think you've taken a good, hard look at your daughter lately. You can hardly call the beautiful, beguiling woman standing before you a little girl anymore."

Julia lifted her chin proudly, pleased that Chad had come so readily to her defense. "That's true, Father. I happen to be twenty-two years old now. I am a grown,

274

mature woman and have been for quite some time and I do wish you would start treating me like one."

"If you want me to treat you like the 'grown, mature woman' you say you are, then you'll have to start behaving more like one," he snapped angrily. "That is *not* something you often do."

"How can you say that?"

To calm the situation, Chad quickly released Julia and held his hands out, as if to indicate surrender. The plan was to make Charles angry with *him*, not with *her*. "We didn't come here to argue with you, sir. We came here so I could have my first look around the mill. Are you ready to show me how this place is run?"

Charles blinked at Chad's sudden willingness to get along. "If that's what Julia wants," he finally relented, heading toward the door. "But we'll have to do this quickly. I have an important meeting with two railroad contractors at one-thirty."

For the next twenty minutes, Chad and Julia followed Charles to the different buildings and Chad listened attentively while Charles explained the uses of the different machinery, told about what safety procedures they used, and pointed out the duties of the different workers. Even though Charles was clearly annoyed to have to show Chad around, the fact that he was proud of all the work going on around them was obvious in his every word, his every gesture.

Chad was duly impressed. He had taken a small water-powered sawmill once owned by his father and had built it into a huge lumber operation. Not only did he mill the timber like his father had, he owned acres upon acres of land where he constantly grew new trees to replenish the old. He also had two large shipping

275

yards where he stockpiled and from where he distrib-uted freshly cut lumber all over the United States.

They stood only a few dozen yards from the huge steam-driven saws, watching the six-foot disks eat through the bodies of large trees with ease. He had to shout to be heard over the resulting noise. "This is some operation," he said in awe. "What's this place earn in a year's time?"

Charles cut his gaze to Chad. "Why do you want to know that?"

"Well, after Julia and I get married, I'll probably end up having to help her run the place. I was just trying to figure out what to expect."

"Have you had any experience helping manage an enterprise like this?" he asked in a way that was de-signed to make Chad feel insignificant.

"No," he answered, although he had helped manage his father's mercantile and their small farm for several years. "But how hard can it be?"

"A lot harder than you obviously think. It would be better to leave the running of this place to Julia."

"I don't know. There's bound to be something I can do to help out," he responded, then smiled at Julia. "Wouldn't want to just stand around and let my pretty little wife run the place all by her lonesome. Wouldn't look right." He reached out and put his arm around her again, this time in front of a whole lumber mill filled with curious workers.

Julia felt the usual shattering of her senses when he again hugged her close, but by now it was something she had come to expect though she could yet explain. It was obviously more than a simple rush of guilt that came with knowing she was allowing another man to hold her close.

"I told you not to do that," Charles said, glowering at

where Chad's arm rested lightly across Julia's shoulders. When his angry words did not bring about the desired response, he reached over and tossed Chad's arm aside. "She is not your property yet."

"But it's only a matter of time," Chad pointed out, then put his arm back around her, as if to challenge Charles's authority. "Whether you finally do agree to our marriage or not, Julia will one day be my wife. You may as well accept that as a given fact."

Chad had made that vow with such conviction, it caused Charles's nostrils to flare and Julia's already rapid pulses to quicken more. A strange feeling of foreboding crept through her while she awaited her father's angry response.

"Don't antagonize me, young man!" Charles warned. He stood tensed, with legs braced, as if prepared for physical battle.

"I'm not trying to antagonize you," Chad responded calmly but firmly, which made him sound all the more sincere. "I just want you to know exactly where I stand. I do love your daughter, and no matter what you think of me, I intend to marry her."

"Why?" Charles's eyes narrowed until they were but two slits of green. "So you can help her take over the running of this mill?"

"I'll do that only if she wants me to. I'll do whatever it takes to make her happy, even if that means running this place alone. I told you. I *love* your daughter. Her happiness means even more to me than my own."

Julia's eyes widened at such a remarkable performance. She had not expected him to sound so resolved while saying such things about her. Her heart continued to hammer fast and hard while she awaited her father's angry retort, knowing that by now he had to be very near his breaking point.

Instead of flying into an instant rage and ordering Chad to leave, she could hardly believe that her father merely studied Chad's determined expression for several seconds then turned away.

"I'll see if I can find someone to follow you two home. Whether you end up married or not, I don't think it is appropriate for you to be seen alone together until you are."

Chad and Julia exchanged surprised glances, then followed Charles silently as far as the main yard. Julia suddenly pulled Chad to a stop. She waited until her father had disappeared into the next building then gestured toward the carriage. "Come on. Let's go."

"Before your father gets back?" Chad questioned, glancing at the building Charles had just entered.

"Yes. Before Father gets back. The whole idea behind having Pearline stay home was to make Father worry about what all might happen between us during the ride home."

Chad smiled, then willingly let her take his hand so she could pull him toward the carriage.

Keeping the horse at a quick canter, Chad waited until they were far enough away that they could barely hear the constant whine of the steel saws and see the stark white pillar of steam that constantly hovered above the mill before he asked his next question. "What happens when your father sees that we've already gone and decides to send someone out after us? What's to keep a man on horseback from catching up with us and escorting us on home—making sure nothing happens?"

"The fact that the rider won't find us. As soon as we top that next hill, I want you to turn off the main road," she said, then glanced back to make certain they were not already being followed. "Since your foreman said it was okay for us to travel across his boss's land, we'll take a shortcut that will take us over to one of my father's lumber trails. Once we are back on Father's land, we'll stop for a few minutes. That way we won't arrive back at the house right away." Her eyes sparkled at her next thought. "Father will be furious when he finds out that not only did we not stay for the escort he wanted to send with us, we also did not go directly home."

"Are you sure you want him that angry with you?"

"He won't be for long, not after I tell him that it was your idea we go ahead and leave. That should focus all his anger on you."

She glanced back again to make certain no one yet followed, then nodded toward a narrow lane that veered off to the left. "Take that road. It will carry us through to my father's land where we'll be surrounded by enough woods no one will see us."

Chad did what he was told and waited until they could no longer be seen from the main road before slowing the horse from a quick trot to a steady walk. "But what happens if this Patrick fellow finds out that we were out alone like this?"

"He won't. I've sworn Pearline to secrecy, and after Father meets Patrick and discovers what a nice, competent man he is, he won't want to do anything that might jeopardize our budding relationship. He'll be too afraid I might try to find someone else like you to marry instead."

Chad pulled the horse to a slow halt when they approached the first gate, then held out the reins to her so she could drive the carriage on through.

Julia looked curiously at the new fence while she accepted the reins. "Did you help build that?"

"Sure did," he answered proudly as he, too, looked

out over the new fence. "I drove in more than half those posts by myself."

No wonder his arms are like rock, she mused, watching him climb down from the carriage and take several long, lithe steps toward the gate. Smiling to herself, she noticed how his clothes hugged his body in all the right places when he walked, bringing attention to his tall, lean body. She also noticed how dark his skin had become in the past few weeks, making his eyes look even bluer. Evidently a lot of his work was done directly out in the sun.

"How long until Mr. Andrews starts putting cattle on his land?" she asked in an attempt to force her thoughts elsewhere. When she did, she glanced out across the pasture they were about to cross and noticed that most of the scrub bushes and smaller trees had been cleared away and that the dirt looked and smelled freshly tilled. A lot of work had gone on since she had last seen the place.

"The way Solomon has been talking, that could be any day," he answered, then bent to unlatch the gate, unaware of the keen interest Julia had in his movements. As soon as he had the gate opened, he stepped back and gestured for her to drive on through. "They have this pasture nearly ready to seed and another well under way. In fact, they're going to buy the grass seed later this week. Should be ready to scatter that seed by the first of next week. Within a month, the grass should be pretty well established."

Julia snapped the reins lightly and drove the carriage until it cleared the gate. She then pulled it to a halt again. "In a way, I'm sorry to hear that. Once the grass has been planted and those cattle are in place, your boss will be less likely to sell my father the land."

Chad scowled when he swung himself back up onto

the seat beside her and took the reins back. "Your father has enough land. Why can't he let Mr. Andrews keep his? Why must he keep hounding a man who obviously does not want to sell?"

"Because that land is important to him," she answered honestly, but then quickly changed the subject. She had problems of her own to worry about at the moment. "Shortly after we've traveled past the creek, this road should divide into two small trails. Take the one that veers to your right."

Knowing exactly the trail she meant, he nodded. "And then what?"

"We wait until we're on Father's land again, then pull over for a few minutes."

"You mean just the two of us?" he teased, his blue eyes sparkling.

"No, I mean the *three* of us," she responded, exasperated. Her heart was hammering at too rapid a rate to put up with any of his playfulness. "I was thinking that maybe we should include the horse."

"Good idea," he said with another nod. His dimples appeared immediately. "We might need that horse when it comes time to leave."

Julia blew out a heavy breath and glanced back over her shoulder to make certain they still were not followed. It was possible the rider her father might have sent would notice a set of buggy tracks turning away from the road and realize the tracks were theirs. But then again, that road *was* well traveled.

She saw no one behind them, and by the time they had passed through their second gate and were back on her father's land, she felt safe.

"You can pull over now," she said, and indicated a small, grassy clearing ahead. Now that they were again on her father's land, they were surrounded by hundreds of acres of towering pine trees that for the most part had been planted in perfect rows. They would stack the timber on the field when it came time to cut.

"But what if one of your father's work crews came by? Wouldn't they notice us right there by the road?" he asked. "Wouldn't it be better to veer off a little farther than that?"

Julia glanced at him suspiciously, wondering why he was suddenly so concerned, then shook her head. "The only time work crews come into this area is when Father is ready to cut some of the larger trees or when they are out surveying storm or insect damage. No one will be along today. And even if someone *did* come along, he wouldn't see much. It's not as if we really plan to do anything we shouldn't."

"We don't?" He pulled gently on the right rein to turn the horse into the clearing, then pulled on both reins to bring the carriage to a stop.

Julia felt a tingling sense of foreboding when he turned to face her then. His blue eyes glimmered with the same intensity she had seen on at least two other occasions. Those times he had ended up kissing her.

Her heart leaped at the thought of what might happen if he tried kissing her again now, while they were alone together. "Of course not. We are just here because I want to make a lasting impression on my father."

"But what if it turns out he's not the only one you make a lasting impression on?" Chad wanted to know while he slowly wrapped the reins around the tether bar out of the way.

Julia's eyes widened. "What do you mean?"

"Well, what if it turns out you also make a lasting impression on me?" Having secured both the reins and the brake, he turned his attention to her. His gaze never left hers while he slowly removed his hat, then raked his fingers through his hair to take out any dents.

Julia swallowed while she watched him toss his hat haphazardly into the small compartment behind the front seat. His gaze stayed level with hers while he slowly closed what little distance lay between them. "What do you think you are doing?"

"Getting ready."

"For what?" She glanced at the seat beside her to see how much room she still had, but quickly brought her gaze back to his.

"For that lasting impression," he put forth with a fleeting smile.

Julia's heart responded with such force that she could barely hear anything above the wild rush of her own blood. It was clear by the disturbing look on his face that he planned to take personal advantage of their moments alone. She stuck out her right hand to prevent him from coming any nearer.

"I think we are close enough," she said in a voice that sounded far more controlled than she had expected.

"That's where we differ," he said, and gently pulled her hand off his chest and held it in both of his. "I don't think we are quite close enough."

To Julia's further dismay, Chad continued to hold her hand so she could not use it against him while he resumed moving closer.

"Chad, you are making a grave mistake," she said. He looked so dangerously attractive while sitting that close to her, she was not all that sure she would be able to resist him should his intention really be to kiss her. "I did not ask you to pull over so you could try to kiss me again. Don't think that I did."

"Very well," he responded in a deep-timbered voice. "If it pleases you, I won't think at all." He continued to edge his way closer, all the while holding both her hand and her gaze with his.

Julia's stomach twisted into a hard knot when she realized how devastatingly handsome he looked with his blue eyes glimmering like that and his long brown hair catching the tiny splashes of sunlight that filtered through the surrounding trees. She had never seen a man look so tempting in all her life! If it were not for the fact she was still devoted to Patrick and the life he had promised to give her, she might allow Chad to have his kiss with little or no struggle. But as it was, she had to keep him from kissing her at all cost. She could not take the chance of being caught up in her own confused emotions again.

Why, just the memory of the kisses he had bestowed on her earlier made it hard for her to breathe. And made her all the more determined to keep a safe distance between them. Her heart continued its rapid drumming while she fumbled for the latch on the carriage door nearest her with her free hand.

"Maybe this was a bad idea," she said, her whole body now quivering in response to his nearness. She had to stop this madness before it went any further.

"But then again, maybe not," he countered in a tone so deep and so sensual, it made her want to close her eyes. He was already bending to take the kiss he wanted.

Aware that within seconds those splendid lips would once again be molded against hers, leaving her as weak and as wanting as before, Julia jerked her hand free, opened the door, then quickly stumbled out of the carriage. She waited until she was at the very edge of the small, grassy clearing before turning back to face the carriage. Her heart slammed hard against her chest when she saw that he had followed her, his eyes still glimmering with intent.

Knowing she could never outrun him and would not want to stop him once his mouth had again claimed hers, her next breath caught deep in her throat, where it seemed permanently trapped. She knew she should say something to him before he came any closer—something clever or demanding that would change his mind about kissing her—but the words simply did not form. Nor did her trembling body allow her to run away from him, despite the fact he now stood only a few feet away.

It was as if somewhere deep inside, she *wanted* him to kiss her, wanted to be overwhelmed by those same fiery passions he had aroused in her during his first few days there. As if she wanted to feel that same delicious ache deep in the very core of her and be reminded yet again that she was every bit a woman.

But that was ridiculous. Why would she want such things when she was practically engaged to marry another?

While Chad again locked her frightened gaze to his, he continued to move slowly forward. His lips parted when he stood but inches from hers, indicating again that he intended to kiss her. Julia's gaze fell to those lips while she waited with aching anticipation.

She knew she should again try to resist the allure of his soft mouth. Should do something to let him know another kiss was not to be tolerated. She should cross her arms and turn a stiff shoulder to him or make a dash for the carriage and try to drive away, but instead she startled herself by leaning slightly forward to meet the coming kiss partway. Her racing heart gave another strong surge when his arms slid around her and their lips finally met in what started out a surprisingly tender kiss for a man so powerfully built.

The moment his arms had closed around her and

brought her body gently against his, Julia was overcome by a remarkable sense of belonging, although there was no reason for such a feeling to exist. She was to marry Patrick Moore. Not this man. Still, it felt wonderful to be in his arms again. Enough so that she closed her eyes to enjoy the cozy warmth building inside her while his pliant mouth continued its tender assault.

After several seconds of such gentle mastery, she started feeling light-headed. She lifted one of the arms she had kept limp at her sides and rested her hand lightly on his shoulder, suddenly needing to touch something solid to keep her bearings.

Chad responded by tightening his hold around her, pressing her body more firmly against his. When Julia again felt the strong, powerful planes of his body press even harder against the soft curves of hers, she moaned softly. Any resistance she might have had melted away, and in its place grew a longing so deep and so strong, she knew she could never control it.

She listened to the soft pounding in her ears while she focused on the wondrous onslaught of desire and emotion that spread slowly through her body. A gentle, seeking warmth moved through her until it invaded all her senses.

Shortly after she succumbed to the gentle, probing warmth, the potency of his kiss slowly deepened. Her pulses throbbed in every part of her body with an alarming yet thrilling intensity. She had an immediate and overpowering desire to be closer to him, despite the fact their bodies were already melded as one. Still, she slid her other arm around him so she could at least try to hold him closer.

Her earlier misgivings were completely gone. All she felt was the turbulent desire to know more about the strange new passion he had so quickly brought to life within her. She pressed yet harder against him and met the escalating kiss hungrily.

She continued to respond to his every movement. Her body moved with his body. Her lips parted beneath the gentle pressure of his tongue while she slowly allowed her palms to roam over his neck and shoulders. Stopping to explore the corded muscles with the tips of her fingers, she marveled again at how powerful he felt.

Chad groaned at her touch, and ready to take full advantage of Julia's parted lips, he dipped his tongue into her mouth. He teased the inner edges with quick, light strokes, going ever deeper with each probing entry.

Julia had heard of such kissing when she lived in St. Louis. At the time the idea had repulsed her, but now that she was actually experiencing the gentle tingles that resulted from such an action, she could not believe the pleasures such an exchange wrought.

Entering his mouth shyly at first, she savored the tantalizing taste and enjoyed the shuddering response it had caused in him.

Like Pearline had wondered about Solomon, she wondered what it would be like to be married to such a man. She hoped that Patrick would be able to bring her that same sort of pleasure. Once experienced, this was not something she wanted to live without.

Julia was so lost to her confused thoughts, she was not aware that Chad had lifted one hand to her hair and started to pull out her hairpins one at a time. Within seconds, he had most of them removed and placed in his pocket. He then tugged at the long shimmering brown tresses until they fell softly across her shoulders and down her back. Unable to resist the softness, he plunged his fingers into the dark mass and allowed the silky curls to caress his hands while he slipped them downward.

287

When Julia did nothing to prevent him from such an intimate action, his hands moved next to stroke the inner curve of her waist. There he found her sash and tugged at it until the bow gave way. As soon as he had the ends dangling, he pressed his hand against her, bringing her body back against his. While he continued the kiss, he edged the other hand slowly upward from the back of her waist around to her rib cage, slowly making his way to her breast. He noticed that her breathing became increasingly more ragged the closer he came to his treasured prize and realized she was his for the taking.

Although he had started out just wanting a kiss, his own desire had grown until he now longed for much more. He longed to possess more than just her sweet mouth. He wanted more than to touch the outside of her clothing. He wanted to feel her naked skin pressed against his. He wanted to possess her entire body. He wanted to make her his forever. And he wanted to do so now.

His whole body trembled with expectation while he continued his slow ascent to her right breast, knowing if he went too quickly he might frighten her. He drew in a deep, shuddering breath when he found it to be every bit as full and as firm as he had expected. The sensual moan that escaped her throat when he next grazed the sensitive tip let him know that he would not be chastised for what he had just done. For the first time in their relationship, he was in command. And knowing that excited him more.

Chapter Sixteen

Powered by an overwhelming desire to see her glorious breasts at the same time he caressed and molded them in his hands, Chad continued to kiss her hungrily while he moved his free hand to the tiny pearl buttons that held the back of her dress and worked frantically to release them. His heart pounded with growing anticipation when the back of the dress finally gaped enough to allow him to slip his hand inside and feel the velvety-warm skin beneath.

Quickly Chad found his way beneath the ruffled camisole she wore and soon caressed the breast with his hand, causing yet another current of mind-dazing warmth to shoot through her.

Julia gasped in response. But instead of pulling away and scolding him for having touched a place no other man had ever touched before, she responded to the fascinating sensations he had wrought by pressing heavily against his palm. Lost to such ecstasy, she ran her hands hungrily over his body, wondering if it was possible for her to bring him the same sort of pleasure he had just brought her. Did men react with that same volatile intensity or was this something reserved only for women?

Gently he played with the tip of the breast until it

grew rigid with a need so powerful, it caused her to gasp again with unexpected pleasure. Meanwhile, he used his free hand to ease the loosened garment down over her shoulders until it hung limply just below her waist. He followed by untying the tiny white satin sashes of the camisole so he could push that garment down out of his way as well. Finally, exposed to his view, was that which he so wanted to see.

Pulling away briefly, he allowed himself a leisurely view of her firm young breasts and her creamy white shoulders and found her every bit as exquisite as he had known she would be. He stared a long moment before bending forward to kiss first the nape of her neck, then the top of her breast before he returned his mouth to hers.

Again Julia leaned heavily against him, only this time he did not support her with his strength. This time he bent and gently lowered her to the ground, finding an instant bed in the thick green grass. He continued to supply his wondrous magic with a pliant kiss while he worked adeptly to remove the rest of her clothing. She did not fight him. Nor did her eagerness lessen when he reached to unbutton his own shirt and trousers. She was as lost to her passion as he was to his.

Wanting to feel her body pressed intimately against his, he broke away just long enough to remove his clothing, then quickly returned to her side. He possessed her mouth again and rolled partially on top of her, so overcome by his need to possess her completely, he could barely restrain himself. But it was important that this be a memorable experience for her, too. He wanted her to look back on this day with no regrets, which was why he held back his own response while he worked to bring her from one new height of arousal to another.

Chad continued to ravish her mouth with hungry

kisses while allowing his hands to explore every gentle curve of her body. She was soft and pliant to his touch, which made it increasingly harder for him to keep her pleasure before his needs, especially when he knew he could take her at any moment and find complete fulfillment.

Instead, he continued his exploration, tormenting her by trailing his fingers lightly over her delicate skin. While memorizing every contour of her body, he teased and he taunted, coming ever closer to the more sensitive areas with slow, circular motions, but never quite touching them.

Unable to bear such gentle torture, Julia arched her back, thrusting the breast high, wishing frantically that his hand would hurry and reach its destination. She wanted to feel that same wondrous feeling she had felt earlier when he had first dipped into her clothing.

Although somewhere in the hazy back regions of her mind, she knew that what they did was wrong, she was helpless to stop him. And when moments later, he again broke off the mind-dazing kiss, she moaned aloud with disappointment. How could he bring her to such a fine state of madness and not fulfill her needs—even though she was not all that sure just what those needs were! She just knew that her body ached for some form of release.

She moaned again and reached out to bring his magnificent mouth back to hers.

Chad obliged her with another long, ravaging kiss, but then pulled his lips away again. Only this time he did it to trail feathery kisses across her neck, then down her body. When he reached the nearest of her heaving breasts, he gently closed his mouth over the tip and drew deeply. Julia could not believe the wondrous effect that had on her. She curled her hands into tight fists to keep from crying aloud with pleasure while he worked a whole new kind of magic on her.

While his lips held the hardened tip in place and his tongue deftly teased the end with short, tantalizing strokes, his teeth nipped until she could no longer hold back her cry of pleasure. Just when she felt certain she could bear no more, he moved to her other breast and did the same. Again, he brought a cry of ecstasy from her lips. She shuddered repeatedly from the delectable sensations that continued to build inside her until she felt certain she would burst.

A luscious ache centered itself low in her abdomen and her whole body craved release from the sensual onslaught that burned uncontrolled inside her. She bit the sensitive flesh of her lips to keep from yet again crying aloud her need.

Chad could not keep silent a moment longer. He had to tell her what he was feeling. He had to be sure that she felt the same. "I want you, Julia. I want you more than I've ever wanted any woman before in my life. And I don't mean just for today. I want you for all time. I have fallen in love with you and I want you to marry me. This pleasure must be ours forever."

It was his mention of marriage that finally caused an alarm to sound, drawing Julia far enough back into the realm of sanity for her to realize what was actually happening. To Chad, this was more than just an act of passion. This was an act of love. He loved her. He wanted to *marry* her. But she couldn't marry him. She planned to marry Patrick. Patrick was the one who could offer her the sort of life she wanted. Chad could never do that. He had no money. He had no business skills. He wasn't even the type to stay in one place.

About the only thing Chad *could* provide her was this wondrous feeling of ecstasy. And the laughter they shared whenever they were together. But those weren't enough to sustain her. She needed much more.

Appalled by what she had allowed to happen, especially when she did not even want him to kiss her, she immediately shrank back and turned away. Shame burned her cheeks when she sat up and snatched her strewn clothing to her. She was not completely innocent of the ways of men. She had known from the onset that a kiss like that could lead to such intimate behavior. But she had allowed it anyway. She had not pushed him away nor had she tried to flee to the carriage and escape.

"That should never have happened," she said, her voice trembling. Her hands shook as well while she hurriedly slipped her camisole over her head then pulled her bloomers up over her legs and tied the waist back into place. She was barely able to find the arm openings of her dress when seconds later she yanked the garment down over her head.

"But it did happen," Chad responded. His eyes were still dark with unfulfilled passion when he reached forward to help her with the openings in her dress. "There's no use pretending that it didn't."

"Still, it shouldn't have." She sucked in a sharp breath when she finally worked her head through the top of the dress and she saw that his hands were lifted in her direction. Her first thought was that he intended to finish what he had started by pulling her back into another passionate embrace, then felt a different kind of shame when instead he helped her with the many buttons of the garment. "I never should have allowed it. I am in love with another man and if he ever finds out what happened, he will think the very worst of me. I could end up losing the very man I hired you to help me marry."

Chad's expression hardened while he continued to

help her with her clothing. He seemed oblivious to the fact that he was still naked. "I don't understand how you can do that. How can you sit there and tell me that you're in love with another man and that you still want to marry him after what just happened? After having responded to me the way you just did?"

"That's just the point," she said, and lifted her troubled gaze to his the moment her dress was refastened. Her thoughts were still spinning in all directions and her heart still pounded with a great force. "I never should have responded at all."

"But you did. you responded in such a way that I have to question the claim that you are still in love with another man."

"Why?" She frowned deeply while she glanced around to see what had become of her hairpins. Finally she remembered he had them in his shirt pocket. "Do you think just because I responded to your kiss that I am in love with you? That's impossible!" she said, trying to deny even to herself the importance of what she felt for this man while she snatched up his shirt and dug into the pocket for her hairpins. "You just caught me off guard is all."

He watched while she lifted her fumbling hands, twisted her hair back into place, then quickly jabbed the twisted pins into the bulk. "I think it is more than me having caught you off guard. A lot more. Don't you think it's just a little possible that you are in love with me, too?"

"No!" she refuted. She looked at him directly and felt a strong shiver of dread wash over her when she noticed how intently those pale-blue eyes stared at her. And how he did not seem at all concerned with the fact that he was still naked. She tried not to look down at his magnificent body. "I'm *not* in love with you. And what's more, I don't *want* to be in love with you."

"Why not?" He finally reached for his underwear and trousers.

"Because it would ruin everything." Tears burned her eyes. "Don't you understand? I *have* to marry Patrick."

"No, I *don't* understand," he answered calmly, though a tiny muscle pulsed near the back of his jaw letting her know just how upset he really was. "Why do you think you *have* to marry Patrick Moore?" He jammed his legs into his underdrawers then pulled the garment lithely over his hips. His trousers followed. "What makes *him* so special? The fact that he has agreed to run your father's businesses for you so you will be free to stay home and paint whenever you want? Or is it because he obviously has plenty of money and can provide you with the sort of life you've lived with your father? Or maybe it's because he has vowed not to be a controlling husband like some men might and has agreed to let you make all your own decisions?"

Julia's eyes rounded. She paused in the middle of buckling her boot. "How do you know all that?"

"I have my ways," was all he would say, not wanting to get Pearline into trouble. "It's true, isn't it? The real reason you want to marry this man is because he has promised to take over your father's businesses and leave you free to pursue your art."

"But those are not the *only* reasons."

"What other reasons are there?" He kept his gaze directed at her though he had to give part of his attention to the tiny buttons down the front of his shirt.

Julia lifted her chin proudly. "Well, for one thing, it just so happens he loves me very much. He also respects me and has promised to take care of me in every way a husband should. Yes, it's true he intends to take over Father's businesses for me so I can be free to do whatever I want, but that's only because he understands how important my art is to me. He knows the joy I feel when I am putting images on canvas. He also knows that I have no desire to spend the rest of my life running Father's businesses."

She paused to watch Chad. He was dressed now except for one boot, which he had trouble tugging over his heel.

"If I marry Patrick, I won't have to worry about managing Father's businesses at all. Patrick has a very good head for business and is willing to sell everything he already owns just so he can come here and eventually take over Father's lumber companies for me. Patrick loves me that much. He loves me enough that he's willing to devote the rest of his life to making me happy. Which is something I doubt very seriously you will ever be able to say about anyone. You are too much of a loner and a drifter to ever devote your life to *anyone*."

After finally tugging his second boot into place, Chad studied her for a long moment, then shook his head. "You are wrong. I would be more than willing to devote the rest of my life to making you happy in any way I could. I really have fallen in love with you. I love you more than I have ever loved any woman."

"Don't say that!" she replied with a look of sheer horror, then stood and headed immediately for the carriage. "It's not true! We haven't known each other long enough for you to be in love with me."

Chad followed a few feet behind, determined to have his say. "Oh, but we have. And I do. I'm sorry if you don't like hearing it, but I know how I feel, and I do love you, Julia." He turned her to face him again just as she was about to lift her foot and climb back into the carriage. "I love you every bit as much as Patrick does, if not more. And it is obvious that you love me, too. At least to some degree."

"Don't say such things to me." She covered her ears in childlike protest. Her heart raced at an excruciating rate. His words had too much of a ring of truth to them. "I am not in love with you. I am in love with another man. I have my life all planned out and I don't need you stepping in trying to upset everything. I don't want to hear anymore. Take me home. Take me home, *now!*"

Chad grabbed her by the wrists and pulled her hands from her ears, then held them out to the sides. "Not until I make you understand that you *do* have feelings for me. Despite your strong desire not to, you *do* care for me—deeply. Julia, you are *not* the type of woman who could have allowed such a thing to happen with someone she doesn't care for."

Julia's shoulders slumped with defeat. "All right," she finally relented, then dropped her gaze to his shirtfront. "If I admit that I do have feelings for you, will you take me on home?"

"Immediately." As an act of faith, he let go of her wrists and put his foot on the carriage footstep to show he was ready to climb in and take her wherever she wanted. "All I want to do is hear you say it."

"Then I admit it." Reluctantly, she lifted her gaze to his. "I do have feelings toward you. Very strong feelings. But that does not mean I love you. Nor does it mean that I would be willing to give up my plans to marry Patrick just so I could be with you instead."

"But you do admit to having strong feelings for me," he stated, as if to verify the fact, then looked oddly contented when he climbed into the carriage and held his hand out to her. He was ready to keep his promise and carry her home. "Knowing that you've finally admitted it is certainly a step in the right direction."

Afraid to touch him again while her heart was still hammering, Julia ignored his hand and climbed in beside him unassisted. She needed time to collect her thoughts and come to better terms with the startling emotions Chad had stirred to life. She sat quietly beside him during the ride back to the house.

As soon as the carriage rolled to a stop in the side yard Julia climbed down. She told Chad to be on his way, explaining that she wanted him to be gone when her father returned so the man would not be able to confront him with his anger just yet. With Chad already gone, her father would have no choice but to sit and stew for at least one more day. Either that, or ride all the way into town to confront him at the hotel.

But aggravating her father further was not the real reason she wanted Chad to leave. She was ill prepared to sit across the dining table from him so soon after what happened between them that afternoon.

"You want me back over here tomorrow afternoon?" Chad asked, taking his orders in easy stride.

Having expected an argument to stay, Julia looked at him curiously. "I suppose so. But not until it is nearly time for Father to arrive."

He showed no disappointment at having to wait until then. "And what about Wednesday? Are we still headed to Marshall to repeat the performance on Wednesday?"

Julia's eyes widened, not sure which performance he meant—the one at the mill or the one that followed. "Yes, I still want us to visit Father at his shipping yards and be seen at one of our favorite restaurants. But I think we should plan on having Pearline along with us. I don't think we'd be able to get around not having her with us a second time."

Chad paused, his expression unreadable beneath the

shadow of his wide-brimmed hat while he studied her. "Whatever you say. After all, you're still the boss."

Julia looked toward the house, making certain no one had come outside. When she returned her gaze to his, she spoke in a voice just loud enough for him to hear. "I'm glad you see it that way, and if whatever I say still goes, then pay attention when I tell you that what happened today will never happen again. I don't want you thinking that it will."

"Whatever you say," he repeated, but did not look too terribly convinced when he gave the front of his hat a polite tug, then snapped the reins and started the carriage rolling again.

Julia watched while the carriage slowly turned toward the main gate. She fought a very strong desire to call out to him. But she knew that would serve no purpose other than to cause him to turn around, which might allow her to see his handsome face again, but would lead him to believe that she was having second thoughts about having asked him to leave.

She could not let him know what was in her heart for fear he would take that knowledge and use it to control her like he did earlier. Just the thought of being lost again to his charms made her legs ache and her pulses throb.

Julia waited until Chad was through the gate and almost to the main road before slowly heading toward the house. She was a little surprised when only minutes later, before she had come up the veranda steps, her father came riding in on a borrowed horse, his face red with rage. He rode the animal right up to the front steps.

"Where have you been?" he demanded even before he had dismounted.

"With Chad," she answered, her eyes round with surprise. She had not expected her father to leave his work to follow them. Because he had mentioned having an important meeting at one-thirty, she had expected him to send one of his workers instead. Obviously, he was a lot angrier than she had predicted.

"*Where* with Chad?" he demanded, then lifted his weight up off the saddle and dropped to the ground. "I've ridden down both roads here and did not pass you on either one." His eyes narrowed into two angry slits when he marched toward her.

"That's because we took the short way across Mr. Andrews's land." Although the little girl in Julia cowered at the black rage she saw in her father's eyes, she faced him squarely and stood her ground.

Charles took the steps two at a time in his haste to confront her. "The short way? If it was so much shorter, then why is it you are just now arriving?" He stopped directly in front of her, his arms stiff at his sides. "And don't you dare try to tell me you've been here for quite some time because I've already been by once. Besides, I saw him turning onto the main road just a few minutes ago."

Not certain whether she should be pleased or worried by such unexpected rage, Julia swallowed hard, then gave the answer she had intended from the onset. "Chad drove slowly. I told you, we had a lot of things we wanted to discuss."

"Like what?" he asked, his tone clearly accusing. "Like how beautiful he finds you? Or perhaps he wanted to discuss how tempting your lips are. Did he kiss you?"

"Oh, Father," she replied, sounding duly annoyed.

300

"Of course he kissed me. We happen to be *very* much in love." She blinked when she realized how convincingly she had just declared their love. "There is nothing wrong with me kissing the man I love, and don't try to tell me that there is. People in love kiss. It is as simple as that." She cocked an eyebrow. "Didn't you ever kiss Mamma before you two were married?"

Charles's angry expression became a little less intense. "Don't try to turn this around by changing the subject. Besides, *that* was different."

Aware that she had him on the defensive she knotted her forehead into a questioning frown. *"How?* How was you kissing Mamma different from Chad kissing me?"

"Well, for one thing I was a lot older then than you are now. I was twenty-seven when I met your mother."

"That may be true, but *Mother* wasn't twenty-seven. She was much younger than I am now when you two married. She was only nineteen."

"That doesn't matter. The situation was different." Even though much of the anger had left his voice, his eyebrows had pulled together until they formed a thick white line. "Robert Freeport was trying furiously to convince both her and her folks that she should marry him. But she didn't want to and was afraid if we didn't act quickly, her parents might do something to force her into such a wedding." He looked away for a moment, his gaze distant. "Like me, your mother knew from the very moment we met that we were made for each other. We were so very much alike." He looked at Julia again. "You and Chad are not."

"That's *your* opinion." She narrowed her gaze to show intended defiance and wondered why his anger had so suddenly calmed. If she wanted her plan to work, she had to get him angry again and keep him that way.

"That's right. It *is* my opinion and as your father I'm entitled to give it. I realize that Chad is a very handsome young man, but he is also rude and he's brash. He is not the right man for you. He could never make you happy."

Although that was exactly what Julia had wanted her father to think, she felt oddly compelled to argue in Chad's favor. Instead, she tried a different approach. "Aren't you forgetting your promise, Father?"

"What promise?" Charles fidgeted and looked away again.

"The promise to wait until at least Saturday before passing any final judgments concerning Chad," she reminded firmly. "This is only Monday."

Charles drew in a quick, sharp breath, then released it slowly. "You are right. I did promise you that. And I will keep that promise. I will try my best not to judge him *if* you will promise me that you won't go off alone with him again during that same time. It really is not a good idea for a pretty young lady like you to be off alone with an attractive man like that."

Smiling, aware she had already reached that same conclusion herself, she paused so he would think she was reluctant to award such a promise. "All right, Father. If it will make you feel better, I promise not to go off alone with Chad again before Saturday."

Turning her mouth into a pretty pout in an effort to look as she had just made a major concession, she turned and headed into the house with her shoulders slumped and her head down.

She wanted her father to feel sorry enough for her to leave her alone for a while so she could go to her room and collect her thoughts. She needed the chance to think through all that had happened in the past few weeks and find some way to come to terms with the powerful new emotions that still raged inside her.

Although she knew Pearline was waiting in the back of the house to hear about everything, Julia went directly to her room, closed the door, then flung herself across her bed. She was still too horrified by what had nearly happened between her and Chad during the short time they were alone to want to talk about it with anyone.

She needed to find a reason for her behavior. She had never allowed such intimacy before, so why had she allowed it that afternoon, and from a man she hardly knew? That sort of behavior was reserved for those people who were deeply in love and completely committed to spending a lifetime together—which they clearly were not. Although he had professed to having fallen in love with her, and she had admitted caring deeply for him, the emotions they felt for each other were not the sort that led to marriage.

She propped her chin in her hands and stared off at the open window with a worried frown. What would she do if she suddenly found herself in love with *two* men? How would she ever decide which one to marry?

But then, that question was pointless. She had *already* decided who she would marry. She would marry Patrick. Fervently, she closed her eyes and tried to bring his blond-haired, green-eyed image to the forefront of her thoughts so that she could remind herself why she remained so determined to marry him. But for the life of her she could not push aside Chad's handsome face long enough for a lasting image to form.

Angrily, she pummeled her pillows with her fists. "How dare you do this to me," she raged at Chad silently. "How dare you come into my life and confuse me like this when everything had already been so neatly planned."

Opening her eyes again and flopping over onto her back, she fell remorsefully silent knowing he had not come into her life uninvited. She had *asked* him to become part of it.

What had since happened between them was just as much her fault as it was his. If not more so. After all, she was the one who had thought of such an odd scheme. And she was the one who had laughed with him about some of the things he'd done while pretending to be her sweetheart and had encouraged him to do more. She was also the one who had let him touch her in such an intimate manner, even when her father was not around to witness it. She should have slapped him soundly for trying to kiss her again, but she hadn't. Nor did she try to get to the carriage and drive away. She had simply stood there like some mindless schoolgirl and let him have his way.

She moaned aloud her misery when she realized just how much of the blame lay with her. She had to admit that she had liked the feeling of passion that had so suddenly flared between them. She enjoyed falling victim to the powerful sensations he had awakened inside her. As badly as she hated to admit it, even to herself, she had wanted him to touch her. She had wanted him to make her feel like a true woman.

Julia shook her head in disbelief.

Despite the fact that Chad was not the man she planned to marry—and despite everything she still felt for Patrick Moore—some unknown part of her had wanted to know what it would be like for him to make love to her. What was worse, she knew in some small way, that she still did—even though allowing such a thing would ruin her chances of ever marrying anyone like Patrick. No man wanted a spoiled woman. At least not one worth having.

Yet she longed to find herself back in Chad's strong yet gentle embrace. At least once more.

Chapter Seventeen

Julia spent that entire night and most of the following morning trying to decide just what it was she felt for Chad. And despite a renewed resolve made in the wee hours of the morning not to fall victim again to Chad's undeniable charms, knowing it could serve no purpose other than to ruin her life, she caught herself at the window waiting eagerly for his arrival that following afternoon.

It had been only twenty-eight hours since she had last seen him, yet in that time she had missed him dreadfully. She had missed his playful teasing, and she had missed that deep, dimpled smile that always followed. But mostly, she missed being able to gaze into those strikingly blue eyes of his while she wondered who he really was and why he felt it so necessary to keep his identity from her. All she knew was that he was from Charleston, South Carolina, liked to work outdoors, had a special craving for Ruth's apple pie, and was about as handsome as a man came.

Sighing, she pressed her cheek against the cool windowpane with a forlorned expression while she continued to watch the main road from her bedroom. Even though she did not really expect Chad for another hour, shortly before her father was due back home at six o'clock, she had hoped he would have missed her enough to come early. But obviously, that was not to be the case. He had not missed her enough to bother.

She wondered if that was because he had spent last evening in the company of his other lady friend. The one Pearline had told her about the day before. It was possible, for he certainly had had the time. But there was no way for Julia to know for sure.

Julia wished now she had sent Pearline on into town later so she could be certain where he had gone. The thought of him with another woman made her ache. She hated to think what it would be like when the day eventually came that he left there forever. No, she did not just *hate* to think about it, she *refused* to think about it. Refused to think about those empty days without him. They still had two weeks to be together, two weeks to enjoy each other's company while they worked together to make her father hate him. That was all she would focus on for now . . .

That and the guilt she felt because she no longer thought about Patrick, even though he was due to arrive in only a couple of weeks. She had tried to keep him in her thoughts for loyalty's sake, but she had found it so much easier to think about Chad instead. Especially after what had happened yesterday. Since then, he had claimed her every thought.

Julia tapped her foot impatiently while she continued to gaze out across the front lawn toward the main road, waiting to catch her first glimpse of his carriage. In the distance she could hear the faint chugging of the sawmill but heard no sounds that could be attributed to an approaching carriage.

She had tried sketching for a while, to help get her mind off him coming but that had only served to focus her thoughts more. She might have started out to sit by her open window and sketch a large, leafy red oak down near the river's edge, but what she had ended up sketching were the strong lines of Chad's face instead—in minute detail. It was then she realized just how much her feelings for him had grown in the past few days. Why, that morning she had even caught herself wishing *he* could be the one she planned to marry instead of Patrick!

But that was a ridiculous notion. Chad was a drifter. A man with a hidden past and not a penny to his name. He would never make a good husband. Still, she could not help but wonder what it would be like for him to become a permanent part of her life.

Sighing again at the futility of such frivolous thoughts, she continued to watch the empty road. If only he would come early. Then perhaps they could spend a little time together before her father returned and Chad once again had to pretend to be the crude, overbearing buffoon her father thought him to be.

Her thoughts wandered to the night she'd first met him and at how shocked she had been to see that Pearline had found her someone so handsome. She became so lost to the memory of him standing there in the moonlight looking at her as if she were one planting short of a row that she was only vaguely aware that a carriage had just appeared over the hill and was now headed toward the house. Her heart jumped when her thoughts finally resurfaced and she realized Chad was on his way.

Exhilarated by the realization he had come early after all, which meant he had to have missed her at least to some small degree, she hurried to the mirror to make sure every hair was still in place. She also checked the sapphire-blue gown she had chosen to make sure it hung just so, then decided not to wait for Abraham to announce him. She snatched the sketchbook and charcoal she left lying beside the window and headed for the front stairs, wanting to pretend she was headed outside to sketch the lilies in the garden when he arrived. Her hope was that he would follow her and they could be completely alone for a while. Or at least out of earshot of the house.

With her heart hammering at an impossible rate, she scampered down the stairs like an eager child and did not slow her pace until she was nearly to the front door. Then, as if someone had pulled a brake to slow her gait, she eased into a graceful walk. Hoping to look as if she did not expect to find him already on her front lawn, she opened the mesh door that prevented insects from invading the house and swung lithely outside.

When she turned to catch a quick glimpse of him, her heart slammed abruptly against her chest with such force it left her feeling suddenly dazed.

Chad was not the one who had just driven up. Patrick was. And she could tell by the gleam in his eyes, he was extremely pleased to be there.

Chad had thought a lot about everything that had happened over the past few weeks and decided the time had come to convince Julia that not only did he truly love her, but, like Patrick, he longed to marry her. He could not allow Julia to continue thinking of him as a man who could be cast aside after only another couple of weeks, did not want her to continue thinking of him as merely a man she had hired to do a job for her. He had to find some way to convince her that what had happened between them yesterday was meant to be. It had been the result of a deep, growing love—not simply an act of casual passion. He had to find some way to make her see that what they shared was special.

Even though he was not quite ready to tell her who he really was—he did intend to do what he could to make her see that he was not the loner or the drifter she claimed him to be. He had to make her understand that he had both the ability and the desire to provide for her every bit as well as her beloved Patrick. Also he wanted her to know that he, too, would be very willing to take over the everyday running of her father's timber businesses, especially if it meant being able to come home to her at the end of each day.

With Solomon and Raymond to help with the running of his new ranch, he could easily find enough time to manage both his new place and all three of Charles's timber businesses. It would take dividing his time accordingly, but he really saw no problem in taking on everything. Truth was, he looked forward to it. He had always loved a challenge and would enjoy seeing both his and her father's concerns continue to prosper under his direction.

Now, if he could only convince Julia of all that without letting her know he was the hated new neighbor who did not want to sell his land. Convince her before it was too late. Before the impeccable Patrick Moore showed up and lured her away.

Chad climbed into the carriage to go on over to her house thinking that he had only two weeks left in which to win Julia's heart permanently. Two weeks to prove himself worthy of her and to become a vital part of her life.

And two weeks was not all that much time.

* * *

"Is that you, Patrick?" Julia asked with a puzzled expression, and crossed the veranda to have a closer look. Her stomach knotted with instant foreboding when she realized that indeed it was him. "But you weren't supposed to arrive for at least two more weeks. Why have you come so early?"

"I couldn't stay away any longer," he said, hurrying across the yard to greet her. He studied the house behind her when he neared the steps. "I had to see you."

Julia shook her head, as if that might help clear away the unwanted image. "But you promised to give me at least a month," she reminded him, her voice filled with apprehension. "I'm not ready for you to be here yet."

"You want me to leave?" He looked deeply insulted and pressed a hand against the front of his immaculately pressed day coat. As always, he was dressed in the latest of men's fashions. Today he wore a white summer suit with matching vest tailored to fit his slender body perfectly above polished black round-toed boots. She noticed that his blond hair had been recently cropped in the latest style. "Why? Is your father against me coming here?"

"No," she answered honestly, all the while trying to figure out just how to go about telling him what she had done. She was not all that certain he would approve of such a devious plan. "But then Father doesn't know too much about you yet."

Patrick looked even more insulted. "You've been home for nearly three weeks now and you haven't bothered to tell your father about us? What am I? Some shameful secret?"

"No." Julia offered a weak smile, knowing he had every right to be so upset. "I have mentioned you a time or two. Just like I've mentioned several of the other people I met while I was in St. Louis. But I haven't yet told him that you are special."

Patrick's look of concern faded then, as if that were a minor problem. He replaced it with that deep, winning smile of his. "Then we'll just have to tell him together."

"He's not here. He doesn't usually get home from the mill until nearly six. Sometimes later."

Patrick slipped his watch out of his vest pocket and glanced at it. "Then that should give us about half an hour to decide just how we plan to go about telling him." When he glanced back up and saw that her gaze had dropped to the watch, he held it out so she could view it better. "See? I still have it."

She smiled when she recognized the delicate etching, but the smile was short-lived. Patrick was two weeks early. That could ruin everything. Her father was not ready. *She* was not ready. And Chad was due to arrive at any minute. She had to convince Patrick to leave before Chad got there. But she had to do so without hurting Patrick's feelings.

She decided the best thing would be to admit what she had done and quickly explain her reasoning. "Patrick, I have something to tell you."

"Can't it wait until I've had a welcome hug?" he asked with a boyish pout and held his arms out to her to show his eagerness.

Thinking he deserved at least that, Julia went willingly into his embrace. Oddly, she did not feel the vibrancy she had expected when his arms closed around her and held her for a brief moment. It was that lack of vibrancy that caused her to frown when he released her and pulled away. Why hadn't she thrilled to be in his arms again? After all, it had been over a month since he had last held her.

"Now, what is it you wanted to tell me? Whatever it

is, it can't be as serious as your beautiful face makes it out to be." When his green eyes dipped to take in all of her, his gaze caught the sketch pad still in her hands. He turned his head so that he could see what she had drawn, then frowned. "Who's that?"

A tight knot formed deep in Julia's chest. She had not wanted Patrick to know what Chad looked like.

"That's what, or rather *who,* I have to tell you about." She gestured toward a nearby wicker chair, the same chair Chad liked to sit in when they came outside after eating. The knot in her chest twisted tighter when her mind placed Chad's image there instead of Patrick's. "Perhaps we should sit."

"I'd rather stand," he said firmly, his frown deepening. He snatched the sketch book out of her hands and glowered at the carefully drawn lines. "Just what is it you have to tell me and what does it have to do with this man? Who is he?"

Julia's legs ached with the need to sit, but if Patrick was determined to stand, then she would stand, too. She tried to take the sketch pad away from him for fear he might become angry and destroy it once she had admitted what she had done, but he held it just out of her reach.

"He's a man I hired to help me convince Father to let me marry you," she stated, her mind whirling with several different ways to explain what she had done. She decided the best way would be to start at the beginning and tell him just how the unusual ploy came about. "An idea came to me while I was on the train coming back home. Remember when I told you how Father had always found fault with the men in my life? How he had always found some reason for me not to marry them?"

Patrick nodded that he remembered, but did not pull his gaze off the sketch Julia had so painstakingly drawn.

"Yes, but you admitted that in most cases he'd been right."

"In most cases he was. But still, I was afraid he might do the same with you, and I didn't want that to happen. So I came up with a plan that might persuade Father to be more receptive to the idea of us marrying."

"And what sort of plan was that?" When he finally looked at her again, his expression was grim. Clearly he did not like what he knew thus far.

"I decided the easiest way to get Father to approve of you was to trick him into it by first pretending to be in love with someone else. Someone I *knew* Father would never tolerate. Someone who would pretend to be deeply in love with me all the while doing everything possible to provoke him. Someone Father would never approve of, who would be willing to pay call on me during those crucial weeks before your arrival. I wanted him to be abrasive enough that when I finally agreed with Father that perhaps he was not the man for me after all, Father would feel so relieved, he would gladly agree to let me marry you instead."

Patrick's eyebrows arched when he again looked at the drawing. "So you chose *this* man?"

"Actually, no. Pearline chose him. I sent her into one of the saloons in town to find someone who needed the work and that's who she came out with."

Patrick shook his head while he continued to look grimly at Chad's image. "I don't like this. I don't like this at all."

"Even though I did it for us?" she asked, wanting him to see that her intentions had been pure. "Even though the reason I hired this man was so you would end up looking like a sheer godsend in comparison?" She placed a hand on his arm to soothe his concern.

"There had to be another way to convince your father that I'm worthy. One that would not include this other man."

"If there was, I didn't think of it," she said in an attempt to dispel the guilt she felt, knowing he had every right to feel threatened. "But then again, the plan I came up with seems to be working. Chad keeps my father steaming."

"Chad?" Patrick repeated the name and glanced again at the sketch.

"That's his name. And it turns out he is a very good actor. He's played his part perfectly."

"I can hardly wait to meet him," he replied, although he did not sound all too sincere.

"Well, I'm afraid you are going to *have* to wait. At least for a little while because he has not yet quite accomplished all that I need for him to accomplish. That's why I want you to leave. Now, before Father gets home."

"Why?"

"Because I'm not ready for him to meet you. Chad has not yet made what I think will be an everlasting impression."

"But why does that mean I can't be introduced yet? I think having me around would give your father something to compare this Chad to. By having *me* here on my best behavior while this other man is here at his worst, it can only end up making me look all the better."

Julia frowned. "I hadn't thought of that."

"Well, think of this. It is the only way I'll let you continue with your farce. I want to be around to make sure this man you've hired understands his bounds."

Julia felt another sharp stab of guilt and decided it was the best way to handle the situation. At least with Patrick there, Chad wouldn't feel free to kiss her again. "You won't do anything to give us away?"

"Not as long as it is to my advantage not to," he answered as if that should have been obvious, then stepped inside the house. "Now show me where to put my things, then you can take me on a quick tour. This is sure some place your father has. Nice to see you told the truth when you described it to me."

Julia's eyes rounded at the thought of Patrick being in the same house with her father over the next several days. Surely something would happen to give her away. "Oh, but you can't stay here. Father would never allow it. Besides, you didn't let me know you were coming. We don't have a bedroom made ready."

Patrick smiled indulgently, as if talking with a small child. "How long can it take to put linens on a bed and set out a few towels?" he asked as he set the sketch pad on a nearby table, suddenly forgotten. "Besides, you have proved to be such a clever girl this far. You should be able to think of a way to convince your father to let me stay." He then turned and headed back outside to get his things.

Julia closed her eyes to fight the frustration building inside her, then hurried to follow.

Chad wondered about the other carriage when he first pulled into the yard. Never in the three weeks he had been visiting Julia had the Thorntons had other guests. He figured Charles did not want their friends knowing what an oaf Julia had picked.

Pulling his own carriage up beside the other, he wondered who the visitor might be and if that person would be easily aggravated should he need to make the person dislike him.

Annoyed to find that he would not have a moment alone with Julia before her father arrived, he hopped down from the high-backed seat and tethered his horse to the same iron railing as the other horse.

Thinking it now more important to impress Julia than it was to *un*impress Charles, Chad smoothed the sleeves of his new light-blue shirt, then bent to make certain the pant legs of his black trousers fell smoothly over his new boots. He had spent all afternoon purchasing this new outfit and was curious to see Julia's reaction.

Eagerly, he headed toward the front door and was not quite halfway across the shaded veranda when he heard Julia's voice within. Curious to see who she was talking to and to get an idea of the sort of visitor to expect, he stepped closer to the nearest window and peered inside. He was not at all pleased to find her standing in the entry with her back to him and her hand resting lightly on another man's arm.

While he watched them, a cold, pricking sensation washed over him. Though he had not seen any pictures to verify the fact, he knew immediately the man was Patrick Moore. It had to be. Why else would Julia be dressed like that, in a gathered gown made of blue silks and white satin? It certainly could not be because *he* had been expected. She did not dress like that when it was going to be just him there entertaining her.

Evidently dear Patrick had taken it upon himself to arrive a couple of weeks early and must have wired ahead to let Julia know, which dampened Chad's hopes considerably. He would not be given the opportunity to try to persuade Julia to his way of thinking after all—at least not without unwanted distractions from Patrick. That part of his plan was lost. A strong sense of defeat pulled at him while he continued to watch the two. He had not acted quickly enough. Now he was in direct competition with a man who had already stolen her heart.

But then again, the race was not run yet. Just because the opposition was now there in the flesh did not mean he had lost all chance to win her heart. It made the goal far more difficult, but not impossible. He should not consider Patrick the victor just yet.

With his resolve instantly restored, he backed away from the window. Aware he had not yet been noticed, he waited a few seconds to decide his plan of action, then stalked determinedly toward the front door, which had been left partially open.

He rapped sharply on the door and held his breath while he awaited her response. He so hoped not to see annoyance on her face when she spun around to face him.

Upon hearing his knock, Julia's hand flew from Patrick's coat sleeve to her throat when she twirled toward the door. Her brown eyes were stretched wide with what had to be fear. Clearly annoyance was the last thing she felt at that moment.

"Chad. You're here!" she gasped, stating the obvious. He could tell by the roundness of her eyes and the slight parting of her mouth that she was extremely nervous. Obviously, she did not like the idea of the two men, who both claimed to be in love with her, suddenly coming face-to-face.

"That I am," Chad responded, then forced a pleasant smile just before stepping inside. "Here again, ready to resume my duties."

Rather than wait for Julia to introduce them, aware of how awkward the situation was for her, he stuck his hand out to the blond man standing beside her and continued forward.

He was pleased to see that Patrick was at least two inches shorter than he and not nearly as fit. Judging by the tone of his skin, Patrick rarely spent any time out-doors.

"Let me guess," he continued with a friendliness he did not feel—especially when he spotted a large valise sitting just inside the door. Obviously the man planned to stay right there in the house with them. "You must be Patrick Moore. I've certainly heard a lot about you."

Looking as if every last drop of blood had drained from her face, Julia's dark eyes turned to Patrick while she waited to see if he would accept Chad's handshake. For several seconds it appeared he would not, then finally he lifted his hand and met Chad's with a firm grip.

"Looks like you have the advantage here," he answered. His green eyes locked with Chad's, as if to convey some secret message. "It seems I am just now finding out about you." Clearly Patrick was not pleased with what he had been told thus far when he gestured toward a sketch pad that lay faceup on a nearby table.

Chad glanced at the pad and was amazed at the perfect likeness he found there. He looked at Julia, truly impressed. Pearline was right. Julia was *extremely* talented. "You drew that?"

She nodded, then shrugged as if hoping to make light of it. "I had nothing to do this afternoon so I decided to draw you. I thought you might like to have a sketch to send to your lady friend in town."

She did not wait for Chad's comments. "So are you ready to face Father again?"

"That depends." He kept a light, conversational tone, for her sake. He knew by her pale expression that the last thing she needed at that moment was to have both men upset with her. "How angry is he over what we did yesterday?"

"Pretty angry. He did not like your behavior while

you were at the mill," she answered, choosing what she said carefully.

"Imagine that," he replied with a knowing laugh, aware that Charles had to have disliked what happened *afterward* even more. After all, they were off alone together for quite some time.

"Why?" Patrick looked at them with a curiously raised brow. "What happened yesterday at the mill?"

Julia glanced both at Chad and Patrick before answering. "Let's just say that Chad was not on his best behavior."

"Can I help it if his secretary doesn't like people poking around her desk?" he asked, as if not understanding what he had done wrong. He then looked at Patrick and shrugged. "He seems to think I'm only interested in how much money the place makes," Chad explained. "I think I may have come across as being a tad too curious about the financial end of things."

"How's that?" Patrick asked, obviously wanting clearer answers than he was getting.

"I will explain it to you later," Julia said, then gestured toward the front parlor. Chad noticed that some of the color had returned to her cheeks. "Why don't you two go in and make yourselves comfortable while I go warn Ruth that we will have one more guest for supper."

Chad wanted to chuckle at how easily Julia had avoided having to admit what else they had done to anger her father. He turned toward the main parlor, already headed for his favorite chair.

Chapter Eighteen

Julia did not know whether to feel relieved or worried that her father had agreed to let Patrick stay with them for the next several days.

After the way Patrick and Chad had behaved toward each other during dinner, she could not be sure that Patrick would continue to keep his promise to go along with her scheme. She worried he might become just angry enough with Chad's behavior toward her to reveal the truth to her father just so he could put an end to Chad's employment.

Clearly, Patrick did not like Chad—nor did Chad particularly care for Patrick. All through supper, the two had behaved like a pair of bandy roosters, each keeping a careful eye on the other. Patrick's feathers had ruffled noticeably each time Chad behaved boldly toward Julia—to the point she feared Patrick would come across the dinner table and strike him.

It did not console Patrick to know that Chad was being paid to behave like that. Nor that the end result could very well be to his own advantage. He clearly did not like the way Chad looked at her, nor did he care for the manner in which he occasionally reached out and touched her.

Patrick and her father already and one thing in common. Neither liked Chad. And because of the way Patrick bristled each time Chad did something that could be considered forward, Julia knew she might have a problem keeping Patrick from saying or doing something that might in the end reveal her scheme.

Chad seemed to be trying to provoke Patrick's anger. Evidently, he hoped that by causing a rift between them, Patrick would become disgruntled enough to leave, which in turn might give Chad a better chance to take up where they had left off the afternoon before.

Julia could tell by the piercing looks the two gave each other that each wanted the other out of the picture permanently. *She* wanted neither one out of the picture. She wished she could find some way to have them both be a part of her life.

"So, tell me Patrick, what brings you to east Texas," Charles asked as soon as he had lit the sulphur lamp to ward off the mosquitoes and settled comfortably in his favorite chair on the brightly lit veranda. Having moved his seat so that it faced the other three, he pulled out two cigars from his coat pocket and offered one to Patrick.

Julia tensed, hoping Chad would not feel insulted that he had not been offered a cigar while at the same time she prayed Patrick had not become so fed up with Chad's bold behavior that he might answer that last question with the truth. Her heart froze while she awaited his response.

"I'm not really sure," Patrick leaned back in his chair, having accepted the smoke offered him. He looked curiously at Chad, who seemed not at all surprised that he had not been offered one. "I guess I just wanted to come down here and see if Julia was right about this area. She had made the idea of living here sound so inviting, I thought I might check into the possibility of moving here myself."

"But aren't you pretty well tied down with that shipping company you own?" Charles asked. He bent forward to offer Patrick a match, then fell back into his chair, bit off the tip end of the cigar he had selected for himself, and lit the other end. Julia noticed that her father purposely left Chad out of the conversation.

"Not really. You see, my partners have been after me for quite some time to sell my third of the company to them so they can enjoy a larger portion of the profits. And I'll have to admit, their latest offer was quite generous." Having accepted the match, he struck it against his thumbnail, then touched the resulting flame to the end of his cigar. He took several long draws, then closed his eyes while he let out a large puff of smoke. "Good cigar."

"Chad there prefers a pipe," Charles said, as if that bore explanation. He then glanced at Chad and frowned. "By the way, where is your pipe? You are usually smoking that thing by now."

"I didn't think to grab it before leaving the hotel," he answered with a shrug. His expression remained unreadable when he met Charles's questioning gaze. "Guess that will have to wait until I get back."

"And when do you usually leave?" Patrick reached into his pocket and took out his watch. "It's after eight."

After seeing how quickly Chad's shoulders tensed, Julia decided to be the one to answer that. "He usually stays until after nine. Sometimes he's here until nearly ten. But that's because we do so enjoy having him here. Don't we, Father?"

Charles grunted rather than answer, and turned his attention back to Patrick.

"So, now that you've seen the place, do you think you might be interested in settling in this area after all?"

"Yes. Very interested." He cut his gaze to Julia. "But to be perfectly honest with you, sir, my main interest lies with your daughter."

Chad and Julia both sat forward as one, as if they had been charged by the same bolt of electricity.

"My daughter?" Charles asked, and looked clearly amused while he studied the growing length of ashes at the end of his cigar. "You find my daughter attractive, do you?"

"Yes, sir. Very much so. I have since the first day I met her."

Charles took several more puffs while he considered that last comment. "And just how did you meet my daughter?"

Julia's heart lurched. She could not let Patrick answer that. Her father would find the similarities far too peculiar.

"We met in a restaurant," she answered quickly, then cut her gaze to Patrick to let him know he was to go along with her on that. But Patrick's gaze was on Chad.

"No we didn't," he responded, and finally looked at her but too late to notice her meaningful expression. "Don't you remember? We met in the park. You were strolling along the walk nearest the river and accidentally dropped one of several letters you carried at the time. Because I was walking along right behind you, I picked up the letter and returned it to you. It was at that same moment, when you smiled to say thank you, that I became instantly smitten by your beauty."

Julia's stomach twisted into a hard knot while she tried to think of some rational explanation for how she had ended up meeting both these men in the exact same fashion. But nothing logical came to her.

"Daughter, you seem to have dropped a lot of letters while walking through the park," her father stated while he studied all three of them. "Is that the only way you know to go about meeting men?"

Julia glanced at the hands folded in her lap then again at her father and smiled sheepishly. "Well, it does tend to work."

Several seconds of awkward silence followed before Charles spoke again, this time to Patrick. "How long have you known Julia?"

"Several months," he answered, cutting a questioning gaze to Julia as if to ask if that was an acceptable answer.

"Oh, then you came here knowing that she was already in love with this other man?"

Julia closed her eyes briefly while she turned her thoughts heavenward, pleading silently for some form of divine intervention while awaiting Patrick's answer.

"Yes, but I came with hopes of changing her mind," he answered, looking quite pleased with himself for that answer. "To tell you the truth, sir, I can't see her marrying someone like this Chad Sutton. He's not the right sort of man for her."

Chad's shoulders stiffened, but he said nothing to defend himself. Instead, he waited for Charles's comment.

Charles's eyebrows had shot skyward at the young man's audacity. "And you are?"

Patrick met the older man's questioning gaze directly. "Yes, sir, I am. I have both affluence and a good, working knowledge of the social graces. Traits I'm afraid Mr. Sutton here does not possess. Clearly, I am the one who could provide a better life for her."

Julia did not like the direction of their conversation, so she tried to change it. She pointed out into the yard.

"Oh, look. Did you see that? A firefly. And so late at night. Can you imagine?"

No one seemed to care that there might be a misguided firefly out trying to light up the night. The conversation continued as if she had not spoken at all. Chad was next to comment.

"You may have plenty of money and know a lot more about manners and the like, but it just so happens she loves *me*," he said. His expression grew rock hard while his icy blue gaze clashed with Patrick's angry green. "We plan to be married just as soon as we can get her father's approval."

"Which might not be coming," Charles pointed out.

"But then again, it doesn't really matter if you approve of our marriage or not. We love each other. We'll get along just fine even without your permission."

Charles studied him a long moment, then leaned over to thump his ashes into the surrounding flower bed. "You do know that if Julia decides to marry you without my permission, you will get no money from me? Unless Julia marries someone I approve of, she will be immediately written out of my will."

Patrick's green eyes expanded until he finally managed to blink, but he made no comment. Instead, he waited to hear what Chad had to say.

"It just so happens we won't be needing your money. I'll provide for her just fine. Truth is, I got quite a bit of money of my own stashed away. Enough to take care of us both for many years to come."

Charles looked at him, clearly doubtful. "On a liveryman's wages?"

"I think you'd be surprised by what this liveryman has earned and put away in the last few years."

Aware the two were on the verge of a full-scale dispute, during which Patrick would undoubtedly side with her father, leaving Chad sorely outnumbered, Julia stood and held out her hands to stop them from saying anything else.

"Father, Chad already knows that if I marry anyone without first getting your approval, I am to be written out of your will. He also knows that we'll risk never being allowed to visit here again. There is no point in discussing this further."

She turned to Patrick at an angle where her father could not see her face, then narrowed her brown eyes to give clear warning. He was causing complications. "And I'm flattered that you have these feelings for me, Patrick, but I'm sure it is not something Chad wants to hear. Therefore, either we talk about something that is agreeable to *all* of us, or we don't talk at all."

For the next several minutes no one spoke. Each merely stared angrily at the others. It was Ruth who eventually broke the brooding silence.

"Mr. Thornton?" she called. She stuck her graying head out a nearby window rather than go all the way to the door. "If you are through with me, I'll be heading on off to my bedroom now."

Having finished his cigar, Charles stubbed the ashes against the bottom of the banister, then tossed the butt carelessly into the nearby flower garden.

"That'll be fine, Ruth." He slowly pushed himself out of his chair and carefully stepped around Julia, who did not move out of his way. "Considering the day I've had, I think I'll be heading on off to bed, too."

He walked on toward the door, but paused after having gone only a few feet. "Glad to have you as a guest, Mr. Moore. If you need anything while you are here, just let me know."

Julia knew that the only reason her father had said that was because he had wanted to remind Chad of the annoying fact that Patrick was to be their guest and he was not. She glanced at Chad to gauge his reaction and was not too surprised to see a very grim expression.

Not wanting to face time alone with these two, and not about to leave them to each other's company, she quickly stepped forward and presented her elbow to Chad. "I'm tired, too. Come, let me walk with you to your carriage."

When both Patrick and Chad stood at the same time, she knew she had yet another problem. Patrick intended to be included in whatever they did.

"No, we will *both* walk him to his carriage," he stated firmly, then crossed his arms to show the decision was final.

"But that might raise questions with Father," she countered, wanting a chance to apologize to Chad for some of what had been said that night and explain that she'd had no idea Patrick planned to arrive early. "Father will be expecting Chad and me to go alone."

Patrick shook his head. "Not when you consider the fact that I have already declared my feelings toward you." Patrick's voice was edged with anger and impatience. "On the contrary. He will think me very clever not to let you two go off alone. That is why we will *both* walk him to his carriage."

Unable to think of another logical reason for Patrick to have to stay behind, she finally relented. "All right. We'll both walk him there. But, remember, it should look as if I am more interested in pleasing Chad than you."

"As long as you remember who it is you *really* want to please. Don't go forgetting that it is *me* you are in love with and plan to marry." He looked at Chad pointedly. "Or that the whole reason you hired this man was so your father would better approve of me."

Chad studied Julia's apologetic expression for a moment, then shook his head to prevent her from saying anything else. "There's no need for either of you to walk me. I can find my way easily enough." Then, without allowing further discussion, he started in the direction of the stairs.

Julia's heart wrenched while she watched Chad cross the yard with long, even strides, as fascinated as ever with the man's easy movements.

Before she could think of a logical reason to call out to him, he had lit the lanterns attached to his carriage, climbed into the front seat, and was gone.

Pearline opened the door to Julia's bedroom and slipped inside without bothering to ignite any of the lamps. Just enough light spilled in from the hallway to let her make her way to Julia's dressing table, where she kept her expensive perfumes.

Soundlessly, Pearline picked up a small, cut-glass bottle, sprayed the delicate scent across the base of her neck, then set the bottle back down. Even though it could be hours yet before Chad left and she would be allowed to follow him, she wanted to be ready. She did not want to miss even a minute of her time alone with Solomon.

Having so quickly accomplished what she had come into the darkened room to accomplish, she turned to leave through the same door she had entered. But before she had spun completely around, a light outside caught her attention. Curiously, she stepped over to the window.

"Oh, my!" she gasped when she realized Chad had already prepared his carriage and was about to climb inside.

She wondered why he had decided to leave so early, then realized that it probably had something to do with the fact that Mr. Patrick was now there and would be directing all their actions. Mr. Patrick had always been very possessive of Missy and would not want Chad hanging around her any longer than was necessary.

Which was perfectly all right with Pearline. Her heart jumped excitedly at the thought of being able to leave early. It meant she could spend an extra hour or so with Solomon, which she longed to do. Because Chad had not been there for her to follow the night before, she had not had her usual excuse to leave the house.

Grabbing her skirts and hiking them well out of her way, she hurried through the door, toward the back stairs where she could slip outside without being noticed. She could hardly wait to see Solomon's face when she arrived at his door over an hour early.

Solomon glanced at the clock when he entered the back door. Eight-forty. That should give him just enough time to take quick bath and put on some clean clothes. Having worked outside in the hot sun most of the day, he was sticky with sweat and knew that the accompanying odor would not be conducive to the sort of kiss he planned to steal from Pearline this night.

Smiling at the mere thought of seeing his beautiful Pearline again, knowing it had been two long days since he'd last set his gaze upon her, he hurriedly set the laundry tub he used for his bath in the middle of the kitchen floor and filled it with cold water before peeling out of his clothing. Knowing from past experience that Pearline could arrive as early as ten o'clock, he did not take the time to light a fire in the stove or heat a kettle of water. He wanted to be dressed and ready when she arrived.

Because the tub was too small to allow his large frame to sit comfortably, he merely squatted in the water while he worked a quick lather over his body and in his hair. It wasn't until he was nearly through cupping the water and rinsing the soap away that he realized he had forgotten to grab a towel out of the cabinet.

Pearline was so excited over the prospect of seeing Solomon again that she could hardly hear above the rapid pounding of her heart when she climbed down from the horse she had ridden and hurriedly wrapped the reins around the post nearest to Solomon's house. Because Chad had left so unexpectedly, her brother did not have one of the carriages ready for her as he normally did. Rather than wait for him to rig one out, she had decided to have a horse saddled instead.

Even though she knew how to ride bareback, having been taught by her Indian grandmother Weeping Branch, she chose not to. She knew that riding next to the animal's bare skin might cause her clothing to pick up the horse's smell and she didn't want to take that chance. Not after having gone to all the trouble to sneak into Missy's room and spray herself with her most expensive French perfume.

Stepping away from the post, she took just a moment to smooth her skirts, which this time were her own and not Missy's. She had spent her last month's earnings on this gown and wanted to make certain she looked her very best before approaching the house where Mr. Thornton's old overseer used to live.

Remembering the stories of what a contrary old man that overseer had been, she was glad the place was now

Solomon's home, though she hated to think that it no longer belonged to the Thornton family. But then, she was there to help change that, wasn't she? She was there to work on getting the place back for Mr. Thornton and earn herself that acre of land in the process. Her heart fluttered at the thought of being a landowner and eventually having a small house of her own.

The fluttering became even stronger when she thought of Solomon sharing that house with her. What a fine thing that would be! Smiling at the images that thought produced, she stepped up onto Solomon's porch, and heard him singing happily inside. Pleased with how deep and resonant his voice sounded, she rapped lightly at the door, then stepped back to wait for him to open it for her.

A second later, Solomon called out something from just the other side of the door, but she could not quite make out his words. Thinking it must have been orders for her to come in and eager to see what the inside of his house looked like, she took a deep, calming breath, then turned the knob and opened the door.

Her hands went immediately to her throat when she spotted Solomon standing inside a small laundry tub, buck naked and dripping wet.

"Pearline!" He glanced around for something to cover himself with but found nothing. "What are you doing here?"

"I—I came early." Although she knew she should turn away, at least long enough for him to find his clothes, she could not. Her unblinking eyes were frozen to the magnificent male body that stood before her.

"So I see," he said, then, as if aware it was too late to cover himself anyway, stepped over Ruby, who slept on the floor nearby and walked calmly over to the cabinet and pulled out a large towel. Slowly, he bent to dry himself.

"I—I wanted to surprise you," she continued, thinking her brash actions needed further explanation.

"Well, you did that," he admitted, then with the towel still dangling from his hand, he gestured casually toward the door, as if it was an everyday occurrence to have a woman in his house while he dried off from his bath. "I'd appreciate it if you'd shut that. It's creating a draft in here."

Too embarrassed to argue that the door should remain open, for propriety's sake, Pearline did immediately as told, then wet her lips nervously when she turned to look at him again. "I'm sorry to have disturbed your bath, but when I knocked, I thought I heard you tell me to come in."

"No. What I did was ask who was there," Solomon explained in an oddly relaxed tone while he headed over to the table where he had left his clean clothes. Because the house was so small, there were no walls dividing the kitchen where he stood and the parlor where she stood only a few yards away. "I thought maybe it was Raymond coming to return the gloves he borrowed earlier today. The man wore a hole clean through his own pair."

Pearline continued to watch Solomon's movements, truly fascinated, while he unfastened the front of his underdrawers, then slipped the soft white garment up over his well-muscled legs. "I guess I should have waited to make sure what it was you'd said."

"Doesn't matter. I'm just glad your here." He then gestured toward the tub before looking down to close the front of his drawers. "You're the whole reason I was willing to take that cold bath. I was pretty sweaty from all the work we did today and knew you wouldn't be too taken with the way I smelled."

Pearline was flattered to know he wanted to please her. "I appreciate the deed," she said in a playful tone. "But I didn't come over here to smell you."

"Oh?" he asked. He had just pulled on his trousers, but paused to meet her gaze before actually buttoning them. "And just why *did* you come?"

"Why, to see if Mr. Andrews had made an appearance yet, of course," she answered with a false innocence. "Why else would I bother comin' all the way over here so late at night?"

Solomon stopped working with his trousers, leaving the top two buttons undone, and headed directly toward her. His dark gaze locked with hers while he slowly closed what little distance had lain between them. "I was hoping that by now one reason might have to do with wanting to see me."

Pearline's smile deepened while he came closer, knowing that *he* was the reason why she had come. She had not expected Mr. Andrews to be there. She had wanted to see Solomon, although she had not expected to see quite so *much* of Solomon upon her arrival.

While he continued toward her, her gaze roamed across his broad shoulders, still damp with the tiny droplets of moisture the towel had missed, then moved up to take in the handsome lines of his face. When he came to a stop only a foot away, something in the shimmering depths of those coal-black eyes held her captive, making her stare at him like an enamored child.

"I guess that might have a little somethin' to do with it," she finally admitted. Her legs quaked at the thought of his being that close to her while still mostly undressed. She swallowed hard when he reached out to touch her cheek with the curve of his hand.

Tremoring from his gentle caress, she continued to gaze longingly at his handsome face, wondering why he had felt it necessary to stand that close when she could have heard him just fine from across the room. "It just so happens I am right partial to your company."

"As I am right partial to yours," he said, his head already bent to claim her lips in a long, sweetly violent kiss.

A waterfall of tiny shivers cascaded over Pearline when she felt his possessive mouth claim hers. Knowing it was exactly what she wanted, her heart beat a crazy rhythm, causing her legs to quiver more and her senses to spin alarmingly. This was the kiss she had dreamed about for weeks now, ever since he'd taken that one from her in his boss's kitchen. She responded by slipping her arms around his bare shoulders and holding him tightly to her, drawing him closer.

Solomon moaned, and the kiss intensified. Before Pearline realized what was happening, he had bent to gather her into his arms and was headed for the bedroom door, which stood open. She knew that if she had any intention of protesting what was about to happen, she had better do so right then; but no protest was forthcoming. Truth was, she had never felt so driven by any man and was eager to find out what passion lay between them.

She returned his kisses with fiery hunger, and when he bent to lay her gently upon his bed, she refused to let go of him. She brought him down with her.

While snuggling securely in his arms, she met his kisses with the ferocity of a starved woman. Instinctively she parted her lips to allow him easy access into her mouth. The pleasurable feelings when his tongue dipped lightly inside drove her to the point of sheer madness and she responded by pressing her hands into his back, urging him on. She was ready to give herself fully to this man. She was ready to become a woman.

Chapter Nineteen

Solomon needed no further urging from Pearline. Eagerly, he slipped his hand between their bodies and felt first her waist then her rib cage before moving upward to cup one of the firm round breasts that rose and fell rapidly beneath her clothing. The tip was already rigid, making him aware of her needs—needs that in no way surpassed his own.

While lying more to the side than atop her so as not to crush her with his weight, Solomon allowed his hand to continue its easy exploration of the soft curves of her body. He ran his fingertips across the smooth, satiny fabric of her bodice while he imagined what lay beneath. Then when he could wait no longer, he dipped his hand behind her to unfasten the buttons.

Just as soon as he had an opening large enough, he slid his hand inside, working his way underneath her cotton chemise until he again cupped the velvety-brown treasure that awaited him. He found deep pleasure in hearing her sharp intake of breath the moment his thumb came into contact with the hardened tip.

While his mouth continued to sample the sweetness of her lips, he continued to tease the peak of her breast lightly with his fingertips. She moaned aloud with pleasurable response and she trembled in anticipation when he reached around and finished unbuttoning the gown. Soon he was able to tug the loosened garment up over her head and toss it easily out of the way. A scant second later, her undergarments and boots followed, then his own trousers and underdrawers.

He pulled her to him, pressing her soft, warm curves against his hard frame. Her fingers dug deep into his back when his mouth left hers to trail hungry kisses down the slender brown column of her neck, pausing at the pulse point in the hollow of her throat before resuming the path downward. The closer he came to his destination, the shorter Pearline's breaths became and the harder her hands pressed into the muscles along his shoulders, urging him on.

Seconds later, when his mouth moved to claim the straining breast, Pearline quivered in response. She arched her back to give him easier access to the sweet mound he had so eagerly sought.

Tenderly, he suckled one breast while fondling the other with his hand, bringing her more and more unbearable pleasure, until her head tossed restlessly from side to side. His desire grew with each tiny moan that escaped her lips. Soon he knew he could wait no longer.

Gazing down at her beautiful passion-filled face, he moved to take her gently. He was pleased when he met with resistance and his first gentle thrust brought forth a tiny whimper of pain. He was her first lover. And he would be her last. He would see to that by convincing her to marry him. He had finally found the woman with whom he wanted to share his life.

"I'll be gentle," he vowed, his words but a warm whisper against her cheek. With deliberate slowness, he moved within her, allowing her to get over the initial pain and become used to the feel of him. After he sensed her body gradually relax, he moved with more force until she finally moved with him. Before long, they reached the same frenzied level of passion.

"Solomon. Oh, Solomon," Pearline called out between short, raspy breaths as she soared ever higher into the unknown. Her entire body trembled with a deep need for release. "Solomon, please."

Seconds later, at almost the same earth-shattering moment, the two lovers crested the zenith of their passion. They gasped at its body-shuddering force again and again before drifting into the hazy realms of fulfillment.

For several moments, Solomon lay beside Pearline, holding her in his arms like a precious gem. He was still too stunned by the sheer power of what had just occurred between them to find the words he needed.

Pearline was the one who finally spoke, her tone filled with awe as she stared at the newly patched ceiling. "I knew from the many books I've read that it would be wonderful, but that was even more glorious than I'd ever imagined."

Solomon lifted up on one elbow and gazed at her. Her eyes when she turned to gaze at him looked like two black jewels in a sea of brown velvet.

"Yes, it was," he agreed serenely, then reached out to rest his hand on her stomach, aware of how possessive he felt of her. "But I'm surprised you let it happen, considering we've only known each other a few weeks. Why did it happen? Why did you let me make love to you so soon?" he asked, hoping to encourage words of love. He wanted to know exactly how she felt about him before mentioning the possibility of marriage. He didn't think he could bear being turned down by her.

Pearline blinked at such a question, then looked away. "I thought it was what you wanted."

Solomon fell silent while he thought about his answer. "And why do you suppose it was so important to do what I wanted?" When the words of adoration he had hoped to hear did not follow immediately, his stomach knotted with the sudden, sickening awareness that love had had nothing to do with it. At least not on her part. Quickly he shoved away from her and climbed out of the bed.

Angry, and feeling used, he turned his back to her while he bent to snatch up his clothing. "I understand. You thought that by giving me what I wanted, I'd be a little more willing to help you convince my boss to sell his house and at least half this land to your boss." He hurried to dress. "Well, I hate to disappoint you, but you thought wrong. I have no intention of interfering in this matter either way. The only reason I ever agreed to let you even talk to him is because I wanted you to have a good reason to come back over here. I thought I might like getting to know you better."

When Pearline did not respond, he turned back to face her, not surprised to find that she had already gathered her clothes and, like him, was busily yanking them back on. She already had her chemise on and was wriggling into her underskirt.

"You flatter yourself, Mr. Ford," she said angrily while she hurriedly tied the sash of the underskirt. "Your intervention is not that important. It just so happens I can handle this matter without any of your help at all."

"Then why did you do what you just did?" He paused to watch while she continued to pull her clothes back on. "Why were you so willing to give me what I wanted?"

Her eyes narrowed while she strained to grasp the buttons behind her. "I have no intention of answerin' that."

"Why not? What are you hiding?"

"I'm not hidin' nothin'. It just so happens that it ain't none of your business what my reasons are. All you need to know is that nothin' like that is ever goin' to happen again between us."

Solomon felt his heart breaking into tiny pieces while he watched her finish refastening her dress then hurriedly sit forward to pull on her boots. "Will you at least tell me why it is so important to you that your boss get his hands on my boss's land? What's he paying you to do this favor for him?"

"That ain't none of your business, either!" she said, lifting her chin proudly after making sure her boot was securely fastened.

Solomon noticed her lower lip trembling and he felt as sorry for her as angry. She had so hoped her scheme would work. "And just what is my business?"

"Nothin'. Especially nothin' to do with me." Tears filled her eyes while she smoothed her skirts. "I am right sorry about what happened here tonight, but you don't have to worry about nothin' like it happenin' ever again. I won't be back over here until I know for certain Mr. Andrews has finally arrived, and then it will be to speak directly with him and not to you."

She stood then, gave a quick look around to make sure she left nothing behind, then walked proudly out of the room. She paused only long enough to yank open the front door before marching directly toward the horse.

Solomon followed only as far as the front porch, then stood with his hands curled into hard fists against his hips, wondering how he could ever have considered marriage to such a confounded woman.

* * *

When Julia heard the light rapping at her door shortly after having pulled on a lightweight cotton gown, she was not sure whether she would find Pearline or Patrick on the other side. But because she did not want her father knowing that either one had paid her a visit so late at night, she hurried to slip into her dressing robe so she could open it and have whoever it was come inside.

She hoped it was Pearline. She was curious to find out if Chad had gone to that other woman's house again after having left earlier than usual last night. She was also curious to find out whether Pearline's evening with Solomon had gone as agreeably as she had hoped, glad her maid had a chance of finally finding some happiness. She wanted to hear every last little detail of what had happened between them and was a little disappointed when she saw Patrick standing in the dimly lit hallway instead.

"I wanted to talk to you," he said in a hushed voice.

Julia stuck her head out into the hall to make sure her father was not where he could see them, then hurriedly stepped back. "Come inside."

Glancing both ways as Julia had just done, Patrick waited until she had closed the door before saying anything else.

"You look lovely in white," he said, referring to the satin robe she had slipped on over her night clothes. "You'll make a beautiful bride."

Julia turned back to face him and saw that his gaze had dropped to take in the bare feet and ankles her night clothing exposed to his view. Self-consciously, she bent her knees just enough so her dressing robe would touch the floor. "What do you want?"

"To talk to you alone for a few minutes. I have a few questions I want to ask." He glanced around at the elegant furnishings in her bedroom. His eyebrows arched when he took in the oversize mahogany bed with its intricate broadleaf design carved into both the head- and footboards. The same design could be found in the dresser, chest, and vanity. "After that hired man of yours left, you were in such a hurry to get back inside and on up to your bedroom that I didn't get the chance to ask you anything."

"I wasn't aware you had any questions." She hoped that would explain why she had been so quick to leave. But the truth was, she had wanted to get upstairs where she could sort through all her confusing emotions. "What did you want to know?"

Patrick brought his attention back to her. "Well, for one thing, I wanted to find out why you never told me anything about the fact that you would be written out of your father's will if he doesn't approve of me."

"I didn't want to worry you," she answered honestly. "Besides, it doesn't really matter that much. It's not as if we really *need* his money. You already have enough for us to live comfortably."

"That's not the point." His face showed the first signs of anger. "The point is that you chose to keep something like that from me. Don't you think it's important to me that you be able to inherit everything that's rightfully yours?"

Julia's eyebrows knitted while she tried to figure out why Patrick was so angry with her. It wasn't as if she had lied to him. She had just omitted certain information.

"And if losing your inheritance really doesn't matter all that much, as you put it," Patrick went on, his expression angrier still, "then why are you going to so much trouble to keep that from happening? Why did you hire that arrogant bastard Sutton if it really doesn't matter to you what happens between you and your father?"

"I didn't say it didn't matter to *me*," she corrected, getting a little angry herself. What right did he have to accuse her? "What I said was, it shouldn't matter to *you*. You have plenty of money. And the only reason it matters to me is because I love my father. I don't want to lose him over something so inane."

"You consider marrying me to be inane?"

"No. I don't consider marrying you to be inane. I consider my father's demand to approve of the man I marry to be inane. Especially in these modern times when most women are allowed to make their own matrimonial choices."

"And you're sure that's why you hired Sutton? Because you want him to help you get around your father's ridiculous terms?"

"Of course it is. Why else would I be paying him five hundred dollars."

"*Five hundred dollars?*" Patrick repeated, then swallowed hard as if unable to believe such an amount. "You're paying that man five hundred dollars?"

Julia met his startled gaze. "Yes. I'm paying him the money I have left from what Grandmother Zilphia left me."

"But I don't understand. Why so much? It's not as if you've asked the man to rob a bank or kill someone."

"No, but I've asked him to pretend to be someone he's not, and not let anyone know the truth about who he really is."

"And who is he really?"

Julia's forehead wrinkled. "I don't know. He won't tell me. All I know is that his first name is Chad and that he came here from South Carolina. I made up the name Sutton."

Patrick tossed his hands as if dealing with a child. "You mean to tell me you've entrusted a job like this to a man who won't even tell you what his name is?"

Julia paused to consider her response, but realized there was really only one answer she could give. "Yes."

"What kind of fool are you? Don't you realize what could happen if he suddenly decided not to cooperate?"

"If that happened, I would not pay him," she said, though she knew the problem he referred to ran deeper than that.

"Oh, yes you would. Just to keep him quiet. Unless, of course, you don't mind your father finding out what you've tried to do."

"But we'll only need to keep him quiet until after we are married and Father finds out for himself what a nice person you are. After he's had the chance to get to know you, it won't matter what anyone else tells him."

"But don't you know how much we could be forced to pay him before then?"

"You are worrying about something that is not going to happen. True, I should have considered all that before I hired Chad, but I didn't. And I will admit the thought did occur to me shortly after I'd hired him, but as it turns out, it was a needless worry. Chad is completely trustworthy."

That opinion angered Patrick more. "How can you say that with such conviction when you don't even know the man."

"I know him well enough." She crossed her arms stubbornly.

"You don't even know his last name," he was quick to remind her.

"But I know the *man*. We've been together almost every day for nearly three weeks. In that time, I've managed to get to know him pretty well."

345

Patrick shook his head. "The more I hear about what you've done, the less I like it. I do not like the situation you've created, and I don't like the man you hired to do the job. I *especially* don't like the way he goes around leering at you and pawing you all the time."

"He doesn't *paw* me. He knows better than to do something like that. He merely reaches out to touch my hand or my waist from time to time, and the reason he does that is because he knows it bothers my father. That's also the reason he leers at me. It's all a part of his job. His only interest is earning that five hundred dollars," she said, though she knew that was not true. He had proved to be interested in much more than just the money. He was interested in having her, too. She wondered if that might not partly be because of the money. It had to have crossed his mind that if she had that kind of money to spend on something so frivolous, then she must be worth plenty. But then again, he knew that if she married someone her father did not approve, she'd never see another penny.

Again, she had to wonder why Chad was suddenly so interested in her. Or was it sudden? She had so many questions that needed answering. "He's interested in the money I've promised to pay him and nothing more."

"I don't know." Patrick lowered one eyebrow in thought. "It looked to me like he's interested in a whole lot more than your money."

"That's just your imagination getting the better of you," Julia said, then, hoping to encourage him to leave, she placed her hand on the doorknob. "You're just tired and haven't had enough time to think about what I've done. You'll see things differently in the morning." She then turned the knob and opened the door just wide enough to allow him to slip out.

"I doubt it," he muttered, and headed obediently toward the opening. He paused just long enough to warn her, "Just you remember who it is you are in love with here and who has the means to make you happy. Just don't you go letting yourself get confused about who it is you're in love with."

Too late, she thought while she watched him duck his head into the hall to make sure her father was nowhere around then lean back to look at her one last time. *I'm already about as confused as one person can get.*

"I won't," she answered, hoping she sounded more confident than she actually felt.

"Just see that you don't," he said, then offered a quick smile and slipped quietly out of the room.

Sadly, Julia watched while he crept silently down the darkened hallway, back toward the adjoining hall that led to his own bedroom.

Just you remember who it is you are in love with here, he had said, obviously thinking to help her keep her mind straight. But she was already in love with both of them. She loved them for two entirely different reasons, but she loved them both just the same.

After closing the door, she pressed her back against the cold, hard surface and shut her eyes to hide from her anguish. How would she ever decide which one of them she loved the most?

For the next several days, Chad and Patrick managed to behave civilly toward each other. While Chad continued to do what he could to annoy Charles, until the man wanted to pull out his hair, Patrick worked busily to please him in every way.

Chad thought it aggravating what an obsequious sort Patrick had turned out to be, always agreeing with whatever Charles said, no matter how ridiculous or mundane, and always scurrying about eager to help him in some way.

Obviously that sort of behavior pleased Charles immensely because he had begun to call Patrick either by his first name or simply "Son," and had started to ask Patrick's opinions concerning certain business matters. Either Charles could not see or did not care that Patrick was an obvious manipulator.

What bothered Chad even more was finding out that Julia was so blindly attracted to him. What prevented her from seeing right through him? Clearly, Patrick was a man of many faces—none of which seemed very appealing to him.

What bothered Chad the most about Patrick Moore was how quickly he could change from being so utterly charming and eager to please to being completely cold and indifferent to what was going on around him. It was like watching a whole new person materialize from inside him, a person who was most likely a lot closer to being the *real* Patrick Moore. Clearly Mr. Moore was not the refined and gentle person he pretended to be. Twice during the past few days, Chad alone had seen the personality transformation.

He had seen how easily Patrick could drop his bright smile and replace it with a rumpled scowl. What also bothered him was what the man had to say about Julia and her father when neither was around to hear.

"That old man is about as stupid as they come," he had said to Chad the night before, looking completely disgusted. Charles had left the room to make quick use of the privy and Julia was still upstairs changing out of a dress on which she had spilled wine sauce. "How can he be so easily manipulated?" he had asked in a voice loud enough for Chad to hear but in a way that made Chad wonder if he'd meant to say it aloud.

"Why do you think he's so easily manipulated?" Chad had asked.

Patrick looked at him as if unable to believe the question had been asked. "That man is as easy to play as an old deck of cards. Watch him. He lets you irritate the hell out of him, even though he knows he's never going to give his permission to let the two of you marry. As for me, all I have to do is say a few nice things to the old goat and I have him practically eating out of my hand. The man can't see beyond what's put right in front of him, which I suppose is to both our advantages."

Chad was still angry about what Patrick had said about Charles, but his nostrils flared with pure rage when he remembered what he had said next about Julia.

"Fortunately the daughter is the same way," he'd said with a contented smile, but then had blinked several times as if suddenly realizing it was Chad he'd spoken to and immediately changed the subject to the weather, wanting to know how anyone stood such heat.

Patrick's true personality was revealed again, when, instead of swatting at a particularly annoying fly, he had captured it in one hand then squeezed the life out of it with his fingers. It had been a repulsive act, and something the man never would have done had Julia or Charles been present.

Patrick had stared at him while he crushed the fly to a gritty pulp, and Chad had realized then that Patrick wanted Chad to know exactly who it was he was dealing with without having to come right out and spell the situation out for him.

But that wasn't all that bothered Chad about Patrick. He also did not like the way Patrick treated Julia when her father wasn't present, never showing her sufficient respect. Nor did his conversations ever center around her or were his eyes filled with a suitor's adoration, like one would expect of a man who was supposed to be so deeply in love.

When Charles was not there to talk about some facet of business, Patrick preferred to talk about himself, or the many plans he had for himself. He loved to discuss such topics as the value of the land Julia would one day inherit or the things he intended to do while running her father's businesses. Rarely did he mention any plans that included her. Never did he mention such things as having a family, nor did he ask about her painting. Clearly, no one mattered to Patrick but himself.

So why couldn't Julia see that? What was it about the man that kept her so blind? If only there was some way to make her see Patrick for the cold, conniving opportunist he really was.

While Chad headed for yet another night of listening to Patrick woo Julia's father and of watching Julia sit quietly while everyone participated in the conversation but her, Chad decided he would find some way to be alone with her, if only for a few minutes. He had to make her see Patrick for what he really was.

Patrick sighed heavily while he lay in bed assessing everything that had happened since his arrival. He was tired of waiting for Julia's father to come to his senses and order Julia never to see Chad again. Tired of waiting for his chance to marry Julia, get rid of Charles, then live the sort of life he had always wanted. The sort of life he had left home to find back when he was only sixteen.

According to Julia, Chad had been coming to the house and acting badly for well over three weeks now, yet Charles continued to put up with the man's boorish behavior. Patrick had only been there three days and already he was tired of Chad. He was also damned tired of having to play Julia's little game.

He did not want to wait any longer. He did not like being poor again. He was ready to get his hands on some of the money he saw evidenced around him—but was not quite sure how to go about it. He figured his best chance would be to convince him to invest in some scheme to get rich quick, but he was not sure which one would work on a man like Charles. Although Thornton was not too terribly bright when it came to judging people, the man had a real knack in knowing just where to spend his money.

Perhaps he could get him to invest in putting a store in town. Or maybe in some bogus railroad. Or maybe the man would be willing to invest in a fake mining company. After all, this land was rich in red clay and many times that meant there was iron ore to be milled. Perhaps he could fake a few geologist reports and pretend to be interested in starting a small steel operation somewhere close by.

Or it might be easier to simply come right out and ask for Julia's hand in marriage. Charles had had three days to note that he was the better man. Surely he would be ready to choose him over Chad by now.

But *no*, he had agreed not to do anything like that without having talked it over with Julia first. He had promised to see her silly plan through and he did not want to do anything to anger her at the moment. Not when he was so close to winning both her heart and her money—forever.

If only he could think of some way to speed matters along so he could finally have control of all that wealth and at the same time convince Charles to throw Chad out of his house forever.

* * *

Julia was only half listening when Patrick told her father about some business deal he had going in town. Her thoughts were on Chad. He was late and she worried that he might finally have had enough of Patrick's rough treatment and decided not to spend another Friday night in their company.

Her heart ached at the thought, so much so that she was only vaguely aware of the conversation still going on around her.

"Perhaps you'd like to go in with me on this little venture," Patrick said, sitting back in his chair with all the ease and comfort of a friend who had been coming there for years.

"I'd sure like to hear more about it," Charles admitted, then glanced at the clock and frowned. "Look at that. It's after seven. I'm too hungry to wait for Sutton another minute." He looked at Julia with a stern expression. "Go tell Ruth we are ready to eat." He did not await her response before speaking to Patrick again. "We can discuss this further in the dining room. How much did you say you'd need to get this thing started?"

"To get started, we would only need a few thousand. But that will just buy the permits and the right-of-way land we'll need. Once we have those, we'd need about fifteen thousand more to start the actual dredging. But just think how much we could make if we were able to open a waterway wide enough and deep enough to allow barges to get through. Think of how much you'd save in shipping costs alone if you were suddenly able to ship your lumber by water instead of rail."

"And you say all we'd have to do is tie into Caddo Lake then ship to Shreveport through the natural system?" he asked, already rising from his chair.

Julia noticed how easily her father had started to say *we* instead of *you* and wondered just how serious he was in investing in something that sounded a little unrealistic to her. If the Little Cypress could truly be made to bear barge traffic, then why hadn't someone thought of that before? And why was it so important when shipping by railroad was so cheap?

But then again, she knew Patrick to be a man of incredible vision. It just might be that it took someone with his foresight to see the possibility.

"Father, can't we wait just a little while longer before we eat?" she asked, knowing it was expected of her to plead Chad's case—though she was not all that certain Chad wanted to spend another meal sitting idly by while Patrick and her father purposely ignored him. "I'm sure he'll be here any minute."

"When he gets here he can join us. But I'm hungry. I'm not waiting a minute longer," Charles said firmly, then, without waiting for her to get up out of her chair, he headed toward the door. Patrick followed only a few steps behind, eager to continue his discussion of the forced waterway.

Sighing, Julia stood and headed toward the back of the house to do as she had been told. But when she arrived in the kitchen she noticed Pearline heading out the back door. Knowing how despondent her maid had been ever since her return from the Andrews ranch late Tuesday night, Julia decided to follow her.

She knew her father would be angry with her for not returning right away, but she did so want to know what was wrong with Pearline. She wanted to know why her friend seemed on the verge of tears, and decided that if she approached her outside, away from the others, she might get the truth out of her yet.

Even if Pearline was not yet ready to talk, she could

at least let her know how concerned she was, and assure her that if she ever did want to talk about her problem, she would be available.

Chapter Twenty

Chad knew he was late and he knew Julia would be angry with him even though his tardiness could eventually work out to her advantage. Charles hated people who were not punctual, just as he hated people who were clumsy and awkward or arrogant. And wasn't the whole point of his coming over there day after day to do everything he could to annoy the man?

But still Chad did not want Julia angry with him, not when he continued to be so close to losing her to a man like Patrick. A man who would make her life miserable.

Chad rode hard, not having taken the time to hitch up the carriage after the accident that afternoon. Forcing his horse to jump a small fence so they could take a shortcut across Thornton's land rather than follow the main road around, he ended up approaching the house from the back rather than the front. He was surprised to find Julia and Pearline standing in the side yard, only a few yards away from the back porch. Charles and Patrick were nowhere in sight. That gave Chad the opportunity he wanted.

"I'm sorry I'm late," he called to them even before he had brought his horse to a dusty halt several yards away. It had not rained in over a week and the ground was dry. "But there was an accident at work. I had to stay long enough to make sure Solomon was going to be all right."

Pearline was the first to react. "What happened to Solomon?" She hurried to the edge of the lamplight to find out more.

"He fell out of the barn," he answered, already down from his horse and tying him to a nearby tree since there were no hitching posts in the back. "He was up in the loft trying to repair a broken hay pulley when he leaned out too far and lost his balance."

"Is he all right?" She searched Chad's face in the darkness.

"Far as I can tell," he said, headed toward her. "Fortunately, he landed on a stack of grass seeds we had piled nearby. Didn't break anything, but he sure twisted his left ankle, and that's going to make him awfully sore for a few days." Now that he was closer, he could tell that Pearline was genuinely concerned.

"But you're sure he didn't break nothin'," she repeated, as if she didn't quite trust Chad's assessment.

"Nothing but his pride," he admitted. "But then I think that was already pretty bruised. He won't tell me what happened between you two that last time you were over there, but he hasn't been the same since. I'm surprised something like this didn't happen any sooner. Just what is it you did to that man?"

Pearline looked away, refusing to let Chad see her troubled expression.

"It's more what she thinks he did to her," Julia put in, obviously believing Chad deserved an explanation. "We were just talking about what happened, among *other* things," she said, and gave Pearline a meaningful look. "It seems Solomon has accused her of trying to do something that had no truth to it. It's his claim that the

356

only reason she was willing to . . ." She paused for just the right word for what she wanted to say. "Be so *nice* to him was because she wanted his help with convincing your boss into selling that house and part of his land to my father. He claims it wasn't because of any feelings she may have developed toward him, which is ridiculous. It is obvious she cares for Solomon a great deal."

"So *that's* what's been wrong with him these past few days." Chad rubbed his chin thoughtfully. "He's not suffering from broken pride. He's suffering from a broken heart."

"So is she," Julia admitted. "She's been moping around here like some lost little puppy. Says she can't be happy again without finding a way to get Solomon back in her life."

"Missy!" Pearline admonished. Scowling, she cut her gaze from Julia to Chad, then back to Julia. "Mr. Chad ain't interested in hearin' about my misery."

"Oh, but I am," Chad corrected. "And I know someone who would be even *more* interested, and that's Solomon. Why don't you ride over there and tell him how you feel? It would sure make him feel a lot better."

"I can't do that. I can't go running back, acting as if nothin' ever happened. Not when he accused me of tryin' to use him like that."

"Why not?"

"Because for one thing, it ain't proper for a woman to go chasing after a man. What'll he think of me."

Chad shook his head in disbelief. "What's not proper here is for the two of you to continue being angry with each other when it is so obvious you both want to make amends and start over. If it'll make it easier for you to go talk to him, tell him that I told you about the accident and sent you over there to check on him, to see if he needed anything."

357

"He'd believe that?"

Chad smiled when he saw her hopeful expression. "Of course he would. Especially if I stopped back by later and mentioned that I sent you."

"You'd do that?"

"Of course I would. I do owe you a favor, remember?" he reminded her, referring to the fact she had kept secret what she knew about him. And because she trusted him, she had not bothered to follow him into town like she was supposed to do.

He gestured toward his horse. "Go ahead. Take my horse. Just get back here in time for me to have a way to get home."

Pearline looked at Julia hopefully. "Can I? Can I go over there? I'll be right back."

"Just *be* back, so Chad can leave."

Pearline wasted no time. She headed immediately for the horse. Julia waited until she had climbed onto the saddle and was on her way to the front gate before saying anything else.

"That was nice of you." She gazed at him appreciatively.

"That's because I'm really a very nice fellow." He smiled. How beautiful she looked standing in the outer circle of the soft lanternlight. "Or haven't you heard?"

"No. I'm afraid the people around here don't talk too highly of you," she said with an answering smile that caused her dark eyes to glitter. "They seem to think you are a very rude and very crude human being."

"Which I guess is to my credit, since that's what they are supposed to think," he said, and waved his head proudly.

Julia laughed. "You certainly do take your insults well."

"As long as you are not the one insulting me, I don't

care about anything anyone has to say about me." Unable to resist her smiling beauty, he reached out to hold her cheeks in his hands and to observe the way she closed her eyes. Despite all that had happened between them, and despite the fact that Patrick was now back in her life, she still responded to his touch.

When she opened her eyes again, she gazed at him a long moment, then her forehead wrinkled with thought, as if something had just occurred to her. "What did you mean a minute ago when you said something about owing Pearline a favor? What has she done for you that merits you being so kind to her?"

Chad shrugged. His blue eyes took in every intricate detail of Julia's beauty, heightened now by the silvery glow of the half moon that had just slipped from behind a fat cloud. "She introduced me to you, didn't she?"

"And that was *good?*" Julia teased, smiling so deeply now that her cheeks formed dimples beneath his thumbs.

"For the most part," he admitted and let go of her face so that he could better view her smile. "Although there are times when I rue the day we ever met."

Her eyebrows arched with surprise. "Why?"

"Because I've grown to care for you too much. And because I worry about you."

Julia blinked. "Worry about me? Why?"

"Because of Patrick," Chad said, hurrying to have his say before someone came outside to interrupt them. "I know you don't want to hear this, but I really don't think he loves you. Not like he should. Now that I've met him, I think that the only reason he's here is because of your money. He's an opportunist, although I know you don't see that. If you do marry him, you'll be making a grave mistake."

Julia's frown deepened into a dark, angry scowl and

her arms stiffened at her sides. "You are just like my father, aren't you? You think I am too inept to make any of my own decisions. All you want to do is find fault with what I do."

Chad was perplexed. Although he had not expected her to be pleased with what he had to say about Patrick, he had not expected her to lash out at him so angrily. Not when he was trying to warn her of the truth.

"You are wrong," he said, trying to reason with her. "The only thing I've found fault with is your selection of a husband. There is just something about that man that isn't right. All I'm saying is that maybe you should think about it a little more before actually agreeing to marry him. The man is not what you think. He is not worthy of you."

"There you go again," she said with a wild toss of her hands. "You sound just like my father. You think that because I'm a woman, I'm not capable of making a sound decision on my own. Well, you are wrong. My decision to marry Patrick Moore is quite sound."

"I didn't say anything about your ability to make decisions," Chad argued.

"You think I've made a bad choice in selecting Patrick don't you?" she challenged.

"Well, yes, but—"

"And Father thinks I've made a bad choice in selecting you. But then again, Father thinks all my choices are bad. He thinks I never think things through well enough. He thinks I am too quick to follow my heart instead of my head, which makes me wonder why he's so eager to entrust his businesses to me."

Chad kept his voice calm, hoping that might help quiet this unwarranted outburst of anger. "Have you ever considered the possibility, however remote, that your father is not out to ruin your happiness? That instead, his only desire is to protect it and possibly promote it? Isn't it entirely possible that he actually does have your best interests at heart?"

"Oh, so you've joined sides with my father now," she said. "I should have known that would happen. The only person who ever had any real faith in me or in my ability to think for myself was my mother, God rest her soul." Tears welled in her eyes. "I just wish she was here now. At least there would be *someone* who believed in me."

Without giving Chad a chance to plead his case, she spun about and marched angrily toward the house. She climbed the stairs, then paused before crossing the back porch when she realized he had not followed. "Aren't you coming? You *do* still have a job to do."

Chad threw up his hands, unable to figure out what had caused her to react so strangely, then followed several yards behind.

Julia hurried ahead of Chad. Her whole body shook while she tried to bring her rage back under control. It had been bad enough to hear Pearline say such disparaging things about Patrick, but to have Chad try to convince her of practically the same thing had been too much.

Why did everyone have something to say against Patrick? What had he done to make everyone suddenly question his intentions and his virtue?

First, Pearline admitted to having gone through his things while straightening his room and had discovered two loaded derringers, a wooden club, and a large ivory-handled knife in a valise he kept near his bed. She claimed he had to be a very violent man to carry such things around with him.

Then Chad arrived only a few minutes later and tried to convince her that Patrick didn't even love her.

361

What was wrong with everyone? Didn't Pearline know that it wasn't so very unusual for a man to travel with such forms of protection? Not in these violent times. True, he might be overdoing it a little by carrying quite so many weapons, but he had every right to try to protect himself from road thieves.

And how could Chad possibly decide that Patrick didn't love her? The man had proved unable to stay apart from her for even one month. He had traveled hundreds of miles just to *be* with her, and was willing to sell his part of a profitable business just so he could *stay* with her. Didn't sacrifices like those account for anything? How could Chad possibly believe that Patrick was only after her money?

She clenched her hands in frustration. Chad had sounded just like her father when he had said that about Patrick. How many times had her father denied her permission to marry some young man for just that very reason? Couldn't anyone accept the fact that maybe, just *maybe,* someone might want to marry her for all the right reasons? After all, she was not an unattractive woman and could be very pleasant when she wanted.

What was so wrong with Patrick that suddenly everyone was finding fault with him? Wasn't he everything a woman was supposed to fall in love with? And what did the high-almighty Chad have to offer? Nothing. No money. No freedom. No undying love. No luxuries of any kind. And he had certainly shown her no respect. How could he dare pass judgment on someone who had promised to give her all of that and more?

Julia was too upset by all that had happened to eat. Turning to face Chad who followed only a few paces behind her, she lifted her chin and spoke to him in a short, clipped voice. "Tell Father I've suddenly come down with a terrible headache and don't plan to eat after all. Tell him that I'm going to my room to lie down instead." She could always return downstairs later, *after* she'd had a chance to get over her anger.

"You're sending me in there alone?" he asked, clearly not wanting to spend an entire evening in the sole company of the other two.

"Well, you can't very well leave, now can you? Not when you just let Pearline leave on your horse. She won't be back for at least an hour, she said, probably more." There was a mutinous set of her chin. "I guess we both have a problem when it comes to making poor choices, don't we?"

She turned her back to him and started toward the stairs, eager to get as far away from him as possible.

Because Pearline had not yet returned, Chad had little choice but to lean back in his chair and watch Patrick and Charles puff leisurely on their after-dinner cigars while Patrick rattled on about the profits to be made by simply enlarging the Little Cypress River a few dozen yards. Knowing he was not a part of their conversation, he remained silent for as long as he could. But finally he had to say something, for about half of what Patrick said just did not make sense to him.

"Are you sure the Little Cypress could really be made suitable for barge travel as crooked and as winding as it is? What's to keep the river from filling in again after you've finished dredging it? There's a lot of watershed going into that river that carries a lot of silt with it. And silt isn't easily washed away when the water moves as slowly as it does through this area."

Patrick cut his gaze toward Chad, as if unable to believe he had just spoken out against him.

"I wouldn't be asking Charles to invest in such a project if I didn't think it was sound." Patrick sat slightly forward, his voice edged with impatience. "Nor would I be planning to put some of my own money into the venture."

"Oh?" Chad met Patrick's venomous glare with a look of cool reserve. "How much are you planning to invest?"

"That's really none of your business." Patrick narrowed his green eyes in warning. "I haven't asked you to come in on this, have I?"

Chad was unimpressed by Patrick's attempt at intimidation and let him know it by his flat expression. "I don't have to be asked to participate in the matter to have an opinion."

Charles studied the two men for a moment, then nodded toward Chad, though he continued looking at Patrick. "Maybe you *should* ask him to come in on it, since Chad says he has quite a bit of money put away."

Patrick rolled his eyes behind closed lids, clearly unable to believe Charles's gullibility. "If he has so much money, why does he have to work every day at your neighbor's ranch."

Charles looked at Chad. "Why is that, Chad? Why would you want to work for Andrews if you really have all that money?"

"I enjoy working," was all Chad was willing to admit, then looked at Patrick when he heard him let out a cynical snort.

"And we are supposed to believe that you enjoy working so much that you're willing to work for a man you know your supposed future father-in-law hates?" Patrick asked snidely.

"That's who was willing to give me a job," Chad answered calmly. "Besides, I never have understood why Mr. Thornton despises the man like he does."

Patrick stared at him, dumbfounded. "He has refused to sell him the land or the house he obviously needs and you don't understand why he doesn't like him? Are you without a brain?"

Chad refused to be provoked. "I didn't say I didn't understand why he doesn't *like* him. I said I didn't understand why he *despises* him. There's a difference."

"Not the way I see it," Patrick said in ready defense of Charles. "The way I see it, he has every reason to despise him. Isn't that right, sir?"

Charles did not respond but continued to watch and listen to the two closely.

Chad shifted his weight in his chair. "I don't see why you think disliking a man and despising him is the same. I also don't see why you are always so quick to come to Thornton's defense when you've only known him a few days. How do you know what he's thinking or feeling?"

"Because we are very much alike and *somebody* needs to defend him." Patrick narrowed his gaze further. "Especially the way you attack him all the time."

Chad knew Patrick was still trying to goad him into an argument but refused to let it happen. "I wasn't aware I had done any attacking. All I remember was asking you a simple question about the channel you keep talking about."

"And I believe I answered it," Patrick said with finality. "Now, if you don't mind, Charles and I were discussing something important."

"No we weren't," Charles surprised them both by saying. He had kept so quiet for the past few minutes, they had almost forgotten he was there. "*You* were. And to tell you the truth, I'm growing tired of talking about it."

"But I thought you were enthusiastic about this idea,"

Patrick argued, his green eyes suddenly very round with concern.

"I am—in a way. But it's not something I'm likely to jump into without first having looked at it from every angle," he answered honestly. "I don't throw my money around quite that easily."

"But this is something that will make us both a lot of money."

"How do I know that? All I have is your word that it will work, and to tell you the truth, I haven't known you long enough to know the value of your word."

Patrick stiffened. "My word is sound."

"It probably is, but I don't know that for sure. At least not yet. For now, all I can promise is that I'll give your idea some thought. But I won't promise to put any money into it until I've looked at the possibilities from all sides."

"I hope you won't hesitate too long. The sooner we get started, the sooner we'll see a profit."

"I realize that. But I'm afraid I've always been slow when it comes to letting go of money."

When Patrick's response was to fall back in his chair, his body tense and his eyes narrowed, Chad fought a sudden urge to grin. It looked like "old Thornton" wasn't quite as easy to manipulate as Patrick first claimed.

Now if only the same could be said about Julia.

Patrick was not about to take any chances. He knew that there was still the possibility, however slight, that Charles would refuse permission to let him marry Julia. If that happened, Julia could end up cut off without another cent and he would have invested all that time and money in her for nothing.

That was why he wanted to try to get as much money as possible out of Charles beforehand, just in case the marriage approval fell through. But that meant convincing him to invest in his fraudulent river scheme as quickly as possible.

Not wanting any further interference out of Julia's hired sweetheart, Patrick waited until Chad had finally left before trying one last time to get Charles to commit himself. When that failed, he realized he needed to do something drastic to get on the old man's good side. Having found out how important it was to both Charles and Julia that they convince Mr. C. W. Andrews to sell what they kept calling "the old place" back to them, he decided to see what he could do to help matters along.

Knowing if he could somehow get Andrews to sell the land, Charles would be forever in his debt, he waited until Charles had gone up to bed before tapping lightly on Julia's door. When she did not respond right away, he tried the handle and found the door unlocked. He wasted no time entering the darkened bedroom.

"Patrick?" Julia spun around to see who had entered. Because she was dressed in only her sheer cotton nightgown, she stood and made a quick grab for her dressing robe, which was on the table beside her chair. "Why didn't you knock?"

"I did. But evidently you were so lost in thought you didn't hear me," he said, coming forward to grab her hands before she could slip into the satiny white robe. He took the robe away from her and tossed it back across the small table. "What were you thinking about? How to break it to your father that you are really in love with me?"

Julia's forehead wrinkled when she realized he planned for her to stand there before him in just her nightgown. She was glad she had not bothered to light a lamp. She felt awkward enough knowing how much light filtered in through the window. "No. I was still thinking about Pearline." She crossed her arms protectively over the front of her gown. "She was just in here telling me about her evening."

Patrick wondered what Pearline could have done that was so interesting. He grasped Julia gently by the shoulders. Smiling, he looked down at her, pleased by the way the moonlight highlighted her pale skin. He decided himself very lucky, for not only was Julia in line to inherit a small fortune, she was beautiful, too. It was the first time he'd found a woman who had both wealth *and* beauty. "What sort of evening could your maid have possibly had?"

"A very good evening," Julia answered. "Pearline and the fellow she's been sweet on these past couple of weeks had a falling out. But they've patched things up now. Looks like their love is back on course."

"As is ours," he said, then, thinking it might help better his situation, bent to kiss her. But before their lips made contact, there was a knock at the door. He frowned when he glanced in the direction of the unwanted sound.

Julia gasped and pulled away from him.

"Oh, dear. That could be Father," she said in a fearful whisper. "You have to leave."

"How?" Patrick asked. He did not want to chance Charles being angry with him for any reason.

"Climb out the window," she said, already hurrying over to pull the lace curtains back. "Climb out onto the brick ledge and follow it around to your own room."

Patrick's stomach knotted when he looked out the window and saw that the ledge she spoke of was only about six inches wide and about eighteen feet from the ground. He had never liked heights. "But I need to talk to you."

"We'll talk tomorrow." Her brown eyes widened further when another knock sounded. This one louder and more persistent than the first.

"But I need to talk to you alone, and tomorrow is Saturday. Your father will be home all day."

"We'll find a chance to be alone," she promised. "Sometime in the morning. Now, go!"

"All right. But don't forget. Find some way for us to be alone." He bent forward to place that kiss he had originally intended for her mouth on her cheek, but when the knock sounded a third time, louder than before, he decided to forego the kiss altogether and get on out the window instead. He knew the door was still unlocked and, just as he had done, whoever was there might try the latch at any moment.

He was already on the narrow brick ledge working his way toward the edge of the building when he heard Julia finally call out. "Who is it?" She followed that with an, "I'm coming."

Because of the unwanted distance between him and the ground, he did not wait around to see if the visitor was indeed her father or perhaps just Pearline returning to tell Julia something she'd forgotten. He hurried along the narrow ledge, toward the corner of the house, knowing the safety of his own bedroom lay just around the edge.

It looked as if he would have to wait until tomorrow to tell Julia about his latest scheme. He just hoped she could come up with the money he would need to finance it.

Chapter Twenty-one

Having had such a hard time falling asleep the night before, Patrick was the last one downstairs the following morning. He arrived at the breakfast table too late to eat with the others. He ate what the housekeeper brought him, then headed out to find Julia, annoyed that she had not waited to talk with him as she had promised.

He had barely stepped out the back door when he heard Charles call out his name. He glanced over in time to see Charles headed toward the house from the stables.

"Patrick, come see the new colt. He's as frisky as a young pup."

Although Patrick would have preferred to find the small field where Julia had gone to paint, he decided it might be better to try to appease the old man instead. After all, Charles was still the one with all the money and Julia was under his control.

"What kind of colt?" He had already altered his course to join Charles in front of the stables.

"Quarter horse," he responded proudly. "Good lines, too. Plan to make a stud out of him. There's good money in that, you know."

Charles had just said the word that always got Patrick's full attention. *Money*. He went along with him willingly.

"Do you know much about horses?" Charles asked just before they entered the large barn, then headed toward the bigger stalls near the back.

"No, sir. I'm afraid I don't. But I'd be eager to learn. I've always been fond of horses." Although in truth, he could never understand a man being completely devoted to a horse. It provided transportation and labor and an occasional thrill at the racetrack.

"Good. Maybe I can teach you a few things."

"I'd like that," Patrick said, and continued to follow Charles to the furthermost stall where a sleek, light-brown horse stood letting a gangly, reddish-brown colt nurse sloppily at her teats. Although Patrick tried to be attentive while Charles explained just what had gone into this particular colt's breeding, he could not keep his mind on what Charles had to say about his fool animals. He was too eager to get away and find Julia, so he could try to put his latest ploy into action.

He was only half listening when he realized Charles was changing the subject.

"Good blood lines are important. Don't ever let anyone tell you anything different. Especially in people," Charles said, finally pushing away from the stall gate where they had stood for the past several minutes. "I have always believed that. I have always believed that traits like honesty and fortitude have to be bred into a person. Don't you agree?"

"Yes, I do," he answered, eager to remain in Charles's favor. "Which is why I worry so about Julia. Chad Sutton isn't exactly what one would consider good stock. If she marries him, I shudder to think what her children will be like."

Charles nodded, then smiled to reassure him. "Don't worry. She won't marry him. I have no intention of letting her."

Patrick's eyebrows perked. "If that's true, then why put up with him like you do? Why not go ahead and toss him out of here?"

"Because I'm hoping Julia will come to her senses on her own and see for herself that Chad is not the sort of man she should marry. Besides, I think she may have brought him here as a way to spite me, even if she doesn't realize it. That's why I've decided to let her have her little rebellion. At least for now. But in the end, she'll do exactly what I tell her to do. She always does."

When Charles headed back toward the front of the stables, Patrick followed, eager to hear what else he had to say.

"Then you don't believe that she really loves him?"

"If she does, it's not the sort of love that would last a lifetime," Charles explained. "Don't get me wrong. The young man does have some good qualities. For one thing, I believe he truly does love my daughter and would probably do anything *and* everything within his power to make her happy. But that seems to be his main shortcoming. There isn't much within his power he *can* do to make her happy. Not in the long view of things, which is what I have to consider. I have to worry about what will make her happy forever."

"*I'd* sure like to have a chance at making her happy forever," Patrick said, and paused to look Charles squarely in the eye. "I may not have gotten the courage to ask her yet, but I did not come here just to keep her from marrying Chad. I'm not quite that noble. I want her to marry me instead."

"I figured out that much from what you said the

372

other day," Charles told him, but remained noncommittal when he stopped to show Patrick yet another horse.

Wearing his best broadcloth trousers and a white cotton shirt and with his hair freshly washed, brushed back, and just starting to dry, Chad headed toward the Thornton place a couple of hours earlier than he usually did on Saturdays. He hoped to find Julia in the field where Pearline claimed she did much of her painting.

He had made no headway with her the night before and wanted a second chance to talk to her about Patrick. But because he wanted to talk with her alone, he prayed that if he did find her still out painting near the river, he did not find Patrick with her. He did not think he could stand finding the two of them alone like that. Especially after having heard everything Julia had said about Patrick the day before.

Chad was not normally the jealous type, but whenever his mind envisioned Patrick and Julia together, he felt a cold rage inside him that could be only that. Jealousy. Mixed with a little fear. Fear that Julia might end up actually marrying him.

He knew by the way she defended Patrick yesterday that despite how obvious it seemed to him, she did not yet see the man for the cold, conniving opportunist he really was. And that worried Chad. Enough so, he was willing to try one last time to make her see the truth. Even if it meant alienating her forever.

With that purpose, when he neared the clearing where Julia was supposed to be spending most of her mornings, he slowed his horse to a walk so not to startle her, but was disappointed to find her not there.

Evidently she had preferred to stay home and be with Patrick than paint.

Again he felt the cold fingers of jealousy pull at his heart and turned his horse toward the house, eager to make sure she and Patrick were given few opportunities to be alone.

Julia had spent the past several hours trying to sort through her confused emotions but still had not come to terms with exactly what it was she felt. Part of her already wanted to forgive Chad for what he had said the night before, for he had known Patrick only a few days and could not know the person he really was. But another part of her wanted to strangle him for having proved to be so much like her father.

She'd had enough of domineering men to last her a lifetime. Which was why she still so liked the idea of marrying Patrick. At least *he* believed in her enough to accept her ideas as being sound and he did so without question.

If only Chad could be like that.

Feeling sulky to have discovered that Chad had turned out to be just like most of the other men she had ever known, Julia set her canvas at the far end of the back porch to finish drying in the sun, then went on inside the house.

Although she had expected her father to be off at the stables or out in the barn, she found that both he and Patrick were standing in the main hall near the front stairway. Judging by their spotless white attire, they had been inside most of the day. Probably talking about business.

"You missed lunch," Charles pointed out needlessly when he looked up to find his daughter headed toward them. "We ate hours ago."

"I know, but the colors are so beautiful right now. I

wanted to capture as many of them as possible while I could," she said, hoping to slip right by them. Having spent the last six hours outdoors in the hot May sunshine, all she wanted was to go upstairs and bathe, then change into a fresh, clean dress.

When it became obvious that she was headed for the foot of the stairs instead of the dining room, he asked, "Aren't you planning to eat? Ruth has prepared you a plate and is keeping it warm for you in the kitchen."

"Tell her I'll be down later to eat it," she explained, and continued past them. "I'm not really hungry right now. I ate too much at breakfast."

"Trying to make up for having missed supper no doubt," Patrick put in, not wanting to be left out of the conversation. "Are you feeling better?"

"Yes, I am," she answered, though she avoided looking at him. She knew he had to be angry with her for having disappeared, especially after having promised to have a talk with him that morning. "The headache went away during the night. I guess all I really needed was a little rest. It has been a trying week for me."

"Still, you should not miss a meal," Patrick continued. "If you're worried about having to eat alone, I'll sit with you."

Julia's mouth pressed into a flat line. She had so wanted to be left alone for at least another hour, but then again, she had promised to talk with him privately. If her father did not join them while she ate, they would be given the perfect opportunity. "All right. But tell Ruth it will be a few more minutes. I want to change out of this damp clothing first."

She pulled at the sleeve of her bright-yellow dress to show how hot she had gotten, then headed upstairs. By the time she returned with her hair pinned into a simple twist high on her head and wearing a freshly laundered green-and-yellow cotton dress, her father was gone and Patrick was seated in the dining room. He waited until she finished eating before mentioning the events of the previous night.

"So, who came knocking at your door?" he asked, watching while she lifted her napkin out of her lap and placed it with neat folds beside her now-empty plate.

"It was Father. He wanted to make sure I was all right. He worries about my headaches."

"Do you get them often?"

"Often enough, I guess." She pushed her chair back. Now that she had finished eating, she was ready to get up and move around. Glancing back to make sure Patrick had also risen from his chair, she headed toward the back of the house so she could check to see if her painting was dry yet. She hated leaving it in the sun for very long. "But last night I was more tired than anything else."

"You looked tired," he agreed, following close behind. "Even though it was dark when I slipped into your room, I could see that your eyes looked a little red and swollen."

Which was probably because she had been crying, but she decided not to tell Patrick that. There was no sense having him angry at Chad, too. She paused just inside the back door, ready to hear what he had wanted to discuss last night. "What was it you were so eager to talk about?"

"A plan I came up with while lying awake last night," Patrick said, then explained the problem he had getting her father to like him. "Don't misunderstand me. Your father's been nice enough to me. It's just that he seems to be holding something back. That's why I need to do something drastic. My best choice would be to try to do something that might convince your new neighbor to

376

sell the house and land your father wants. Then I would have no problem winning his favor."

"Getting Mr. Andrews to do that may be a lot harder to do than you think," she cautioned, not wanting him to get his hopes up. "Just what is it you plan to do?"

"I really don't want to say just yet," he told her, but his eyes sparkled with the enthusiasm he felt for his plan. "If something went wrong, I'd end up looking like a fool. But what I *can* tell you is that I've done this sort of thing before and it is almost certain to work."

Julia looked at him questioningly. "If you don't want to tell me your plan, then why are you even mentioning it to me?"

"I guess because I want your permission to do something about it. I don't want to jump into this without you at least knowing about it."

"You want my permission?" She blinked several times while she tried to come to terms with that.

"Yes. Don't you remember? I promised to include you in any decisions I make. That's why I want to know what you think."

Julia stared at him a long moment, wishing Chad had been there to hear him say that. If nothing else, Patrick was a man of his word. "I think that if you really do have a good plan that could eventually get Father that house, he would be devoted to you for life."

"There is just one problem, though. I need to act quickly."

"Why is that a problem?"

"Because I need money to get things going, and for safekeeping, I deposited all of my traveling money into one of the banks in Marshall when I first arrived. This being Saturday afternoon, the banks are all closed and won't open again until Monday morning. That's why I hoped you might have some money I could borrow until then."

"How much will you need?"

"A hundred dollars should do it."

"I have what's left of my grandmother's inheritance tucked away, but I've promised most of that to Chad."

"That's not a problem. I don't plan to keep it long. I'll replace it just as soon as I can get to the bank and withdraw some of my own money."

Julia studied him a moment while she tried to decide if she should let him have the money. She knew it would help change Pearline and Chad's opinions of him if he were able to convince Mr. Andrews to sell her father the house and land, but then again, it was money she had promised someone else. Finally, her desire to give Patrick the chance to prove himself won out. She had to show Chad that he was not the only man with his heart in the right place.

"All right. I'll loan it to you. Wait for me outside. I'll run upstairs and get it."

Patrick glanced toward the stairs, as if about to ask to go with her, but then nodded. "All right. I'll be out on the back porch."

Julia hurried upstairs and counted exactly one hundred dollars from the money she kept inside her favorite kid ballroom slippers. Within minutes she was back downstairs with the money tucked neatly in her hand.

"Here," she said. "Just be sure to replace it by the end of next week. Chad's month will be up about then."

"Don't worry." He quickly counted the money. "You'll have it back long before then."

It was not until he had slipped it into his trousers pockets that she noticed Chad coming across the back lawn with long, steady strides. Not wanting him to know what she had just done, she hurried forward to greet him.

"You're early," she said, stating the obvious as she came to a halt several yards away. She could tell by looking into his deep blue eyes that something troubled him. She decided he was still upset about some of what she had said last night.

"We quit work earlier than usual," he offered as an excuse for being there, then gestured toward Patrick, who was headed across the yard toward the stables. "Where's he going in such a hurry?"

"Into town," was all she answered, thinking it none of his business where Patrick went.

"To spend the money you just gave him?"

Julia's forehead notched high enough so that the soft curls that fringed across it touched the tops of her eyebrows. "You saw that?"

Chad's expression was grim but there was little emotion in his voice. "Wasn't too hard to see. How much did you give him?"

"That's really none of your business," she answered, feeling suddenly very defensive. She knew there was a very good chance Patrick intended to bribe a judge or a county clerk to change a few records. That was the sort of thing wealthy businessmen in St. Louis did all the time. "Besides, he has promised to pay me back just as soon as he can."

"I don't doubt that. What did he claim to need money for?"

"That is none of your business, either. But if you really must know, he has come up with a plan that will get Father back both his house and his land."

That certainly piqued Chad's interest. "What sort of a plan?"

"A very *good* plan," she said, not wanting to admit

that he had not entrusted her with that information. "One that can't possibly fail."

Chad lifted one dark eyebrow. "And why not?"

"Because Patrick happens to be a very clever person. But then, that's not something you really want to hear, is it?"

"Not really," he admitted, but with far less hostility than she had expected. "But then who am I to judge someone of Patrick's obvious caliber? We'll just have to wait and see how successful he is in getting Mr. Andrews to change his mind."

"You sound as if you don't think he can do it."

"I work there, remember? I may not have met Mr. Andrews face-to-face, but I do know from talking with the other men how determined he is to hold on to his property. He has waited a long time for the chance to make a success of the place."

"Still, I think if anyone can convince him to sell, Patrick can."

"What if he fails?"

Julia lifted her chin and met his gaze directly. "He won't."

"But what if he does? Would you be willing to admit then that Patrick is not the perfect person you seem to think he is?"

"He won't fail," she stated again. She narrowed her brown eyes to show her determination. "Patrick has done this sort of thing before. He will convince our new neighbor to sell. You'll see. After Patrick gets through with him, Mr. Andrews will be *begging* to sell us his land."

"I really don't like to argue with you, but for the record's sake, my money's on Andrews," he said with an unexpected smile.

"Why, when you have never even met the man?"

"I've heard enough about him to feel that I know him as well as I know myself," he told her. His eyes sparkled. "Besides, I do know Patrick and I can't say that I have much confidence in him. He'll never convince Andrews to sell even one acre of that land. I think you just wasted your money."

"You're wrong. Patrick is very good about getting exactly what he wants. He'll be successful," she said, and clenched her hands with frustration. She hated the confidence she'd heard in his voice. "You just wait. Andrews will be signing over that house and a good part of his land, if not every last acre of it, within a matter of weeks. And Father will be singing Patrick's praises when he does."

Having said that and not wanting to hear any more caustic remarks, she spun about and marched back into the house, leaving Chad to wonder if he should follow or remain where he was. In the end, he decided to follow, but said nothing else to her until her father entered the house nearly an hour later wanting to know where Patrick had gone.

All Julia told him was that Patrick had gone into town to make a few personal arrangements but that he would be back in time for supper. Nothing was said about the money or the land.

When she went to bed Julia was still fuming over the confident manner in which Chad had denounced Patrick's ability to follow through with his plan. She was just glad Chad had still been there when Patrick returned from town smiling contentedly. Although she had not yet gotten the chance to talk with Patrick about what he'd done, it was obvious that things had gone well for him.

She just hoped that Chad realized the same thing. And she hoped that he would be man enough to admit he was wrong when Patrick did indeed convince Mr. Andrews to sell her father the property he wanted.

Knowing there was a good chance that Patrick might come to her room to tell her what he had done while in town, she waited to put on her nightgown and was still dressed and the bedroom still well lit when he did indeed appear at her door. She opened it quickly to let him in, eager to hear his report but not wanting her father to catch him at her door. That would never do, not when they were still trying to convince him that Chad was the one who interested her the most.

"How did your business go?" she asked just as soon as she had closed the door and turned to face him.

Patrick's green eyes sparkled with childlike excitement and his face broke into a wide smile. "Perfectly."

Julia returned his smile, pleased at his answer. She did not want Chad to have a reason to gloat.

"I found exactly the help I needed," he went on to tell her, then suddenly swept her into his arms and held her close. "Your father's troubles will soon be a thing of the past." Then, without warning, he kissed her.

Although Patrick had kissed her before on other occasions, his kisses had rarely been on the mouth, and Julia had not expected him to kiss her there now. Knowing the strong effect kissing had had on her these past few days, she immediately closed her eyes so she could enjoy the effect of the unexpected kiss more fully. Since Patrick was the man she intended to marry, there would be no guilt to get in the way, which should make the kiss all the more enjoyable.

But to her disappointment, the kiss did not set her blood to racing like Chad's did. Nor did it make her feel weak and wanting. In fact, it did very little to her at all.

She wondered why that was, then decided Patrick had not had the experience in kissing Chad had had, but that in due time, with due practice, he would become just as ardent a kisser as Chad. She would just have to be patient with him. Eventually she would respond to him in much the same manner she responded to Chad. Or so she hoped.

"Looks like everything is going my way for a change," he said when he finally broke the kiss. His eyes continued to sparkle with boyish excitement. "You and I are going to be married, then I can take over your father's businesses just like we planned."

Julia looked at him for a minute and wondered why that no longer made her feel as happy as it once did. Something had changed, but she could not determine exactly what that something was.

Chapter Twenty-two

It was just turning dark when Deborah Porterfield, Raymond's wife, stepped outside to announce that supper was ready.

"Ready to end it for the day?" Solomon asked, glancing over at Raymond who stood on a narrow ladder only a few feet away. "About to get too dark to see what we are doing anyway."

"If you want the truth, I was ready to quit an hour ago," Raymond said, already putting the lid back on his paint tin, then rested his brush across the top. He reached up to wipe the sweat off his face with his shirtsleeve. "How'd I ever let you talk me into this?"

Solomon shrugged as if he hadn't a clue while he, too, prepared for the climb down.

Since it was Sunday, the rest of the workers had the day off, but it had been such a pretty day, Solomon and Raymond decided to go ahead and paint the outside of the barn, which was the only building left unpainted.

With them both working, they had expected to be able to cover the entire structure in only a couple of hours. But because the barn was mostly original wood and had not been painted in years, the walls drank far more paint than they had expected and the chore had quickly turned into an all-day job.

"Time to eat!" Raymond called to his sons, who had spent most of the afternoon building forts out of the large sacks of grass seed and strewn hay in the loft, then groaned when he started his slow climb down the ladder. He had been up there long enough to have developed sharp muscle aches in his back and arms.

Solomon climbed down from the stack of crates he'd used to boost his height and stopped to slip his green shirt back on. He stood at the back of the wagon they had used to store the paint and was busy washing out his brush by the light of the only lantern they had bothered to light when he heard horses approaching from the northwest.

Because the road just north of the house stayed pretty busy on Sunday afternoons, he did not think much about it until he looked up and noticed that a small group of riders had already turned off the main road and was headed in their direction.

"Looks like we are about to have a little company," he told Raymond just before he grabbed up their only lantern and turned to face them squarely. All he could make out at that distance were black shapes, but he could tell by counting those shapes that there were at least seven riders headed in.

"Figure they are bringin' you another letter for Mr. Andrews?" Raymond asked as he set his paint brush aside, then followed Solomon out into the yard.

"I don't know. Maybe." Although there was no way for Solomon to know yet if the men meant any serious trouble, Solomon's stomach curled into a tight knot while cold fingers of apprehension pulled at his gut. Chad had made a point of warning him there was to be yet another attempt to buy that house and land. "Seems those people don't give up too easily. But until we do know for certain what it is they want, it might be a good idea for you and the boys to stay out of sight. Hurry and get them into the house."

"But what if those men mean trouble?" Raymond asked hesitantly. "I don't like the idea of leaving you here to face them alone."

"I can handle them," he assured them, already headed to the feed bin where he had left his rifle propped in a corner. "You just make sure the boys go out through the back so they don't get in the way."

Raymond hesitated, then headed into the barn. Only a few seconds later, the men on horses rode into the yard.

Solomon picked up the rifle and held it loosely in his right hand while he continued to hold the lantern with his left. He did not want to frighten the riders but did want them to know he was ready to protect himself should the need arise.

When the group eventually came close enough for Solomon to see their faces, his heart fell to his stomach with a sickening thud. The men in drab clothing wore either white pieces of cloth or brightly colored bandannas over their faces. All of them.

He clutched his rifle tighter.

"What can I do for you?" he asked in a surprisingly calm voice. A quick scan of the group let him know they were not the same men who had come before and that they were all well armed. Some had handguns strapped to their thighs while others had rifles and shotguns protruding from their scabbards. The man closest to him already had his pistol drawn.

Solomon did not dare raise his rifle now. Unlike the lumberjacks who had visited them earlier, *these* men were dangerous. Slowly, he lowered the lantern to the ground to free one hand.

"You can tell me why that stubborn boss of yours won't sell this house and part of that land to his neighbor," the man said while waving the pistol in Solomon's general direction. By now, several others had taken their pistols and rifles out of their holsters and scabbards and held them in their hands. All of them stared at him intently.

Solomon's gaze moved from one man to the next trying to decide who represented the largest threat. He decided the spokesman did. He seemed like the type who was constantly trying to prove himself to the others.

"My boss doesn't want to sell because he needs the house and the land for his own use," he finally answered.

"Keeping this land is a bad thing for him to want," the spokesman said, his words puffing at the bright red bandanna he wore across the lower half of his narrow face.

Unlike the lumberjacks who had harassed him before, these men were smaller in stature. Smaller, but clearly meaner. Although he could not see the lower halves of their faces, he could see the viciousness in their eyes. Every muscle in his body grew taut in preparation for the worst while the leader continued his speech.

"In fact, it's a *real* bad thing for him to want. And it's goin' to end up costin' him plenty."

Solomon's heart beat a frantic rhythm when he realized how much danger he was in, but he remained outwardly calm. He knew better than to let these men see his fear. "Are you threatening him?"

"No. Just statin' a fact. Simple as that." The spokesman climbed down from his horse and signaled for some of the other men to do the same.

It was then Solomon realized that none of the horses carried a brand.

A tight knot twisted in his chest while he watched four of the other six men quickly join their leader on the ground. "Have you come with yet another offer from Mr. Thornton?"

"No." He cut his gaze to his men briefly. Solomon could tell by the way the man's red bandanna lifted and by the crinkles that had formed around his eyes that he was now smiling. "It's more like we've come to make a statement in his behalf."

"And what statement is that?"

The spokesman leaned back to untie something from the back of his saddle. At first Solomon had thought it was a club, but it turned out to be a torch, which the man promptly lit.

A blue flame swirled around the tip, then turned yellow, letting Solomon know it had already been soaked in coal oil. When the spokesman turned to face him again, an orangish glow flickered eerily across his masked face, causing deep shadows to dance at the corners of his dark eyes.

Two others brought out similar torches and lit theirs from his. Remembering what an angry mob could do with fire, Solomon kept his eyes on the three and did not notice that the other man on the ground had slipped around behind him. It wasn't until he felt a sharp crack against the back of his skull and saw the resulting white flashes that he realized his mistake. He spun around to face his attacker only to find a shovel coming down at him for a second blow. He ducked in time for it to miss his head, but it struck his shoulder, causing him to let go of his rifle. It clattered to the ground only a few feet away.

When he bent to recapture it, one of the other men

came forward and kicked him on the side of the leg. The force sent him sprawling into the dirt in the opposite direction of his rifle. His dog, Ruby, who had been in the barn with the children, came charging across the yard, growling.

"Get his rifle!" one of them shouted an instant before another swung forward to do just that. By the time Solomon had recovered enough to make another grab at it, the rifle was gone.

Still growling, Ruby made a lunge for the man who held Solomon's rifle and the first shot rang out, dropping the dog in midair.

Solomon watched in horror while Ruby fell to the ground, jerked twice, and was dead. In one second, the life of the friendly animal was extinguished. With a rage Solomon had never felt before, he turned and charged the man who had shot his dog.

A second shot fired, this one from one of the men still on his horse, and Solomon felt his leg buckle under him. He stumbled forward to the ground. Although he did not feel any real pain from the wound, this time he did not get up. He knew they would kill him if he did.

He looked up at the pair who stood nearest him. "You've shot me and you've killed my dog. What else do you want?"

"I told you. We're here to make a point. One your boss ain't as likely to ignore," one of the two answered, then glanced at the other. "Go ahead." He jerked his head in the direction of the barn. "Torch it."

Solomon's heart pounded so fiercely in his chest he could hear little more than his own heartbeat while he watched the man take a torch in each hand and head toward the barn.

"No, don't," he pleaded, knowing that Chad's new equipment, his grass seeds, and part of their furniture were stored inside. There were also three horses in there.

"Shut up, nigger," the man nearest him said, then for no apparent reason, kicked Solomon in the chest.

Solomon closed his eyes against the sharp spasm that followed but reopened them when he heard Raymond's voice come from somewhere just to the left of him.

"That's enough."

He turned in time to see Raymond walking cautiously across the yard with a shotgun held with both hands. Solomon's heart plunged to the pit of his soul when he realized just how outgunned Raymond was.

"You men done enough here. Time for you to be movin' on."

"You the boss?" one of them asked, clearly surprised that anyone had come to Solomon's aide. They had obviously expected to find Solomon alone.

"No. The boss ain't here. But I'm a friend of this man here, and because I am his friend, I'm not going to let you hurt him anymore."

"And you plan to stop us all with only that one shotgun?"

"Might not get you all, but I should be able to take down one or two of you," Raymond said, narrowing his gaze while he stepped closer.

Solomon wanted desperately to tell Raymond to go back inside, that this was not his fight, but because of the pain that surrounded his chest from that last blow, he could hardly breathe.

"You're makin' a big mistake," one of them said just before Solomon heard the clicks of several handguns, all in preparation to fire.

"Raymond, don't," he rasped, finally getting enough air to push his words out. "They mean business."

"So do I," Raymond said just a half second before a

shot was fired and his shoulder slung back. Although Raymond did manage to fire the shotgun, the shot went wild and no damage was done. He had one shot left but was not given the chance to use it.

Instantly two of the men were on top of Raymond and wrestled him to the ground. As soon as they had him pinned, the same man who had kicked Solomon in the chest came over and kicked Raymond several times in the stomach and once in the head.

Solomon made one attempt to stop them, but before he could cross the yard, the other men were on top of him. While two held him down, two others delivered blow after bone-shattering blow to his body. It was not until he was completely crippled by his own pain that they finally stopped.

"Pick those torches back up and burn that barn. Get to it."

Though Solomon's vision was hazy and one eye had swollen shut, he lay in a position where he could see one man go inside the barn while another opened a can of what looked like kerosene. He splashed the pungent liquid across the freshly painted walls.

As soon as he was finished and had stepped away, and the man inside had come out with the three horses he found inside, a third man ran up and threw two torches against the wet area. The resulting flames spread across the wall like water spilling across glass. Because the paint was still wet, the flame fed on the oils in it, and in less than a minute, the fire had engulfed the entire structure.

The group started backing away because the heat was almost immediate. Two climbed up into the wagon where Raymond and Solomon had been washing their brushes so they could have a better view of what they had done.

Solomon continued to watch with helpless outrage, while the bright yellow-and-orange flames licked high into the darkness.

"We takin' the horses?" he heard one of the men ask, but he didn't have the strength to try to figure out which of them had spoken. It was all he could do to stay conscious.

"No. They're branded. Leave them. I don't want nobody being able to trace none of this back to us."

Having said that, the man used his foot to roll Solomon over on his back to face him.

Solomon was in too much pain to fight them, but was lucid enough to realize they had done the same to Raymond. Now they both lay within several yards of each other, helplessly staring at the men who hovered over them.

One of them nudged Raymond with the tip of his boot. "Hey, you. I've got a message for you to give Mr. Andrews when you finally see him. Are you listening?" He paused for Raymond's response, which came in the form of a grunt. "Good, because here's what I want you to tell him. You tell him that unless he signs that land over to Charles Thornton within five days, we will be back to give out more of the same, only next time it will be the house itself that burns."

He turned and pushed Solomon with that same boot. "But as for you, you uppity nigger, you don't have to worry about it. You won't be here to see it happen." He took the can that held kerosene out of another man's hands and turned it upside down, splashing Solomon with what remained of its contents. Solomon screamed when the stinging liquid soaked through his torn clothing into his many cuts. Instinct told him to roll in the dirt to get it off him, but his body could not respond.

He heard Raymond scream just before the man who

392

had doused him reached into his pockets for the same matches they had used earlier to light the torches.

The pain searing Solomon's body was too great and slowly he allowed the resulting darkness to descend over him, but not before he heard two piercing gunshots. His last thought before slipping completely away was that Raymond was dead. He just hoped that Deborah and the boys had enough good sense to stay hidden until it was all over. He hated to think what these men might do to them.

Because Chad had wanted to look his very best that night, knowing that he now competed directly with Patrick, whose clothing was always impeccable, he had left town later than he wanted. Because he had decided to put on his nicest dinner clothes and had had a hell of a time finding his string neck tie, he knew he was going to be late again and kept his horse at a high gallop. He was only half a mile away when suddenly he saw an orange dome of light fill the late-evening sky. He knew immediately that a fire had erupted somewhere in the vicinity of his house.

With a breath lodged deep in his chest, he turned toward the glow. Slapping his reins hard, he headed his horse across the pasture rather than continue following the road. Riding hard, he soon crested the hill overlooking his house. Although he was still too far away to see exactly what was happening below, he knew something was wrong. Something other than the fact his barn was completely engulfed in flames. Something to do with the many men in his yard, none of whom seemed to be concerned with the fire.

Instinct told him to let his presence be known. He

reached immediately for his rifle and fired two shots into the air.

The shots sent the men below scrambling for their horses, and by the time Chad had started down the hill toward the house, they were riding off as a group in the opposite direction. It was not until he reached the yard and saw Solomon and Raymond lying on the ground that he realized just exactly what he had interrupted.

He hurried toward Solomon at the same time that Deborah and the boys came out of the house.

He tried to get Solomon to tell him what had happened, but neither man was lucid enough to do more than mumble incoherently. It was Raymond's boys who finally managed to tell him what had happened through their loud, rasping sobs. The three had watched from the front windows of their house and had seen almost everything. Eric sobbed uncontrollably when he told about Ruby being shot.

"We tried to make her come with us," he said, his cheeks streaming with tears while he and the others knelt at his father's side. "We tried, but she wouldn't come. She wanted to help Mr. Solomon."

"And we tried to stop Papa from coming out here, too," Craig put in, then bent to press his cheek against his father's bloodied chest. He pressed his eyes closed and wrenched a cry of anguish. The wavering light from the fire fell over him. "Oh, Papa, why didn't you listen? There was too many of them for you to do any good."

Chad was so furious by what he heard, he could hardly think, especially when little Jeffery told him about the threats to come back to do more of the same later in the week. "Eric, you boys help me get your father and Solomon into the house. Then I'll want you to take my horse and ride into town and get the doctor."

With all three boys and Deborah helping, they managed to get first Raymond then Solomon inside Raymond's house, which was the closest structure not in danger of catching fire. He helped Deborah tear off the men's clothing so she could cleanse their wounds, then hurried outside to wet down all the roofs as best he could so the fire would not spread to other buildings.

Both men remained unconscious and unaware of the extent of their injuries until after Eric returned with Dr. Mack and about a dozen men who had come to put out the fire.

With enough men there to quell the danger of further damage, Chad stayed just long enough to make sure he was no longer needed inside, then headed directly to the Thorntons' house.

When he arrived, he did not bother to tie his horse. Nor did he bother to knock. Instead, he charged directly through the front door and headed for the dining room where he expected to find everyone still eating.

He was halfway down the hall when Julia came through the dining-room door with a look of pure annoyance.

"You're late again," she pointed out, then came to a sudden halt when she noticed Chad's clothing. "You're covered with blood! What happened?"

"As if you didn't know," he said through clenched teeth, then grabbed her by the shoulder and dragged her down the hall toward her father's study.

"What is wrong with you?" she demanded to know and pulled free just as soon as they had entered the empty, darkened room. Because it was so cloudy that night, the only light came from the lamps just down the hall.

"You know damn well what's wrong with me." His eyes were black with fury. "What I want to know is how you could allow Patrick to do such a thing."

"What did he do?" Again she looked at his bloodied clothing, as if she expected to find the answer there.

"Don't act innocent with me." His nostrils flared and his eyes narrowed while he looked at her with disgust. "You know exactly what I'm talking about."

"No I don't. What did Patrick do to you?"

"It's not what he did to me, it's what he did to my foreman. Or rather what he *had done.*"

"Your foreman? I don't understand." She shook her head while she tried to make better sense of what he had said. "Why would you have a foreman?"

Aware she had not yet made the connection, his lips tightened against his teeth. He held his fury back long enough to explain. "You've been after me from the beginning to tell you my last name. Well, let me do that for you right now. My last name is Andrews. As in Chadwick Wayne Andrews, your despised new neighbor."

"You're C. W. Andrews?" She stared at him unblinking.

"Yes. Now you know why I didn't want to tell you who I was. And *now* you know what I mean about Patrick, don't you?"

"No. I don't. All I know is that you've just admitted you are the man who keeps refusing to sell my father the property he wants. I have no idea what Patrick has done." Her eyes widened with sudden realization. "You said something happened to your foreman. Do you mean Solomon?"

"Of course I mean Solomon," he ground out bitterly, his fury still roiling inside him.

"Pearline's Solomon?"

"What's left of him."

"What do you mean, what's left of him?" She again looked at his bloodied clothing, this time with a trace of fear. She ran her hands nervously over her dark-blue skirts. "What happened?"

"Why don't you go ask Patrick? As you might recall, he's the one who arranged it all."

"Patrick is not here. He went for a ride just before it turned dark and hasn't come back yet."

"You mean he went out to watch? It wasn't enough for him to know what his hired men had done. He had to see it happen?"

"See *what* happen?" She looked more and more frustrated.

Chad stared at her a long moment and decided she was far more cunning than he'd given her credit for. Though she was the one who had handed Patrick the money for his "fail proof" plan, she looked completely innocent. "You sure had me fooled. Right from the start."

"*I* had *you* fooled? How can you say that? *I'm* the one who's been duped. I'm the one who has been lied to from the start."

"I never lied to you," he answered with explosive calm. A tiny muscle in his cheek pumped rhythmically, indicating a barely controlled rage. "In fact, the only lies I've told to anyone were the lies you ordered me to feed to your father."

"That's not true," she argued. "You never told me who you were. You never told me that you are the man who has been causing all the trouble."

"I may have neglected to tell you who I am, but I never actually *lied* about my identity." He stepped closer so she could better see the anger in his eyes.

"And why is that? Why did you hide that fact from me? And if you really are Robert Freeport's nephew, then why did you ever hire on as my pretend sweetheart?" Her eyes rounded when she suddenly hit upon an answer. "You're after part of my father's land, aren't you? That's why you pretended to be in love with me. Those five hundred acres your uncle sold you are not enough. You want more. And since my father's land surrounds yours on three sides, you figured we were the ones you needed to get to know better. You wanted to find some way to trick us out of more land. You're just like your uncle."

Chad's gaze cut her to the bone. "And just what did my uncle do that was so bad?"

"What did he do that was so bad?" she asked, as if unable to believe he had asked such a question. "Do you mean besides having cheated my father out of his home and five hundred acres of prime timberland then forcing us to move out?"

"He cheated him? How?" His dark, determined gaze remained fastened to hers.

"My father used to be a terrible drinker and Robert Freeport knew it. He waited until he caught my father drunk one night in town and lured him into a card game. He then tricked Father into putting up five-hundred acres of land to cover a bet. He'd waited until he knew Father had a good hand, but knew he had one that was better. He then coerced my father into agreeing in writing that should he win, he could have his choice of acreage and would be allowed to keep whatever was on that land. Father thought he meant timber, so he signed the paper.

"When the hand was played and Father lost, Robert called in the bet. Because he had been given his choice of any land Father owned, he picked the land on which our home sat and the family cemetery lay. He would have taken the sawmill, too, but it turned out that land was in the name of all my grandfather's descendants and therefore did not belong directly to Father and was not his to lose."

Chad stared at her a moment, unable to believe his uncle could do something so vile. "Why would he do something like that?"

"Because he is a cruel and hateful man. And because he is so cruel and hateful, he refused to sell back the land and buildings later when Father tried to buy them back at three times their worth. Instead, your uncle moved into our house and made it his home. It turned out Robert Freeport had been harboring a grudge against my father for over fifteen years, all because my father was the one my mother chose to marry instead of him."

"My uncle was in love with your mother?"

She nodded. "Until my father came along, my mother was letting your uncle pay an occasional call on her. But after only a few weeks of my father courting her, she realized he was the man she loved. They were married shortly thereafter, leaving your uncle seething with jealousy. He tricked Father out of our house and the land as a way of getting even with him. I still have a hard time believing that he gave back the cemetery when Mother died."

"And you think I want to do the same," Chad said with a grim shake of his head. "If I wanted more land, I would not find it necessary to trick you out of it. I would have simply made an offer to buy it. I'm not exactly penniless. I have over fifty thousand dollars deposited in a Marshall bank, and because my lawyer just sold the rest of my family's holdings in Charleston, I have another one hundred and twelve thousand still to come."

"You're wealthy, too?" she asked, and glared at him

with even more anger. "Then *everything* about you is a lie, isn't it?"

Chad met her angry gaze, then curled his lips into a tight frown. "I did not come here to discuss me. I came here to discuss you. I came here to tell you just what I think of you and Patrick. And to warn you never to step foot on my land again."

"I haven't been on your land. Not since that day we . . ." She paused and looked away, unable to say it.

Chad cringed at the memory. He had thought himself in love with her. "That's only because you and Patrick are not the type to do your own dirty work. You hired others to come onto my land instead." He grabbed her again by the arms and shook her. "It's bad enough my barn is now little more than a pile of glowing coals, but let me assure you that if either Solomon or Raymond dies, I'll have you both brought up on charges of murder. You will be held accountable for what those ruffians you hired did to my friends."

Julia stared at him but did not offer any excuses for the terrible actions.

"You'd better pray that both those men live," he stated, then shoved her away. "Because your life isn't going to be worth living if either of them dies. As it is, I plan to see that every last man you two hired is locked away in jail for a long, long time. And if I can find a way to prove that you two were involved, you and your future husband will spend the first few years of your marriage in jail right along with them." He then headed immediately for the door, eager to get far away from her.

When he turned to head back down the hall, he found Charles standing several yards away, his face twisted into a questioning frown.

"What was all that shouting about? I could hear you

two all the way outside." His eyes widened when he looked down and saw Chad's bloodstained clothing.

"Ask your daughter," Chad answered while he continued walking toward the door. He was in no mood to go through all the details again.

Charles followed. "I'm asking *you*." He reached out to catch Chad by the arm.

Still seething from his confrontation with Julia, Chad brushed the man's hand away, but did stop long enough to tell him what he wanted to know, focusing on the fact that Julia and Patrick had hired a band of thugs to set fire to his barn while they beat his foreman and one of his ranch hands to a bloody pulp. "And if either man dies, I will find some way to prove that your daughter and her future husband were the ones responsible."

Charles's face paled as Chad continued.

"One man was shot in the leg and the other in the shoulder, then beaten senseless. And if I hadn't noticed the glow from the blaze and shown up when I did, the men also would have set fire to Solomon. They had already doused him with kerosene and were reaching for a match."

"My God." Charles reached out to grasp a table by the edge. "What sort of animals are they?"

"The sort who will do anything for money," Chad answered. "Money Julia supplied them."

"How do you know that?" he asked. Clearly he doubted his daughter's involvement.

"Because I saw her hand it to Patrick late Friday. When I asked her what the money was for, she admitted to having given it to him because he had come up with some sure-fire plan to make me want to sell my house and land to you. He needed money to pay the men and I guess he didn't want to use any of his own. Julia obviously liked the plan well enough to supply the money.

She even admitted that after Patrick saw his plan through, I—or rather Mr. Andrews—would be begging to sell you that land you want. In turn, you'd be singing Patrick's praises enough to finally let her marry him."

"She wants to marry Patrick?"

"That's why she hired me. To make such a bother of myself that Patrick would look like a godsend in comparison. She wanted to make certain you appreciated Patrick's many 'fine' qualities. They set that other plan into motion for that same reason. They hoped to frighten me into selling that land so you in turn would feel grateful to Patrick for having accomplished something you couldn't."

"I can't believe Julia could be a part of anything like that," Charles said, then swallowed hard while he let all the facts soak in. "Of course I'll replace your barn and anything that was in it, and I'll pay all the doctor's fees."

"I don't want your money," Chad said. "You just keep that conniving daughter and her future husband off my land, because if they or any of Patrick's men show up there again, I'll shoot them on sight."

He pushed past Charles then and headed straight for his horse. He would have waited to confront Patrick himself, but he was too eager to get back and find out if the doctor thought Solomon and Raymond would live.

Chapter Twenty-three

Charles was too stunned by what he had just learned to follow Chad outside. Instead, he stood where he was staring into the darkness that lay beyond the door Chad had not bothered to close.

It was baffling enough to find out that Chad was Robert's nephew, but to be told that his daughter had purposely deceived him and might even have had a part in something as vile as arson and assault was inconceivable. Still, Chad's words rang in his ears.

Because I saw her when she handed the money to Patrick, he had said with such black rage, Charles still shuddered from merely having witnessed it.

You just keep that conniving daughter of yours and her future husband off my land, he had warned. *Because if they or any of his men show up there again, I'll shoot them on sight.*

Charles wondered how he could not have known that Patrick was the one Julia really wanted to marry. Patrick was much more like the men she normally chose, only a little older. Suddenly he realized just how dead wrong he had been about Chad. Dead wrong because they had wanted him to be dead wrong.

He glanced at the room where Chad had confronted Julia and found the strength to go inside and do the same. Although he dreaded hearing the truth, he had to know.

He found Julia standing motionless in the dim glow from the hall light. "Did you and Patrick have anything to do with what happened over at his place tonight?"

Julia turned confused eyes to him. "I don't know."

"What do you mean you don't know?" he asked angrily, too frustrated to put up with such nonsense. "Did you or did you not give Patrick money late Friday so he could go into town and hire a pack of hoodlums to go and burn down Chad's barn as a way of convincing him to sell out?"

"I gave Patrick some money," she admitted, her forehead notching. "But I didn't know what he intended to do with it. All I was told was that he needed money to carry out a plan that was sure to get you the land and house. He did not tell me what the plan was because he didn't want anyone knowing of his failure should it fall through. I thought he planned to use the money to hire a lawyer or maybe pay off a judge. I had no idea he planned to hurt anyone."

With tears in her eyes, she pressed her hand to her throat. "Pearline is on her way over there right now to see Solomon. She has no way of knowing what happened." Her whole body trembled. "What if he's dead?"

"You'd better pray that he's not," Charles said, unaware that Solomon meant anything to Julia's personal maid other than a means to get her that acre of land she wanted. "Because if either man dies, you and Patrick could very well end up in jail for having hired those thugs to go over there and hurt them."

"But I had nothing to do with that. I had no idea that was what Patrick had in mind."

"But you gave him the money he wanted," Charles pointed out. "You should have asked what it was for."

As Julia pressed her eyes closed, a tear rolled forlornly down her cheek. "I wish I had."

Charles stared at her a long moment. He wondered how his daughter could ever have trusted Patrick Moore. He knew from the very day Patrick arrived that the man was a deceitful opportunist. The only reason he had put up with all that foolish talk about investing in a river canal that would cost more to build than it could ever save him in shipping was because he knew that Patrick's presence annoyed Chad. At the time that was all that mattered. He should have followed his instincts and sent the man packing that very first day.

"Where *is* Patrick?" he asked, remembering that neither he nor Chad had been present during supper. For the first time in weeks, he and Julia had eaten their evening meal alone.

Julia shrugged to indicate she did not know just seconds before they both heard the sound of a horse entering the yard.

Charles walked over to the window to catch a glimpse of him. But he had not ridden around to that side of the house.

Knowing that Patrick would come looking for them, he and Julia did not move. When Patrick entered the house through one of the side doors only a few minutes later, it was Julia who called out to let him know where they were.

Julia bent to light a table lamp while Charles walked across the room to join her near the door.

"Why are you both in here?" Patrick asked as he entered the room. His blond hair was windblown and his green eyes were wide with repressed excitement. For the first time, his clothing was rumpled. "I expected you to be outside enjoying this beautiful night. Haven't you eaten yet?"

Charles was in no mood for any unnecessary talk. He got straight to the point. "Chad was just here."

Patrick looked down to straighten the lapels of his white summer coat and smooth the front of his shirt as if unconcerned by such a statement. "That is nothing new. He comes over every night, doesn't he?"

"Yes, but tonight was different. Tonight he came to admit who he really is and to tell us what happened at his place."

Patrick cut his gaze to Julia, then returned it to Charles. "Why? Who is he?"

"He's Robert Freeport's nephew. The one who bought the land and house I want."

"Chad Sutton is C. W. Andrews?" he asked in disbelief, then looked again at Julia, this time accusingly. "You hired the very man your father despises?"

"I didn't know who he was until tonight," she admitted.

"Neither of us did," Charles put in. "But that's not what is important here. What's important is what happened at his place just a few hours ago. How could you have done something like that?"

Patrick took a tentative step toward Julia, as if hoping to find protection with her. "I did it for you. Didn't I, Julia? I did it so you could get that land back. I did it so you would finally see a reason to like me."

"And you think that going out and hiring a band of thugs to burn down someone's barn and beat his men senseless was going to make me like you?"

Patrick's body tensed. "Yes. If it got you your land back. After all, didn't you do practically the same thing?"

"All I did was send a group of men over there to act in an intimidating fashion. I didn't order anyone hurt or any damage done."

"That's because you have no real foresight and I have. I've dealt with people like that all my life. I know what it takes to get through to them."

Charles was too angry to discuss such foolishness further. He needed time to think. Time to figure out what could be done to rectify the situation. "Get out of my house."

"Sir?"

"I said, get out of my house. I want you to pack up your things and leave! I will not have you living under my roof another minute."

Patrick blinked, truly perplexed. "But I don't think you understand. I did it for you. And for Julia." Again he looked to Julia for help. "You can't let your father send me away. Tell him what a mistake he's making. Explain to him how very much you love me."

Julia glared at him with clear contempt. "How could I possibly love you? I don't even know you. You are not the man you've pretended to be. That man never could have done what you just did. That man never could have caused such harm to Solomon Ford, the man Pearline is in love with."

As angry as Charles was, the fact that Pearline was in love with Chad's foreman barely registered. "I told you to leave."

"Not until I have a chance to explain to Julia why I did what I did," he said, then grabbed her by the arms as if that might help him hold on to her affection. "Please, Julia."

"There can be no explanation for having done anything so vile," she responded, and jerked free of his grasp. "You might as well do what Father said and leave. The sight of you disgusts me."

With tears in her eyes, she fled the room, leaving Patrick and Charles facing each other.

Calmly, Charles walked over to his desk and pulled out a drawer. "I think I know what it will take to convince you to leave."

Patrick's interest perked and he moved forward when Charles bent to get something from inside. "What's that?"

"This," he responded, and brought out the pistol he kept there for just such occasions. He relished the look on Patrick's face when he realized no money was forthcoming. Instead, he now had a pistol aimed at his stomach. "Now get out!"

"I don't think you understand. Your daughter *loves* me. She loves me and she wants to marry me."

The muscles in Charles's face flexed, indicating just how angry he really was when he slowly cocked the hammer back. "I said to pack your things and get out!"

Patrick's eyes narrowed a moment, then widened again. "You'll live to regret this night, Thornton," he stated, then turned to do as he had been told.

Once alone in her bedroom, Julia had time to fully consider what had just happened and was amazed at how little remorse she felt knowing that Patrick was not the man he had claimed to be and had just been ordered out of their house. All she felt was anger. Anger toward Patrick for what he had done and anger toward herself for having been the one to invite him there in the first place.

She had been so eager to have things go her way, she had not seen Patrick for who he really was. She had not *wanted* to see him as anyone other than the man who could give her the sort of life she had always longed to have. She should have known that Patrick was a fraud.

Staring off into the shadows that surrounded her, for

she had not bothered to light a lamp, she remembered how Chad and Pearline had both warned her that Patrick was not who he seemed to be. But she had been too stubborn to listen.

Now what was she going to do? How could she ever face Pearline again knowing that she was the one who had not only brought Patrick there but had given him the money he needed to see to his evil plan.

She closed her eyes and prayed fervently that Solomon would live and that one day Pearline would forgive her for what she had done.

Still holding his pistol, Charles watched from the doorway while Patrick flung his clothing and personal effects into a large valise that lay open near the foot of his bed.

"I hope you know that you are making a grave mistake," Patrick said, then paused in his task long enough to meet Charles's angry gaze.

"So you've said."

"I'm not as guilty as you think I am. True, I hired those men to go over there, but I did not know they intended to hurt anyone. Obviously, the men misunderstood my orders. It was their idea to get rough, not mine. All I wanted them to do was frighten everyone a little."

"Keep packing." Charles tapped the pistol with his fingertip as a reminder of what might happen if he didn't.

Patrick's eyes glinted dark green. "Why can't you believe me?"

"Because I've lived in this world long enough to know a liar when I see one. I don't believe a word that comes out of your mouth."

"Well, Julia will believe me," Patrick said with a stubborn lift of his chin, then headed toward the door to go to her. He paused when he realized Charles blocked his way.

"No she won't."

"Yes she will," Patrick argued. "She loves me."

Charles had seen the anger and the hatred in Julia's eyes just before she had fled to her bedroom and knew that this was not the time for Patrick to try sweet-talking her again. Any attempt to do so now would surely end with Patrick getting his face soundly slapped, at the very least. Julia was a smart woman and was not about to fall prey to this man's lies a second time.

"If she loves you so much, then take her with you," he offered, finally stepping aside to allow Patrick to pass. "But don't you stay another minute in this house and don't you ever try to return here. You are not to step foot inside my door again."

"You'll have to let me back in if I marry Julia," he said with a cocky wave of his head. "I'll be her husband. You'll have to open your door to me."

"No I won't," Charles responded simply. "Nor will I have to open my door to *her*, either. I don't know if she explained it to you or not, but the truth is, if Julia ever marries someone I have not first approved, then she is no longer welcome here. I'll not be a witness to her having ruined her life. That means if she does marry you, she will not get another penny out of me—*ever*. I'll have her struck from my will the minute your vows are spoken."

Patrick clenched his hands in frustration. If he stayed and tried to convince Julia to marry him, he could end up with a wife who had no money. But if he left willingly, he might never have the chance to worm his way back inside that house. He could lose his only chance at someday inheriting all the Thornton money.

"You'd do that?" he finally asked. "You'd cut your daughter off without a cent?"

"If she married you, she would no longer be a daughter of mine."

Patrick studied Charles's determined expression for a moment and realized he'd meant what he said. Frustrated, he returned to the bed where he had left his valise and finished throwing his belongings inside.

Minutes later, he stalked out of the house with his valise in one hand and his hat in the other. His mind was already working on a way to rectify the mistake he had obviously made. He needed a new plan, and quick.

Wishing now he had not returned the horse and carriage he had hired the day he arrived, he trekked across the yard, toward the front gate. He stopped just long enough to look back at the house to see if Julia might be peeking out her window and noticed Charles standing on the veranda watching his every move. When he saw the anger still pulling at the old man's face, he knew that instead of winning Charles Thornton's gratitude as he had hoped, he had just made a lifelong enemy of him. *And that was one enemy he did not need.*

Charles waited until Patrick was well down the road, before grabbing up a lantern and heading off toward the stable. He did not trust Patrick and wanted to tell Sirus and the others to keep a watch for him. They were not to let that man step foot back on his land.

After warning the others to be on their guard, he walked out into the backyard and sat on a small wrought-iron bench to think through all he had heard and seen in the past hour.

411

Gauging by how angry Chad had become with Julia for the part he thought she had played in the earlier incident, and by how angry Julia had been with Chad in return for having kept his true identity from her, he knew somewhere along the way those two had come to care for each other. They were not just angry with each other, they were heartbroken. It also occurred to him that should Julia and Chad finally acknowledge their feelings and marry, the house would once again be brought into the family and his grandchildren would be free to play in the same yard where Julia had played. In that way, he would have fulfilled his promise to his wife.

The following morning Charles approached Julia as she gathered her paints and canvas and casually encouraged her to mend the rift with Chad. To his dismay, she refused to even consider such a thing. It was her belief that Chad was the one who had misrepresented himself from the beginning, and since it was Chad who had falsely accused her of having done something so horrible, he should be the one to apologize to her.

Unable to get her to see Chad's side, he next tried to convince Chad to apologize. But Chad did not believe *he* had anything to apologize for, although he had seemed pleased to hear how angry Julia was with Patrick. He was also glad to hear that Patrick not only had been forced to leave the house but had been seen purchasing a one-way ticket at the train station earlier that morning. Even so, Chad sent Charles on his way with no hint of being willing to apologize to Julia, ever.

Not knowing what else to do to help matters along, Charles went on to work at the mill. After several hours of getting nothing done because of the problems that weighed heavily on his mind, he decided that what he needed was a woman's viewpoint and sought Jean Boswell's advice.

When he opened the door to his office to ask her to come in for a talk, he discovered she was not at her desk and realized she must have gone outside to get the morning reports from the foremen. Not wanting to wait for her return, he headed down the hall and had just stepped outside when suddenly he felt a horrendous explosion behind him. The sound was deafening and the force of it so severe, it jerked him right up off the ground and sent him sailing through the air like so much debris.

He was so stunned by the incident, he was barely aware that his clothing had caught fire or that the building behind him now scattered in all directions. All he knew was that there had been an unbearably loud noise that made him feel as if he had been whacked in the back of the head by a two-by-four and that his feet were no longer on the ground.

With incredible slowness, his body turned over and over in the air, letting him see first the sky then the ground, then the sky again. It was not until he finally landed nearly thirty feet away that he realized any severe pain, and then it was just for a moment because within seconds the flames engulfed him and he lost consciousness.

Julia had just returned to the house and was gingerly washing out her paintbrushes when she heard the explosion. Dropping her brushes in the pail, she raced back outside to try to figure out what had caused such a noise. First, she noticed a cloud of black smoke off in the distance followed almost immediately by a large pillar of

413

white smoke and realized there had been an accident at the mill.

Not about to wait long enough for a carriage to be rigged and seeing that the horse Sirus had used earlier when he went into town to make sure Patrick intended to leave town was still saddled, she untied the horse, then quickly swung herself into place. Because it was a man's saddle, she had to yank her skirts to her knees and ride astride. With bloomers showing, she took off immediately for the mill.

Barely ten minutes later she arrived at the smaller road that would take her from the main road to the mill. Shortly after she turned, she met a wagon carrying something in the back. When she got closer, she realized the cargo was her father and someone else. Because she was headed in the opposite direction at such an impossible rate, it took her a moment to turn her horse and catch up.

"What happened?" she asked Tommy Sanford, who along with two millers kept the wagon moving at a quick but steady pace.

"There was an explosion at the mill. Looks like someone set off a pack of dynamite under your father's office. Completely destroyed the building. But fortunately your father was just leaving out one door and Miss Boswell had not quite yet entered another when the blast went off. Otherwise they'd both be dead right now. As it is, they are hurt real bad. We're taking them into town to the hospital so a doctor can have a look at them."

Julia's heart leaped to her throat when she glanced into the back and saw just how blackened and bloody they both were. Jean Boswell's body was so badly burned, she was almost unrecognizable. "I'll ride on ahead and warn them you're coming so they can be ready for them."

With fear paralyzing her heart, she dug her heels into the horse's sides then hung on for dear life.

Sheriff Andrew Bellomy and Deputy Tony Brooks entered the hospital only a few minutes after Tommy had arrived with Charles and Jean's badly burned bodies. He waited until both had been carried inside and work started on them before asking any questions of Tommy and the two millers who had ridden with him. It was then that Julia found out about the note one of the men had found nailed to a wooden hitching post out front.

Knowing it was important, they had brought the note with them. Although rumpled from having been in Tommy's pocket for over half an hour, the words had been neatly printed on plain white paper in black pencil: *This is for what happened to Solomon!*

"Solomon," the sheriff repeated after having read the note for himself. He glanced at his deputy with a puzzled expression. "Isn't that the name of one of those men Doc Mack brought in here last night?" He looked at a nurse who stood nearby. "Wasn't that Negro's name Solomon?"

She nodded. "He's been taken over to the old building if you want to talk to him. That's where we had to put him."

Julia knew the building she meant. Because Negroes were not allowed to stay in the main hospital with the other patients, they had been provided a hospital building of their own just down the block.

"Probably would be a good idea," the sheriff commented to his deputy, but said nothing else to Tommy or Julia before heading immediately out the door.

Tommy waited around for half an hour more before it dawned on him that he and the other two men might be needed back at the mill. Knowing there was nothing else they could do, Julia agreed to send someone out with word of her father and Miss Boswell's conditions as soon as she knew something definite.

Because she was not allowed to be with her father or his secretary while the surgeons worked to repair some of the damage done by the blast, she stayed in a small waiting area nearby. With nothing to do but think while she waited to hear if her father would live or die, she realized just how selfish and foolish she had been.

She had never loved Patrick. That was obvious by how little it had hurt to lose him. She had obviously been using him as a means to prove something to her father. Having brought Patrick to the house had been more an act of defiance than anything else. By trying to trick him into approving someone he otherwise might not have approved, she had actually been trying to control *him* rather than allow him to continue controlling her. But she had given no real consideration to the eventual cost of her forced liberation.

What if she had succeeded in tricking her father and he had allowed her to marry Patrick?

She shuddered at the thought.

Chapter Twenty-four

Julia was still at the hospital awaiting word of her father when Sheriff Bellomy and Deputy Brooks returned.

"About half a mile up the road from your father's sawmill we found an abandoned wagon with a broken wheel that had a small roll of dynamite fuse hidden under a blanket in the back," the sheriff told her, then pushed his hat to the back of his head rather than take it off like he should. "Because the wagon looked to be pretty new and had the Smith Brothers' mercantile brand burned into the back, we went there to find out if they knew who it might belong to. They said it had to belong to your new neighbor, Chad Andrews. The man whose barn burned to the ground last night. The man Solomon Ford works for."

Julia stared at the sheriff a moment while she let what they had just told her sink in. "Surely you don't think Chad Andrews had anything to do with the explosion at the mill."

"Yes, ma'am, I do. It was his wagon we found with fuse still in it and it was two of his work hands who got beat up so bad. Who else could have done it?"

"I don't know, but it wasn't Chad," she said, wishing she did have some idea of who might have set that blast.

If Sirus had not watched Patrick go into the train station that morning and buy that one-way ticket out of town, she would have suspected him. But as it was, she didn't know who could have done such a thing.

"Sorry, ma'am, but all the evidence we've found so far tells us it was Chad Andrews. We just wanted you to know what we'd found out and that we are on our way out to arrest the man now. You won't have to worry about anyone coming around to hurt your father again."

"But you can't arrest Chad," she pleaded, knowing in her heart that he was innocent. "Chad could never be guilty of such a terrible thing."

"If he's really innocent like you say, then that fact will come out at his trial. But until a jury tells me different, I'll be keeping that man locked up in my jail," the sheriff told her with certainty, then nudged his deputy with his elbow. "Come on, Tony, we got us a job to do. Better get to it."

Unable to argue against the evidence the sheriff had found, yet still believing Chad to be innocent, Julia felt a hard and throbbing ache deep inside her chest while she watched the sheriff and deputy stride out of the room.

She knew there had to be a logical reason for Chad's wagon to have been found along that road with the roll of fuse hidden inside. There just had to be. If only she could figure out what that reason was.

Returning to the small chair she had occupied off and on during the past several hours, she tried to figure out what might have happened. She was still sitting there, her mind alternating between thoughts of Chad and thoughts of her father, when Pearline came into the room looking dejected and exhausted.

"Thought I'd find you here," she said as she trudged

across the room. She was so drained from her overnight vigil at Solomon's side that she was barely able to lift her feet off the floor when she walked. "How's your father?"

"I don't know," she answered, and glanced at the clock near the door. "He's been in surgery for nearly five hours, but in all that time no one has come out to tell me what, if any, progress has been made. How is Solomon? Sirus told me you stayed with him all night."

Pearline offered a weak smile, then sank wearily into a nearby chair. "I stayed by his side until just a little while ago and I think he's finally doin' a little better. He's come to twice now, but he don't stay to for long. Because of all the pain, they got him and Mr. Raymond both pretty drugged."

Seeing Pearline's troubled expression and knowing exactly how she felt, Julia got up and knelt in front of her. "I'm glad you're here. I wanted to tell you how very sorry I am for what Patrick did." When Pearline looked confused by her apology, she dampened her lips and continued. "You did know that Patrick was the one who hired those men, didn't you?"

Pearline nodded, but still looked confused. "Mr. Chad told me. He was at the hospital until early this morning waitin' to see if either Solomon or Mr. Raymond was goin' to wake up enough to tell him anything. But what's that got to do with you? You ain't responsible for what that sorry man did."

"In a way I am. I gave him the money to hire them."

"But you didn't know that was what the money was for. Mr. Chad done told me that."

Julia blinked, unaware Chad had finally come to believe her. "He did?"

"Sure did. He told me while he was waitin' for Solomon and Raymond to wake up and talk to him."

"And did they?"

"Solomon did. Told him everything that happened, and hearing it just made Mr. Chad angry all over again."

Julia felt a quickening of her pulses. "How angry?"

"Not angry enough to go stickin' no dynamite up under your father's office buildin' if that's what you're wonderin'. I tried tellin' the sheriff that, but he wouldn't listen."

Julia felt another quickening of her pulses. "Where is Chad now?"

Pearline took a deep breath and looked away. "That's what I come to tell you. The sheriff's done up and arrested him. Says they got proof that he's the one who set off that dynamite at the mill."

"But that's ridiculous," Julia insisted.

"I know. Solomon tried tellin' them that there's no way Mr. Chad could be involved in something like that, but they just didn't want to listen. Solomon tried explainin' how he's known Mr. Chad a long, long time and how he knows him to be a good and honorable man. He said Mr. Chad don't even like to tell a lie. Bothered him something fierce just havin' to pretend to be your sweetheart from St. Louis."

Julia closed her eyes, knowing that was true. After having had time to think about everything, she realized how wrong she had been when she'd accused him of having lied to her. The only lies he had told were the lies she had ordered him to tell, lies that had to do with being her sweetheart. As for who he was, he had never really *lied* to her about that. He had just never bothered telling her the truth.

"I wonder why he ever took the job I offered him when it obviously goes against his nature to tell lies?"

She looked to Pearline for an answer. "Especially when he did not need the money."

Pearline smile tiredly. "I think maybe it was because he's so attracted to you. Solomon says he never stops talkin' about you."

A sharp pain filled Julia's heart when she realized that not only had she misjudged Patrick, she had misjudged Chad, too. Sadly, she stood and pressed her hands against her cheeks while she tried to come to terms with what she felt. "What are we going to do? Chad is clearly innocent. We can't let him sit in that jail for something we all know he didn't do."

"Nothin' we can do. They already arrested him. He's already sittin' there. They got him just as he was comin' to the hospital to see Solomon again." Her mouth twitched. "I sure hate the thought of havin' to tell Solomon about that when he wakes up again. He's got enough to worry about."

Julia thought about that for a moment. "Then don't tell him yet. Or if you do tell him, explain that I'm headed over there to have another talk with that sheriff. There's been a terrible mistake made and Sheriff Bellomy has to be made to see that."

Pearline followed Julia to the front door, but as soon as they were outside, Julia headed off in one direction, toward the jail, while Pearline headed in the other, toward the other hospital.

By the time Julia reached the sheriff's office, she was so angry that she marched directly into the sheriff's front room and demanded Chad's release.

"I can't go let him out, ma'am," the sheriff said, clearly surprised to see her there pleading Chad Andrews's case. "He tried to kill your father."

"No he didn't. He's not guilty." She waved her arms

as a way to vent her frustration. "I know Chad and he's not capable of doing anything like that."

"Some people can fool you," the sheriff said. "They can act one way but be another."

Remembering that Patrick had done exactly that, Julia hesitated a moment, then shook away the idea. "Not Chad Andrews. He's too honest. You can't let him waste away in jail for a crime he did not commit."

"Sounds to me like you got your cap set for this man," the sheriff said, not at all swayed by what she had said thus far. "Sound like maybe it's your heart that's doing all the talking instead of your head."

"You're wrong. It's nothing like that," she insisted, refusing to admit even to herself that she might actually be in love with him. Especially after having just gotten over being so angry with him. "It's just that I have learned to respect him. He really is an honest man." She spoke those words with complete conviction, knowing now that he had never lied to her. He had just failed to volunteer the truth about certain matters. "I've known him nearly a month and I know he is not capable of something so vile. Please let him go." She could not bear the thought of him in that jail.

"He is guilty of having destroyed part of your father's mill and of having injured your father and his secretary in the process. He has to be punished," the sheriff told her in no uncertain terms, then offered a condescending smile. "I know you think I'm wrong, but you may as well get used to the idea of him spending quite a bit of time in this jail."

"But he's not guilty," she tried again.

The sheriff's smile faded into an annoyed frown. "I think you better get on out of here. You've got a father in the hospital to worry about. I'd think that's where you would want to be."

Aware she was getting nowhere with this man, Julia finally left, but not before trying one last time. "An innocent man is in there."

The sheriff let out a short huff, completely out of patience. "Good day to you, Miss Thornton," he said, then turned his back to indicate he had nothing more to say. Julia had little choice but to leave.

Chad leaned heavily against the bars, straining to hear every word that was said. Although he was disappointed to learn that Julia would not yet admit any true feelings for him, he was touched by the confidence she had shown in him. And he was glad she did not believe him capable of having brought any harm to her father. He had worried that the evidence, phony as it was, would make her believe him guilty. Especially as angry as she had been with him last night.

He sighed, dejected, when seconds later he heard her leave. He was not even going to get to see her.

What he needed was to get out of jail long enough to find out who really had set off that dynamite—though he already had a suspicion. Pearline's brother might have followed Patrick to the train station and watched him buy a ticket, but Sirus had not stayed to see him actually board a train. He had been too eager to get back to the hospital to see Solomon.

Because he believed Patrick would not leave until he was certain he had gotten some form of revenge, Chad thought someone should be out searching for him. If only one of his men would come by to visit him, then he could send him out to do just that. But for now, all he could do was sit there and feel helpless.

Hearing footsteps headed in his direction, Chad stepped away from the bars and waited.

"I suppose you heard all that," the sheriff said, his face drawn with anger when he stepped into the narrow hall that linked his office to the cells. "Julia Thornton believes you're innocent."

"And you still don't," Chad said, knowing the answer to that.

"Of course I don't. I know better. You may have that pretty little lady fooled with all your sweet talk and your flashy smile, but not me. I know your kind. And I know you did it. And if that father does die like they say he might, then I'll see you swing from the gallows for his murder."

"I didn't do it," Chad told him, though he knew the statement would do no good.

"That's what they all say," the sheriff said, then turned and walked away, leaving Chad to wallow again in his frustration.

After having been told that the earliest she would be allowed in to see her father or his secretary would be that following morning, Julia took the doctor's advice and returned to the house rather than stay the night at the hospital.

It was just after eight o'clock when she returned, and even though she had not eaten a bite since early that morning, she had no desire for food. Because Sirus had gone back to town, she quickly unsaddled her own horse, then went directly up to her room.

She found that Ruth had gone up ahead of her, had lit a bedside lamp and turned back her covers. Thinking it a good idea to try to get some sleep, she immediately started to unfasten her clothing.

When she bent to toss her outer clothing over a nearby chair, she noticed her sketch pad lying there.

Sadly, she picked it up and studied the image she had so lovingly drawn of Chad the week before. Tears filled her eyes while she hugged the pad to her and remembered what it was like to be held in his arms. Remembered what it was like to be caressed in such a loving way.

How foolish she had been to stop him that day after they'd returned from the mill. How foolish to have ignored his glorious declaration of love. He had admitted being in love with her, enough so he wanted to marry her—and she had foolishly pushed him away. All because she thought she was in love with Patrick when in truth the only thing she was in love with was the sort of life he had promised to give her.

Tears filled her eyes when she thought more about that day. It broke her heart to know that someone that caring and that gentle was now sitting alone in a jail cell, all because he had been falsely accused of having brought harm to her father. Her pain became unbearable when she realized what would happen if her father should die from those injuries.

But she refused to consider such a thing. She refused to consider what life would be like without her father and without Chad.

Finally she set the pad aside, knowing someday she wanted to transfer the image to canvas, then finished getting ready for bed. After saying prayers for her father, his secretary, Solomon, Raymond, and Chad, she turned out the lamp and slipped between the covers. She was so exhausted, she fell almost instantly into a fitful sleep. Not much later she was awakened by a dull light shining in her face.

Groggy from having been asleep for such a short time, she blinked her eyes open and looked around to see why her room was no longer dark. Surely it was not morning already.

"Patrick!" she gasped when she noticed him standing beside her bed, lamp in hand, looking very rumpled but extremely happy. "What are you doing here? I thought you left Texas early this morning."

"I considered it, but that was before I realized just how much I had to lose by leaving," he said, then sat down on the edge of her bed as if he had every right to be there in her bedroom. "I had already bought my ticket and was waiting for the early train when I realized what a big mistake I was making. I decided I would be a fool if I didn't stay and try to do something to fix things."

He reached for her hand, but she snatched it away and used it to clutch her bedcovers to her.

"Such modesty," he said in a teasing voice. "I like that."

"You shouldn't be here."

"But I wanted you to know that our problems are almost over. I just came from the hospital and was told by one of the staff that your father has had a drastic turn for the worse and probably won't live to see morning."

Julia stared at him, unblinking. Such obvious happiness on the part of Patrick and the frightening fact that her father might die did not coincide.

"And that means Chad will eventually hang for murder." Patrick chuckled, thinking himself quite clever for what he had done.

Julia cowered against her pillows and clutched the covers to her more tightly, unable to make full sense of his rantings.

"Just think," he continued and arched his shoulders proudly. "With one simple act, I will have gotten rid of the two men I hate most and yet no one will be any the wiser. After all the clues I've left, Chad is sure to swing from the gallows for having murdered your father."

The devastation Julia felt upon hearing that Chad really *could* hang for murder was so overwhelming, she could hardly stand hearing it. It was painful enough to know she risked losing her beloved father, but to lose Chad, too, would be her emotional undoing. She could not let Chad die for a crime he did not commit. She had to find some way to get away from Patrick so she could go tell the sheriff what she now knew: Patrick was the one responsible for that blast.

But would the sheriff believe her? To be better able to convince him of the truth, she decided she should try to find out exactly what he did so they would know where to look to prove him guilty.

"*You* set off that blast?"

Patrick nodded, then wagged his head, clearly pleased with that accomplishment. "After I realized what needed to be done, and then finding out that Chad was still in town seeing after those two men of his, I went back to his place early this morning and took a wagon I remembered noticing out in front of his barn last night. I found what I needed to hitch it up to my horse right there in the carriage house, then drove it about halfway to your father's mill. I then ran it into a ditch to give it a reason for having been abandoned like it was.

"Then I unhitched it again, put some of the dynamite fuse I'd stolen out of a wagon in town into the back, and covered it up so it would look like it was not supposed to be found. Next I headed on over to the mill and did the deed." He rubbed his hands together with obvious glee. "I even thought to leave a note worded so the sheriff would think Chad was the only one who could have left it."

"How did you get in and out of the mill yard without anyone seeing you?" She pressed her lips together, hoping to discover there *had been a witness*.

"With all the noise that goes on around there and all people running around the place, I managed to walk right up to the building with the dynamite up under my coat and no one ever even noticed me. Even if they had, all I'd have had to do was tell them I was there to see your father, to beg one last time for his forgiveness."

His smile widened. "Pretty clever, how easily I solved the problem of you being cut off. Now we don't have to worry. We can have everything. Because I acted as quickly as I did, your father never got the chance to cut you out of his will like he threatened. We can be married as planned and not have to worry about that father of yours keeping us away from all his money. And the beautiful part about it all is that Chad Andrews will take all the blame."

Julia was so stunned by his confession and so frightened by his behavior that she could only stare at him, her mouth wide with horror, too dumbfounded to comment.

Thinking Julia had parted her mouth because she was so very pleased with what he had done and beckoned a kiss, Patrick moved closer and wrapped his arms around her.

"Now we can be married. Just think how happy we will be," he said just as he dipped his head to kiss her.

Horrified at the thought of his mouth touching hers, Julia shoved him away and kicked back her covers.

"You are dead wrong about that, Patrick," she said, rolling off the bed onto the opposite side. She flung her hair out of the way as her feet hit the floor. "There is no way in hell I'd marry you now."

Patrick's eyes darkened with fury when he made a

grab for her but missed. She headed for the door without bothering to reach for her robe and he hurried to head her off. "Get back here."

When she did not slow her pace, he made a wild dive for her legs. He struck her behind the knees and knocked her to the floor. Before she could get up, he had her pinned to the rug by the shoulders.

"You *will* marry me," he said, then angrily grabbed her gown and tore the front. "You *will*—even if I have to put a baby inside you to make you do it."

"Leave me alone!" she screamed just before she slammed her fist against the side of his head in an effort to free herself. When that did not work, she tried to kick him. "I will not marry you." Realizing she needed help in fending him off, she called out to the only other person in the house. "Ruth! Ruth, get Father's gun! Help me!"

"Don't bother calling your housekeeper. She can't hear you. She's busy taking a little nap on the kitchen floor," he said angrily, and rolled over on top of her until his mouth hovered just over hers.

"Get off me! I don't love you and I won't marry you."

"Oh, yes you will," he said, then let go of one shoulder long enough to tear her gown further, exposing her breasts to his view. "You will gladly marry me once you realize you'll be needing a father for your baby."

Aware he fully intended to take what he wanted, Julia reached for a nearby table, causing it to tumble over, its contents scattering on the floor. Grabbing a metal picture frame, she used it to strike Patrick across the side of his head. The blow caused him to let go of her long enough to make another run for freedom.

Knowing she would never make it downstairs before he caught up with her again, she hurried instead into her father's bedroom where she knew she could lock the door. If only there was some way to get down to her father's study. Then she would have a gun to protect herself. She looked at the window and wondered if she could make it around to where a large oak tree grew near enough to the ledge to provide her a means down before Patrick realized where she had gone.

Chad paced the floor of his cell. He didn't understand how the sheriff could be so stubborn. Not only was he unwilling to believe that someone else could be to blame for that blast, he refused to send someone over to the hospital to check on Julia. He also refused to believe that Julia was in any danger, especially since she was inside a large hospital with so many people around to protect her.

But Chad knew that if Patrick was capable of almost murdering Charles at a crowded mill and getting away with it, then he was capable of trying the same with Julia. The man was obviously insane.

"Sheriff, what's it going to cost you to send someone over there to check on her?" he shouted loud enough to be heard in the other room, but the sheriff did not answer. Finally, he gave up and just waited for someone to come see him. To his relief Pearline appeared only a little while later, *asking to see him*. When the grumpy sheriff refused to give her permission to go on back, she turned on the tears until finally he gave in.

"But just for a few minutes," he warned. "As soon as I get through reading what's on these latest posters, I'm headed home."

Chad's heart raced wildly while he waited for Pearline to appear around the door. "Am I ever glad to see you," he said, and stretched his arms through the bars to show her how very much.

Pearline reached out and took one of his hands. A deep frown marred her face. "Mr. Chad. I'm worried. Just a little while ago, Julia stopped by the part of the hospital where I was wantin' to see how Solomon was comin' along and said she was headed home to get some sleep."

An immediate feeling of apprehension crept over Chad. "Why didn't she just sleep there at the hospital?"

"Because they told her she wouldn't be allowed to see her father until sometime tomorrow anyway, so she decided to go home. That alone didn't frighten me. But then just a few minutes later, I was headed down the street to get somethin' to eat before everythin' closed and I saw Patrick Moore comin' out of the other part of the hospital. Knowin' he was supposed to be already gone, I waited until he was down the street, then went inside to see why he was there. They told me he had come in askin' about Mr. Thornton. Said he was real concerned about him." Fear reflected from her dark eyes. "That don't make no sense to me. Not when Mr. Thornton all but threw him out of his house last night."

"So Patrick Moore *is* still in town." Chad's expression was suddenly hard as granite.

"The nurse told me something else that didn't make no sense. He told me that Mr. Patrick asked to be left alone with Mr. Thornton for a few minutes because he was almost family. He wasn't allowed to do that because a nurse has to be with him all the time." Pearline's grip tightened. "Mr. Chad. That don't sound good to me. Now that I know Mr. Patrick is still in town, I think he might be the one who set dynamite off."

"I do, too. But there's no convincing the sheriff that anyone did it but me," he said, then felt a fresh surge of fear. "Do you know if the doctor or one of the nurses might have mentioned to Patrick that Julia had gone home?"

"I don't know. I didn't ask them nothin' about that."

Chad shoved away from the bars. "Pearline, you have to help me. Julia could be in serious danger."

"Help you? How?"

"I need to escape. You have to help me get out of here."

Pearline's eyebrows dipped a moment, then arched questioningly. "How?"

"Find me a gun. Bring it to me under your skirts."

Pearline nodded, then with no further questions, headed out the door. She returned not fifteen minutes later with the story that she had dropped her supper money while she was talking to Chad and needed to go back and look for it.

The sheriff was still busy reading and waved her on back.

She waited until she was near Chad's cell before bending over and pulling the pistol she had just stolen out of the bottom of her bloomers.

Chad let out a relieved breath as he stuck his hand through the bars for the gun. He looked confused when she did not hand it to him.

"No, sir. You call him back here and I'll get him to open the door."

Aware it would be more effective for the person not incarcerated to be the one holding the gun, he agreed.

Within minutes they had the sheriff locked in one of his own cells. Chad took the gun from Pearline and headed down the street to get his horse. He was relieved to find it still in front of the hospital where he had left it.

Knowing that time was important, Chad rode like a madman. His mind raced wildly with fear. He knew there was a good chance that Patrick was already on his way to the Thorntons' house. He just hoped he could get there in time to save Julia from harm.

Chapter Twenty-five

Chad's blood pounded in his ears with such force it drowned the clamor of his horse's hooves while he rode as fast and as hard as he could to save Julia. Finally he had the house in sight and it felt like someone had speared his heart with a knife when he saw an unfamiliar horse tied to one of the nearby hitching posts.

Dropping out of the saddle even before his horse came to a halt, he hurried inside the darkened house. Before he was able to call out Julia's name, he heard several hard thuds just over his head. He bolted up the stairs, taking them three at a time.

When he reached the second floor, he heard a loud, shattering crack near the back of the house and turned immediately toward the sound. With his pistol drawn, he moved with catlike agility down the darkened corridor, fully prepared to do whatever was necessary to save Julia's life.

When he neared the door that had just been smashed, and through which the only light on the floor came, he heard Julia's loud scream.

"Leave me alone. I told you. I don't love you. I love Chad and there is nothing you can do to change that fact."

"You don't mean that," Patrick responded, clearly in a rage. "You are just angry with me because I didn't consult you first with my plans."

Chad swung into the room with the pistol Pearline had stolen ready to fire and felt a sickening blow when he found Julia penned to the bed with Patrick on top of her.

"Get off her!"

Patrick's head snapped up. "How did you get out of jail?"

"That doesn't matter. I said to get off of her. Do it now!"

Rather than obey Chad's command, Patrick snatched Julia to him, using her like a shield. That rendered Chad's pistol useless, for he didn't know this gun well enough and did not dare risk a bullet striking Julia.

Angrily, he tossed the pistol out into the hall to get it out of his way and bore down on Patrick with his bare hands. As angry as he was, he figured he could take him one to one.

Lunging forward, he grabbed Patrick by the shoulders and broke him away from Julia. Together they fell to the floor and rolled several times, each trying to get the better of the other by inflicting as much pain as possible. Neither seemed to be gaining much of an advantage until suddenly Patrick managed to get his hand down into his boot and came out with a small double derringer.

Chad immediately froze, aware of the new danger.

Julia threw her hands to her face and screamed when she realized that Patrick was now armed. The scream caught his attention long enough to cause him to look toward her briefly. Seeing his chance, Chad made a grab for the pistol but Patrick jerked it out of his reach, then pointed it at him again. His green eyes were dark with continued rage.

"You never should have tossed away that gun," Patrick said, although clearly pleased that Chad had done such a foolish thing. "You should have known I'd come here armed."

He stood for a moment, glaring at Chad, who was again stone still. "Come on. Give me an excuse to shoot you." When Chad did nothing, he slowly started backing away, never taking his eyes off Chad. "Julia, get off that bed and come with me."

"No," she responded angrily. "I'm not going anywhere with you."

"Yes you are," Patrick told her calmly but firmly while he continued to back away from Chad. "Because if you don't, I'll put a hole right through the heart of old lover boy here. Now get on out the door. But do it slowly."

Julia glanced at Chad hesitantly, then finally did what she was told. Clutching her torn gown, she headed cautiously toward the door.

Dividing his attention between Julia who was nearly to the hall and Chad who remained on the floor where they'd last struggled, Patrick made it halfway across the room before something struck him in the back of the shoulder, causing him to stumble forward.

Turning, he was surprised to find a kitchen knife protruding from his right shoulder. He glanced around to see who could have thrown it and noticed Pearline standing just inside an open window, barefoot and wearing just her bloomers and camisole.

Angered by the intrusion, he turned the pistol on her. "That was a foolish thing to do. If you were going to go to the trouble to throw a knife at me, you should have aimed a lot lower. As it is, you barely got me."

Pearline saw the danger she was in but lifted her head proudly. "I did aim lower, but the knife veered. My grandmother would be ashamed of me. And I used the wrong knife. All I had was a kitchen knife and I had to try to save Missy. She's my best friend."

"How noble," he said through clenched teeth while he pulled the knife out and held it in his free hand. "Too bad you failed. It's also too bad you didn't consider that I'd have more than one bullet in here," he said, then narrowed his eyes while he prepared to squeeze the trigger. "That gives me one bullet for you, which I can claim was delivered in self-defense." He nodded toward his knife wound to indicate why. "And one bullet for Chad, who will undoubtedly do something foolish before this is over with, giving me a reason to kill him, too." He held up the knife still stained with his blood. "And, thanks to you, I'll still have this to persuade Julia to do exactly what I want."

Aware Patrick was no longer looking in his direction and afraid he truly meant to kill Pearline, Chad made a dive for the backs of his legs, but did not get there before hearing the shot.

Pearline screamed and seconds later sagged to the floor, but not because she had been hit. Because Patrick had.

Trembling with relief, not expecting to still be alive, she looked toward the door and found Julia standing there with Chad's gun still in her hands. She looked at Patrick again and saw that he lay on the floor, still holding both the pistol and the knife. He was not moving.

"Is he dead?" Julia asked, her voice steady though her hands shook violently.

Chad eased up on him and first removed the knife then the pistol before reaching for his throat to feel for a pulse. "No, he's still alive, though he doesn't deserve to be."

"Then I—I guess then we should send for a doctor," she said, and continued to stare at Patrick in horror.

"And the sheriff," Chad rose and gently pulled the front of her torn gown together, then put his arms around her. "That was a brave thing you did. You just saved Pearline's life. Mine, too. I want you to know how truly grateful I am for that."

"Me, too," Pearline said, and finally found the strength to stand again. "I'll get dressed and go for a doctor and the sheriff just as soon as I've had a look at Ruth. She's down there lyin' on the kitchen floor with a nasty bump on her head. He must have hit her pretty hard to make sure she didn't get in the way."

Julia waited until Pearline had left before speaking again. "I'm sorry."

"For what? For saving my life? What a thing to say."

"For having called you a liar. For not having listened when you tried to warn me about Patrick. Can you ever forgive me?"

Chad looked at her for a long moment while he continued to hold her close. "Only if you'll promise me one thing. That from now on, you'll believe everything I say. Can you promise me that?"

Relieved he was not still angry with her, she nodded, her lower lip trembling. "I promise."

"Then you'll believe me when I tell you that I love you and that I never meant any harm to come to you?"

She nodded again. Tears had filled her eyes.

"And you'll continue to believe me when I tell you I want to marry you?"

She nodded again.

He cocked his head to the side. "Well, since I've already got you nodding your head like that anyway, maybe it's time to ask if you feel the same about me. Is it possible you love me, too?"

With the first evidence of a smile playing at her lips, she nodded again.

"And is it at all possible that you love me enough to be willing to marry me?"

Her eyes sparkled when she lifted her chin to nod yet again, but found it was an impossible task, for at that very moment, Chad brought his mouth to hers in an amazingly tender kiss.

Julia closed her eyes to enjoy his mouth more fully, aware she had finally taken her fate in her hands and in the process had found the happiness she had been looking for all along.

Epilogue

Julia lifted the painting and placed it on an easel so it would be the first thing Chad saw when he entered the house.

"Do you think he'll like it?" she asked Pearline, who stood nearby with her arms resting across the top of her rounded stomach.

"Of course he'll like it. He likes all your paintin's."

"But this one is special. This is that field where we had our first picnic. Remember?"

Pearline nodded and grinned. "Sure I do. And as I recall, it's also where he stole several very passionate kisses from you."

Julia spun about and looked at her with raised eyebrows. "You were watching?"

"Let's just say I saw more than I should," Pearline admitted. "I was feelin' a little guilty about havin' run off and left you two alone like that and was on my way back when he leaned over and took that kiss from you. And I knew right then, by the way you responded, that you two was destined to be married."

"And did you know then that I was destined to carry his child?" Julia asked, and gave her own rounded stomach a glance.

"Let's just say I had me a feelin' you might." Pearline laughed, then changed the subject. "So where is the birthday mister? Doesn't he know you spent all after-noon cookin' his favorite supper? That you wouldn't even let your cook bake the bread?"

"He'll be along in a minute," she assured Pearline. "I told Father to go ring the bell. Meanwhile, help me turn this so that it faces the door better."

Pearline moved forward to help. "Just keep in mind that Solomon and I have to leave early. We still have a long way to go if we want that house ready before the baby comes."

"Don't worry. Everything is ready. All we need now is for Father to bring everyone inside."

Pearline glanced in the direction of the dining room. "You sure you have enough chairs?"

"Yes. Eleven chairs for eleven people."

"Does that include your stepmother?"

"Yes, that includes Jean."

"Then it looks like we're ready for them," she said, and followed Julia to the window to see what was keep-ing everyone.

When they looked out they saw that Charles had just wheeled himself to the edge of the veranda, where he could reach the bell cord without having to stand.

Because of the explosion, Julia's father had lost part of his left leg and was now confined to a wheelchair. But that had not kept him from remaining a happy and pro-ductive person. Far from it. All it had changed was what he was able to get done in a day's time. And all Patrick had accomplished by setting off that dynamite was land-ing himself a long prison term.

But because of Charles's injuries, Chad now took care of the timber businesses and was doing quite well, while Charles, Raymond, and Solomon took care of the cattle business, which was the main reason her father and Chad had traded houses.

Charles needed to be where the cattle were if he was to be a help running the ranch. Especially now that he'd lost one of his main workers. For the past few months, Solomon had only been able to help part of the time because he was now very busy building a house of his own for his expanding family.

"Here comes Chad," Pearline said about the same time Julia noticed him walking slowly across the yard.

"So I see." Julia smiled, still as fascinated by his easy movements as she had been the first day she'd met him. Her heart hammered anxiously while she waited for him to come inside. She was eager to see his reaction to her latest painting.

"Looks like everyone's about ready to come in," Pearline said, then stepped away from the window so she could watch Chad's reaction, too.

As planned, Chad entered first, followed by Charles, then Jean, Solomon, Raymond, Deborah, Eric, Craig, and Jeffery. He made it only halfway across the entrance before he spotted the painting.

The second she was certain his eyes had caught the canvas, Julia called out, "Happy Birthday!"

"Julia, it's beautiful," he said, and hurried forward to have a closer look. His eyes twinkled when he recognized the location. Smiling, he reached toward the rough texture. "But something is missing."

"Missing? What?"

"I don't know. Perhaps it needs a blanket and a picnic basket."

"Then you recognize it."

"Of course I do. I just wish you hadn't forgotten to include us in it." He then turned to the rest of them. "Look at the beautiful painting my wife did for me."

When everyone moved forward to have a closer look, Chad stepped to the far side of the room and took Julia with him. "Thank you for the painting, but I was hoping for something more."

"Like what?" she asked, though she knew her husband well enough to already know the answer. Tilting her head back, she closed her eyes and waited for the kiss she knew would follow. That was the amazing thing about Chad Andrews; he never tired of kissing her.

ABOUT THE AUTHOR

ROSALYN ALSOBROOK is a bestselling author whose novels have sold more than a million copies worldwide. A resident of Gilmer, Texas, Rosalyn married her high school sweetheart Bobby. She has two sons and one grandchild—but, she adds, she's a very *young* grandmother! Rosalyn enjoys doing intricate research for the authentic details she includes in her historical romances. Her many bestselling Zebra historical romances include PASSION'S BOLD FIRE, ENDLESS SEDUCTION, WILD WESTERN BRIDE, and MAIL-ORDER MISTRESS. She is also the author of TIME STORM, an exciting time travel historical romance available from Pinnacle Books.

Rosalyn would like to hear from her readers. Write to her c/o Zebra Books, 475 Park Avenue South, New York, N.Y. 10016. Please include a stamped self-addressed envelope if you'd like a reply from the author.

SURRENDER TO THE SPLENDOR OF THE ROMANCES OF F. ROSANNE BITTNER!

CARESS	(3791, $5.99/$6.99)
COMANCHE SUNSET	(3568, $4.99/$5.99)
ECSTASY'S CHAINS	(2617, $3.95/$4.95)
HEARTS SURRENDER	(2945, $4.50/$5.50)
LAWLESS LOVE	(3877, $4.50/$5.50)
PRAIRIE EMBRACE	(3160, $4.50/$5.50)
RAPTURE'S GOLD	(3879, $4.50/$5.50)
SHAMELESS	(4056, $5.99/$6.99)
SIOUX SPLENDOR	(3231, $4.50/$5.50)
SWEET MOUNTAIN MAGIC	(2914, $4.50/$5.50)

WHAT'S LOVE GOT TO DO WITH IT?

Everything . . . Just ask Kathleen Drymon . . . and Zebra Books

CASTAWAY ANGEL	*(3569-1, $4.50/$5.50)*
GENTLE SAVAGE	*(3888-7, $4.50/$5.50)*
MIDNIGHT BRIDE	*(3265-X, $4.50/$5.50)*
VELVET SAVAGE	*(3886-0, $4.50/$5.50)*
TEXAS BLOSSOM	*(3887-9, $4.50/$5.50)*
WARRIOR OF THE SUN	*(3924-7, $4.99/$5.99)*

DISCOVER DEANA JAMES!